The Flaming
Cutlass

First paperback edition: 13/08/2025

ISBN: 979-8-89860-033-4 (Paperback)

Cover illustration by Jamie Scully
Left pirate ship © Vecteezy.com
Right pirate ship © Vecteezy.com

Published by Amazon KDP

To Tom, Noah, Adam, Ethan, Zachary, Tudor, Maddy, Amber, Charlie, Neve, Fern, and Henry.

Contents:

Prologue: Highway to Hell

Chapter I

Satan's Peak

The sea was unusually calm on a mild winter evening in the Gulf of Mexico in 1743. A medium to large-sized vessel lay anchored beside a small island from which a grotesque and dragon-like peak erupted. Not a single member of the ship's small crew remained on deck, as every last one followed their captain on land, for they were in search of treasure. Not your typical buried gold and diamonds and coins, the last act of a great sea captain, no, this was a treasure so powerful it had slipped into folklore. In fact, the map itself was the only evidence of its existence, yet the map alone could surely not warrant the belief that this myth was a reality. It is the sheer temptation that this relic creates that encourages countless treasure hunters to search for their demise in the unforgiving cave within the mountain.

It was told that the Devil himself had planted the treasure and the obstacles protecting it, and the depictions of horns and pentagrams upon the map which leads there actually backed this. This may sound far-fetched, but the pirates of the time were often highly superstitious or religious. Because of this, some could not be forced nor bribed to seek this item, while others were only more drawn to its power. Alas, the cave held deadly secrets.

Yet despite the surrounding ambiguity and scepticism, again and again entire crews of sailors would attempt to reap the reward. Why wouldn't they? After all, perhaps I should have mentioned, it is said to grant immortality to the soul who reaches it — and for their entire crew.

A pirate crew of less than 10 (which was unusually small for the size of their ship) stood outside the entrance to the cave, which sat within the mountain. Some carried torches; others had satchels and sacks of equipment. All of them had their heads held back as they gazed in both awe and terror at the two fang-like shards of stone which hung from the roof of the cave. It was like a more humid, tropical version of Aladdin's cave, but no genie in the lamp was to be found within the belly.

The captain, a short, late middle-aged fellow whose once blonde hair was turning silver, named Andrew Glove, turned to his son, Thomas Glove, and said, "We live today, in hope that we will live forever!"

Tom was 23 and taller than his dad, and had flowing blonde hair, causing his 'pirate name' to be 'Goldenlocks.' He had a belt over his coat, from which a scabbard carrying a cutlass, a pistol and a couple of knives hung.

"Today," Tom echoed his father, "together, we will quest to find the famous gift of Satan! The gift which promises immortality for all the crew of he who possesses it!"

"That be it!" Andrew Glove confirmed, "The greatest gift a man like me could wish for. To live forever, and know that his crew, his family, should do the same."

The crew all drew their swords and held them in the air while cheering before lighting lamps and torches to light the way within the caverns they would soon search. Boots thudded and buckles clashed as the entire crew charged into the smothering darkness of the cave, a darkness which resisted the weak glow of the torches.

As the air suddenly cooled, a colony of small bats fluttered from the tunnel ahead. Water from the high tide made the floor slightly damp. The tunnel led gradually downwards, twisting and turning, and already its cold, featureless walls constricted. Each pirate's boots squelched through puddles of muddy seawater.

They were quick to find themselves at a junction, from which the following tunnels emitted a low and ominous drone. The less weathered pirates slowly stepped back. The sudden movement of an immense boulder, which swiftly fell from the cave roof above to fill the mouth, soon foiled their vacation. Every crew member besides Glove and his son jerked their necks around in shock to see what had caused the crashing sound behind them.

"We need no escape route!" cried Andrew Glove, "The only way is forward!"

A small chest sat between the split in the path.

"Perhaps this is it," said a dark-haired man standing alongside Tom.

Tom stated, "Adam, it won't be that straightforward."

Adam Lumberlodge was Thomas Glove's childhood best friend. Both had been brought up upon the deck of *The Lady Mary*, Glove's ship, and taught the ways of seafaring. He was medium height and broad, with dark curly hair to his shoulders and short but ungroomed facial hair.

"I suppose it's a clue then."

"You may be right," replied Tom, approaching the box cautiously. A small parchment, revealed when he lifted the lid, went to Elliott 'All-know' Ethan, another crew member. Elliott was Andrew Glove's first-mate, making him second in command because they had never appointed a quartermaster.

Elliott murmured the paper's inscription: "Heard by many, seen by none. Speak to me and I will reply, and you should follow."

"So, it's a riddle?" Lumberlodge asked.

"A simple one you'll find, but alas, a riddle," Elliott replied, with a strong northern English accent, before stepping towards the first tunnel. He clapped his hands, to which the effect was unclear. He subsequently tried the second tunnel, clapping once more. This time, despite his hands only colliding a single time, applause followed, or rather, a series of echoes.

"Echoes," Elliott thought aloud, "it's this way, people!"

He turned to Andrew Glove before imploring, "If I may, captain."

Glove, knowing that Elliott was indeed logical in his decision, gave a nod, and the crew followed through the second passage. The tunnel was long and winding. Stalactites hung low from the ceiling, creating an increasingly dangerous atmosphere. The cave walls slowly became wider until they had entered a room that possessed walls containing intricate carvings of beasts and birds and flames.

In the centre of the room, there was another small chest. Elliott opened it. A second scrap of parchment read: 'Reaching stiffly for the sky, my fingers I bare in the cold. In warmth I wear an emerald glove and in between I dress in gold.'

"We may as well make the most of it," Elliott joked, "anyone fancy a try?"

"Let me think," Adam said.

"Something tall," Maddison Casserole, the ship's lookout, added. Maddy was short, with a rag of cloth tied to keep her long, brown hair from her face. She was dressed in the same sort of clothes as the male pirates, though this wasn't particularly by choice.

"I know," said Tom, pacing around the room to examine the carvings. He stopped at one at the far end — an oak tree. He had examined that each carving had a thin slot underneath.

Elliott walked up to Tom and reassured him, "I believe you are correct."

Tom drew his cutlass and slid it into the slot corresponding to the oak. Nothing happened for what felt like an entire minute, and then disappointment flooded over him. Then, the walls shook violently as the slot ejected the sword, and the panel depicting the tree fell back, revealing a new tunnel. Elliott handed him his Cutlass, which was not placed back within the scabbard.

"Onward!" Tom yelled.

It is true that the previous events seemed far from deadly, more like something that should fall out of an otherwise disappointing Christmas cracker. Perhaps this rather novice introduction was intentional, to catch the unwary off guard. What other tricks might the devil employ? The entire crew was sure to stay vigilant, but not much could have prepared them for the next stage — the next level, so to say.

Beyond another long, winding, and claustrophobic tunnel lay another circular room with a low ceiling. The ground was dry; no water, no one, had been here for many years. The room's centre held another chest. Again, Elliott Ethan took out the third piece of parchment as the door to the next tunnel fell open. Many stepped forward. With the paper in his right hand, Elliott reached out with his left to stop his associates from progressing.

"Not with such haste," he warned.

He read aloud the writing that he was now accustomed to comprehending.

"You've proven your mind, but is that all you're worth? What you must fight does not dwell on turf," he recited, before adding sarcastically, "how poetic the devil must be!"

"Be prepared!" Glove said.

"Lower the lanterns," Maddy added, "You need swords."

"We're fighting something that doesn't live on turf?" Lumberlodge pondered before going on one of his signature rants, "What is it? A shark? Or worse? Those bloody dolphins. They're after us, I tell you. Too smart for a fish. Bloody dolphins."

"You know, they are not actually fish, more related to cows and pigs." Elliott pointed out.

"Shut up about dolphins! It isn't bloody dolphins," Thomas said, before adding solemnly, pointing his cutlass to an ominous fiery glow spilling from the tunnel, "It's far worse." Almost every crew member drew their swords, except for the captain, who had a pair of flintlock pistols, and Lumberlodge, whose weapon of choice was a 5-foot musket.

As the glow neared the opening, they could just begin to discern its source. Amongst the fiery light, a small silhouette was visible. Then, out of the tunnel came first a hand, dark and skeletal. Next, a foot, bent and beaten. Now an arm, followed by a torso. Little flesh hung upon the frame, but what did was burning, producing the glow. But then it stopped. Stopped for a prolonged moment. Finally, the figure lunged forward, and the face was at once revealed. Like the body, it was inhumanly frail and lean. Fire bulged from the eye sockets and the mouth, which was open wide, exposing the jagged and offset teeth. It leapt straight for Glove, who swiftly stepped to the side, shooting the creature with his pistols. It shrieked, glaring at its rival. Before it was ready to attack once more, Thomas plunged his cutlass into its side and elevated it. At first it squirmed, letting out a dying howl before flopping onto the floor as Thomas pulled back his sword. It's blood that coated the weapon was dark and thick and caught fire above the creature's smoking corpse.

Chapter II

Within Satan's Peak

"What... the... Hell... was... that?" Elliott muttered.

"Not a bloody dolphin!" Lumberlodge corrected himself.

Hoping now to progress, the crew took a step towards the tunnel — which was still glowing. Glowing brighter. Glowing harsher. Casting the shadows of twenty or so more beasts. Quiet yet sinister cackles and growls echoed through the cavern. Lumberlodge held his musket close, staring down the sight and ready to fire. He cocked the gun, his finger ready on the trigger. Glove gave him a nod. A cloud of smoke pummelled from the barrel as shot was ejected through the tunnel. The sound of the gun reverberated throughout the entire tunnel system, followed by a harrowing scream. Adam reloaded as the uninjured monsters began to run.

"Brace yourselves!" yelled Glove, firing his pistols simultaneously.

His son, whose sword was now alight, made the next move, pacing forwards as he impaled a second. Between gunfire and the slashing of steel, creature after creature fell to the ground. While Elliott was noted for his mind, he was also large and imposing, so not unprepared for physical challenges. Glove, Thomas, Adam, Elliott, Maddy, and many more had all slain monsters within minutes of the confrontation. Half were already dead, heating the floor as they slowly dwindled. The creatures themselves were not incapable. Many of the crew gained bite marks, scratch marks and burns, which left an agonising sting. Even Elliott had a painful wound down his right arm. While many had found their way to the back of the group, one grabbed the attention of the captain. This one was on all fours, with a bulky skeleton supporting a similarly scarce and burnt hide. It had sharp teeth, and 5-inch red-hot steely claws adorned its feet. The appearance was that of a bear from Hell, striking fear into Glove, though he remained stoic. This was the last to leave the cave, slowly dragging its claws, causing sparks.

Then, also like a bear, it reared up onto its hind legs, letting out a guttural bellow. Unmoved, Glove shot bullet after bullet, to little effect. Each shot was deflected off the beast's flanks, creating an oddly metallic scrape. With its vast paw, it took a swipe at Glove's right leg, flooring the increasingly fearful sailor. With hot and sticky saliva dripping from its skinless face, it hunched over Glove, widening its gape to fit around his head — preparing to crush it. His son was occupied in a fistfight with another monster as his cutlass had been smacked from his hands. Elliott was also fighting. Maddy, being not much larger than the monsters, was fighting viciously, though with success, to stay on her feet. Lumberlodge sought additional ammunition. There was no one able to help their captain.

No one except a new crew member by the name of Doyle Clementini. His amber curtains had earned him the nickname 'Redtop'. Glove had rescued him from a sketchy vessel; his only possessions at the time being an old bandana and leather coat. He fought with neither a sword nor a gun. Knives were his customary weapons. He had some training in martial arts, a strange practice for a pirate. He first hauled his captain back just in time to escape the clashing jaws, saying, "I'm here, captain. Easy now." Then, he kicked the animal in its paw, causing it to collapse to the floor. Sliding to its rear, he sunk a knife into either haunch. Glove once again began to fire at its face, before Doyle jumped onto the beast's back, propelling himself using the already implanted daggers. It reared again with a painful roar, turning while trying to claw the pirate off. With a mighty blow of its paw, the beast tore Doyle off. Wounded and restless, it let out another roar, remaining on its rear legs. The creature clawed at the captain, and the blow knocked him off his feet again. In a desperate last effort, Redtop stabbed the beast in its leg. It fell to its knees, but it still held its front paws off the ground.

Thomas, who had, as had most, succeeded in combatting his previous rival, picked up his still-lit sword and dashed towards his father. The cutlass sank into the rib cage of the beast, but Thomas himself was flung to the ground. The big one was the only remaining monster. Some held back, while others were quick to aid their captain, with the effect being no greater than Tom's attempt. The same sticky saliva dripped from its mouth. It let out one final bellow as once more the sound of Lumberlodge's musket ruptured through the cave. Lead blasted through the beast's open jaws and penetrated the other side of its skull.

It fell to the floor.

The entire crew had dropped to their knees. Smoke still floated from the big one's skull, which lay broken on the floor with its jaw dislocated and blood dripping from the throat. Panting, Doyle Clementini rose and gave it a nudge with his boot, just to make sure.

"Nice shot, Lumberlodge," he added.

"Never miss," Adam replied after standing, half cocky, half joking.

Lumberlodge assisted Tom to his feet, as Elliott did the same for Glove.

Tom pulled his cutlass from the beast's carcass, along with Doyle's knives. As they had before, the blades, which were covered in blood, caught fire. While Doyle blew his knives out, Tom decided to keep his sword burning.

"Off to the next stage, then!" said Maddy.

Glove didn't respond. It was apparent from his face that he was deep in thought. He bit his lower lip and sighed.

"You okay, cap'n?"

"Glove?" Elliott begged.

"Father?" his son added.

Glove blinked and gave his head a shake.

"Me?" he said, "Me, I'm absolutely fine. Onwards."

The crew began to advance through the tunnel from which the fiery creatures they had just fought had emerged. Their eyes were all fixed on the walls and ceiling in case another unholy beast should lay hiding within the cracks. The way was now lit not just by the torches, but by Thomas's cutlass, which did not appear to be fading. Small passages led off in all directions, but none large enough for a person to fit through. The larger tunnel continued forward. They were walking for several minutes, so took to talking. Glove and Elliott were walking ahead (when I say Glove, I am most likely referring to Andrew, or else I will specify if it isn't apparent), with Tom, Adam, Maddy, Doyle and a man called Tudor Boris walked in a group a few yards behind.

"Something bothering you, Captain?" Elliott asked Glove.

Glove responded in a grave mutter, as to keep it between the two of them, "I was once untouchable, boy, untouchable. One of the big fish in this pond we call the Caribbean. Few men have come close to killing me, but look at me now. I almost died, that bastard almost crushed my head like a mere apple."

"That 'bastard' was a twelve-foot-tall beast, not a man; you can't compare it. Could have easily killed the best of men. Don't get yourself down. And besides, we're here, aren't we? Searching for the gift of the Devil. Once you have it, you won't have to worry anymore."

"Aye, I know that to be true. It was more of an observation. It's no secret the hand of time is pulling at my string of fate, the man I speak of expired long ago. No, boy, it's not me I worry for," Glove turned and looked at his son.

"I don't think you need to worry about Thomas, sir," Elliott assured.

"Perhaps, but he is the closest thing I have to," he paused, "to her. It be he I want immortal."

As they walked further and further in, this time the walls became closer and closer together. After walking for about ten more minutes, they had reached a dead end.

"Bugger!" Tom yelled.

"Bugger again!" Lumberlodge added, pointing behind them. From the holes in the walls, metal spikes were now protruding, forming a barrier in a gradual, Indiana Jones-esque fashion. They had time; the wall ejected new spikes only every thirty seconds or so, and they were about 30 yards clear.

"What to do?" Elliott pondered.

Glove felt the walls, hoping for a switch or button or secret room. Tom turned around with his cutlass lighting new areas of the wall, also searching. He jumped. He had lit up a face on the wall. This time though, it was not a monster, just a carving. Its expression was one of dread, with its eyes staring upwards. Tom followed its gaze. He pointed his sword towards the ceiling, revealing a small opening above.

"Up here!" he yelled. Fifteen yards separated them from the spikes. The ceiling was over 10 feet tall, meaning everyone would need a leg-up.

"Son?" Glove inquired, "you help everyone up, and I'll be waiting up top to assist."

Tom dropped his cutlass and cupped his hands for his father to place his boot. Glove then projected himself towards the opening, grabbing the edge with both hands before swiftly lifting himself through.

"C'mon!" he then shouted.

His son then proceeded to leg-up every crew member, as Glove pulled them up at the top. Lumberlodge threw his trusty musket up for Glove to catch before jumping up himself.

The spikes, now ten feet off, multiplied with alarming speed. As the crew was small, only a few more members required help up: Doyle, who required little assistance from his captain but thanked him nonetheless; Elliott, who was rather apologetic about being less nimble than the others; Maddy, who struggled to reach the ledge so jumped onto Tom's shoulders; one Tudor Boris, who insisted that he didn't need Tom's help but still took the leg up; and Tom. He placed his cutlass back into its scabbard, presumably putting out the flame, and stepped back to take a run-up. Another row of spikes shot out from the walls, missing Tom's back by hardly an inch.

"Jesus!" he exclaimed.

"Hurry, Goldenlocks!" Lumberlodge warned. He turned around in shock, his heart pounding from the surprise. He took a step back — in the nick of time too, for yet another set of blades had burst out. Using what little runway he had, he sprinted towards the opening, and prepared to jump. He reached his hand out towards the ledge, but narrowly missed. He landed with his ankle bent, causing him to fall.

The spikes were closer, only five feet away. Standing this time directly underneath the hole, he squatted down, readying again for take-off. But again, he couldn't reach high enough. Now, spikes shot from both ends of the tunnel, encasing him with only two feet of space on either side. Once more he jumped, and once more he missed. One foot away. One last time. He could hear the mechanisms within the walls winding, ready to deal a fatal blow. With one last bounce, his feet left the floor. His hand was almost at the ledge, about to make it. Higher and higher he went. His fingers were ready, ready to grasp whatever surface they could. He was almost there, about to do it. But he went no higher. His fingers brushed the ledge, but he failed to hold on to anything.

Another hand reached out — his father's. His worn, dry, and tired hand, with bony fingers, wrapped tightly around Tom's wrist. Suspended in the air by his father's grasp, he was able to raise his other arm to hold on to the ledge. Lumberlodge bent down to reach for his arm, and so did Elliott. Between the three of them, they pulled Thomas Glove to the top, leaving him on the floor to catch his breath. He rolled to look through the hole they had just lifted him through. With a quick slashing sound, the last rows of spikes scraped past each other.

Tom huffed in both exhaustion and relief. He wiped his dirty wrist over his sweat-dripping forehead before flinging his arm back to the ground where he lay. Lumberlodge reached out to help him up. Tom rose to his feet and stretched almost every appendage of his body, which let out a series of stiff cracks from the joints.

"Well, this is a step up from riddles," Elliott began.

"Fear not," Glove insisted, "we still have much fight left in us all."

Now, the proceedings occurred as previously. A circular chamber held them once more; inside, a small wooden box contained another scrap of parchment. Elliott, having assumed the role of riddle-reader, took the paper and read.

"There be six doors ahead,

Only three doors tell the truth,

The others are a-lying,

One door leads to freedom,

The others, to your demise.

And some friendly advice: the doors tell and lie in absolutes, believe everything or nothing which they say."

Around the edge of the room, just as the paper had told, hung six large doors. One red, one blue, one yellow, one green, one black and one white. On each was engraved a message. Tom went to withdraw his cutlass once more, to find to his surprise the metal scabbard was almost molten. He lifted the sword, and a gust of smoke burst from the scabbard, accompanied by glowing sparks. If his jacket had not been leather but rather had been cotton or linen, then Tom may have noticed quite sooner, for the red-hot scabbard had left a burning black mark on the side. The weapon itself was burning away as brightly as before, if not brighter. Gold plating on the writing reflected the light from the cutlass. Six keys on chains fell from the ceiling above the chest. The colour of each key matched a door. A deep and mysterious, only partially human, voice filled the room.

"Choose only one!"

Glove turned to see who had spoken. No one. No longer averse to any supernatural concept, he accepted that the voice had no apparent source and carried on the investigation. Tom read the first door, the red door's message:

"Don't trust sapphires – they be fooling you,"

"Very insightful," scoffed Elliott.

The blue door read:

"I'm not safe,"

The yellow:

"Ebony and crimson be lying,"

The green:

"I will lead thee out,"

The black:

"Beware of the beast that lies behind the door,"

And the white:

"Certain death awaits this way,"

If you are one for riddles, perhaps you may wish to pause reading in order to figure it out for yourself. I cannot summon a medal from within these pages for completion, but you can get the smug feeling of getting this right, perhaps even before our protagonists.

"What the Hell is all that?" Lumberlodge burst out in disgust.

"A puzzle of deduction," Elliott replied, "but where to start?"

"Well, red and blue cannot both be true," Glove began.

"And they cannot both be false either," his son finished.

"A worthy conclusion," Elliott assured, "meaning there are only two more lies and two more truths." He carried on muttering to himself for some time, then he continued by explaining how they should next evaluate the possibilities surrounding yellow.

"If yellow is lying, then red is telling the truth, and so is black. This means that blue is lying, which leaves us with one true and one false door."

Tudor interrupted: "I say we just pick a door. Whatever might be behind it hasn't met me yet."

"Stop it, Tudor, let him think!" Maddy scolded.

"He can't think if you're shouting, Maddy," Doyle added, as he had contributed nothing to the other conversation.

"Anyway," Elliott wrapped up all bickering and continued himself.

"Green says it will lead us out, and white says certain death," Maddy said, trying to return to the 'adult' conversation.

"So if one is lying, then neither are to be trusted, as they are either both safe or both deadly," Tom realised.

"Which means yellow must be telling the truth," Elliott couldn't help himself but develop.

"But could not yellow lie by saying both are lying, when in fact only one is?" Doyle chirped in.

"It says the doors lie in absolutes, so both the ebony and crimson must speak fiction,"

"So, if yellow is true?" Tom asked to which Elliott was delighted to continue,

"Then Black and red are lying, like I say. This would suggest that black is the door we want, as it is lying about possessing a beast, but for argument's sake I shall go on. This leaves one lying door left. Blue and yellow are telling the truth, leaving green and white. Green says it is the escape, while white says it leads to death. If white is lying, green is telling the truth, which means there are two safe doors, which we know is not the case. Therefore, green is lying and white is telling the truth, so neither is the correct door. So, it's definitely black,"

"Are you certain?"

"Certainly, captain,"

"Son, grab the black key!"

Tom reached out and snapped the rusty chain that suspended the ebony key. At the same moment, all the other keys lifted beyond reach. The key itself appeared ancient and magical, crooked but elegant. It was so dark that it almost appeared two-dimensional, reflecting none of the light which came from any torch or mysteriously burning sword. It was also strangely cold, almost freezing to Tom's fingertips. He pushed it into the lock and twisted it once – nothing. Twice – nothing. Three times – nothing. Four times – nothing. Five times – click. He used both hands as he had to combat the typical resistance felt just before you unlock a door. A series of cranks and creaks and clunks followed this. Finally, the door swung open, revealing another passage, this time not forwards, but upwards.

The tunnel was narrow, only one person could fit at once, meaning they would all have to climb single file. The wall did not seem too difficult to scale, with ledges and rocks quite conveniently placed for gripping, but one false move could spell disaster. In a hurry, they climbed one behind the other, rather than letting each person reach the top before the next began. Should one person slip, they may not just cause themselves to perish but also all below them. But no member of the crew was an amateur, and so they ascended. Glove suggested that Tom go first, so he could take with him a rope to throw down to the others. Tudor stepped forward at this moment, saying, "I'll do it, I'm a better climber."

"Be my guest," Tom said, so Tudor took the rope, completing the forty-foot climb in under a minute, and the others soon followed.

"Easy does it, lads. The rock will hold if you're not clumsy."

Chapter III

Atop Satan's Peak

Murphy's law states that if something can go wrong, it will. But as luck would have it, the entire crew reached the top with relative ease. There were odd stumbles here and there, sometimes a rock would fall from below a careful boot and hit the next person on the nose, but there were no major accidents or injuries. One by one, the members of the crew hauled themselves out with the rope and congregated again at the top. This time they did not find themselves in another dark cave or long, winding tunnel; they were at the summit of the mountain. It was a weird sensation – both the feeling of finally being out of the encompassing darkness and the fact that they had been travelling mostly downwards — except for the jump up and previous climb, which had only been about 40 feet – yet they were already at the peak of a monolithic rock formation.

Chiselled onto the peak was an altar, approximately 20 feet wide. This altar displayed images of horned demons, skeletal figures, and a great serpent, along with an ancient, indecipherable script. The altar's centre featured a pentagram etched with the final, small, familiar chest. Elliott again lifted the lid and picked out the parchment. As soon as the paper had left the box, the table began to change. A weathered, fierce devil statue emerged as the pentagram's parts folded inward. Both arms were outstretched. The crooked fingers of one open hand beckoned for an exchange; the other hand remained tightly clenched. Elliott stepped back so as not to get caught in the moving pieces.

"All yours, Elliott," Glove insisted,

He cleared his throat with his fist to his chest,

"I was stolen from on high,

In a season of frost, I help thee flourish,

A foe and an ally dwell within me,

I am a thing of sound, smell, and sight."

"Nonsense!" Lumberlodge butted in with his usual enthusiasm, "Nothing more to blow the brains out of? More riddles?"

"I'm afraid so," Tom replied.

"Stolen? On high?" Elliott asked himself, "help thee flourish? Foe and an ally?"

He shook his head in despair; the feeling was unfamiliar — the feeling of not knowing straight away. He had always been an academic person, studying ancient texts and myths, but also scientific breakthroughs and political affairs. It was not, however, that this particular riddle is extremely difficult, especially for a scholar, instead, it had perhaps caught Elliott off-guard. He was expecting an epic duel or great escape — instead; he got yet another riddle. Also, the potentially satanic magic at play does not seem to lend itself to a reference of Greek myth. In fact, in any other scenario, it is probable he would have figured it out in a heartbeat, but today it just wouldn't come to him.

"Ay-up!" Tom yelled as he pointed to a silhouette on the horizon. Two pirate vessels side by side, one vast and the other far humbler. The smoke formed as the smaller ship withered into the sea, collected as a great black cloud. Glove took out his telescope.

"It's him." He observed, and his first-mate exactly who he meant by 'him.'

"The *Revenge*?" Elliott asked, though he knew the answer.

"Aye-aye. *Queen Anne's Revenge*. Captained by that sly old dog Edward Thatch. He has no honour, no restraint, only greed. And believe me, that makes him the most dangerous man you'll ever meet."

"But he died over twenty years ago," Tudor Boris added, "Sunk his ship and took his head."

"Whoever the poor bastard that head belonged to, it certainly was not Edward Thatch," Glove insisted, "Thatch lives, mark my word."

"Look at all the smoke!" Casserole added.

"All that smoke must mean there's one hell of a…"

"Fire!" Elliott triumphed, "The answer is fire!"

"The answer to what?" Tom asked, somehow so preoccupied with the sight of *Queen Anne's Revenge* that he had completely forgotten about the task at hand. Elliott just looked at him. The exchange lasted about 5 seconds before Tom had realised what he was talking about.

"Oh, the riddle! So, fire, you say?"

"'I was stolen from on high' – in Greek myth, Prometheus was a titan who stole fire from the gods.

'In a season of frost, I help thee flourish' – fire helps us stay warm, pretty self-explanatory. 'A foe and an ally' – fire can keep us warm, cook our food, but also burn us. And 'sound, smell and sight' – fire is bright, you can smell the fuel burning and hear the crackling."

There was another long pause as Tom comprehended what Elliott had just explained. He joined his father in staring again into the distance, to see the mast and sails of Blackbeard's prey collapsing finally into the devouring ocean and as a last flurry of sparks billowing into the sky. It was as if neither ship had ever been there, for *Queen Anne's Revenge* had now sailed off past the horizon. He turned to his dad, who had a rare and solitary tear crawling down his cheek. He placed a hand on his father's shoulder.

"The world is cruel, son," Glove told him.

"But there's good in it, too. Are you not the man they call 'Robin Hood of the Seven Seas'? Was it not you who kept Blackbeard at bay for so many years?"

"Three years, son, that's all. Then I lost mi ship 'n' mi crew to the Navy. Twenty-three years he's had to recover. He's a scourge, that man, to all people who have any business in the Caribbean. He's bested me, now he will never get the better of you."

"What do you mean?"

"Come on, son, let's claim this treasure."

The crew had taken this time to relax a little, some had even taken to sitting. Lumberlodge stood beside Elliott with his musket vertical and used it to take some weight. Elliott just waited patiently for his captain to come around.

"Thomas," he began, nodding to the cutlass, "I think you may have the honour."

Tom stepped forward and placed the glowing blade of his cutlass into the stone Devil's hand. The fingers snapped shut. Slowly, the fingers became red as the stone became molten. Eventually, the heat had spread down the arm before the entire forearm snapped off and fell to the floor. Then, the rest of the statue began to crumble, initially slowly, but this sped up at an increasing rate. The disintegration occurred now from the top, the bottom and the side. The break finally merged at the second arm. While cracked, the structural integrity kept the arms suspended as it too started to fall apart. Just as it was about to fall, nothing more remained but fragments. As the debris collapsed in a heap, light shone through the dust. Glove put his wrist above his eyes to shield them from the red glow. Remaining where the devil's closed hand had been, floated a jagged, thin, luminous crystal. It resembled a piece of agate, yet the patterns and layers of radiant sediment were even more enthralling.

Glove reached out and seized the jewel. His son turned to him, the pair beamed and embraced each other.

"We did it, son! We did it!"

"We did it, Father!"

"I will never lose you now, my dearest child! I needn't worry about losing any of you!"

The entire crew let out a tremendous cheer followed by a laugh.

"Well done, old boy," Glove said, patting Elliott on the back.

"For Elliott Ethan!" Tom announced, "whose brilliant noggin has brought us to triumph!"

Again, the crew whooped and whistled and applauded their ally – their friend.

"And to the one, the only Adam Lumberlodge, whose shot with that damned musket has no equal!"

The applause continued as Glove Sr. began the congratulations.

"To Doyle, to Doyle 'Red-top' Clementini, whose famous kick saved my soul this very night!"

Lumberlodge, in excitement and in victory, held his loaded gun to the air and fired with only one hand, with his other cupped around his mouth to yell.

"And to Maddy Casserole's tenacity, and Tudor Boris' strength, and to each one of you fools who dared accompany me on this quest. And especially to my son, Thomas 'Goldenlocks' Glove, who I know will make a great captain one day."

Tom smiled and blushed, for the attention embarrassed him. To turn the praise away from himself, he said, "And to the man who brought us here, brought us together. My father, Andrew Glove!" Anyone throughout the area would have heard hooting, calling, screaming, whistling, and clapping; sound travels far from a mountain peak.

"Let us venture down, my friends," Glove said, already forgetting about the sight of Blackbeard, "I fancy a spot of rum for us all!"

The crew secured ropes and threw them down the mountainside. You may wonder why they waste time taking the precautions of a mortal. The thing is, they were so ecstatic about their victory they had mostly forgotten about exactly what they were victorious about.

Chapter IV

The Lady Mary: below deck

Once the crew abseiled the mountain, they paddled to their vessel in small rowing boats, and all made their way to the cabin. Tom rolled in a cask of rum from the storeroom. Someone hammered a dull brass tap into the barrel, and they filled an odd assortment of glasses and old bottles one at a time, passing them to crewmates with congratulations or friendly smacks on the shoulder. The crew knew better than to drink straight away; they expected a toast from their captain. Glove had found himself a large gold locket. The treasure, being only about two inches tall and a few millimetres in depth, fit in the accessory, which he fastened around his neck. Tom handed him his usual large, handled glass, full of rum. He lifted it into the air and cleared his throat.

"Gentlemen," he began, addressing Maddy as well as the men — his seafaring vocabulary wasn't the most inclusive — "Gentlemen, I believe you'll all agree that you have heard enough of me today, so I'm going to hand you over to my son." He nodded to Thomas, who was less prepared for a speech. It was no relief, however, when he discovered he wouldn't need to give one.

No one word could create the effect the crashing sound which followed had. The entire boat rocked to the side. A second hit. This time, fractions of slats and beams of wood flew from the wall, leaving a cannonball-sized hole in the wall. The projectile itself had flown past Doyle's face, who had just leapt back in the nick of time. The sun had set, yet scarily little light shone through the break. Both Gloves rushed to the deck. It was *Queen Anne's Revenge*, Blackbeard's ship. It was 25% larger than *The Lady Mary*.

"Lumberlodge, Clementini, Boris and Casserole on deck! Ethan on cannons…"

Chapter V

The Lady Mary: **main-deck**

Tudor Boris raised the anchor as *Queen Anne's Revenge* approached. The ships were now side by side. A tall and imposing figure walked into view. He wore his dark hair plaited under a showy captain's hat.

In his coat hung six loaded pistols and a sword. He had a lit torch burning in one hand. His face was a furious pink colour, pierced by two ghostly blue eyes. His beard was too plaited at the ends but fell down to his chest. It was jet black.

"Captain Andrew Glove — a fall from Grace indeed. We shared a kingship, our ships once equal, yet see your diminished state. The rumours were true," he mocked. His voice was deep and cold, commanding respect and striking fear simultaneously and effortlessly. The accent originated in southwest England, though not as far southwest as Cornish pasties. He was not thoroughly well-spoken, but he spoke slowly and deliberately, pronouncing each letter.

"Captain Edward Thatch, I know too well you too live up to your reputation as a revolting beast."

"Dare insult me, old man! And you, you must be 'Goldenlocks',"

"Blackbeard," Tom responded briefly but respectfully.

"Play nice, Thatch," Glove warned.

"I believe you have something for me, Glove,"

"And what is that?"

"The darned gift of the Devil."

"Oh, this," he procrastinated, "I'm afraid not."

"You have my respect, Glove. You managed to conquer Satan's little game; you've earned it."

"Thank you, Edward."

"I hadn't finished! You know how much I'd enjoy burning your ridiculous ship to ash, but if you hand it over, you can go free, you can live."

"We will live nonetheless, have you forgotten? This jewel brings the gift of eternal life?"

"Shall we test that, you old fool?"

"Don't do this, Thatch."

"Too late!"

"Okay, boys," Blackbeard ordered. Three men pushed forward a catapult loaded with a wooden barrel. They released it; the barrel burst, and greyish powder coated the floor. Blackbeard then tossed his torch onto the pile, and it exploded – it was gunpowder. Tudor Boris dived out of the way of the fire, forward rolling on the floor.

"Cannons!" Glove yelled with terror on his face.

Gun-deck

Elliott Ethan, who was on the gun-deck alone, had loaded all the cannons and lit three pointing towards *Queen Anne's Revenge*. He placed a finger in each ear as the cannons fired. One, two, three. He didn't care to aim each one manually, assuming that at least one would hit the other ship, as they were so close. The enemy replied with three more shots. One, two, three. Both ships rocked and even collided violently. The ships were so close, Elliott could look out his little window and see the faces of Blackbeard's cannon firers staring right back at him.

Main-deck

Back on deck, the battle was also intensifying. Members of Blackbeard's crew were swinging onto *The Lady Mary*'s deck with ropes suspended from the flagpoles. There they were combatted by Glove, with his pistols ready to shoot; Tom, who had drawn his still flaming cutlass; Doyle, who was putting his Martial-arts skills into practice (even against guns and swords) and Lumberlodge, who was now in the crow's-nest firing his musket from afar. Maddy was tying the ropes, which she had caught from the incoming attackers, in-place to be used by the protagonists. While the idea was no longer original, Tudor had gone below deck to retrieve a cask of rum or brandy. Once back, he tied cannon-fuse around the barrel and then a rope from the enemy ship as well. Tom lit the fuse with his sword and then Tudor ran forward to give the barrel a push. The flaw in this plan was that the barrel would swing back and forth. Despite being short, the fuse was long enough for the barrel to swing halfway between both ships before igniting the alcohol. Both sides found themselves affected by the explosion, both caught fire. *The Lady Mary* was still worse off.

"Not the drink!" Lumberlodge yelled, "Use the powder! Not the bloody drink!"

A gust of wind blew the ships further apart. *Queen Anne's Revenge* rocked to one side, angling its cannons upwards. One fired. This shot was perhaps unintentional, but it hit the mast of *The Lady Mary*'s mainsail, causing it to snap cleanly in half. The sail, along with the crow's-nest and Adam in it, came tumbling down. The crow's-nest was too high to hit the deck, rather, the mast collided with the edge of the deck and snapped again. Lumberlodge plunged into the sea, followed by burning debris. An opposition also treaded water nearby, pistol in hand. He fired, missing Lumberlodge's head by a foot. He fired a second time, missing again through the difficulty of staying afloat. With no time to load his musket, Lumberlodge pulled out a double-barrelled pistol and fired back. The sea was choppy now, and one particularly powerful wave submerged both pirates for a moment.

Tom took hold of another rope, took a deep breath, and swung towards *Queen Anne's Revenge*. A challenger met him midair. He held his cutlass out and sliced through the rope, assisted by the added firepower. The rival splashed into the water to join Lumberlodge. Tom planted both feet on his foe's deck. Two men ran at him. At the same time, he caught one with his sword and the other with his left fist, knocking him backwards. He drew his sword from the first man's body, pivoted and got the second while dodging a hook to the face. A third man shot at him, but the bullets deflected off the sword. From the deck of his own ship, Doyle threw a knife, which landed directly in the third man's chest. He dropped his gun and Tom hit him to the floor.

"Thank you!" Thomas yelled to Clementini in a way that was joking without undermining his actual gratitude.

Gun-deck

Elliott thought he'd save some time by loading multiple cannonballs into the cannons at once, and maybe three times the amount of gunpowder necessary. He had a great barrel full to the brim of cannonballs, so found no reason to use them sparingly.

The men at Blackbeard's cannons began to throw lit torches out of their windows and into Elliott's, who placed them in a bucket of water to put them out. After a while of this, in between further cannon fire, he ran to the cabin and brought back on a tray: glasses of rum. The next one to throw a torch, or to fire their cannon, got a glass of rum in the face. Rather than putting out the torches, now he chucked them back, as well as his own. If he were lucky, it would land in rum and catch fire. This differed slightly from the kind of warfare either crew was used to.

The sea below

Back in the water, Lumberlodge rose and spat the salty water from his mouth. He was about to take another shot, as he realised there was someone behind him. The second swimming pirate lunged at him with his cutlass. Lumberlodge avoided it by falling backwards. He then spun around and shot his pistol underwater and took out his surprise attacker. The first man then shot again, skimming his jacket.

"You just can't hit me, can you, man?" He dug at his opponent. Adam would not miss again, he was adamant. He drew a second pistol and fired both rounds quickly. Both hit. The sea was red around him. He swam to both corpses and took their guns and ammunition. Eventually he grabbed hold of part of the mast to keep him afloat. In this moment of rest, he reloaded all the guns in his possession with what little dry gunpowder he had.

Main-deck

Tom stood for a moment to catch his breath.

"Let's see what you've got, Goldenlocks Glove!"

From behind, Blackbeard had made a dash towards Tom with his own cutlass drawn. Blackbeard, while he carried many guns, liked to fight the old-fashioned way. He believed it was the truest test of skill — no long — range weapons, just hand to hand, or sword to sword combat.

"Was about to say the same thing about you, Blackbeard!" Tom replied, holding out his cutlass to block his enemy's. Blackbeard stopped, both swords forced against each other.

"A flaming cutlass?" he asked, partially jealous. Truth is, Thatch had already seen this before, as he watched Thomas battle his crew, but he had paid little attention to it, perhaps passing it off as a torch or losing it in the glow of burning timbers. The bizarre nature of the weapon left him rather awestruck. Tom used this to his advantage.

Gun-deck

Back on the gun-deck, Elliott was still juggling between rum chucking and torch throwing and cannon firing. There were now several major punctures in the walls of both boats. During the highest waves, or when a large piece of the boat would fall into the sea, water splashed up and ran across the floor. There was now only one enemy left on the gun-deck, for all the others had abandoned, burnt, or got caught up in the fight above. They both attempted to rush to the closest cannon to their rival, while undetected, to deal a finishing blow. However, unlike Doyle, stealth was not Elliott's area of expertise, especially with a wet floor. Time after time he tried to catch his opponent off guard, but each time he would detect his movements and get out of the way, only then to respond with his own foiled shot. This game continued for a while, each round weakening both ships. But soon Elliott found himself with no cannonballs to spare, he had already depleted the once plentiful supply. After his last shot, which was no more effective than the others, he dashed to a crate in the corner to search for more. He scrambled around, throwing all sorts of items around in an unusual, disorderly fashion. He tipped over boxes and tossed around ropes and tools.

The hold

The Lady Mary had two small rowboats. One was in need of repair. The other gave Tudor Boris an idea. He rushed down the stairs again to haul up two more barrels, one of gunpowder, one of rum, one on each shoulder. The recent events led to the invention of a whole new form of warfare — rum bombs. Tudor tied both barrels to the boat and shoved it off the deck. He lowered himself down with a rope. He grabbed the oars and began rowing with great power around his own boat and to the back of Blackbeard's (the back being the side not facing *The Lady Mary,* the side which was being given no attention). Taking a hammer, which he had put in his pocket, he began to break through the side of the ship. The gap he had made grew larger and larger as he pulled away now loose slats. The ship was already beginning to fill with water, pulling the rowboat in too. Tudor ducked as the rowboat fell into the cargo hold.

Queen Anne's Revenge: **main-deck**

Thomas pushed with his cutlass and knocked Blackbeard back. Thatch, who was no longer hypnotised by the flames, retaliated with a swipe of his. Tom dodged and thrust with his sword again. Thatch, who lifted Tom's arm up by swinging his sword to the side, blocked this. He gave a kick to Tom's knee with the entire sole of his boot. Tom fell to his knees but held out his sword just in time to survive another blow of Thatch's sword. With their weapons once again together, he slowly rose to his knees, forcing Thatch back as he did.

He took a swipe with his cutlass and caught Thatch's coat, tearing it. His opponent counterattacked and cut Tom's forearm. Thatch kicked Tom a second time, then punched him in the face with a strong right-hook. He fell to the floor, dropping his cutlass, which slid into the sea, finally being put out as it sizzled weakly.

"A noble effort, boy," Thatch remarked, "I'm glad I could trust you to find that treasure for me,"

"You don't know me."

"Better than you think."

"Thatch!" Glove yelled, grabbing hold of a rope hanging from the flagpoles of *Queen Anne's Revenge.*

"Glove!" Thatch turned away from Tom to confront Andrew Glove, "Are you ready to surrender?"

"I'd sooner die!"

"Good man!"

Gun-deck

On the gun-deck, Elliott had not yet found any more cannonballs.

"Bugger!" he exclaimed. The enemy vessel fired another shot. The angle of the shot was almost 45 degrees to *The Lady Mary*, bursting first through the wall and then through the ceiling above. Planks of wood fell in front of Elliott, causing him to fall backwards. The boat rocked terribly, sending him and the wreckage sliding across the floor, straight towards the ruined wall. Due to all the cannon fire, the wall was so weakened that it gave way as soon as Elliott collided with it. In a desperate effort, he reached out to slow himself. His palm only continued to slip on the sodden floorboards, and Elliott fell to join Lumberlodge in the water. As he was falling, Lumberlodge yelled to him, "Elliott, man!" He descended into the depths headfirst, becoming completely submerged. Lumberlodge watched, waiting for him to emerge from the water. After 30 seconds, Elliott still had not reappeared. A series of bubbles floated vigorously to the surface.

"Elliott?" he yelled, reaching into the sea, "Elliott?"

Elliott's hand suddenly burst out of the water, shaking desperately. Lumberlodge dived from his float to assist, but the hand darted back down. Elliott Ethan was gone.

Queen Anne's Revenge: the hold

The cargo hold of *Queen Anne's Revenge* was dark and full of rats, which sat atop crates, avoiding the incoming seawater. Tudor lit a torch with flint and steel to see where he was going. He rowed the boat to where even more alcohol was being stored in huge drums and tossed his torch into the alcohol to ignite it. Then, he hammered against a barrel to break it. He had done this with significant effect, too much effect. The barrel burst open, and rum poured out, not yet reaching any flame. He sprinted for the exit. The entire room suddenly went up in flames as alcohol burnt in a chain reaction, causing the next barrel to burn too.

Tudor dived into the water to avoid the fire. He trod water, watching the havoc he had just caused. Slowly, the end of a strange appendage lifted itself from the water. It was partially like a turtle's flipper, but had claws like a lizard or bird's, with a larger hooked one being from the thumb. Barnacles had grown on it, though it was hard to tell what was barnacle and what was scale, for those too were large and rugged. The claws gently, slowly, brushed Tudor's face, and he was too terrified to move. He closed his eyes in fear, and then the second flipper rose to grasp him in between them. He whimpered, petrified; the flippers gently nudged him.

Surprisingly, both flippers released the man and disappeared within the waves. Tudor sighed in relief and put his hand on a cross that he wore around his neck. This relief was, however, premature. Jaws six feet wide and like a crocodile's lunged out of the water, swallowing him whole. The scutes on its head were like armour plates, and its teeth were fangs almost as tall as a man. The head fell back below the depths, and bubbles followed like the sea was boiling. Tudor Boris was no more.

Both ships: main-deck

Both Thatch and Glove stood with rope in hand, ready to swing into action.

"Thatch!" Glove began, "Come and get me!"

Each let out a battle cry as they leapt from their ships. Each held their swords out as they swung past each other. The collision's velocity knocked Glove's weapon from his hands. Using the momentum they had gathered, they swayed back again. This time, Glove clenched his fist and punched down on the flat side of Blackbeard's cutlass. Thatch reached out and snatched hold of the locket Glove had the jewel sealed in. Glove seized the chain, thus preventing his neck from being pulled. The two remained suspended together above the crashing water below. Glove let go of the rope, causing him and his foe to fall into the water.

The waves

Thatch drew a pistol and attempted to fire. Glove had quickly reacted and forced the barrel down, so it fired into the water. Glove threw a punch. Thatch ducked. Thatch tugged. Glove tugged back. Glove would not let go. Thatch wouldn't either.

Glove couldn't help but ask, "If you want it so badly, why'd you not get it yourself?"

"Mortality brings fear to us both, it's no secret. I once thought making my name immortal would do, but when I'm told of a treasure that brings true eternal life, I couldn't resist. I couldn't resist. Intoxicating, the gamble of a few decades against forever. But you know that."

"You didn't answer my question."

"Hope. There's your answer. I ran out of that years ago. The slightest risk seems all too great when you don't have hope, especially when you're wagering your life. But you still have some hope left somewhere, you have to, as do your men. I am thankful, Glove, you know. I may be out of hope, but I had faith in you."

"Flattered," Glove interrupted.

"And your crew! Your brilliant crew! No matter how great the odds, they always come through," Blackbeard paused in thought, and his tone became rather sinister for what he was saying, "because they have passion. And that passion comes from you."

"Don't tell me about passion, Thatch," Glove added, surprisingly gravely.

Despite Glove's order, Thatch continued as if he hadn't heard, "and as everyone knows, each and every member of your tiny crew has the passion you burnt into them. All I had to do was wait until you plucked up the courage to search for it and come and take it off your hands."

"That much faith in us?"

"My men lack the spirit of yours, and the motivation. All I needed to do was give you, their captain, a little push."

"What kind of push?"

"Don't act like you've forgotten! Don't pretend you don't know! I know you haven't put it behind you!"

"Don't say it," Glove muttered.

Thatch paused for a moment, and an eerie silence followed. He looked Glove directly and harshly in the eyes and moved his lips like somewhere between mouthing and a whisper.

"Mary."

Glove let go of the chain and gave Thatch the hardest punch in the face he'd ever felt. Thatch spat and yelled, "At-a-boy!" He then dived back and began swimming away with the locket. Glove soon caught up. He placed a hand on his shoulder and pulled him from the sea.

"You don't deserve this!"

He pulled the locket from Thatch's hand, but he still clung to the chain.

"Let go, you murderer!" Glove barked.

"Murderer? We're all murderers here!"

Now, a large, serpentine body had coiled around both ships. It had scutes like a crocodile's, fins like a fish, but was constricting the boats like a snake. Further masts with their sails crashed down as the wailing sound of strained wood and steel struck fear into all ears. Slowly and ominously, a reptilian head ascended from the depths. The head of a fanged alligator, wider than a man is tall and as long as three.

"Leviathan!" one crewmember screamed.

The Leviathan opened its mouth, and its throat glowed with a flame of blue.

Glove and Thatch froze, both holding the locket. The boats were squeezed closer and closer together as they began to collapse. The body, which was ten-foot-thick, slithered around each mast and around the sides of both ships, which groaned in agony. All the pirates in the water swam desperately to escape the impending doom of being crushed between two large vessels. The locket remained in the possession of both adversaries.

"Musket!" Glove yelled to Lumberlodge, who was letting water spill from his gun's barrel, "Musket! Musket, man. Musket, man!"

Lumberlodge's musket was fired for one last time as both ships came crashing down over their owners. There were no survivors.

Act 1: Riders In the Sky

Chapter I

Hell

Five years had passed since the unspoken conflict that led to the demise of both *Queen Anne's Revenge* and *The Lady Mary*. In a distant solar system, on a scorched planet, a pinkish sun dipped below a sage green sky. This planet was not so different from Earth, but some details were quite peculiar. The first is that this was no green planet; everything soon burnt, and almost all the trees had been stripped of any foliage. There was less water on the surface, though vast oceans still existed. But these seas were not blue — they were a translucent scarlet colour. They appeared as if they'd be hot. And they were — for oceans, being about 30 or more degrees Celsius (that's 86+ in Fahrenheit), but just something about their hellish appearance would lead you to assume they'd be as equally hellishly warm.

The animals here were also scorched, many identical to those the crew of *The Lady Mary* had fought within the mountain. They mostly appeared nomadic, possessing no form of settlements or even houses and occasionally fleeing at the sight of some form of larger creature. In fact, there were many larger creatures. Many resembled fiery versions of familiar Earth-dwelling species; others, not so much.

This world seemed quite idle, free of anything in particular, merely existing with no sense of hurry or direction. That was until a single bull sprinted doggedly into view. As expected of a creature of this location, fire displaced his eyes. As the beast snorted in exhaustion, smoke sprayed forward as red sparks fluttered past his furious face. His hooves were metallic and refused to tremble under the ton weight. The beast bore a burning orange pentagram branded on its flank, which continued to burn on its ragged, leathery, black hide, and even blacker horns twisted from its skull. He let out short and sharp lows as his head rocked forward with each tremendous stride. Finally, his legs gave way as the animal collapsed to the floor.

As he struggled back to his feet, the earth (or rather, not the Earth) rumbled. Pebbles on the barren floor began to jump up and down and roll around as the ground below them shook. Now, more snorts, pants, and lows were audible. The bull rose to his feet and began running as a stampede of several hundred, perhaps thousands more followed. These cattle shared the first bull's general appearance: some larger, some faster, some with bigger horns, and some with snapped off ones. And some were flying. Not in a flapping wings sense, or in a gracefully gliding, Santa's reindeer way. No, they appeared to be charging as all the others were, just no feet touched the ground. The creatures felled naked trees and trampled them to oblivion within seconds, while other creatures dashed away to avoid the same fate. For anything to stand in the herd's way would be a catastrophic mistake.

More and more cattle flooded the landscape. Over a meandering red river. Over an empty plane. Through a lifeless forest. Then came creatures that were not bovine. Horses. Perhaps I needn't describe these horses to you, for they are as you likely imagine. Angry, tired, fiery horses. They also snorted fire. Rusted iron tack fastened around their starved bellies, and chain reins tugged on a foul bit. On their backs rode people. You may guess what these people look like — fiery, bony, and exhausted. Wrong. They were indeed bony and exhausted, but they were not at all on fire, nor did any flame erupt from any crevice of their bodies. They were regular people, mostly. To be precise, they were cowboys. Cowboys from Earth, not space cowboys, whatever they'd be.

"Steady, boys!" One yelled with a strong Texan accent, "We're nearly there."

"Why are we doing this?" asked another.

"To get back to the darned Earth!"

"Should never 'ave taken that stupid crystal!"

"Shouldn't've got killed by that son-of-a-gun sea monster!"

They continued chasing the herd for miles. Past a valley. Around a lake. Even through a small bay where an old but repaired early 18th century ship lay at anchor. Clear alterations, such as glass windows above each cannon and additional windows to brighten each floor, had occurred since the ship's original construction. The sails, however, remained old and un-repaired for linen and cotton were in short supply — and by that, I mean there was none.

Chapter II

The Lady Mary

The crew of the ship were doing nothing. Just sitting around waiting for something to happen. Just the same as they had done for the past five years. After they had repaired their ship and done enough exploring to conclude that there wasn't anything worth exploring, they had found themselves left aimless. No idea of what to do next or how to get there. I expect you already know the individuals I am about to introduce — so I won't. Tudor Boris lay lazily in a hammock, rocking calmly in the breeze as he wrapped his curly, dark hair around his finger. Doyle Clementini leant against the ratlines and sharpened two knives against each other. Not that they weren't already razor sharp, but rather he had nothing else to do, and sharpening knives can make a man feel important. Maddy Casserole lounged in the crow's-nest of the mainsail, dining on one of her latest concoctions, a water biscuit with a layer of salted beef on top. She ate it with her hands and tried to ignore how awfully dry it was.

Elliott Ethan sat atop an empty barrel on the main-deck, with a piece of parchment stretched out across the top of another. He busily sketched away on the parchment — a map. Mapping the landscape they had ventured into became his self-appointed mission. He had discarded many attempts, striving for great perfection. The pencil he used was now short and had a diagonally flattened edge from the way he drew with it. Like the herd of cattle had ended the idleness of the plains, something ended the idleness of the ship.

"Clementini!"

"Boris!"

"You up for a game of cards?"

"Yup!"

"Lumberlodge!"

"What!"

"You in?"

"Gimme a minute! You two coming?"

"Sure."

"Why not?"

That brief exchange concluded, they all abandoned their former positions, congregating around a barrel on deck. They each pulled up their own barrels to sit atop. Maddy had brought with her a stash of crackers and leftover bred. Sitting on the tallest barrel to compensate for her stature, she shared the food among the crew as the cards were dealt. She then removed the band of cloth from around her forehead, revealing a streak of paler skin that was less familiar with sunshine.

Elliott Ethan was always first to deal. Not that he was eager to volunteer, it was more of an unspoken rule formed from the fact that he was indeed always first to deal. He shuffled two packs of 54 cards (each pack had two jokers alongside 1-10, jack, queen and king of four suits), not dissimilar to the cards you will be familiar with, except no genius had thought to give the face cards two heads so that they appear the same from both ways around. Rum had stained some, rats had nibbled others, but they were readable and did not affect the outcome of playing (except for a four of diamonds, which had been so yellowed that it was instantly distinguishable from both the front and back).

The game they were playing was of their own creation but shared many aspects with the branded card game Uno or a card game known as blackjack, which differs from the more popular game of the same name. Elliott dealt seven cards to each player, with a single card placed face up beside the face-down leftover deck. It was a three of spades. The game involved placing a single card of the same suit or number on top of the top card. Jacks switched the order of play from clockwise to anti-clockwise/vice versa, queens made the next person pick up three cards (and miss a go), and kings skipped the next person's turn. If a player played a joker, the next player picked up seven cards but still took their turn afterward; also, the player who played the joker chose the suit. If you could place no card, you would miss a go, and pick up from the top of the deck. Lumberlodge, seated to Elliott's left, began by playing a four of spades. Tudor then placed a four of hearts.

Then, Thomas climbed onto the deck from the kitchen, and pulled a stool beside the table. Tom was, and had been from a young age, the ship's cook, but found himself free while his food was cooking to join in the game. With him came Glove, who also wanted to join in.

"Give us some cards then!" Tom said, as Maddy began counting two piles of seven cards from the top of the deck.

"Whoa, whoa, no!" Elliott interrupted, "If you're going to play, I am to re-deal."

"Come on!" Maddy insisted, "How does it matter?"

"It just does, come on, give me your cards."

"Aye, I agree with Elliott," Tudor added, "It's only fair."

"How is this unfair?" Adam complained as Tudor collected the cards in for the dealer.

"Just do as you're told," Glove said to those complaining.

"Now, are we all present and correct?" Elliott asked.

Elliott dealt each player seven cards; afterwards, the game lasted over half an hour.

"And I win!" Lumberlodge yelled, placing his last card over a six of spades.

"Oh, for God's sake, Adam!" Thomas replied, too on his final card. Maddy chucked her pile of cards onto the table in defeat.

"Hang on," Elliott began, that card is not a spade.

"What do you mean, of course it is," Adam rejected, attempting to pile up the cards. Elliott stopped him and pointed to the card he had placed.

"It's the seven of clubs, not spades, just the gaps between the three circles making the club have been pencilled in."

"How'd that happen?" Lumberlodge bluffed.

"I think you know very well how."

"Alright, I did it, but this game has gone on long enough!" Adam admitted before ordering, "Give it to me then, Boris, your turn."

"You need to pick up first." Tudor told him. Lumberlodge held up his first two fingers to Tudor under the table as he picked up a card from the top of the pile.

Tudor placed down the true seven of spades, then he added, "Oh, I'm the best at this game! Now, I can't lose."

"You don't know yet," Elliott argued.

"I do know — I really can't lose."

"So, you've got a joker, then?"

Tudor paused, realising his mistake, "Well, you don't know yet."

"Haha, we know your card now!" Maddy laughed.

"Well, I know yours too because you threw them on the table."

"Yeah?"

"Yeah! You're about to put down the seven of hearts."

Maddy flushed as she did indeed place down the seven of hearts, leaving her with only one more card.

"And now you're left with the king of diamonds," Tudor said far too boastfully, saying it required nothing but a single functioning eye to know. Maddy punched Tudor in the leg.

Next, Glove placed down a card, though he was not so close to winning. Doyle had only one card left, the eight of diamonds, but could not place it, so he went to pick up. Instead of one card, he picked up two, hoping that he would gain at least one valuable one. He gained a queen of hearts and an ace of spades. Tom was next and placed a two of hearts over his father's six of the same suit. Completing the cycle was Elliott, who had six cards, five were hearts and one was a joker. Rather foolishly for such an intelligent man, he placed the joker down, making Adam pick up seven. He chose the suit to remain hearts, confusing the others a little.

"I thought you couldn't lose, Boris?" Adam mocked as he placed down the king of hearts.

"You must be cheating again!" Tudor complained.

"It's the king of hearts, plain as day," Elliott confirmed.

"But I already placed it earlier!"

"But there's two packs, knob-head!" Adam said, mimicking Tudor's tone.

"Yeah, but…"

"No, sod off and miss a go. You're going to lose now!"

"At least I didn't cheat," Tudor said proudly, "Shows I'm still better at the game."

The game continued again with everyone placing cards besides Maddy, who could not, for the suit remained h. Glove put the queen of spades down.

"Pick up three, Clementini!"

"Pick up six, Thomas," Doyle said, placing another queen on the pile.

"Stop right there!"

"Whoa, what are you doing?"

"Excuse me!"

"What?" Doyle insisted in a suddenly high-pitched voice that made it obvious he knows he's guilty of something.

"You can't do that!"

"Says who?"

"No one has ever done that, and we've played this game for ten years!"

"I haven't played it for ten years."

"You've played it for long enough."

"I think it's a good idea," Tom interjected, "I'll pick up six cards."

"Tom, you're throwing away your victory."

"Yeah, but it's a better game now. And anyway…"

Tom placed his ultimate card down — the queen of hearts.

"Pick up nine, Elliott! And I win."

"Well played."

Tudor shook Thomas' hand, and Doyle patted him on the back.

"Thank you, you card-playing moron," he joked before sniffing the air for the smell of his baking food, "I better go and get that bread out."

Captain's cabin

Glove had returned to his quarters after playing cards and sat in his old chair. He tossed a familiar object up into the air and caught it repetitively. It was the same crystal that he had attained atop the mountain — the same crystal that left him stranded in Hell, or at least half of it, for the other half was in possession of one Edward Thatch. While he did this, he never looked at the object directly, for his eyes were fixed on something else. He gazed entranced at a painting on the wall. A painting of his wife, Mary.

His son entered a few minutes later to inform him that the meal was ready. Glove did not respond directly to this piece of information, and instead said, "You know, son, if I could, I'd try to find her."

"Mother?" Tom asked, curious about this sudden train of thought.

"Aye, but there is not a chance that she'd be here. No, this is a place of sinners, for people like us. Angels like her do not come near here."

He waited for a response, but Tom had no reply.

"But at least we went down together, we're still together, together with my crew."

"And at least we can't die," Tom added, mostly because he didn't know what else to say.

"We are dead."

"I like to pretend we aren't."

"'Tis Hell, ain't it?"

"Yeah, but it's nicer pretending."

Glove dropped the crystal, and it shook. A mist floated above it, and the mist began to move. It moved to show a vision of Earth. It felt to Glove as if it were neither the past, nor the present, nor the future; though it was presumably one of them. The vision was one of the Middle Ages, in England. The weather was pleasant, and the sun beginning to rise. A small village lay closely within the valley between two smooth, green hills. A white carthorse with a small man on its back rambled calmly towards the town. Smoke drifted from chimneys and fires to meet the reddening sky. As the steed plodded further along the trail, which had been trampled in the clay dirt by footsteps and hooves, a ringing bell became apparent. The man did not appear alarmed; he took to admiring the sunrise over the hill he had just travelled over — it was like the sun had followed him.

Neither pirate knew what to think of this, so just kept staring into the mystical cloud for further revelation. For a few more minutes, the man just progressed towards the town, seeming rather content. When he got there, however, he was less cheerful. He remained on the back of his horse, which was walking more cautiously as its shoeless hooves tiptoed on cobblestones. A new sound had now drowned out the ringing bell. Crying. The man could not tell from where, but it was unmistakable. He turned a corner to find the path full of people sitting against the walls of buildings. A terrible cough and an awful rash racked them. It was obvious that a plague had struck them. They were queuing for something. And that something was the doctor's surgery that sat on the corner of the street. It was a small building made of brick, unlike the even smaller houses, which were made from older stone.

It was the other side of this building that was reached after the horse turned another corner. This side was a sight even sorrier than the front. A wooden cart full of bodies sat outside a side door to the surgery. They ordered the carthorse to stop just in front of the cart before someone from the hospital rushed out to help attach it to the horse's harness. The man quickly told the animal to continue, and they left the village with their cart of bodies, heading back over the hill towards the sun. Finally, the ghostly vision ceased, leaving Glove and his son to decipher it.

"It's never done that before," Glove remarked.

"Do you ever wonder if we could get back?" Tom asked, though his dad looked at him blankly, "What if we could get back to Earth?"

"And give up everything we worked for? Give up our safety, our eternal safety?"

"But we didn't work for this, did we? We were conned, bested, fooled. We were promised eternal life, this is hardly life!"

"Don't be so ridiculous, boy! We are safe, we have our family, we have nothing to fear!"

"But plenty to want!"

"You don't know what you're talking about. We all have everything we need, what more could you 'want'?"

"More than this! More than the same thing everyday forever. What point is eternal life if we have nothing to live for?"

"I'll hear no more of this, son," Glove said finally, "Let's go and enjoy our supper."

Tom did as his father asked and walked to the kitchen ahead of his father to start dishing out the meal of chicken and bread, while Glove went to inform the rest of the crew.

Crow's-nest

In the crow's-nest, Maddy saw something out of the corner of her eye. Something big and fiery. She took her telescope and extended it to see into the distance. It was a herd of cattle charging as a group across the land. Elliott prized the telescope from her to look. Adam took his own too and observed the herd.

"People!" he exclaimed, "Bloody people!"

"Where?"

"On horseback alongside the Hell-spawned cows."

"People!" Maddy yelled down to her crewmates.

Glove rushed from the cabin onto the deck, and like the others, drew his telescope. The sight had quickly diminished over the horizon but remained frozen in their minds. They were no longer alone. But they were also hungry, so went to get their supper without delay.

Queen Anne's Revenge

Blackbeard sat in his office on his flagship. The room was not lit by the windows, for the curtains were closed, and no lamp flamed. Two unfamiliar figures sat opposite him, facing away. The only source of light was around each of these men's heads. A purple ring of light around one, yellow around the other, each split at the top. They were not bright, but obviously magical. Both men wore cloaks concealing their wings. Physically superior to the pirate, but they came with information superior to themselves. The three had talked for a while, but their conversation was coming to an end.

"I must thank you both," Thatch said genuinely, as he swatted away a fly, "the secrets you have revealed to me being a great opportunity. In fact, I might even go so far as to say they bring me hope."

"It is our duty, sir. Our goal is to inform all worthy men of this information, to help them make their own conclusions," the one with the purple light said.

"I have no doubt you will become a wealthy man indeed, if you play your cards right," said the one with the yellow light, "Your destination lies north of here, follow the coast and you will find the canyon. And in the canyon lies Pandæmonium."

"Very well, I shall see you there," Thatch replied, looking at his compass.

"Perhaps," one said as Thatch looked up, but they were already gone. The door remained unused, but they were gone.

Chapter III

Hell

The group of cowboys continued to herd the cattle. In the sky above, the black silhouette of another planet hung ominously close, making the sky appear even darker. It blocked out all the surrounding stars.

One cow broke off from the herd. A herder spun a lasso as he chased her down.

"Bring her in!" someone shouted. He approached the cow from its left flank, attempting to push it back into the group. When he was close enough, he tossed his lasso, narrowly missing her neck because of her wide horn-span. Again. Got her. The cow stopped, clashing her hooves on the stony ground, creating that horrible noise similar to nails on a chalkboard. The horse did not stop, so the rider tried to tug the cow with it. She refused. Another wrangler came up from behind and cracked his whip against its rump. She was furious, letting out a shocking roar. Without warning, she took off, flying above the ground at an alarming rate away from the herd. The ability of flight was apparently unique to the cattle, but the horse was too massive to be lifted. Being unprepared, the horse failed to keep up and toppled over its forelegs, sending its rider loose. At first, the horseman was dragged across the ground, but then he rose. Letting go of his lasso, he fell to the ground. The wrath of the herd soon devoured him under the pounding of steel hooves.

They approached a stone structure. It was round, and the sky above it was lit by lights both rising from it and towards the neighbouring planet and from the planet to the table. Immense and rectangular pieces of rock protruded to form a series of circles, sitting within each other. More rocks sat horizontally upon these, connecting them to form a circle, like a complete Stonehenge. In fact, the pattern was almost identical to that of the English landmark should it have remained completely intact.

"We're here, fellas!"

"Easy does it!"

As if it were from the sight of this phenomenon, the herd shot off in every other direction without care to their pursuers or their steeds or whips. They bellowed and snorted and moaned, leaping over each other and clashing horns in their rebellion. All the riders' work had been for nothing. The herd was wild, uncontrollable — almost uncontrollable.

"Son of a…"

The Devil's Canyon

The cowboys we have been following rode now through a canyon. No herd followed, and they moved slowly and cautiously. A horse whinnied as pebbles fell from the top of the gorge, which was so dark it was indistinguishable from the black of the sky. The first rider held out a lantern to guide the way.

"Perhaps we should turn back," one rider began.

"No, he'll find us anyway, and he'll be worse."

The horses reared as the lantern went out. There was an eerie chill that was unmistakable in the usually warm air of Hell.

"Whoa!" the riders yelled to steady the horses, but they refused to continue.

"Dismount! It's just a little this way."

So, they did dismount and tied the horses to pegs, which they hammered into the ground — yes; they were indeed carrying all of this.

"Back so soon?" spoke a voice from behind. The leader turned around. There was no one there. He then carried on walking to find a figure less than a yard in front of his face. The figure was tall and lean, with pale skin that was wrinkled like an elephant's. Not that his frame was particularly slender, in fact, it was quite the opposite, rather that a metaphorical yet uncontrollable hunger had not been satisfied and had somehow manifested itself into a physical starvation.

"I have some bad news to, erm, report, Mister, erm, Mr Satan."

"Is that so?" The figure was well-spoken, talking in a slow and careful manner. His clothes were basic and white, appearing darker and greener in the night sky, yet somehow the silver tips of his slightly curled hair reflected white light. Handcuffs locked each of his hands, but the chain connecting them was broken and rusted. Two warm blue eyes stared sternly into those of the Riders' leader.

"You have failed me."

"Wait a darned minute!" the leader argued, as his reply was at once received through a look that could not just kill but devour one's soul.

"You have failed. You, the so-called master of cattle-wrangling, have failed to do the one thing you say to have mastered."

"They're uncontrollable, I swear, lost a man trying."

"Not just one."

Satan swiftly grasped the cowboy's throat and pushed him against the wall of the gorge while lifting his feet off of the ground.

"God."

"God?"

"God. Help. Me."

"What God?" Satan asked with a smile, "You made a deal with me, you knew what to expect from your failure." His eyes glowed as his victim's last breath puffed painfully away.

"You've lost your soul to me today. We made a deal, and you failed. Who could possibly drive my herd to the Gate of Ubyvis?"

A single round of shot landed on the cowboy's forehead. Astounded, Satan dropped his body and slowly twisted his neck to see which of the five riders had deprived him of his kill. But it was no rider.

"I could!" yelled a weathered voice from behind. A long pause followed.

"Have you come to challenge me, the Devil?"

"Come to make a deal!"

"Blackbeard?"

"You know me?"

"Call me a fan."

"Flattered!" There was another long pause.

"Okay then, lay out your terms." Satan agreed as Thatch reached into his pocket and drew the other half of the crystal.

"This bloody stone torments me! It's done so since I found myself here after battling Glove. Shows me the riches I left behind — on Earth and elsewhere."

"So, you're what? Jealous?"

"Furious! What good is eternal life if you can't find eternal good! And what's more, I have been told of secrets of the skies, the Universe. But that also makes me gladdened. Good messengers have told me of the wealth that lies on endless planets, wealth most men will never dream of! "

"So, you think you can drive my herd of cattle in exchange for what? Authority over the alien worlds? Access to all their treasures?"

"Exactly, but I would not drive the herd, but deliver," Blackbeard explained, stepping closer to Satan, "There be three ships in my fleet, with some reinforcement each could hold a hundred oxen."

"Know something, if I agree, you must promptly destroy the first planet you have plundered, by releasing the herd."

"I don't see that as a problem, just tell me where."

"You must start where you left off — your home world, Earth. The Gate of Ubyvis can lead you there."

"I see, and I respect that decision. Just assure me I cannot perish in the midst of this procedure."

"That stone grants immunity to your soul, and with it, you can return to Hell at any time. I am indeed beginning to like this plan of yours, Mr Thatch."

"Well, I'll need some wranglers, ain't that so, boys?" Blackbeard began, turning to the four cowboys. Thatch had cared not enough to realise one minor detail: there were supposed to be five riders. Satan, however, was calculating and observant enough to pick up on this.

"Where on Hell did the other one go?" he asked. They all looked over both shoulders and saw that they were a man down.

"Leave him!" Thatch insisted, "yous will be enough."

"Show me the crystal," Satan demanded. Thatch held out the jewel, still out of reach of the Devil. Satan beckoned for him to place it onto his palm. Slowly, the pirate obliged and dropped the item from his long, brown fingernails into the dry hand.

Satan tutted as he ran his fingers around the stone's edges.

"This will not do."

"What be ya saying?"

"I am saying that this crystal will not do. I enchanted the crystals both as a key here and as the key out. You must present it before the Gate of Ubyvis in order to open the portal. But this one is not whole, it is a broken key, so will not do."

"You boys got a key?"

"Erm, I believe Noah had it, sir."

"You Noah?" Blackbeard asked, pointing at the next cowboy.

"No, sir. Noah's the fella who just ran off, sir."

"What y'all talking 'bout? Carl had it,"

"So, you must be Carl?"

"No, Carl's dead, sir."

"Who gave Carl it?" the cowboys began arguing amongst themselves.

"Why, Noah did."

"And who even gave Noah it?"

"Boss did."

"End your bickering. There is another, or rather, the other. The other half to this," Satan said, placing the crystal back into Thatch's hand.

"Glove."

"Indeed, indeed. Beelzebub! Get me a map." Next, a tall, dark silhouette with two dark and feathered wings upon his back flew into view as if from the walls of the cave. Flies buzzed around him, though he seemed entirely unbothered by them.

"Beelzebub!" Thatch greeted.

"You know him?" Satan questioned, though it had been he who had ordered Beelzebub to acquaint Thatch in the first place. Specifically, he had done this to encourage the pirate to do exactly what he had done — come and make a deal.

"The map, my dear Beelzebub." Sure enough, Beelzebub handed Satan the map. The map depicted the geography of the planet. Satan pointed to a spot.

"We are here, okay? And *The Lady Mary* is anchored here. Take the *Revenge* to retrieve the stone, it should take you about half a day to reach them. I will ensure that the two remaining ships are prepped and loaded for your return, and the map shall guide you from there."

The two continued discussing technicalities for a few more minutes, ensuring every aspect of the plan was ready.

"Then I'll be off, boys."

"Just one minute."

"What?"

"I have yet to lay out my terms."

"And what are they?"

"Your soul."

"My soul?"

"Yes, should you fail, your soul is mine. Should you not deliver the herd through the Gate, your soul is mine. Should you break our accord, your soul is mine. And not just your soul, but the soul of every member of your crew."

"Alright, we have a contract." Blackbeard agreed confidently, offering to shake Satan's hand.

"We ought to make this official, don't you think?" The Devil rejected this handshake.

"Must we?" Thatch complained slightly, for he was used to a firm handshake being the most official way of making an agreement. To this, Satan just stared.

"Once you are prepared, we will reconvene in my palace, Pandæmonium, and I shall call upon The Fates to witness our treaty and hold our souls accountable."

Chapter IV

The Lady Mary

"Dinner is served!" Thomas yelled to his crew as they entered the kitchen. They sat themselves around a large dining table, which hung on chains from both the ceiling and floor to stop the food from sliding as the ship rocked. Tom opened a reasonably sized oven, from which a chimney took smoke outside the ship. He had taken the time to roast a whole chicken, and a fresh loaf of bread cooled on the table.

Elliott Ethan had kept a small flock of chickens in a pen in a section of the cargo hold. A window had been fitted beside the coop to keep up egg production and let any hens sit on eggs to ensure a stable population, as Adam Lumberlodge had the habit of going in the pen, wringing one's neck, and getting Tom to pluck, process and cook it. Elliott had even fitted raised beds on the sides of the quarterdeck to grow wheat, barley, oats, and potatoes for both his chickens and Thomas' cooking (and for attempting to brew ale).

As Tom was carving the chicken, Doyle swooped in and took two big slices of breast meat. Elliott had already cut two very thick slices of bread. With much laughter, ruthless pirate banter, and reminiscing, they quickly devoured the chicken and bread. As if it were through no fault of his own, the crystal fell from Glove's locket and bounced on the floor. A mist rose as it had before, and a similar series of events followed. This time the entire crew was present. The mist swirled around and parted to reveal a second vision. Again, the vision was of the past, though it was the future for them should they return in the time they left. The year was 1916 in France. Hundreds of men held themselves against ladders in 6-foot muddy trenches, each holding a bayonet rifle.

Adam, who had never seen a bayonet, remarked, "I like the look of those."

"The guns or the men?" Maddy joked.

"Both. I love that dude's beard."

The joking ended when a piercing whistle blew. So terrified that there was no hesitation at all, every man ascended the ladder and together charged forward from the trench, climbing over barbed wire and avoiding falling into craters left by shells. Then it began. It sounded like one of those needlessly screechy fireworks, but more terrible. They were under attack, yet not one tried to retreat. A great shell pulverised the ground upon impact. The crater it left was twenty feet across and took at least seven men with it. But from the explosion projected thousands of tiny lead balls in all directions. Twenty more men fell because of the shrapnel. Machine guns soon joined in. Bullets cut down the soldiers like a lawn trimmer. The artillery fired shell after shell, and the machine guns shot bullet after bullet. You couldn't hear their screams because of the sound of gunfire.

The time moved forward as if it were being fast-forwarded. Despite the surrounding bodies, a man atop a bay stallion held his head high. Men in the ground heaved the dead into a cart pulled by the horse, but it was impossible to retrieve the most disfigured.

Silence followed the vision's disappearance for over five minutes. A tear fell down Tom's cheek. He remained deep in thought for a while. His father picked up on this and awaited his response.

"We should try," Tom began.

"Try what?" Maddy questioned.

"To get back. Back to Earth."

"But how?" Elliott asked, "We've mapped all we've explored and found nothing. No gateway, no portal, no magical ladder out of Hell."

"But we haven't explored everything; we've never even encountered other people," Tom argued, before remembering his earlier briefing about the riders and correcting himself, "well, until today."

"Son, we've been through this already, we are staying put. We are better here; you've seen Earth now."

"Yes, I have seen it, awful stuff happens all the time. But maybe I could help. Perhaps we could help. That stone is showing us the world we shouldn't't've left behind."

"Nonsense!" his father stated.

"Let us set sail at sunrise, and we shall voyage to escape Hell!"

"Over my dead body!" Glove rejected the command.

"Then so be it," Thomas said before instantly swallowing his words.

Glove rose from his seat, the legs of the chair scraping awfully against the floorboards. He paced towards his son and drew his own cutlass, pointing it threateningly at him.

"That is enough, boy. Any more, and there shall be grave consequences."

"Father, are you not the man you once were?" Tom tried to reason as he dodged his father's furious stare.

"Fine," he turned away to sit back down and away from his father at the other end of the table.

"As the captain of this ship, I command we are to go nowhere — nowhere!" Glove yelled as he walked out of the kitchen. An awkward silence filled the room until the crew had scrubbed the plates and wandered off to their sleeping quarters.

Pandæmonium

"Come, Beelzebub," Satan told the demon as the two strolled to the end of the gorge. (I am going to refer to fallen angels as demons.) They reached two massive stone doors, engraved so delicately it was clear no human instrument could rival this precision. Beelzebub pointed to the golden doors, and they swung open slowly, the hinges groaning as they did so. This revealed a round chamber. Unlike the canyon before it, complex structures of gold and volcanic glass formed a roof over it. A kind of skylight was present in the centre of the ceiling. Within the walls were seven grand seats, one for each of the Seven Princes of Hell, four of which were occupied, and in the middle was a throne for the Devil. Neither Satan nor Beelzebub sat down though; they paced around the room, talking.

Satan declared to the entire room, "The pirate has made his wager. Thank you, Maloch, Prince of Hell, for seeing to this affair, for scouting this worthy candidate. And thank you to Beelzebub, Prince of Hell, for helping me seal this accord."

You may expect that large applause may follow such a speech, but these attendees were the Princes of Hell, they cared far more for their own achievements than anyone else's. There was, in fact, only one demon clapping: Beelzebub.

"The plan is in motion," Satan said as he turned back to speak to Beelzebub privately, "Thatch has set off for Oblitos, and Glove soon for here. Two wagers, each bound to foil the other. Soon, their souls shall be mine, soon I shall have my resurgence, and then, only then, my Revelation."

"It shall be a glorious day indeed, sir. Seventy souls labour upon that boat."

"It's a good start, I require the Fates' presence to account for every one of them."

"Why must you associate with them? I feel it is not an affair so worthy of the Moirai," Belphegor — another demon — questioned, not rising from his seat, "wouldn't we just be wasting their time?"

"They have no time to waste, they exist beyond it. They know all that has and is and will happen."

"Okay, but are not we wasting our time?"

"Seventy souls are at stake; I will not let them escape me. When they fail, I need to be assured that those souls are mine. So, I shall ensure their souls are bound to contract, witnessed by those with dominion over all souls. Tell me, am I wasting my time?"

Chapter V

The Lady Mary

The pink sun rose over the dark and lifeless horizon. It shone through a tiny window in the quarters where Glove slept and fell directly upon his eyes. He woke and stretched his arms, every joint from his neck to his knuckles cracking. For about ten minutes he lay rocking comfortably in his hammock, before throwing on his coat and slipping into his untied boots. Always the first to wake, he stumbled outside onto the main-deck to watch the sunrise. Leaning against the railing, he stared out to watch the now familiar sight. Despite the illumination, the blackened and slate-coloured rocks remained dark, cold, and dull. The sky, patterned with dark grey clouds, changed from the colour of broccoli heads to the colour of pond water. Should there have been a sprawling green forest and clear blue water in a calm sea – oh, and perhaps a singing blackbird – it would have been tremendously pleasant. But there wasn't. It looked like what it was. Hell.

But today, he wasn't the first to wake; he looked up to the quarterdeck and saw his son, also admiring the sunrise. Glove walked cautiously towards his son and opened his mouth to speak before he was interrupted.

"Hello there?" said a voice from the shore. Glove descended the stairs and moved to the other side of the ship to see who was calling. He did not recognise their voice, an American voice.

He cautiously asked, "Hello?" Shocked by the sight of another person — a cowboy from the future, no less. (The cowboys are really from the past, just the crew is from an earlier past, which means the cowboys are from what would have been their future, though they are now existing together in the present. Just believe me when I say this makes sense.)

"You Glove?"

"Indeed, I am."

"Thank God," he followed with an awkward pause, "erm, may I come aboard?"

Thomas, not at all averse to new company after speaking to only the same six people for five years, replied, "Aye, hold on." He lifted the wooden ladder, which had been leaning against the railing, and slid it down to the cowboy. Glove reacted to his son's invitation with a frown, but did not intervene. The man climbed up the ladder and onto the deck. When he boarded, they could get a better look at him. He was quite short and lean, though the latter may be because of hunger, and had short brown hair, a thin beard, and eyes which Tom struggled to tell the colour of.

"Sit down, sit down," Thomas attempted to be hospitable.

"Thank you, name's Noah Beard, and I have something to ask. Well, a few things really."

"Go on."

"Do you know a Blackbeard?"

"You could say that."

"You've duelled him, ain't that so?"

"Too many times," Glove said.

"So do you have half the stone?" Noah asked.

"Yeah, just half," he answered, pointing to Glove, "My father has it."

"I thought as much, Blackbeard has the other half."

"So he's alive?" Tom interrupted.

"He is close. I abandoned my fellow riders as he contracted them. But I heard every word. He is coming. Coming for the other half of the crystal so that he may use it to open the Gate of Ubyvis."

"I'm sorry, what?"

"He seeks to open the Gate of Ubyvis, a portal on the furthest planet, Krykrakon. It can take you to Earth when opened with one of these stones."

"To Earth?"

"That's what the fella said."

"What who said?"

"Satan."

Neither Glove nor his son even bothered to seem like they followed. Tom's face was completely and utterly dumbfounded. Yes, he knew he was in Hell, but he hadn't really considered the whereabouts of this key figure.

"Satan?"

"Yeah, he has this herd of cattle. Angry, fiery bastards. He first asked us wranglers to herd them, but we failed. Blackbeard has made a deal to have the beasts loaded on two of his ships, and he'll sail them to the Gate."

"He has two ships?"

"Three."

"So what of the other?"

"One has already set sail for here."

"And what does he plan to do with these cattle?"

"They are to be released, and Earth shall fall under their fury. Satan seeks to bring about the Apocalypse."

"Surely even Blackbeard would not wish to end the world?" Tom asked.

"Don't underestimate him," Glove cautioned, "Of course he would."

"Indeed, he longs for the treasures of all the world. And it seems he's willing to destroy the entire planet to do so."

"And what happens to him after?"

"Satan agreed to let him plunder planets across the universe, I'm not really sure what he's on about."

"Across the what? What other planets?" Tom was rather confused, his eyebrows proving it. It is, however, excusable since he is from the eighteenth century and grew up with no more of an education past 'how to be a pirate,' which itself is more of a learn on the job kind of deal.

"I'm no genius myself, I'm afraid. He might as well be making it all up," Noah admitted, "but I have a feeling something terrible is going to happen if he succeeds."

"So why are you telling us?" Thomas wondered, more eager to respond than his father.

The sound of Elliott's rooster suddenly interrupted the two from within the brig. He was engaged in a crowing-battle — with himself. Tom regretted Elliott's decision to give the chickens a window; otherwise, he wouldn't have known it was dawn.

"So, Thatch comes for ours?" Glove said, now he had thought the information through.

"Yeah."

"So, if we surrendered it, he would be off?"

"I imagine so."

"Then that's what I'll do. No more cursed visions, no rotten trophy to show all we fought for was a lie."

Tom and Noah didn't know what to say at this conclusion. They looked at each other awkwardly, as if they both knew that each was expecting an alternative outcome. Though they were strangers, Tom got the sense that Noah had something more valuable to reveal. Because of this, he was relieved when his father departed. At once, he moved closer to Noah and questioned with a whisper, "What did you truly want to ask?"

"Well," Noah said, chuckling, "I was hoping you would, could, might stop him?"

"What if I got to the Gate?" Tom didn't answer directly, "I could open it and go back to Earth?"

"Right, but not with your stone," he said, "No, it is not complete. But I have one."

When Noah took the item from his pocket. Tom's eyes lit up at once, and he held his hands to Noahs to get his hold on it. "If I could just have this, I promise I'll try to stop him. Then I can get home. Come with me if you want."

"I suppose this could work," Noah said, reluctantly letting Tom take the stone from him, "but you don't have a map."

"Where do you get a map?"

"From Satan — well, from Beelzebub, but obviously Satan's in charge."

"So, you could take us to Satan and Beelzebub and whoever else dwells in Hell?"

"I could."

"Well then, thank you, kind sir. I guess my father is going to let Blackbeard take the stone, so I need to start planning. Make yourself at home, you can stay as long as you want."

"Do you not think we could get rid of the other half of the stone, so Blackbeard cannot use it?" Noah said, suggesting it was his original plan.

"We'll never get it from him. And I'm not going to fight him — he is my father."

"I guess you're right."

Tom left and followed Glove to his quarters. The rest of the crew — except for Lumberlodge, who remained fast asleep — came onto the deck.

"Who's this?" Tudor asked needlessly threateningly.

"This is our new crew member, Noah," Tom replied, patting the cowboy on the back and beginning to walk away too, "I'm sure you can handle them, they don't bite – except Tudor."

Hell

The herd of cattle now grazed the remains of a field of grass in a valley conveniently close to Pandæmonium. (How lucky!) The remaining four riders watched just out of sight.

"Steady boys, this is our last shot," one spoke softly, raising his hand, "on my signal." A horse then snorted, and the closest cows raised their heads. The cowboy dropped his hand, and the riders took off. One on the left, one on the right, and one following behind. One just trotted steadily after.

"Frank!" another yelled.

"Was that the signal?"

"Yes, that was the signal!"

"Yeehaw!" Frank yelled as he kicked the sides of his mount, which promptly sped up into a gallop.

The herd quickly concluded their grazing and too ran. The chase now proceeded similarly to before, so I needn't go into great depths to describe it again.

The Lady Mary

The crew carried on typical idle activities in anticipation of Blackbeard's arrival. The crew, including Adam, who had finally awakened, attempted to teach Noah how to play cards, but he already knew how to play other cowboy card games and accidentally played by the wrong rules. This particularly frustrated Doyle, despite himself making up his own rule the day before. The crew prepared for a large meal, though there was not a great deal of protein available. Tom refused to allow Lumberlodge to slaughter another chicken, as he had already slaughtered all but one male. This was a consideration even

Elliott himself had failed to make. Luckily, his little flock was not the only source of poultry nearby.

Hell's unusual fauna included a species that was particularly disturbing. Not fiery as the others, hens stood at three feet and roosters at almost five. Their large red combs had black burnt tips, and their thin plumage hugged their bodies. They were tall and narrow, like East-Asian game fowl breeds, with thick, triangular beaks. The roosters had reddish-brown breasts and deep black sickle tail feathers with a beetle-green sheen. The scales on their feet were coarse and irregular, and six inch, hooked spurs extended from their shanks. They also had a comical habit of running with their wings extended into the air, or even flapping to propel themselves. Tom, Adam, Tudor, Doyle, and Noah went out to catch one.

This task took more effort than it should have for several reasons, including a rare miss from Adam's musket, and the fiery temperament of the roosters. One notable attack saw Doyle delivering a forward-spinning-elbow to the creature — though the final blow did come from the musket, eventually. After rigour-mortis had kicked in and the carcass fell, Tom and Adam tied up its legs and tried lifting it together. "I'll get that — I'm the strongest," Tudor said, taking the corpse from the other two and hanging it over his shoulder.

"Thought you never missed?" Doyle annoyed Adam as the group returned to the ship, so all could hear.

"Doyle, all you did was elbow the bloody thing!"

"And it was rather effective, thank you."

"It's alright, Lumberlodge. There's a first time for everything," Tudor joined in.

Back on the ship, Elliott helped Tom butcher the chicken. It could not fit whole in the oven, so they seasoned and cooked a thigh and huge drumstick. As usual, everyone dined around the dining table, except for Glove, who remained above deck to wait for Blackbeard.

The Golden Gander

Thatch had boarded his newest, smallest, and fastest ship to locate Glove. This left the *Revenge* behind to be loaded with cattle — since it was the largest of the three, this seemed sensible.

Thatch's quartermaster, Israel Hands, entered the captain's room and sat down opposite him.

"How are we getting the stone, Cap'n?"

"Oh, I'm sure Glove will be more than willing to hand over the stone if it pains him as well. He knows not of the Gate, so has no purpose for it."

"Eternal life?"

"At first I thought perhaps that part referred only to eternal suffering in Hell, I suspect Glove would think the same, or maybe even see it as a con."

"At first?"

"Divine messengers have informed me that the jewel does in fact make the soul eternal. They also, most importantly, explained of the endless realms and lands beyond here, beyond the Earth. And in these lands, I see opportunity. My fleet must deliver Satan's fiery cows to destroy those lands, according to my contract; however, we have the opportunity to take their riches for ourselves. We can take whatever we want. We can then sell it to the peoples of other lands, and then take their goods after we destroy them. The wealth, the riches — they are limitless, my friend. Limitless! But Glove knows not of this."

"I'm not sure I follow, sir."

"This is not knowledge for the ignorant, Hands. You must open your mind if you wish to accompany me on this path."

"I'll try, sir. One more thing?"

"Aye."

"Would you really destroy the Earth?"

"What is there to miss? My fame precedes me; people are prepared. But just you see, the alien folks are unprepared – sitting ducks! We must look beyond the Earth; we can have the wealth of the universe!"

"Ship ahead!" yelled the lookout from the crow's-nest.

"Ship ahead!" another man repeated.

"Ship ahead, captain!" was followed by a knock on the door.

"It's time, Hands," Blackbeard said as he got up and walked onto the deck. He pulled out his telescope to examine *The Lady Mary*. Glove was standing doing the same. Blackbeard held up his half of the jewel for Glove to see, and in turn Glove pulled out the locket from under his coat.

"He has it, Hands, he has it!" Thatch said giddily to Hands, "Oh, old Glove, I've never been happier to see you!"

Pandæmonium

Blackbeard's two other ships had already been reinforced and fitted with metal doors into the cargo hold. Satan's team of fallen angels accomplished this using their ability to manipulate matter.

The four riders had finally herded the cattle to the gorge. Many turned and fled, but plenty continued through the canyon. Seeing the two ships suspended in the air at the gorge's end, the cattle ascended. The fallen angels at the top, however, stopped them. They used their power to order the rock face to close. The riders halted as the canyon closed in front of them, pushing the cattle into the ships. The doors were closed, and the ship had been loaded.

"It's done, sir," Beelzebub reported to Satan.

"Very well, the man can't say we didn't give him a chance."

"You don't think he'll make it?"

"It's not that, no. In fact, I believe the odds are far better than with previous attempts."

"So what of the riders, I don't suppose you're letting them go free?"

"Dear Beelzebub, you know I am a man of my word. A deal's a deal. They wagered their souls against me, and they lost the bet. Thatch already robbed me of one soul and another ran away, so don't think I'm losing any more."

"Should I summon them?"

"If you'd be so kind."

Beelzebub, as requested, gathered the cowboys and led them to Satan.

"I have them, my lord."

"Good, as you were, Beelzebub."

"Thank you, sir," Beelzebub said as he flew away on his black wings.

"Now, gentlemen, do you recall perhaps an agreement we made not too long ago?"

No cowboy spoke, for they knew too well the conditions of the deal.

"Well?" Satan persisted.

"But, but you made the deal with Blackbeard, and let us help."

"Yes, and what use are you now?"

"But Jerry died, he was in charge."

"But, but, but. But did you not shake my hand also?"

"Yeah, but –"

"No more buts, you have a debt to pay," Satan said, with a slight smile on his face. He then grabbed the first cowboy by his throat, as he had their leader. Holding him in the air, Satan's eyes glowed. The cowboy tried to look away, but could not help briefly looking at his killer. Once eye contact was made, his eyes too glowed, and remained fixed, staring into the Devil's. After about ten seconds, all glowing stopped, even the glow of lanterns. The cowboy was dead, and Satan threw his corpse into a pit behind the thrones. One glow, which had not stopped, came from the pit, which was bubbling with lava. The others turned to run, but the fallen angels stood behind them.

The Lady Mary

"He's here, men!" Glove ordered, "On, on a new ship? All hands on deck!"

"Should I man the guns, Captain?" Elliott asked.

"Nay, there shall be no guns firing today."

"You sure? It is Blackbeard, sir."

"Thatch will not waste his fire; we shall surrender the stone and he shall be gone. No questions, no argument, just let him be off."

"Aye-aye."

"Good man."

"Sorry, Captain, would it be alright if I went, just in case?"

"If you fancy, aye."

Lumberlodge leant over to whisper to Tudor, "Are we going to tell him there're no cannonballs?"

"No, I think he can find out himself." Tudor replied.

"Elliott, there's no..." Doyle began before Tudor nudged him.

"Shut up, Clementini," he whispered.

"No what?" Elliott questioned.

Tom came to the rescue with this: "There's no — there's nothing that can stop you."

"Thanks?" Elliott worried as he climbed down to the gun-deck.

"God, Doyle!" Tom joked, "What were you thinking?"

The Golden Gander lowered its anchor about thirty yards away from *The Lady Mary*. It was, unlike Thatch's other ships, smaller than *The Lady*. Blackbeard stood with one leg against the railing. He had an uncharacteristically yet sincerely pleasant smile on his face, for in truth he was happy to see Glove. Not just because he was about to gain the other half of the stone, but also he was truly happy to see a familiar face, especially one of an old friend (though that's probably not the most accurate word choice).

"Glove, old boy!"

"Thatch."

"Oh, it's a treat to see you again."

"I have no words for you, Thatch."

"I believe you might have something for me."

"The stone?" Thomas asked.

"That's the one!"

"About that." Glove took back the conversation.

"What, would you like a repeat of our last encounter? I need that stone, and care not how I take it."

"Father, just…" Tom added, surprised by Glove's hesitation.

"Yes, yes."

"I do not mean to cause trouble," Thatch said, his hands in the air, "though you know I wouldn't be too upset about it."

"About the stone."

"Go on."

"You can have it."

"Oh, good, just chuck it to me then, don't worry about breaking the thing."

What followed was perhaps the most embarrassing moment of Glove's entire forty-five years of piracy, or indeed of his whole life. He did as Thatch asked and threw the locket over to him. Most adults can throw an object of its weight well over fifty yards when done properly. However, through some mishap, Glove did not achieve this distance. It did not skim the side of the ship. It did not hit the side and bounce off. And it certainly did not go over the deck and into the water on the other side. No, it missed *The Golden Gander* by ten feet or more, making a depressing plop as it hit the water. Glove held his red face in his hands and fell to his knees in embarrassment.

Tudor Boris, taking the opportunity to seem important, began, "Need not worry, Thatch. Allow us to send down a small search party in one of our rowboats, and we shall retrieve the stone and surrender it to you."

"No, no, don't bother, my men will do it," Thatch suggested.

"Yes, if you would prefer."

"Fraser Fluffy, Stan Fardon! Come here!"

"Yes, Cap'n?"

"Do you think you two men can go down there and find me the stone?" he asked, massaging their shoulders in the fashion one might when asking a favour the other might not accept.

"Aye-aye! Should we get the longboat?"

"No need!" Thatch said as he pushed both men into the water at once, "Don't even think about coming aboard until you have it."

The men began searching at once, but there remained an awkward silence, broken only when Elliott returned from the gun-deck to announce that there were, in fact, no cannonballs. Tom, Adam, Tudor, and Doyle all disguised a smirk.

"So, Glove, how have these past five years treated ye?" Blackbeard tried to make small-talk. Glove, however, refused to answer. And so his son did the talking.

"Not bad, not bad. It's Hell, of course, but you know."

"Good, good."

"I see you have a new ship; you have three ships now, I hear."

"Aye, three. Not on par with the *Revenge*, the other two, but they'll suffice."

"Well, it's just the one for us still, made a few modifications here and there, the metal here is really strong, you know."

"Yes, we've had a few upgrades too. Who tells you of my ships?"

Tom, never having the best poker face, quickly glanced towards Noah Beard.

"Ah, the fifth rider. Been spilling all the secrets, have ya? Care to join us?"

"No thanks," Noah replied bluntly with an awkward smile.

"Very well, I've given you the choice, and you have not chosen glory alongside the one and only Captain Blackbeard."

"What do you want the stone for, anyway?" Tom tried to prise more information.

"Just between us, okay?"

"Sure."

"I have struck a nice deal where I may deliver a herd of cattle to Earth, destroying it, mind you."

"How are you getting back?"

"The Gate of Ubyvis can take you anywhere you want, using this stone as a key."

"Anywhere?" Glove interrupted.

"Yes, but I wouldn't worry yourself, you're better off here, ain't that so? You are safe and among your friends."

Again, Glove ignored Thatch, leaving Tom to agree for him.

"Is he alright?" Maddy Casserole asked, pointing towards one man in the water. While Fardon trod water, Fluffy was submerged completely, searching the seabed for the locket.

"How we doing, lads?"

"Oh, 'im, he's absolutely top-notch, sir. Ain't that right, Fluffy?" Fardon said as he pulled on Fluffy's leg. The man raised his hand and gave a thumbs-up.

"See, top-notch, sir."

Fluffy then remained underwater for a concerning amount of time. Bubbles rose viciously as he kicked around. But soon he broke from the water with the locket in his hand and a beaming smile on his face.

"I have it, my captain!"

"Good, throw it up, boy!" Thatch commanded. Fluffy did, and the captain caught it by its chain.

"Perhaps you could throw us down a rope, sir?" Fardon suggested.

"Aye, about that," Blackbeard responded with a sinister grin. He drew a pistol in each hand and fired both at the men, landing every shot.

"Don't forget who I am, Glove!" Thatch laughed as the anchor lifted, and *The Golden Gander* sailed away.

"Liar!" Tudor shouted as he held a sword at Noah Beard's neck, "This man is a liar and works for Blackbeard!" In response, Thomas drew his own cutlass.

"He says he abandoned his own friends so as not to work for Blackbeard." To this, Tudor drew his sabre and pointed it at Tom.

"Oh, and you believe that?" From across the deck, Lumberlodge aimed his musket at Tudor and cocked it.

"Hey, that isn't fair!" Tudor insisted.

"What?"

"That thing's a bit overpowered!"

"Shouldn't've brought a knife to a gunfight!"

"Only you made it a gunfight!"

"There shall be no gunfight!" Glove intervened, "What seems to be the problem, lads?"

"This man is an impostor! He works for Blackbeard. Thatch even said so himself," Tudor persisted.

"I've told you, the other riders Blackbeard recruited them, but I ditched them, he never even saw my face until today," Beard defended.

"Aye, this is consistent with what he told us just this morning, you heard yourself, father," Tom agreed.

"Do you trust him, son?"

"Yep. Blackbeard has the stone, so what more would he want from us? This is not the face of a liar."

"Let's hope you're right. Tudor, lower your weapons, do me a favour and man the sails. And Lumberlodge?"

"What?"

"Raise the anchor! Beard, we're in need of a heading."

To defuse the tension created by his own presence, Noah said to Tudor, "That's a nice sword." Tudor smirked for a moment, swallowing the urge to make this comment seem suggestive.

The smile turned into a frown when he explained, "It's my brother's, really. I only got it when he got a better one. He always got the better one."

"You can become better with worse, you know."

Chapter VI

Pandæmonium

Satan sat upon his throne, which was lavishly plated with gold and platinum. Laid out on a table in front of him were four more maps, each one of a different planet. Beside from it was a stone mould, it was the shape of the complete crystal key. Satan sat quietly, tapping his fingers. First his index finger, then the middle, then the next, then the little finger, and repeat.

"Thatch," he addressed without even looking up to see the pirate.

"Satan, I have gained the other half of the stone."

"Good, pass it to me," Satan ordered, though he actually meant both halves, "and the other." Thatch handed over both parts, and Satan fitted them together into the mould.

"Beelzebub, if you would?" he requested. Beelzebub floated down from his own seat within the rocks and held the mould in one hand, holding his other over it. When his hand had passed, it left behind a whole crystal key.

"There you go, my lord."

"Thank you," Satan said, as he tipped the key out of the mould and handed it back to Thatch. He then slid the maps to him.

"What's this?"

"You didn't expect it to be simple, did you?"

"Nay?"

"You shall require four more maps. Four more maps for four more planets. The Gate of Ubyvis lies at the farthest. It is a portal, a portal so powerful it can reach to every corner of the universe. But three other planets lie between here and there. Each has its own pair of portals, but neither is as powerful as the Gate of Ubyvis. They can take you only to the next planet, and only when the planets are aligned. And for the first time in a millennium, all five planets have aligned. Their orbits all briefly synchronised. They become frozen in place like this for ten days, and three of those have passed."

"Ten days to sail across five planets?" Thatch complained, "Are you mad!"

"All beings as old as I am — but that's beyond the point. Hell is the largest planet in this system, and you are already close to the gate. The other planets are quite small, so you have just enough time to make it."

"The time has come then, Mr Thatch. Time to bind our deal with the Fates as witness."

"Where do I sign?" Thatch asked, not understanding the severity of this statement.

"Patience, I am yet to summon them!"

"Summon who?"

And to this, the Devil did not reply, not to Blackbeard.

"I, Satan, the Devil, the First to Fall, Ruler of Chaos, King of Hell, the one they call Hades, call upon the Fates. I call upon you to witness a deal not of flesh nor blood but of soul and spirit."

This was no statement, no request. The words the Devil had just spoken were a ritual. They were a ritual only very powerful beings can perform, or rather a ritual that is only taken seriously when performed by such beings. You may have realised that I haven't described Satan as particularly impressive; he was rather unremarkable in appearance. But it was his soul that was powerful. And because of this, the ritual worked.

At once, the entire sky lit up, and a beam fell through the skylight of the Palace; the beam was the whitest colour possible. Though this light was so intensely bright, it did not diffuse across the black room; it cut through it. In the middle of this beam emerged three figures. They were not covered by cloth, but shielded by light and perhaps some other force that prevented a mortal gaze. But from Thatch's peripheral vision, he could not decide whether these figures were young or old. One could say they were a timeless combination of the two. Each figure was presumably female, and between them they held a glowing, empty scroll.

"The Moirai!" Satan said with a slight smile, "I have summoned you, the three sisters of Fate, from your immaterial realm to witness a deal, and souls are at stake."

The first of the Moirai spoke while she ran a quill across the scroll, "Satan, he who once tried to challenge all of Heaven, is now bound to mortal form. This is a sight to behold."

"And now he plays games with man to win back his power," the second added, reading her sister's writing.

Satan was eager to ask, "And do I? Do I break free from this pathetic vessel?"

"We do not speak of the future," she told him bluntly.

"We cannot," the third stated powerfully, as she cut the end of the scroll with a pair of crooked shears.

The first sister tore away the freshly cut scroll and reached her hand out from the beam of light. Her white hand shook in the darkness, and it snatched back into the beam once Satan had taken the paper from her. He read it conscientiously. The second sister reached a hand out from the light, and the Devil collected a small, white stick of wax. He unravelled the scroll and laid it out across the table before holding the wax out to the third of the Moirai. In response, she held out her own hand, from which a pale and bright flame was burning. Satan hovered the wax in the flame, and as it melted, he let it fall upon the paper. The second sister took back the wax, and the third removed her hand from the shadow of the cave. Using a signet ring on his little finger, he pressed into the wax, which turned first green, then red, but set white. The seal on it was so intricate I cannot describe it entirely – though, as you may expect, there were certainly horns involved. But the centrepiece of the Devil's seal was something rather unexpected. It was a symbol, either a 5 or an S: it was hard to tell which, if it was truly either. And behind this, a faint pentagram, as you could have guessed.

"And you, Edward Thatch, the Tyrant Sailor, cursed to Hell." The first Fate commanded.

"Aye?"

"Your turn," Satan answered.

"Very well," the pirate responded without even reading the paper once. He walked to the Moirai, expecting the wax and flame.

"Do you speak for all your crew?" The third Fate asked him.

"I do, I'm their captain."

"You are the captain of their bodies, not the chief of their souls, this contract binds the soul of every man aboard or fleet to the deal," the second fate told him, "You must ask, and see if they object."

The doors to the cave swung open, and so Thatch walked towards them. All three ships rested outside, the crew of seventy men aboard. He climbed up the ladder on the side of the *Revenge* and began, "Alrighty lads! Do any of you object to this endeavour? Our souls are at stake, and if it's alright with you, I'm about to sign them off."

"Our souls?" one (courageous) man asked, wanting clarification.

"Aye, we wager our escape from this wretched realm against our very own souls."

"You're going to sell all our souls to Satan?"

"Only if we fail."

"I don't –" Thatch gave the man no time to finish this sentence, for he drew a loaded pistol and fired it point-blank, knocking him off the ship.

"Any objections?" Thatch asked menacingly, for he knew the crew knew the consequence of defying him, "No? Good."

The Fates had dropped a splotch of wax onto the paper before he re-entered the room. Using his own signet ring, he placed his seal onto the scroll. His seal comprised a horned, skeletal figure, a demon, but it had no wings. This demon was holding a spear, pointing towards a heart in the bottom right. The wax turned yellow when Blackbeard pressed it, and it set this way.

And as this happened, the scroll set alight, and within seconds reduced to ash, which drifted to the third Fate's flaming hand. After the last particle of the scroll was collected, all mystical light stopped, and the Fates were gone.

Blackbeard stood biting his nails. He didn't really understand why he had had to do all that, and what significance the Fates really had in it. He realised, however, that whatever the reason, there was no turning back. Feeling uncomfortable, he decided he wanted to spend no longer around the Devil.

"I suppose it's time I should get going, then?" he asked.

"Indeed, it is. And Thatch?"

"Aye?"

"Do not even think about showing your foul, red, furfuraceous face here until you have completed our deal, or you will face the true wrath of the Devil!"

The Lady Mary

"Father?" Thomas turned to his dad.

"Aye?"

"Where are we going?"

"You never said that we could get anywhere with that stone," he said, directing this more at Noah, "Why?"

"I didn't know. They mentioned only Earth."

"So? Where are we off to?" Tom said again, "To Earth?"

"Not quite," Glove muttered.

"Father?"

"That stone can take us anywhere we want, right, that's what he said, ain't it?"

"Yeah…"

"Well then," he cleared his throat, "if we be in Hell, and we are indeed, then that must mean there's a Heaven."

"I suppose, but we got Hell. 'Cause we're pirates, sinners."

"Yes, but your mother was no sinner. I have absolutely no doubt that it was Heaven that took my sweet Mary. And so it is to Heaven we must go."

"To find mother?"

"Aye, my son, don't you miss her?"

"I was too young to remember her."

"Surely you have some recollection, she used to line up all the dolls she had bought for you, and you'd give them names. You were only two years old on this very ship and would always give 'em new names each time for you'd already forgotten the ones you give 'em the last time. Don't you remember?"

"Perhaps a distant memory, not vivid."

"It's not your fault, son, she was taken from us too soon. And now we will return to her. We will be a family again."

"What about Earth?"

"What about Earth? Forget Earth! Think about it: you want more than this, more than Hell, better than Hell. And you can't get much better than Heaven! Just think! And besides, don't you want to see her again?"

"Of course."

"Then forget about Earth, we're going to Heaven to find my dear Mary, right after I avenge her death!"

"But you said you didn't know who killed her," Tom reminded, with an anxious frown.

"Aye, 'bout that son. I knew all along whose fault it was, but I didn't want to tell you," Glove answered slowly and guiltily, "but I tell you now, the man responsible for your mother's death is — is Thatch."

"Why wouldn't you tell me?"

"That man is all kinds of sick. Gets in your head, he does. Been in my head for twenty years. He preys on your weaknesses. Weaknesses you didn't even realise you had. Just for the fun of it. Didn't want him in your head too."

"Why would he do it?"

"Son, there was once a time, as you have been told, when I was captain of a ship and of a crew as large as Thatch's. 'Robin Hood of the Seven Seas,' they called me, 'the good pirate.' No matter how tempting, I would never give the order to raid an innocent ship. No merchants, no fishermen, just those who do wrong. Those who make the sea a more dangerous place. But the Royal Navy just saw pirates. We were decimated, my ship destroyed to ash. But I survived, with my wife, and a boy who became my first mate, Elliott. And again, I built a crew, but I didn't want the grandeur, the attention I once had. For she was pregnant. With you. I bought this very ship with the little money I had left and laid low to start a family. And I allowed the desperate, the destitute, if they be good of heart, to join that family. I gave them a new chance in life, and for that they remain loyal."

"So?"

"Well, Thatch's crew is not loyal. Scared, absolutely, but not willing to go through the same level of risks for their captain. And so he knew he could never convince a crew to help him find the treasure. So instead he sent me. He found my weakness. My weakness was Mary, and he killed her. So, knowing what it was like to lose a family member, I realised I must do all I can to keep the rest of my family with me. For twenty years I searched for the map to that island, just to find the Devil's jewel and hopefully keep my family. But I was fooled, and so we are here."

Tom put his hand on his father's shoulder, and the two sat in silence for a while.

Since Tom had the stone that Noah had gifted him, he had forgotten to question his father's plan for the lack of such a key. Perhaps Glove intended to steal the jewel back, or perhaps use brute force. Glove often left out many vital aspects of a plan for the fact that he couldn't be bothered to think of a solution. He was confident enough in his own ability to solve these drawbacks when the time came, not that this had always worked for him. But luckily for him, he wouldn't have to come up with any grand plans to steal it back, though Tom had not thought to mention it. It is rather silly that such a miscommunication can lead to a rather less simple argument, but you'll find that this is rather common. In fact, this has not just complicated the pair's relationship, but both their characters and both their fates. But more of that later.

For yet another day was at its close, Thomas had made his way into the kitchen to prepare a meal for the crew. The chicken had been cooking since earlier, so all that was left to do was prepare some vegetables. Some potatoes grown by Elliott and some kind of carrot-like root found amongst the indigenous flora of Hell (or of what little existed of it). It was thin and knotted, tough and dry, and also dark red with an outer earthy layer that tasted of charcoal. Another problem with this vegetable was the fact that, should it be over-boiled, it almost instantly became rather mushy inside, despite retaining its woody skin. And it didn't take much to overcook it; it would take about half an hour for it to be even chewable, but one minute longer and the only place for it is the chicken coop (or sometimes the mashed potato). But it was sustenance, something that should not be taken for granted, especially in Hell.

Most of the crew found themselves in rather jolly moods. Yes, they hadn't really accomplished much, but there were two things which sparked joy; one was the relief from knowing that while Thatch was still around, he posed no threat to them. And the other was just indeed knowing that Thatch was still around. Their relationship wasn't the best, but it was nice to know that there were other survivors of the very accident that left them in Hell. And I suppose they were a little smug, or at least reassured, that Blackbeard had at least gone to Hell after what he did.

They too entered the dining area one by one as Tom took some food for himself and Noah, who were left to sail the ship.

The helm

Since Noah was needed at the helm for directions, Tom brought Noah a plate of chicken with two slices of bread. He then took the wheel himself. Though he should've been steering, he watched in shock as the cowboy took the chicken and sandwiched it between the two slices of bread.

"You look like you've never seen a sandwich before," Noah said.

Tom, being from pre-sandwich England, said, "No, I bloody haven't!"

Noah took a bite of his sandwich. To Tom's delight, the initial look on his face was just as good as everyone else's had been as they took their first bites, even though the food may not have been as much of a novelty.

"Mmm, that's excellent bread," Noah began, "better than the soggy stuff we make in a pan above a fire."

"Thanks," Tom appreciated this comment until he saw the look on the cowboy's face drastically switch.

"What's up?"

"Nothing, nothing," Noah replied, "Well, now you've asked, the chicken is a little tough, and well, foul."

Tom couldn't keep a straight face for long, "Did you actually just say that?"

"No, no, I don't mean to be rude, it's lovely, really."

"No, I'm not offended. Let's be honest, the chicken is utter shite. That's the problem with getting it from those things, nothing from Hell tastes good. No, I meant that awful joke."

"What?"

"Fowl, really?"

"Ha! Oh, I didn't even do that on purpose."

"Thank God you didn't do that on purpose, or I'd have thrown the stuff at you!"

"I can't say I'd blame you if you did."

"It's a weird name – sandwich, isn't it? Why'd they call it that?"

"Some English fella, I think, Earl of Sandwich or something."

"Never heard of the bloke."

"You're English too, aren't you?"

"Aye, are you not?"

"No, I'm from the United States of America."

"The what?"

"America, I'm American."

"I know America, we've been there and done some pirating. Got a lot of good cargo from the French. But what are you going on about 'states' for? Why on Earth do they feel the need to call themselves united?"

"What are you going on about? The states became united after the declaration of Independence. Kicked you British out."

"You bloody did what? Why would you want rid of us? When was this?"

"July 4th, 1776."

"Are you insane? That hasn't happened yet!"

"I think you're the insane one, it's 1872!"

"Excuse me, I am very certain it is not 1872! It's 17 — it's 17 — I can't bloody remember, but it's 17 something, middle 17 something."

"Don't be ridiculous, it's 1872. Ulysses S. Grant is president."

"Who is what?"

"Sorry, American stuff. Who do you think is the King?"

"King George."

"George the what?"

"George the king."

"No, what number King George?"

"The Second — son of George the very First."

"No, the king is George – but George the fifth. How long did you say you've been here?"

"Five years,"

"Five years? I think it's more like 100 years!"

"I'm telling you, it's George the Second, and it's 17-something!"

"Maybe it was when you left, but I'm telling you now that it's 1873!"

"Well, we'll settle it like this," Tom suggested, "One of us is mad. It might be you, might be me, or it could bloody well be both of us. How about that?"

"I guess it's the only explanation."

An awkward silence followed this debate, as both were forced to contemplate their own sanity. Since this topic of rumination is a heady tonic, Noah ended the silence as soon as he had thought of something to do so with.

"You know that Tudor guy — is that his name?"

"Yeah, what about him?"

"He seems a bit…"

"A bit much?"

"You could say that."

"We're all a bit much, I'm afraid," Tom said, "for some reason or another. Tudor's the youngest sibling, you see. He always got things second, or so he says. When Tudor became an apprentice, his brother started a business. When he became a privateer, his brother became a politician. I think he's tired of being second best. That's why he's always making a fuss."

"That makes sense."

The sleeping quarters

All the crew had finished their supper, so once Elliott had washed the pots and fed the leftover bread to his chickens, Glove left to his own room and the rest of the crew settled into their hammocks and popped a tap into a barrel of rum they had been saving (and in a pirate's terms, 'saving' rum meant just not drinking it on a day when one had accomplished little, but drinking it when they could come up with a better excuse to do so).

Adam lay in his hammock within the smaller room he shared with Thomas, though he left the door open so he could still engage in conversation. Tom and Noah were both above deck, for they had been put on the duty of sailing through the night, so the crew below comprised Adam, Doyle, Tudor, Maddy and Elliott once he had blown out the candles besides the chicken coop. They were collectively the right mixture of tipsy, tired, and full of anticipation to spark a sort of honest, almost child-like chatter.

"We're getting out of Hell, boys!" Tudor Boris stated rather confidently, before turning to Maddy and adding, "and girls."

"Don't get ahead of yourself, Boris," Doyle interrupted, "we've only just begun."

"C'mon, Doyle, don't be so negative," Maddy scorned.

Elliott, who had heard this discussion on his way up the ladder from the brig, advised, "I must side with Doyle. Caution is necessary. We know nothing of what lies ahead. We got here, and that was bad enough. But this is, I needn't remind you, Hell. And I don't think escaping Hell is all that easy, otherwise, everyone would be doing it."

"I dunno," Adam added, poking his head through the doorway, "My mate Lewis Plaque was dead for three years, and then one day, I had a pint with him in that old tavern on Isla de la Cabeza del Sapo."

"He wasn't dead then," Maddy told him.

"Nah, he was. Saw him die. Trampled by his own pet donkey."

"Oh, shut up, Adam."

"One hundred per cent true. There was a funeral and everything. We ate the bloody donkey in a stew."

"What did he say?"

"About what?"

"Did you not ask him about it?"

"Didn't think to ask."

"You didn't think to ask?" Tudor shook his head, "Now I know you're lying."

"Swear."

Elliott ended this discussion by saying, "I think we're getting side-tracked. The point is, whether Mr Plaque did or did not escape Hell, it is not going to be easy."

"We don't even know if he's telling the truth," Doyle said.

"Who?"

"Noah Beard. Strange name, actually."

"You can't make fun of anyone's name, Doyle," Tudor poked.

"Says you, Tudor Boris!"

"Yeah, says me, so what?"

"Gentlemen!" Elliott intervened, "Doyle raised a fair point. How can we trust him?"

"The captain trusts him."

"Why?" Doyle asked, "The captain trusts no one. Only us."

"Tom said he's telling the truth."

"How would Tom know? And besides, that's no reason for Glove to believe him. The Devil and all that — it seems a bit far-fetched."

"Thatch mentioned destroying Earth with cattle," Maddy thought aloud, "seems pretty devil-ly to me."

"I just don't see why Glove would trust him."

"I don't," Glove said a little too loud as he emerged from his own chamber, "I don't trust him."

The helm

"I've never been on a boat before," Noah told Tom.

"Never?"

"Never. There ain't much water to go boating on in Texas."

"Texas?"

"A state in America."

"Ah."

"How long have you been here then?" Tom asked.

"A year, maybe a bit more."

"How'd you get here?"

"Here, to your ship, or here, to Hell?"

"Both."

"Well, I was a bit low on money. Carl's brother had just come back from a trip out east and told us of this treasure. He was talking about the stone. Anyway, my fellow riders and I thought we'd spend what we had between us and take a trip to find it."

"Did you find it on that big old mountain with all the traps and monsters in it?" Tom asked.

"That's right. I assume you know what's inside it, then. But we did get through it all, and got the stone. We even had a buyer lined up for it — but then it came."

"The Leviathan?"

"Sea monster. Like a massive snake thing."

"That's the one."

"Got you too?"

"Yup. I suppose it must some after everyone who goes on that quest."

"Well, it got us, I know that for sure. And now, I'm here."

"So how'd you get to the ship if you didn't have one of your own?"

"Horse. Not my horse. Some fiery, angry Hell horse. Bastard ran off when I dismounted him."

"But how did you find us?"

"Luck, I s'pose. Also, I've noticed your sails before. Didn't want to disturb you before though. But I thought that maybe, since you had a ship, you'd be willing to help save Earth – or try to. I know it's foolish since we don't live their no more, but I dunno, I kinda want to help."

"And that's why I trust you," Tom added, "When my father asked, I said I trust you, because you're a good man. You just want to help, as do I for that matter, and that's why we will stop Blackbeard."

Tom sighed before adding, "But we aren't going to Earth. We'll stop Blackbeard, but we're going to Heaven."

The sleeping quarters

"You don't?"

"Nay, course not," Glove insisted, "You boys know ya cap'n, all I trust is you lot. And do you know why I trust ya? I'll tell ya why I trust ya! 'Cos you lads have worked hard for me, years of service, years of friendship, years of trust. Take yourself, Miss Casserole, you were an orphan girl when you came aboard my ship. Same as Elliott. I gave you a home, and you respect me for that. You're mi family now, boys! And never once have ya stepped outta line. That's why I trust ya! There was a time when I'd have trusted any man, but I learnt, didn't I? So don't you men worry, I ain't trusting this newcomer for a second. He needs to earn mi trust!"

"I agree, Cap'n," Tudor inputted, "All this Devil and getting back to Earth business, it could all well be a scam."

Everyone looked at Tudor with a more than displeased face.

"Aye, ya backtracking bastard!" Glove said as he gave Tudor a friendly slap on the back.

"I think Thomas trusts him, captain," Maddy told Glove.

"Aye, he is young, as are most of you. And he has much to learn. But let him trust, for I was once like him. We have a crew, so we needn't worry about one man."

"What about the Devil?"

"We proceed with caution. Take everything you are told with a grain of salt. But we will discover more when we arrive."

"Do you think he's actually here?"

"Well, this is Hell, ain't it? Where else would the Devil himself be?"

"Let a man sleep, would you?" Adam yelled through the door he had now shut.

"This is important, Lumberlodge," Doyle shouted back, "Don't you care?"

"No, fuck it!"

"What?"

"Fuck it!"

"But we're getting out!"

"Fuck it!"

"Do you not want to escape Hell?"

"Can't be bothered!"

"Can't be bothered?"

"No!"

"But here is just endless nothing. Not much to do, and nothing to care about."

"Exactly, it's class!"

"Oh, come on!"

"Fuck it!"

Glove smiled, "That boy will never change."

The helm

Tom had taught Noah to adjust the sails when asked, as the conditions were kind enough not to need too much attention. The night had planted itself firmly above them, and silence had set in upon the burning planet. Noah yawned heavily.

"You can get some sleep, you know," Tom said to Noah, "We can get someone else to help with the sails."

"No, I'll stay up and keep you company. Anyway, I need to make sure you don't nod off."

"Alrighty, keep us on a steady course and I'll go and get us both something to drink. Fancy some rum?"

"Any whiskey?"

"Oh, nope."

"Alright then, I suppose I'll have to have rum."

Tom got up with a stretch, picked up their plates and went below deck.

A few seconds passed, and Noah suddenly yelled, "I just told you I've never been on a boat, how'd you expect me to steer it?"

The sleeping quarters

Thomas carried the plates through the sleeping quarters to the kitchen. As he passed, he took a crust, which Noah had not finished, and threw

150

it at Maddy for no particular reason. It bounced off her head and hit Tudor also, making Tom even happier with his decision.

The helm

Thomas handed Noah a glass of rum and sat back down beside him. They both clinked glasses and took the first sip.

"We need to be going more this way," Noah pointed, "right of those rocky stump things."

"Take the wheel then, you know the way."

Noah stared at Tom without blinking.

"I'm serious," Tom continued, "How hard can it be?"

"Dunno, how hard can it be?"

"Turn the wheel right to go right, and left to go left. Simple!"

"Seriously?"

"C'mon, get up, get up. One hand here, one hand here. Now turn just a little to the right. A bit more. Woah, too much."

The boat shook suddenly as Noah turned the wheel a bit too sharply. Tom placed his hands over the cowboy's and encouraged them into the correct positioning.

"You memorised the whole route?"

"Pretty much. Of course, I did it on land, along that coast there, but I recognise enough to get us there," Noah replied, "You have to be good at recognising your environment as a cattle herder."

"Don't you just keep 'em in a pen?"

"Kinda, but we have to move them every day to new land."

"Why?"

"Cos they ate all the damn grass!"

"How many cows are we talking?"

"On a big drive, thousands."

"Thousands?"

"That's right, fifteen or so of us men out in the wild looking after 'em. All day, all night."

"What are you doing with cows all night?"

"Keep a lookout for any cougars, bears, wolves, and so forth."

"If you're gonna farm cows you should really do it in England, we have non of that, save you being up all night," Tom added, pretending to understand how cattle farming works, before changing subject, "look, there you have it, you've been steering this whole conversation."

"Guess I have," Noah replied, realising that he had indeed managed to sail the ship.

"Wanna keep at the wheel?"

"No, I think I'll let you have it back."

Tom took back the wheel, and the two fell back into silence as they attempted to comprehend the very different lives they had both lived.

"Maybe you could show me these cows when we…" Tom stopped his sentence as he realised the reality.

"Forgot where we're going, huh?"

"I did, yes."

"Why the change of heart?"

"Well, you only mentioned Earth, so we didn't realise it could get us anywhere else."

"I'm sorry, I only heard them mention Earth."

"I thought as much, but now we know it can take us anywhere, so my dad decided we should go to Heaven."

"Would you not want another chance at life? Then maybe you could earn your place in Heaven. Change your ways, do some good?"

Tom contemplated this for a few seconds until he responded by saying, "My dad can't wait. He wants to see my mother again — we want to see my mother again."

"I see, I'm sorry, I didn't realise."

"Don't be sorry, I didn't tell you. We could drop you off at Earth first or something, if that's how it all works, and if that's what you want."

"I'll have a think about it, thank you. Don't you think it would be nicer to be accepted into Heaven — properly?"

"You may be right, I'm sure my father would say it's a waste of time."

"If you say so."

Queen Anne's Revenge

All three of Blackbeard's ships had set sail, sailing in a triangular formation with the flagship (The *Revenge*) at the front. The captain split the seventy sailors into three crews, one for each ship. The *Revenge* had thirty men, while the second ship, *The Bristol Dragon*, had twenty-five, with a man called Teddy Feather in charge. This left the third and smallest ship with the rest of the men. It was *The Golden Gander*. The crew had constructed the two new ships using resources found in Hell. They were both darker than the *Revenge*, being made of scorched timbers. The crew had even extracted metal from the ground of hell to shape into the frame, albeit through much labour since the metals present in the dirt formed an alloy stronger than any other the pirates had interacted with. It was safe to say that neither of the two new ships was of sublime quality, despite the use of extraterrestrial materials. They floated, and could keep cargo in and water out, but they had obviously not been constructed with the utmost precision like former naval vessels such as the *Revenge*.

After hardly an hour, it was now early morning, though the sun was yet to rise. They were sailing along the coastline of a peninsula, on which the first stone table was located. In the dark green sky, a sphere even darker could just about be seen. Small dashes of light, as well as the occasional pebble, shot up into the air and towards the planet above. Simultaneously, light and matter fell in opposite directions. Not yet could Thatch see the source of this phenomenon, but he knew he was close to the stone-henge.

Then, ahead of them, the captain noticed a figure; a demon was standing on the coastline. Not Beelzebub, not Moloch, but another. He seemed vaguely familiar, but it was hard to tell, for each time Blackbeard had seen him, he had been hiding in the darkness.

"Here we go, lads!" Thatch said as the demon opened his wings. As this happened, a small crack in the land widened. It became wide enough for a ship to sail through, and since water poured in, Thatch took the hint. He adjusted his wheel accordingly. Now, they could see the stone-henge, and the fresh stream of water flowed right towards it.

"Woe to ye, O Earth and sea!" Thatch laughed, rabid from the first, small taste of freedom.

Queen Anne's Revenge departed from the infernal red waters, and shot into the sky, faster than anyone on board could comprehend. The two other ships followed, each glowing as they were transported. Edward Thatch had just escaped Hell. Four planets to go.

Chapter VII

The Lady Mary: the helm

The next thing Thomas could remember hearing was again the sound of the rooster, who had decided to commence his crowing at quarter to five in the morning. He opened his eyes, and wiped the sleep away from the corners, then checked to see if Noah had fallen asleep too. To his relief, he had, so he was able to pretend that he had stayed awake all night. For five minutes. This was because Noah had also awoken to the sound of crowing.

"You fell asleep," Tom told the cowboy.

"You fell asleep first, so I had to get Elliott to help me with the sails," Noah replied. Tom had no response to this until he looked up and saw not the endless ocean but a cliff face. The rock itself, which was of the planet's signature colour: red, appeared to be in the process of decay, and a black vine of ivy constricted the cracks. The waves hit the coast and formed a warm mist, which was lit orange by the rising sun. This helped to wake the two of them up. But they weren't here for the cliff. No, their destination lay within a deep gorge that fractured the land. Light did not fall within this chasm, actually, it appeared to be avoiding it.

"I sailed us here through the night, with help of course, didn't want to wake you up."

"I thought you'd never been in a boat?"

"'Turn the wheel right to go right, and left to go left. Simple!'"

"You're a natural!"

Too, the rest of the crew rose from their sleep, as ordered by their gallinaceous alarm clock. All except Adam Lumberlodge, who had already famously slept through every natural disaster possible: hurricane, earthquake, volcanic eruption, even a tsunami. So, one cocky cockerel would not wake him, and they should be grateful too because if they did it would likely be the last thing they'd do. Unless you include being eaten as a sandwich.

Once Glove had thrown on a fresh shirt, placed on his boots and wiped the saliva from his beard, he stepped onto deck, placed his hands in his pockets and assessed the situation. He brooded for a while, stared into the gorge, and formulated a plan. Or in his regular fashion; it was rather the beginning steps of a plan. He was wary, and that's why he was pondering it with so much care. His gaze began sombre, or perhaps stern, then it became determined. His nostrils puffed as he sighed, preparing himself for the journey ahead, though he knew not how grand it would be.

"Rise and shine, boys!" Glove yelled as he finished fastening his boots, "It be a fine day for cheating Death!"

Doyle replied with a shout but stopped mid call for he realised that no one else was doing the same.

"We all know the plan — find ourselves a way out of damnation, find a way to Heaven! A chance for myself to see mi dearly beloved once again. Husband will be reunited with wife, sons with mother, friends with friends. No more worrying about running out of food, of water. No need to worry about encounters with rivals, and no need to worry about encounters with new ones. No need to worry. It's better for all of us, it's the afterlife we wanted."

"The afterlife we deserve," Tudor added, though Glove just smiled as he knew this was quite a stretch.

"Son," Glove turned to his son and began giving orders heartily, "we need to be cautious. Me and a few men shall stay aboard, ready to receive you should you retreat. You take the rest and go, find out about Ol' Devil, and see what he's about. Make a deal if the price is right."

"Aye-aye!"

"Elliott!" Glove called his first-mate over, "Accompany my son and settle our ticket out of here. Read the situation, you know what terms we're bargaining for. Look after him, both of you, look after your crew, I'd usually put that responsibility on mi-self, but I need to stay here, keeping you safe too in a way, if you need to fall back."

"Of course, captain," Elliott Ethan assured.

"Off you go, men!" Glove ordered, and each pirate climbed down the side of the ship using the ladder built into it, before getting into the rowing boat. Adam, who had still not exited his bedroom, of course remained aboard, but the rest climbed down.

"Wait up!" the captain called to Noah, who was about to climb over the edge of the ship, "You're staying here."

"Why?" Tom asked of him.

"I'd like to have a word with Mr Beard here, don't you worry, son, you can take everyone else."

Tom glanced over at Noah, who glanced back, appearing confused but willing to stay aboard. And so, Tom too followed the rest of the crew and disembarked the vessel.

"In the gorge!" Noah shouted down to the crew, "Just keep going until you find him!"

"Cool!"

"Or he finds you!"

Tudor Boris carried a torch until the dawn's light still ceased to exist within the gorge. Once they had reached the shore and the gorge, Tom drew his cutlass, though a new one, not the flaming one from the prologue because that is in the Caribbean Sea. Maddy too had a sword, and so did Tudor, Doyle had knives, and Elliott had a pistol. Each pirate possessed at least three pistols and a sword each, in order to be ready for all forms of combat. So, with their weapons at the ready, they all proceeded into the canyon, led by Thomas.

Rough gravel rolled under their boots, making it nearly impossible to tread quietly (though Doyle gave it a good go). A streak of glowing morning sky could be seen above, though it appeared that the rock face absorbed the torchlight. Elliott wore an eyepatch, and Maddy often pulled her bandana over one eye. It is common, I believe, to assume that pirates wore eyepatches to cover up a wounded eye, but this was not true, at least mostly. Having one eye cast in permanent darkness encouraged the pupil to dilate, so that it was already adjusted to the dark. This allowed pirates to lift their eyepatches and already be able to see clearly when they went below deck with no light. And to this effect, the two lifted their eye coverings and gained a slight advantage.

Elliott had learnt that the compass was not to be trusted in Hell, but happened to take a look at his own to notice that the needle was spinning violently. He put the compass away but couldn't help but question what had sent it so 'doo-lally' — as he thought in his head.

"This place is strange," he stated, as if it weren't already clear, "a canyon so deep yet so close to the sea, and the compass is spinning like mad. Be careful."

"Elliott, we're going through this canyon to find Satan, did you expect it to be normal?" Tudor said rather coldly.

"I was only warning you, Tudor, calm down."

"You calm down."

"Tudor," Tom interrupted, "shut up."

"Oh, come on, I'm winding him up," Tudor protested.

"No, shut up, look," Tom repeated, speaking through his teeth as he pointed with his sword to two figures ahead.

Each was located on opposite sides of the gorge. They were sitting within the rocks and faced towards each other, the mouth of the first hung open, revealing seven-inch, sabre-like canine teeth from the upper jaw. The other had two horns, which twisted backwards. Batlike wings were raised above hunched shoulders, which supported muscular forelegs. Nothing more could be observed from the distance between them and the crew.

"The Devil?" Doyle muttered.

"Nay, the Devil doesn't come as two," Elliott argued, "but they look to me like they'd make pretty good guards."

"Weapons ready, boys!" Tom ordered, though he probably didn't need to as each crewmember was already holding their weapons as described before. But everyone at least made an effort to raise their weapons, though of course they would have had to if they planned to use them. The approaching torchlight shone through saliva that fell from the first guard's mouth as it yawned, producing a low growl. It flapped its leathery wings and turned its head towards the pirates.

The Lady Mary

"Mister Beard," Glove beckoned, pointing to a barrel on the deck, "sit down."

"Yes, sir," Noah agreed respectfully, "sorry, I mean 'captain'."

Glove too came and sat down on a barrel beside him. An awkward silence lasted a few seconds, as Glove thought for a while. Eventually he began, "Tell me about yourself, Beard."

"Like what?"

"Where you from? What's happened in this life o' yours?"

Noah told Glove of a life as a cattle wrangler in Texas. The captain questioned nothing the man told him, for he knew there was a lot he didn't know and knew that ultimately it wasn't important to him. Frankly, he didn't at all care about Noah's life, rather, he was using the opportunity to observe his mannerisms, and hopefully to understand him more. In fact, he learnt rather a lot from what was maybe ten minutes of conversation. He learnt many mundane things about Noah. None of this was far out of the ordinary, but that was reassuring to Glove.

The Devil's Canyon

 The crew continued progressing towards the two guards, despite the fact that the creatures had noticed them.

"Where's Lumberlodge when you need him?" Tudor muttered.

"You shoot them, Elliott," Doyle said, "you have a gun."

"I don't think that's a good idea," Elliott refused, "don't want to aggravate them."

"Come on, it's worth a shot," Maddy contested as they walked even further towards the creatures.

Doyle began, "Haha, worth a…" before Tom stopped him from embarrassing himself further.

"Doyle, don't you dare. And Elliott, hold fire."

"Aye-aye."

So instead, they all kept walking, though the rate at which they did so was steadily decreasing. The two beasts were obviously aware of their presence, and each had its glance set on the group. As the torch got closer, more detail could be seen. Their faces were like so many things I have described, shrinkwrapped around their skulls — though this time, they were not fiery. The first had a skull like a cat's, its upper canine teeth were long and curved backwards. From its jaws, which it had parted, hung a panting, drooling tongue. Its four legs were also like those of a cat, though very muscular like a bear's. The tail was somewhere between ratty and serpentine, and ended in a diamond, like a gargoyle or other evil spirit. In fact, gargoyles might just be the appropriate noun to describe the pair of beings.

The second had a head like a goat, and also the hooves to match. It shook its head in what could be interpreted as irritation, though it was likely wiser to see it as a threat. The wings of both gargoyles were frayed and torn at the ends, though presumably still functioned. Their skin was the same reddish grey as the rock they sat upon, and looked almost like that of a muddy rhinoceros, hippopotamus, or elephant; it was thick and formed armour plates.

Imagine a panther leaping to the ground from above. That effortless, smooth fashion of jumping, making no sound as it lands. That's exactly what the first gargoyle did. It landed about twenty feet in front of Tom, who gave orders not to stop walking. The second stumbled down the cliff far less gracefully, spreading its wings out to slow its fall. The two stood angled towards the pirates but did not come any

166

closer. Each was a little smaller than a tiger, though certainly larger than any dog. Not that any crewmember had much experience fighting tigers nor dogs.

"Thomas," Elliott spoke softly as he leant towards Tom, "what are you doing?"

"Those things are in our way, and since it seems very much unlikely that they will be going anywhere in a hurry, I'm giving them the choice to move, showing them we're not afraid."

"But they do look quite ferocious."

"They don't need to know we think that."

"What if they aren't all too keen on moving?"

"We'll make them keen."

"We'll fight?"

"What else do you plan to do with those pistols, Elliott?" Tom replied sarcastically.

"Shove 'em up his…"

"Tudor, I said shut up."

As the crew came even closer, the first gargoyle growled, while the other shook its horns some more. The two parties were now barely ten feet apart. Even Thomas was now slowing down, tensing his arm as it held out his sword. Realising now that this gargoyle had no intentions of moving aside, he ordered the crew to stop, just to be safe.

"On my command, Elliott," he ordered, "fire."

"On your command, Master Glove. Though which one?"

"Either, well, both ideally, have another gun ready, just wait," Tom whispered as he crouched down behind Elliott. He felt the ground and picked up a large pebble. Without rising, he bowled it around Elliott and past the two gargoyles, diverting their attention to the sound behind them it had caused.

"Now, Elliott!"

The Lady Mary

"So," Noah began to question Glove, "how'd you get here?"

"How'd I get here?" Glove asked, not expecting to answer any questions himself.

"Uh-huh, I have a feeling you've been here much longer than I have."

"Five years."

"What happened?"

"Twenty-five years ago, I received a copy of a map, the map. The map that leads to the gift of Satan, s'posed to gift eternal life. Well, you know how that went. It took me twenty years to pluck up the courage to find it. We fought monsters and solved riddles, and soon enough we had it. But Edward Thatch ambushed us, wanting to take it for himself. Not that it matters, because neither party left alive, the Leviathan took both ships down, along with all their men. So much for eternal life."

"In a way, Captain Glove, the stone did gift you eternal life, just not in the most ideal location."

Glove just stared, he was not amused by this comment, mostly because he knew it was true.

"Why'd you want to be immortal anyway?" Noah moved on.

"Didn't do it for myself."

"Then for who?"

"My son, I wanted my son to be immortal, he's the closest thing I have — to her."

"To who?" Noah questioned. Glove failed to answer for several seconds, lost in thought.

"Mr Beard, are you aware of the name of this ship?"

"I am not, Captain."

"'*The Lady Mary*' is its name. And it's named after the love of my life. Mary was my wife, and she was taken from me."

"I'm sorry," Noah tried to comfort Glove, but he interrupted to continue.

"Thomas was only three years old when it happened, can hardly remember her. But I can, and seeing that boy grow up to look just like her, and act just like her, it's wonderful. I lost her, and now he's all I have, I cannot lose that."

The Devil's Canyon

Elliott Ethan fired his first pistol at the first gargoyle, hitting its withers, just in front of where the wing rested. He clumsily took a few seconds to draw the second pistol, so when he fired at the other gargoyle, the beast flapped its wings and remained airborne for a moment to dodge the bullet. It was safe to conclude that neither was amused. The first roared in shock and turned back towards its attackers, while the second bleated.

"Again," Tom muttered through closed teeth to Elliott, who was hastily reloading his guns.

"Just a minute, just a minute!"

"Someone shoot the damn things!"

But since no other crewmember had a pistol in hand, the two gargoyles reacted before they got another shot in. The first slowly prowled towards them, its shoulders moving up and down like a tiger stalking prey. The second was more sudden, flapping its wings to propel itself further as it ran forward, like a chicken might. It barged straight through Elliott and Thomas, knocking them both to the floor, it then turned and swung its horns at Doyle, flipping him over but not piercing his clothes nor skin. Doyle retaliated with a jab from his knife, but the beast had already taken off again. Maddy attempted to thrust her cutlass at it, but it leapt over her in flight, battering the top of her head with cloven hooves.

Elliott had finally reloaded both pistols and returned to his feet, shooting the creature while it was airborne. It changed direction in the air and dived towards him, but altered its course at Tom, who had drawn a two-barrelled pistol from his belt and fired at its face.

"Not the face!" Elliott advised, "Aim for the wings! Get it out of the air!"

The sheer obnoxiousness of this gargoyle completely distracted the pirates from the other.

The first gargoyle nearly had its belly against the floor as it so painstakingly reached each paw out in front of it, as if it were stalking prey. And in a way, it was. As it's shoulders raised and lowered with each stride, it looked like waves upon a black sea. Its wings were folded so close to its body they were barely distinguishable from its hide, and its body so low that its silhouette did not attract the attention of the pirates.

Maddy had just successfully landed a pistol shot into the membrane of the second beast's wing when the first pounced. It jumped with both paws flat, and its claws extended. This blow knocked her over, though the creature failed to get a grasp of her. Lying on her back, she drew her sword once again to keep the gargoyle away from her. But it jumped once more and caught the sword in its jaws. Maddy pushed it away from her face by lifting the sword against its jaws. Its claws were now sunk into her coat, and its weight kept her from escaping. She screamed for help as she realised she could not fight back with her sword without allowing it to use the pair of its own swords that came from its upper jaw.

She called for help, and so Tudor made a daring attempt to come to her rescue. He tackled the gargoyle and used his momentum to push it away from Maddy. Her sword, however, remained in the beast's jaws. Both the gargoyle and Tudor had rolled across the floor and then fallen apart from each other. The gargoyle sank its claws into the stony floor to come to a halt. Tudor drew a pistol and fired, reloaded, and fired again. Then, the gargoyle spat out the sword from its mouth and pounced at its adversary, who slid under it. It landed and spun around to once more face Tudor, who was now holding a naval sabre and pointing it towards it.

Meanwhile, the second gargoyle was continuing its more reckless antics, though flying lower and for lesser amounts of time than before, on account of the fact that gunshot had punctured its wings. It spread its wings to slow itself as it flew above Tom, kicking at his head. So, he saw the perfect opportunity to raise his cutlass, piercing the animal's wing and tearing the membrane. The gargoyle then fell from the air, tumbled to the floor, and broke its neck.

Tudor's sabre was far more gracile, longer, and more elegant than the other pirates' cutlasses. He held it out far in front of him, his knees bent and one foot in front of the other. The gargoyle treaded thoughtfully, beginning to circle, so Tudor twisted his body to remain ready to receive an attack, but not to make a sudden move. He noted the creature extending its claws once more, tensing its muscles too. Anticipating a pounce, he thrust his entire body towards the beast. The feet of the gargoyle and the feet of Tudor Boris all left the floor at the same time, and the two parties met mid-air.

Tom walked over to the fallen creature and poked it with his sword, it did not respond. He impaled its chest with his cutlass, just to be safe. It was as if its blood had already clotted, for none spilt from the wound or even stained the weapon. One down, one more to go.

The collision sent Tudor and his foe falling to the ground. A paw struck Tudor's face, claws scratching his eye. He yelled as the gargoyle groaned, for his sabre had pierced its hide. Both tussled on the ground, before Tudor retracted his sword and drove it once more towards the brute, through the wing and then into the dirt, pinning in down. He then took a knife and did the same with the other wing. With no sharp weapon nor loaded gun remaining, he attacked it with his fists. This ended when Maddy picked her own sword back up from the ground, and with one huge swing, cut off its head.

The Lady Mary

"You want to go to Heaven, right?" Noah changed the subject slightly as Glove got up from his seat, "To see her again?"

"Yes, indeed," Glove answered, "It's something I never imagined I would be able to do, but now I know I can, there's nothing I want more than to see her again."

"Do you think you'll do it?"

"I have to. The impossible has become possible, so I have to try."

Glove walked over to the stairs, which led below deck.

"Lumberlodge!"

The tired voice of Adam Lumberlodge, who had just been woken from his slumber, replied, "What!"

"Stay here with the ship!"

"Where are you going!"

"To make a deal with the Devil!"

"Alright!" Adam replied nonchalantly as he tossed himself over onto his pillow and fell back to sleep.

"Come on, man," the captain called to Noah as he climbed down the side of the boat and the two made their way into the canyon to follow the rest of the crew.

<u>Chapter VIII</u>

Pandæmonium

"They're here, my lord," Beelzebub told Satan.

"Already?" Satan asked, "Did someone restrain the guards?"

"That's one way you could put it, my lord," Beelzebub muttered.

"How would you put it?"

"Well, my lord, they've only gone and killed them. The pirates have, they've killed the guards."

"I have to admire that spirit. That fills me with hope, actually. If you'd be so kind, go and receive them, I did enough walking yesterday."

The Devil's Canyon

"Tom?" Maddy began as the group progressed past their previous obstacle, "What are we actually doing?"

"We're getting out," Tom replied plainly.

"But why?"

"What do you mean 'why'? Why would we want to stay in Hell? Heaven is better than Hell, it's like my father said, 'It's best for all of us'."

"But why Heaven?" Maddy persisted.

"Cos there in't no place better," Doyle answered for him, "why would we go anywhere else?"

"Elliott?" Tom asked after thinking to himself, "What do you think?"

"About what?" Elliott replied, as he had been paying far less attention to the prior conversation as he had to his unfamiliar surroundings.

"All this, making a deal with the Devil business. I mean, you're a Christian, aren't you?"

"That be true, though evidently not a good one. We're all here through our own doing, we only have ourselves to blame. God has made his judgement."

"Well, how do you think he'll judge this?"

"Not kindly, I fear."

"Then why are we doing it?"

"Captain's orders."

"I thought you answered to a higher power."

"Look here. If it weren't for your father, I'd be dead. Correction, I'd have died long ago. He may be your father, but he's been just as good to me."

"But maybe he is wrong," Tom muttered.

"You said it yourself: 'It's best for all of us.' He wants to see his wife again; he wants you to see your mother. What's so wrong with that?"

The canyon suddenly felt rather chilly. 'Chilly' is, however, an inappropriate adjective. A better word would be 'bitter,' for the chill was not just unwelcome but unpleasant. The handles of swords stung as they cooled, and the incoming icy wind blew the torchlight out. Though it was dawn, the sky was now apparently darker than before. Despite this, it was not as dark as the figure that stood ahead of them.

The group all came to a stop quickly. The figure then unfolded two large wings, each over ten feet long. They were the darkest objects of all, as if they had cut through the fabric of space itself. Doyle had thought of asking once again, 'the Devil?' but this time, he was too terrified to do so.

"Speak," the figure commanded, though it did so while appearing static. No one, however, did speak immediately, and so it said once more, "Speak!"

"I am Thomas Glove," Tom said reasonably confidently, though he didn't say it quite as loud as he was aiming for.

"Why are you here, Captain Glove?"

"Well, ah –" he stopped himself from correcting this, mostly because he assumed it wasn't important, "We've come to make a deal."

"With whom?"

The crew all looked at each other as if they were looking for an answer.

"With whom do you wish to make a deal?"

"The Devil," Tom muttered under his breath, but the figure, who stood many yards away, could not hear.

"With whom?"

"The Devil," Elliott attempted to help, but he too could not say it boldly enough.

"If you daren't speak his name, you are not worthy of his presence."

"The Devil!" Tom finally yelled, "We're here to make a deal: a deal with the Devil!"

"Good, my master's been expecting you, come."

With some hesitation, Thomas took the first steps towards this figure, who folded his wings to his sides like a bird would when resting. The canyon was then lit with a deep glow. This glow concentrated around the figure and was emitted from a crescent of light above his head. It was like a halo, but split at the top, giving it the appearance of two horns. He also had two material horns protruding from his skull, which were twisted slightly but generally followed the curve of the halo behind them. The body to which these belonged was like a man's and rather tall and muscular, and surrounded by a swarm of insects. He wore black robes, which were greatly decorated with gold, as too was his jewellery. These robes had holes for either wing below the sleeves. He began walking away from the pirates, but at a speed that would allow them to catch up with him.

"I am Beelzebub, First Prince of Hell, servant of Satan: our lord and our King," he said formally.

"I expected Satan to be more impressive," Tudor whispered to Doyle.

"You've not seen him yet," Doyle said.

"What?" Tudor asked, "He is Satan."

"Tudor, Tudor, were you even listening?"

"What?"

"He literally just said that he was Beelzebub, Satan's servant."

"Did he?"

"Just then!"

"Oh."

After this, everyone carried on in silence. The air became even colder as they walked further into the gorge. A couple of men, especially Elliott, suddenly had rather guilty looks on their faces. It looked as if a group of schoolchildren were being escorted to the headmaster's office by a particularly frightful teacher.

Maddy thought that this quiet had become awkward, so attempted to make it less so by asking Beelzebub, "What is that light around your head?"

"My halo," the demon replied bluntly.

"Why does it look like that?" Tom joined the conversation.

"Like what?"

"I thought halos were s'posed to be circles."

"It was, once."

"So why does it look like that?" Maddy insisted.

"Because I am fallen," Beelzebub spoke in such a way that it ended the conversation immediately. He was not overly rude, overly loud, nor overly reluctant, it was just somehow that the matter-of-factness with which he had said this implied that there was no need to get into it. This, as well as the fact that no one else was really aware of what he had meant by 'fallen,' had left enough mystery for them to spend the next few minutes pondering it.

But ultimately, they reached the end of the gorge. And the doors of Satan's palace were open for them. Beelzebub entered the cave first and returned to his seat within the walls. The others hesitated. The room was, as always, extremely dark. Satan was sitting in his chair, waiting. His silhouette was barely visible, but those at the front could just about see him when they squinted. Not the Devil, nor any fallen angel called the pirates in. After what was maybe a minute, Tom realised that they would have to advance.

Pandæmonium

"Ehem," he cleared his throat, but regretted it quickly.

"We've come to make a deal!" Tudor boomed spontaneously.

"With the Devil," Tom added, catching on to his impulse.

"Then what are you waiting for? Enter!" Satan replied.

Still rather cautiously, Tom and Tudor took a few steps forward. The rest remained still for a bit longer, but eventually followed when Tom beckoned them. Elliott looked around the walls, his lip trembling at the sight of fallen angels, and then even more at the sight of the Devil, despite his less remarkable appearance. The dawn sun lit the room dully through the hole in the ceiling, revealing the table with another copy of the maps, identical to those now in possession of Blackbeard.

"Captain Andrew Glove," the Devil started the conversation to end the silence. Immediately, Thomas somehow knew that this figure before him was indeed the Devil.

"No, sir. The captain, my father, remains on board our ship, he has sent me to make a deal." Tom replied, "A deal with you."

"And what would the terms of the said deal be?"

"We were wondering if we could get out, go to the Gate?"

"The Gate of Ubyvis?"

"Yes, that's it."

"That isn't a deal, that's a request."

"What do you mean?"

"If you've come to make a deal with the Devil, you must do his bidding. Otherwise, why would he give you anything?" Beelzebub spoke from his seat above.

"You've allowed Blackbeard to have all the world's riches, I want a similar deal."

"But Thatch is delivering my great herd of beasts for the Apocalypse, you, boy, are yet to offer me anything."

"What do you suggest?"

"Where do you want to go?"

"Heaven."

"Heaven? What do you want from there? You'll find endless luxury boring, eventually. Mindless angels forced to do more than their souls can handle, all to keep safe the souls of the dead. That's all you'll find in Heaven."

"My father wishes to see my mother again."

"And you?"

"The same."

"Very well."

Satan pondered this for a moment, weighing up every option.

"Well, if it's Heaven you want to be, then here's my deal," he said, getting up from his seat and walking towards the back of the room. He opened a hidden door, which led to a tunnel with a fiery pit at the end. Before he reached this pit, he turned and reached into a smaller crevice. When he came out, he was holding a cage. It was just about too small to hold a cat but not tiny. In it was a grotesque critter indeed. Some sort of insect-like creature, it had six legs, but a tail like a scorpion. Its fangs were worse than any spider's, like a big cat's, but its face was maybe the most off-putting part; not quite like a human but close enough to make you think about it. Golden wires of hair covered the areas that were not covered by its exoskeleton, which was made of metal. The wings on its sides were also extremely sturdy, and shiny too. It clapped its wings together in the cage, and it produced the sound of a galloping horse.

"I'll help you get to Heaven, but only if you take this with you."

"What is it?"

"Pain. And justice."

"How can you have both?"

"Because some people deserve pain."

"Who deserves pain?"

"Heaven deserves pain."

None spoke for a minute, and Satan didn't force them to either. It was hard to comprehend, for one they had a deal, but this deal seemed rather pointless. What was the point of reaching Heaven just to cause it 'pain'? And what could Heaven, of all bodies, have done to deserve this pain?

It was the Devil who broke the silence, as he summoned the Moirai as he had before. Again, they appeared in the same place and in the same manner. They were quieter this time, largely because they had got their fair share of insulting beforehand. In the same sequence of events as before, the sisters of Fate produced a contract and handed it to the Devil.

"So, here's the deal: sail to the stone table on each planet to get to the next, then use the Gate of Ubyvis to get to Heaven. Once you get to Heaven, and only then, release this creature of the bottomless pit. You will have a dozen years until anything else happens, so use that time as you wish. After that, that's up to you, but it won't be pretty. It will be Armageddon."

"I thought Blackbeard was starting Armageddon?" Tom asked quietly.

"The Revelation is not about Earth, dear mortal. It's about everything."

"How can we earn the blessing of Heaven with Armageddon?" Elliott frowned, "How can we earn it through you, the Devil?"

"You won't be earning it; you'll be buying it. Buying it with your souls."

"I'm sorry?"

"Oh, yes, that's the other part of the deal, should you fail, your soul belongs to me."

Elliott, with hesitation, approached the Devil's throne and read aloud the writing on the contract. The writing was at first illegible to him, though, to his amazement, the characters reassembled themselves to reform the contract in English. After clearing his voice, he began:

"The signing of this contract, as witnessed by the Moirai (else known as the Three Sisters of Fate, or the Fates), irrevocably stakes the soul of one Captain Andrew Glove, and also the souls of every person formally a crewmember of his ship, *The Lady Mary*, against the execution of the agreed terms. These terms include both the successful escape of the solar system of Hell, via the Gate of Ubyvis alone; and the deliverance of one of Hell's wild beasts upon the destination. Failure in either one or both terms henceforth transfers the rightful ownership of all wagered souls to Satan (else known as the Devil, Lucifer, The First to fall, King of Hell, Ruler of Chaos, or Hades) with no exception unless arranged with Satan directly. This contract is only valid if signed with a seal in wax provided by the Moirai, or with ink provided by the Moirai."

Tom and Elliott looked at each other in terror. Both used every muscle in their faces to produce the look of torment on them. They got the sense that they were about to disagree.

"I'm not sure," Elliott whispered, "I wanted more than a dozen years of heaven. That's the point of it: eternal glory."

"But it's twelve years better spent than here," Tom argued, "Think of it all — better food, I imagine. Better things to do, better things to see. Surely you can see it's better."

"Twelve years and then it's over. And there'll be no eternal reward at the end, not for us, the Kingdom of God has denied us once."

"I thought you agreed with us? Minutes ago, you were trying to convince me."

"Yes, but I didn't know the stakes."

"Were you not listening?" Doyle interrupted, "The angels keeping us safe? Endless luxury?"

"But that's not the point of it! It won't be endless if we help destroy it. We don't have much here, but we have time." Elliott said, frustrated, "I want time. And I want to make sure we're doing the right thing."

Satan, now rather bored, asked, "So what of our deal? All you have to do is sign here." He pointed at the line at the bottom of the paper, "Do we have a deal?"

In an attempt to compromise, Elliott suggested, "Why don't we fetch the captain and ask him what he thinks? We are his crew; it should be his decision."

"His orders were clear," Tom stated, "Make a deal to get us to Heaven."

"Do — we — have — a — deal?" Satan insisted. At that moment, through the doors, which had been left open, a man walked in. It was Glove, and he paced to the table and signed the paper with the quill given by the Fates.

"Deal," he said, as he picked up the maps, turned around, and walked out – all before Noah had even followed him in.

"Good," Satan smiled, as the rest of the crew stood awkwardly. Eventually, they followed their captain. Since Tom was rather reluctant, Tudor picked up the cage and took it with him, holding it slightly away from him since it was so off-putting. Some would never see Satan again. Some weren't so lucky.

Chapter IX

Glove had walked away at a pace that left Tom rather out of breath once he had caught up. It took a few moments before he could start a conversation. The dawn's light had now reached the sky and finally lit the rusty canyon walls. One noticeable feature now highlighted by this was the fact that the bottom of the gorge was darker than the rest, as if it was scorched. A wind was blowing too, whistling as it flew through the canyon.

Glove lifted the maps, which flapped around in the tunnel of wind. After locating the canyon on the paper, he chuckled, realising that the wind was blowing in the direction of his journey. Although Glove hadn't buckled either of his boots correctly, he marched forward without slowing down.

"Father, father," Tom gasped for air in shock and fatigue, "what are you doing?"

"What we set out to do, get out of here. So, hurry."

"But if we get to Heaven, we have to destroy it."

"Do we?"

"Yes, did you not listen before you signed our souls to the Devil?"

"I listened alright — but think. Do we really have to destroy it?"

"That was the agreement."

"But we'll be in Heaven, surely the Devil cannot get us in Heaven."

"He's the Devil."

"Exactly. He can't go to Heaven, Heaven is filled with good, evil cannot tread there."

"Then how can we?" Tom replied, though (to his relief) his father did not hear. They had reached *The Lady Mary* and rowed towards it in two rowing boats: one left by Tom and the crew, the other left by Glove and Noah. The waves had become rather violent because of the wind, making it impossible to remain dry. After some strain to stay on course, they reached their ship, and most boarded. Glove and his son used ropes to haul up the rowing boats.

"We'll discuss it later," Gloved yelled over the sound of the weather, "Raise the anchor, men!" The side of the ship was slimy and covered in barnacles, but Glove gave it a pat as he reached the top, like it was a horse. Tudor and Adam raised the anchor, and *The Lady Mary* set sail with great power and determination; it was on its last journey on the planet Hell.

They were sailing north, the stone table lying just a few miles east-northeast. Land was in the way of the direct path, but the coastline was smooth enough to keep the trip short. Glove stood behind the wheel, observing the surroundings of Hell for the last time. The coast, which was to the port-side (left) of the boat, remained a steep cliff face for almost five miles, at least as far as Glove could see with his eyes. Even the ship itself seemed eager to reach its destination, galloping along the water as if it were trying to outrun even the waves.

Beside *The Lady Mary*, along the coast, a flock of fiery birds flew. They looked sinister and plucked, but their wing feathers remained robust enough to keep them aloft. And underneath the ship: (obviously not fiery) shrivelled and gnarly fish flustered around, disturbed by the keel. No one saw these creatures, however, for Glove's eyes were set on the horizon, which concealed his destination, and Tom's eyes were fixed on the floor.

Elliott walked over to Tom. Both felt a little tense, their gaze and body language proving it.

"You haven't made up your mind, have you?" He asked Tom, who took a deep breath before replying.

"I don't know what to think."

"Me neither, I'm no fan of these stakes."

"Is that what made you change your mind? You don't think it's worth it?"

"Like you said, 'I don't know what to think.' I'm quoting you a lot at the moment."

"It's because I keep changing my mind too. Of course, I want to get out of here. Of course, I want more than this. To tell the truth, there hasn't been a day since we arrived that I haven't dreamt of something better."

"But is this better?" Elliott interrupted, "Is it really better? I agree, something more than this would be lovely, but at least this is predictable, and unlimited. Yes, I was happy to go along with it all, but is it really worth it?"

Then, Andrew Glove trundled towards them, while the ship was briefly on a straight course along the shore.

"What seems to be the problem, lads?" he asked.

"Nothing, Captain, nothing," Elliott assured.

"Now that you've asked," Tom began, "are you sure we've made the best decision?"

"Aye-aye, son. Very sure."

"What makes you so sure? How do you know it won't end terribly?"

"You said the 'best decision,' didn't you? Not the most sensible decision, not the safest decision?"

"Yes?"

"Well then! Of course, there may be dangers, but what of them? Remember, it's a chance to see my Mary again! That's why it's the best decision!" Glove said heartily as he wandered back to the steering wheel.

Elliott thought for a moment, humming to himself. After that, he turned back to Tom and spoke heedfully, "What about this? You want this, sort of. And I want this a little. Doyle wants it, Tudor does, and I'm sure most people do. And the captain wants it. And he is in charge, isn't he? This is the easiest option; it's making the most people happy. So, let's just go along with it, it's only fair. And maybe it is the best option."

"Amen," Tom replied, feeling quite a bit better after hearing that reasoning.

And at last, Adam Lumberlodge, with dark patches under his eyes, made his way above deck. His hair, though never particularly tidy, was even scruffier than usual. Dark curls twisted off in the wrong direction, and there was a flat patch where his pillow had been. He hadn't even dressed: his shirt was unbuttoned, his belt unfastened, and there were no shoes covering his odd and hole-filled socks. However, this was not a rare occurrence, so no one thought to mention it. With a yawn, he asked, "What the bloody Hell's going on here?"

"We're getting out," Elliott answered.

"You didn't?"

"Didn't what?"

"You actually made a deal with the Devil?"

"Yeah, indeed we have," Elliott now sounded terribly guilty for his part in it.

"Fuck's sake," Adam tutted.

"What now?" Tom asked.

"What the fuck are we doing?"

"Getting out!" Elliott repeated.

"But why?"

"Don't you want us to?"

"Why bother? I'm fine here. Leave me be for God's sake!"

"We need a change, Adam," Tom insisted, "we all need it."

"I don't!"

"Don't be selfish," Elliott retorted.

"I'm not being selfish."

"Well, don't be lazy."

Adam, despite his reckless and unorganised nature, was actually rather observant (though sometimes he failed to observe this). He couldn't help but notice the out-of-place item on deck. This was the cage containing the creature that the crew had been contractually obligated to deliver to Heaven. I shall call the creature a locust for the sake of talking about it, though we all know it isn't a typical locust. Actually, I'll call it the Locust, with a capital letter, because that's how important it is.

The Locust had begun running up the walls and ceiling of the cage, occasionally beating its wings to produce a rhythmic thudding sound. It was this sound that drew Adam's attention to it. Without replying to Elliott or Tom, he walked over to the cage, which was placed haphazardly near the steering wheel. The other two followed behind, reminded now of the Locust's role in the plan. Glove noticed the three move over and asked, "Could one of you take that beastie below deck? Don't want it lying about, do we?"

With little thought, Adam picked up the cage. The Locust's body was about ten inches long, with its crooked legs filling up more space of its container. It dashed about frantically as Adam lifted it, its wings clicking loudly.

"No, no, not you, Lumberlodge!" Glove yelled panicked, "Someone take it off of him!"

"Here," Tom offered, as Adam passed him the cage roughly.

"What do you think I'm going to do with it? I'm not a moron, you know!" Adam said; a tad offended.

"Just someone do as I've asked," Glove said.

"C'mon," Elliott said, guiding the other two to the stairs which led below deck. He opened the door to his study, a small room where he kept books and papers and drawings and maps. He had written and drawn some, but most he had collected from other sources for academic purposes. Pipes that carried smoke from the oven out of the ship ran along the wall on one side. Supposing that the creature, being from Hell and all, favoured warmth, Elliott instructed Tom to place the Locust down beside the pipework.

The three remained in the study for a while, avoiding the previous conversation topics. They also, for some reason that they couldn't quite decide, wanted to avoid the others for a bit, so talked for some time about fond memories from Earth. They spoke of many things, but one event in particular was the time when Lumberlodge had walked into four palm trees in one afternoon.

"It was three!" Adam shouted.

"No, no," Tom told him, "It was four, four times you managed to walk into a palm tree."

"All in one afternoon!" Elliott joined in, laughing hysterically.

"Three!"

"No, there was the one as soon as we got off the ship," Elliott reminded.

"And then the one in the tavern courtyard," Tom added, "and the one in the market square."

"And last, when we were getting back in the boat, you walked into the very one you did the first time!" Elliott finished, howling even more than before.

"Thomas, you're wrong!" Adam argued.

"He isn't! I remember it all!"

"No, the one in the market square was a pear tree!"

Unfortunately, all good stories come to an end, as had now this one. This wasn't a problem, for they had many more just as good, often involving the misadventures of Adam Lumberlodge. However, just as one can revel in the past, it is just as easy to question it. Many secrets, and answers to your current and future questions, lie not ahead of you, but behind you. I may be digressing, but bring up the past Tom did.

"Did you know?" he asked Elliott, his senior by a few years, "that he killed her?"

"I beg your pardon," Elliott answered with a now stern face, "that who killed whom?"

"That Blackbeard killed Mary — my mother, I mean."

"Who told you that?"

"My father."

"No, that's not — he never told me that," Elliott was somehow even more shocked than Tom had been, "Oh, dear."

"Why has he only mentioned it now?"

"I can't be sure, maybe because it's important now, now it's motivation, a purpose. Before it was a horrible past," Elliott suggested, before turning to Adam and asking, "You didn't know, did you?"

Adam had been sitting, biting his nails, zoned out of the conversation that neither interested nor involved him.

"Adam!" Elliott repeated, as the man twitched into attention, "Did Glove ever tell you?"

"About Blackbeard killing his wife? No, why would he? Anyway, I wasn't even born when it happened."

"You were, Adam, you were just an infant."

"Was I?" Adam asked, genuinely amazed that the event, which he had often viewed as being long in the past, had occurred in his lifetime.

To everyone's relief, a loud thud came from above. As all three could tell from the pitch, it was Glove's boot against the planks, which were below his own feet but above their heads. Two other thuds followed this. They all knew this was a signal. They were here.

And so, they rose from their brief refuge and prepared themselves for whatever lay ahead – not that they truly could. The land beside the ship had decayed from a steep cliff face to purplish-grey beaches. The land curved slightly east, and so the ship's course had been altered accordingly.

"Almost here," Adam said.

"When did you see the map?" Tom asked.

"Earlier," he said, though had forgotten when exactly.

"The boy's not wrong!" Glove shouted, pointing them to the map at his side. There was barely a mile left to go.

The sky was still dull with the dawn's light and a series of dark clouds. Because of this, the first dash of light was even more visible. From somewhere inland on the tip of the peninsula, a pink light shot up and disappeared within the cloudy sky. Despite its velocity, it did not go unnoticed. All turned their heads west to see it. Then, it happened again. And then one came back down. And again.

"Anyone want to tell me what those are?" Glove asked, though he was not concerned, "what be those lights jumping to and from the clouds?"

"Those aren't clouds," Adam replied, noticing that the clouds had parted, "Clouds aren't round."

"Is that…" Elliott began.

"Our next stop?" Tom finished.

Indeed, this was the next planet. In fact, the outer edge of the one behind it could just about be seen too, poking its way around it. But it was the closest planet they were focussed on, and they'd soon be there.

I could explain the next events in great detail, but you already know what's coming from Blackbeard's turn. The same demon stood waiting patiently on the coast. He opened his wings, and again the land opened with them. As Thatch had, Glove understood this signal. He spun the wheel, and the ship spun around to its left. Her front scraped the bank of the channel a bit, but she returned promptly on course. As water spilt in from the sea, *The Lady Mary* was pulled along faster than even her sails had hauled it.

Not only could the crew see lights coming to and from the next planet, but they could now see pebbles and twigs too. Some twigs had green needles on them — a strange sight for Hell. This was the most natural-looking thing anyone had seen for a long time. The water behind them was rushing in with so much force, it had become impossible for anyone to change their mind; the ship was heading straight for the stone-henge, and nothing could change that now.

And so, just as Blackbeard and his crew had done a matter of hours before, *The Lady Mary* took off from the red waters of Hell and landed somewhere very different indeed. One planet behind them. Like their rival, they had four more to go.

Act 2: Live and Let Die

Chapter I

Oblitos: *The Lady Mary*

The crew found themselves nauseated. They knew they had just been projected at an immense velocity from one planet to another, but it had happened so fast they hadn't had the time for their senses to process it. But they were indeed on another planet. Planet number two (or three if you include Earth, but that was the prologue). But this planet was different from Hell.

The ship (which remained intact despite the momentum you may expect it should gather after hurtling through space) drifted timidly along the delightful shore alongside a luscious coniferous forest. It feels strange to describe conifers as luscious, like this adjective should be reserved for the trees of the rainforests with broad and bright leaves and delicious fruits rather than dark needles. But somehow, the word still fits. These trees were, in fact, trees of a tropical rainforest, just not of the Amazon. Rather than conforming to the typical cone shaped, Christmas tree fashion you're thinking of, they had a large, thick trunk supporting little vegetation until the very tops, which branched out to form a canopy of needles and cones and fruits. And to make them even more verdant, the trunks were also green because of a coat of moss and lichen that grew upon them. Ferns and shrubs also lined the forest floor. If you were to step inside, it is likely that you could look in any direction and see only the colour green.

Glove pulled out the second map.

"Oblitos," Elliott read, "this planet is called Oblitos."

"This is, this is rather different, isn't it?" Noah asked, obviously not actually wanting an answer, as this was apparent.

"Aye, it be a green planet indeed." Glove agreed.

"Feels a bit more like home." Tom remarked.

"Look, birds!" Maddy added, pointing to a flock of about twenty small creatures, which fluttered by before disappearing into the trees.

"They were bats, not birds," Adam argued.

"Adam, it's daytime and we're not in a cave, so why would they be bats?"

"I'm not an animal-ologist, am I?"

"Zoologist, Adam." Elliott pointed out.

"Okay, I'm not a bloody zoologist, but I can tell you they were bats!"

"They were birds!"

"They were bats! Bloody bats!"

"Stop saying bloody bats!" Tom requested as they approached a beach and anchored the ship.

"We need to get a sense of our surroundings. We need to figure out where on this map we are." Elliott said, examining the map.

"How the Hell are we going to do that?" Tudor said — mostly to be argumentative.

Doyle butted in, attempting to lighten the mood, "You mean, 'How the Oblitos.'" Everyone turned and looked at him blankly.

"Were you even trying to make a joke?" Tudor asked, half sarcastic and half serious.

"What? That was good. Do you not get it? You see, he said, 'Where the Hell,' but we're not in Hell anymore, but we were. Now, we're in Oblitos, so 'where the Hell' becomes 'where the Obl...'"

"It's even worse when you explain it," Tom stopped him.

"Oh, come on!"

"It was fucking awful!" Adam couldn't help but add.

"Alright, Adam," Doyle said, offended.

"Men! Seriously now, we know not what is ahead of us, so we need to be on the ball," Glove insisted.

Elliott, however, was indeed taking the matter very seriously. Performing a rather peculiar experiment, he found a bucket and some rope and tied the rope to the bucket's handle. Next, he threw the bucket into the water below and pulled back up a sample in it. He then took a sip of the water. As soon as the liquid hit his palate, his face muscles all contracted, and he spat it out, forming a spray since his lips were sealed. The water was salty, very salty.

"It's seawater, alright!" He confirmed the answer to a question that, thus far, only he had asked.

"You don't say." Tudor moaned.

"You're welcome, Boris," Elliott retaliated, "more help than you're being."

"How is the water salty?" Adam interrupted, "We're in a lake."

"We can't be," Elliott replied, as he took out his telescope.

Tudor did the same and added, "He's not wrong, look."

Elliott looked around. North: land, steep, jagged cliffs. West: land, grasslands. South: land, the forest at the side of them (he did not need the telescope for this). And east: an island, but behind that was land, mountains.

"No," Elliott suggested, "what we have here — is an inland sea."

"That's a lake, mate," Adam scoffed.

"No, it's an inland sea," Elliott retorted.

"That's literally just a lake," Tudor joined in the debate.

"There's a difference."

"Oh, 'There's a difference,' What is it then?"

"One's salty, one isn't."

"Oh, wow, big deal!"

"It is a big deal, because that means we're here," Elliott triumphed, pointing to an inland sea on the south of the map, "and to prove it, look over there, that's the straight that leads us out."

With this, Glove's ears pricked up.

"Well done, boys! Man the sails, we're going West. It's a big ol' journey ahead; it seems we're sailing round the whole wee continent!"

Indeed, they were sailing around, for the tiny planet only housed one large landmass. There were a few notable islands, but only the single continent. The stone-henge was in the North Pole, they were nearer the south. The aforementioned continent lay in between the two, and they were not quite south enough to make a trip around the other side worth it. And so, they set off to go around. They also deduced that the continent, and perhaps the planet, were small by the scale of the rivers on the map. Their meanders appeared on the roughly A3 map to be on average a third of an inch apart, compared to the mostly invisible rivers of a full map of Earth. And so, this journey would take only a couple of days.

The wind was weak and did not blow in the optimum direction, making the boat dawdle slowly. Glove raised his telescope to his eyes to get a better mental map of his surroundings. His eyes were drawn to three objects, which were perhaps ten miles away; Elliott had failed to notice them when observing the more distant geography. There were three ships: Blackbeard's ships. They sailed as they had before – in a triangle. The *Revenge* sailed ahead, and the other two side by side, behind their flagship. They were faint, unremarkable specks to the naked eye, and not much more to look at through the telescope due to the distance. But they were Blackbeard's ships, and travelling the same route *The Lady Mary* had just embarked on.

"Look due west, lads!" Glove instructed, "It be that foul Captain Thatch!"

As one might expect of a group who had found themselves on a new planet, most took to observing their surroundings. Adam, however, as you might also expect, went to bed. Tom walked closer to the side of the ship to look at the forest that lay beside them. Doyle and Noah both followed. The first-mate stayed at his captain's side and helped plan the route, as well as keep a lookout. Glove requested for Maddy to sit in the Crow's-nest and lookout as well. She obliged, and to keep her company, Tudor too climbed up the mainsail to sit in the small wooden shelter atop.

"Look at them there!" Glove yelled in delight, "Thatch is not even an hour ahead of us!"

"Perhaps it's their monstrous cargo weighing them down," Elliott suggested.

"Aye-aye, our Lady be a lighter, more streamlined ship, we should overtake them before the day is over, my boy."

"What about the new one? The little one?"

"Aye, it may have a shot at outspending us, but why would it?" It holds no cattle, so there is no reason for it to leave behind its fleet."

"True, true. Never mind, it was just a thought."

"Don't worry yourself, Elliott. I have no doubt we will triumph over that old hound."

"No doubt at all, cap'n?"

"Non at all. Because we have Passion."

"Look at that!" Doyle gasped, staring at the green coniferous rainforest beside them.

"All of those trees — well, they must be over a hundred feet tall," Noah added.

"They're furry, too," Tom said with a chuckle, "They're covered in green fur!"

"Surely that's moss," Noah argued.

"Yeah, that probably makes more sense," Tom admitted.

The landscape was comfortably similar to Earth, which was pleasant, but also alien enough to seem magical. The mountains behind them were a cool grey, a refreshing contrast to Hell. Snow topped the largest mountain, which had a flat peak. Vast birds, though they appeared minuscule through the distance, flew past the mountains with huge stork-like beaks at the end of outstretched necks. They glided skilfully with little flapping because of the distance. They observed no other creatures at that moment, but it was apparent that life was nearby. The forest swayed in the breeze that carried an aura of sentience. The planet had a sense of being alive. Of course, the planet was full of life, but even the rock itself felt as if it were humming faint songs of existence.

"Why couldn't we have been here all along?" Thomas questioned.

"That's a daft question," Doyle said, "We never knew about it."

"Yes, but it's been here. It's been here all this time."

"But we didn't know."

"But it was here. All this within our reach, and we rotted in Hell for half a decade."

"It's done now," Noah explained.

"Yes, but I wish we did."

"But we didn't. Besides, it's not that great when you think about it," Doyle thought, "I could think of some improvements."

"You don't get it, Doyle, you don't get it."

The helm

Elliott found the time to be alone with his captain and explain, "Tom said that you told him Thatch killed Mary."

Glove shrugged, "I suppose I thought he needed some encouragement. A hard truth can bring encouragement to the right person."

"Do you think he believes you?" Elliott asked.

"Why wouldn't he believe the truth?" Glove said in his plain way of speaking, "He may have a mind of his own, but he knows when his father is telling him the truth."

"I don't think I'll ever understand," Elliott said to make the topic less morbid, "how that man can sleep through something like this, Adam I mean."

"Are you really surprised, Elliott? You know Adam's always been like that. He doesn't care, and that's that."

"I'm a little surprised. Yes, I know how he is, but come on. We just escaped Hell, for God's sake! And all he does is argue about bloody bats and sod off to bed!"

"I don't know what to tell ya."

"But how? How can't he care about this? He seems to have an opinion about everything, so why not this?"

"What can I say? He's a mysterious man, Adam is. I may have raised him, but I can't read his mind. Ask him if you're that worried."

"I wouldn't say worried, cap'n, just curious," Elliott told him, but not very convincingly, "I will go and check on him though."

And so, Elliott trotted off to see Adam downstairs, first taking some time to admire the scenery himself. The gentle breeze carried along with it a feather. Catching the feather with a lunge, he stared at it. Flecks of iridescent black broke up swaths of brown and beige. It smelt strangely pungent too. Not that birds generally smell nice, but Elliott concluded that this was from a large bird of prey. He made this decision based on the smell, but also the fact that it was tipped with blood.

Below deck

The sky was blue — sky blue. That's a strange thing to point out, but I just thought I'd make sure you were aware. The water was also blue; the sun appeared yellow; the clouds were white; and as I have mentioned, the trees were green. This world appeared far more organic, and less supernatural, compared to Hell, and even Earth for that matter. It seemed quite unspoiled, to say the least. Elliott almost felt sorry for it; he thought it was a shame that men like themselves should have the privilege to breathe its pure air, or to tread its unsullied soil. He expressed this to Adam after he had knocked on the door of his private room and entered. Adam, of course, cared little. He was rocking in his hammock facing away from Elliott at first, turning when Elliott continued talking.

"What are you doing, man?" Elliott got to the point, "We've escaped Hell, for Christ's sake! And you're lying in bed looking all sorry for yourself!"

"I'm not hurting anyone, am I?" Adam said in his defence.

"Currently, I'm not worried about anyone else, Adam, I'm worried about you."

"You don't need to worry about me, let me worry about me."

"Well then, let me put it this way, what are you worried about?"

"I ain't worried about anything."

"Then what do you want?"

"I want you to stop bothering me. What's done is done. What'll be done will be done. I'm not fussed either way."

"Do you not want any say in it at all?"

"It's too much effort, and for what?"

"What do you mean 'for what?'?" Elliott was getting angry at Adam's careless attitude.

"What do you expect me to do? I could be standing on deck with you twats, and the outcome will be the same. You'll still sail through this 'inland sea' of yours, and then up the river through the continent and then to the stone-henge in the north. Then to the next planet, then the next, then the next. Then we'll be in Heaven, which will be destroyed in twelve years, and so we'll be dead. Whatever dead means if heaven is destroyed."

"We're sailing through a strait, not a river. Not to be pedantic, but there is a difference."

"I know there's a difference, but surely, we should sail through the river, then we can cut through the continent rather than going around."

"Rivers don't just cut through continents; they start at mountains, not the sea."

"But this one splits, though, one part ends in the south, near us, and the other ends in the north. We could sail straight through."

"No, we couldn't, rivers don't split. They may look like it, but it's just two coming together."

"No, this one splits. It ends in the sea on either side of the continent."

"That's impossible. You didn't even read the map."

"I saw it, and I remember the river splitting."

"Well, it can't."

"I'll bet you my musket it does. My musket against that fat, noisy chicken downstairs."

"Which one? The blue cockerel?"

"There ain't no blue cockerels. I mean the grey one."

"That's what blue means."

"Blue means blue, not grey. Anyway, do we have a deal? You're right: you get my gun, I'm right: I get that cockerel to eat so he can't wake me up no longer," Adam argued passionately, for he knew very well in his head he was right.

Elliott, however, knew that rivers were not known to split, so confidently accepted the bet, despite the fact he was gambling his only remaining rooster.

"Alright then," he said, shaking Adam's hand, "but you've got to come upstairs to check."

"A'ight."

Adam's hair had already become awfully messy, with some of his curls twisting upwards and sideways. He didn't bother or think about fixing this. He walked with his eyes down and his head rocking slightly from side to side as it bobbed up and down with his stride. In a straight line, Adam had paced to the map by Glove's side with intent, holding his arm out to point before he had taken his last step.

Indeed, there was a river estuary to their north. It was a wide river that meandered through the continent and into a lake (I'm describing the river in the wrong direction as this is the way the ship would sail. The water actually flows from the lake out to sea). Three rivers were connected to the lake: the one I have described; another, which was the river that input the water by flowing into it; and another, which led out to sea in the north. So, despite Elliott's claim that it was impossible for a river to split in two directions, that's what was happening. One river, which ran into the lake, split into two that drained it.

"See!" Adam burst out, almost offended that Elliott had not believed him. Elliott had not, however, caught up with Adam, so still could not see.

"See what?" Glove asked, wondering what on Earth Elliott must have said to Adam to make him this lively. This thought put quite an enormous smile on his face, finding out made this even bigger.

"This knob-'ead reckons rivers don't split. But looky here, it chuffin' does! Pay up, Elliott!"

"Knock me down with a feather," Elliott whispered with a strong accent.

"Elliott, boy, the bastard's proven you wrong, you better pay up whatever you bet," Glove told him, less aware of the implications of this cartographical discovery.

"Do you understand what this means, Cap'n?"

"That you've lost yourself a bet, son," Glove liked to poke fun when Elliott occasionally made a mistake, knowing he was willing to play along.

"Yes, that," Elliott chuckled, though his face was red, "but it also means we have a shortcut, a way to overtake Thatch, undetected."

"Do you think *The Lady* could fit down the river?"

"Look at the map, that island there is no more than three times the length of this boat."

"Aye?"

"And the river is drawn to be no less than half the width of that, so presumably, we will fit."

"What about depth?"

"Well, it should be deep enough; it's far enough from the source."

"The wind's not exactly with us now, is it?"

"Not yet, but it is on a good chunk of the meander. We can always let the current take us out if we cannot go on."

"Aye, and lose precious time."

"It's a gamble, captain."

"You've already lost one gamble today, boy," Glove reminded with a smirk towards Adam.

"So do you think I'll let myself lose another?"

"Not at all. We'll alter course! Starboard – due north!" Glove yelled as he spun the wheel clockwise with great might, the crew having to alter the sails afterwards.

"A deal's a deal, Elliott," Adam brought their bet up again with a grin.

"I said you can have him, I didn't say I'd catch him for you."

"Bastard!"

Adam found himself downstairs in the brig. Standing at the gate of the chicken coop, he stared into the pen. And from it, a pair of eyes stared back. They sat two feet and seven inches above the ground, in the skull of a sixteen-pound rooster. It was true that Adam had already taken out a rooster twice this size only a day before, but that was with a gun. He had left his gun upstairs. This particular rooster, Elliott's only rooster, was of a fuller build than the wild chickens of Hell. His breast was almost as wide as his body was long, held up on two widely set legs, which were covered with thick feathers down to the middle toe. Its heavy jacket of feathers was pale grey, with blotches of dark grey and black. His comb was small, compact, and wrinkled, appearing to be made of three miniature roosters' combs folded together; his beak was yellow, long and hooked; and his unblinking eyes were red. Adam stared straight at him, and he stared right back, his head held high as he panted slowly.

Adam groaned at the sight of his spurs, so walked over to a toolbox close by and put on a pair of gloves. He struggled to undo the latch on the entrance to the pen as the bolt was slightly higher than the receiving end. Once opened, he slid through in an attempt to not let any chickens out. The rooster clucked in alarm as the hens scurried away from their intruder. Adam spread his arms out to prepare to catch the bird. That was a mistake.

Roosters, it often seems, are fuelled by one thing alone: testosterone. They often view, or at least the most wrathful of them, any sudden movement or change in body language as a threat, and so treat it as such. This is exactly what Adam's rooster did. It lowered its head and boxy shoulders as it ran at Adam as fast as its feathered feet allowed.

"Ooh, ya bugger," Adam shrieked as he raised his leg in defence. Gaining a second aloft by flapping his heavy wings, the rooster kicked his own legs up and flung his spurs at the man's boot.

Neither spur pierced the shoe, so Adam could push the bird away with a kick of his own. But the rooster wasn't done. It ducked under Adam's boot before it came back down and slinked behind him. Here, it pulled at his trousers with its curved beak. With the same boot, which had not touched the floor, Adam kicked backwards like a horse. Flapping once more, his aggressor gained the airtime to evade this, all while kicking at the back of his other leg. This time, a spur got caught in his trousers, and the two were tangled together as they flustered. Adam dashed towards the gate, and the rooster got free, but pursued him until he slammed the door in its face. It gave one last kick against the wire, perhaps a message.

"Knob-head," Adam sighed, looking at it, displeased. He tossed the gloves to the side and went back to the deck. He would have gone to bed, but wanted to complain.

Chapter II

The Golden Gander

You might expect that the weakest and least important of three ships might be neglected a bit, left with its deck being rotten and slimy. Maybe you also think it would be unfortunate (or fortunate) enough not to be commanded by such a disciplined man as Thatch or the former first-mate. There is a dash of truth in that; *The Golden Gander* was not captained by a man. It was, however, spotless. Its deck was not only clean but glistened with a thin layer of seawater that prevented rot.

The name of its commander was Amber Sings. Her clothes were practical and dark, though clearly tailored for a Georgian woman. She stood on the quarterdeck and stared with doe-eyes out towards her subordinates, who she had scrubbing the main-deck below. At the sight of a slacking worker, she glared at one of the taller men, whom she had appointed officer. He wasn't scrubbing like the rest, but stood above the others, mostly for intimidation. The officer was holding a whip, the infamous cat-o'-nine-tails, and he knew what he had been ordered to do. Commander Sings' almost black eyes directed him to the sailor, who had not been working as hard as expected. The tips of the cat-o'-nine-tails brushed past a different sailor's back, as the officer pointed to him to ensure he had the right man. As this happened, he flinched, despite the fact that the whip had not yet been used to its fullest. Sings did not nod her head, but she didn't shake it either.

Crack! The cat struck the innocent pirate's back with a thud. Only after, the commander shook her head. The officer then moved across to the next pirate. Again, she refused to confirm or deny. Crack! She mouthed, 'No' while she shook her head, half a second before the whip caused another incorrect man to fall onto his chest. Finally, the officer identified the correct pirate, who was by this point whimpering quietly. Once the whip had struck, she nodded her head a single time, and the officer stepped away. The ten or so men scrubbing the deck proceeded to do so with great haste and commitment.

A rather fortunate young man had the nicer job of sitting peacefully in the crow's-nest while this all unfolded. He had been slightly distracted by all the fuss below him, so he hadn't really been doing his job. The job of a lookout was, of course, to look out; he had to watch out for any potential reward or threat. There was, though he wasn't paying attention, a potential threat a few miles northeast of them. The threat may not likely have been a physical one, more of a competitive rivalry.

Out of the corner of his eye, now he could see it. *The Lady Mary*. He wasn't yet aware that it was *The Lady*, but it was a sensible guess. A look through his telescope confirmed it was a good guess. Instinctively, he prepared to call down to his commander and inform her that *The Lady* was catching up to them, so that she could inform the captain on *Queen Anne's Revenge*. Just before he did, he noticed one detail he had missed before. Their rival's ship was not catching up with them. It was moving away. It was moving north, not west like they were. Of course, it was still his job to inform Sings the whereabouts of *The Lady*, so that was what he did.

"Commander!" he yelled down. Amber acknowledged him but did not respond verbally. This was the lookout's cue to reveal whatever he had got her attention for. And so, he pointed northeast of them, at *The Lady*. The commander paced with intent to the starboard side of the quarterdeck. She wore ankle boots with quite a significant heel, which made her footsteps sharp and loud. Other that this, as well as the added height, the choice of footwear was rather impractical. Luckily, she did not need to do anything practical — she had the crew for that.

Taking out her telescope, she looked out at what she could tell with her bare eyes was a ship. It was a ship she had seen before, the only ship she would ever have expected to see. Even now, she remained silent. An officer watched for commands. With nothing more than her eyes, she pointed at one of the flags that were used as signals between ships. And so, the officer raised it; it was the yellow and black flag used to signal for a communication.

Queen Anne's Revenge

The *Revenge*'s own deck was rather less eventful. This was because the men had been ordered to complete various chores below deck. Above deck was six men only: Thatch himself, who had chosen himself over the helmsman to sail; the helmsman, who had been left with on standby until commanded to alter the flags or sails; the lookout, who was sat alert in the crow's-nest; and three others left purely to keep the ship running. The lookout knew he could easily get away with not being so concentrated, but he knew also the man he would have to face should he make a mistake. It was the fear of Thatch alone that kept him working religiously. Because of this, it was not long until he noticed the signal from the smaller ship behind him.

"Captain! Captain!" he called down to Blackbeard, "Captain, *The Gander*!"

Thatch responded immediately and sent the helmsman to take his place at the wheel. He then took out his gold telescope as he stumbled over to the starboard side of the quarterdeck. He acknowledged the black and yellow flag and immediately focussed on the Commander. Sings did not move, but the officer beside her carried a small flag in his hand. He used the flag to point northeast, to the river mouth.

Blackbeard was confused as to why this was worthy of his attention. He understood he was being shown a river, but not its significance. Walking over to the stairs to the gun-deck, he called to the first man he saw.

"Bo's'n! Get up here!," he growled (Bo's'n being Thatch's pronunciation of boatswain).

"Aye-aye, Cap'n!"

Blackbeard then tossed the boatswain a flag and ordered it to be lifted. This flag was a triangle, white at the base and red at the tip. It translated to something along the lines of, 'Signal not understood.' The captain then walked back to the side of the ship and looked over to *The Golden Gander* through the telescope. After receiving his message, the officer on *The Gander* just shook the flag to highlight not just the river mouth, but the ship sailing towards it. In response, Thatch just pointed up to the triangle flag. He mouthed, 'Why?' and hoped that the Commander understood his confusion. After all, why indeed would *The Lady* change its course in the wrong direction?

It was at this point that Amber Sings flailed her arms in frustration, grabbed her copy of the map in frustration and jolted it in the air, prodding it to tell her captain to have a look.

"Bo's'n!" Thatch yelled, as the boatswain handed him the map without further prompt, "A river? A split river?"

Thatch again looked at Sings, who took out a pocket watch and pointed at it.

"They're sailing up the river? But the *Revenge* mightn't fit up the river!" Blackbeard howled in frustration, before reducing to a mutter, "The *Revenge* mightn't fit up the river, but *The Gander* will fit up the river."

He leant as far as he could over the railing and waved his arm at Sings. He pointed in the direction of *The Lady*, thrusting his hand back and forth. It was a simple command: 'Follow them.' This command was complemented by one last action: as he pulled his arm back to his body, he ran his finger past his neck.

"If Glove thinks he can share the riches of the universe, he can think again!" Thatch said to the crew, but largely to himself.

The Golden Gander

"Starboard," Sings commanded the helmsman at the wheel, the first time he had heard her speak all day.

"Pardon?"

The sound of Sings' heels on the ground as she marched towards the helmsman caused him to dive out of the way as if it had been gunfire. She pushed him aside despite the ample room he had created, and, with her other hand, turned the wheel sharply clockwise. In fact, she had turned the wheel with such haste that, had she not been holding so strongly onto it, she may well have fallen off of the ship. The men on the main-deck grabbed onto one another as they slid across the floor they had just polished. A wave clambered up onto the deck as *The Gander* was thrown into its path, drenching them.

"Full sails, men!" the officer yelled at the poor sailors, who pulled down the remaining sails which had not been in use so that *The Gander* did not overtake the *Revenge*. Some men were quick to relieve themselves of the duty of scrubbing the deck, grabbing the line eagerly to fold down the already set sails to their full extent. The wind grabbed the sails immediately and pulled the sailors forward with it. A final flag was also raised from the stern of the ship, though the only reason it was not already flying was for dramatic effect. It was a black flag with a red heart and a white, horned skeleton piercing it with a spear.

It was Blackbeard's flag; the same colours had been flown the night the two rival crews had died.

Queen Anne's Revenge

Israel Hands came to question the summoning of the boatswain. Instead, he questioned something else, for he quickly saw *The Gander* sailing after *The Lady*.

"What's she doing, cap'n?"

"As I said."

"And what d'ya say so?"

"Follow it."

"And?"

"Follow it and kill them. We can't be doing with them interfering — and I'm not willing to share."

The Lady Mary

"It's a cock!" Adam shouted at Elliott across the deck.

"That's what you bet on!"

"No, it's a proper cock. Couldn't catch it, but I will get it, mark my words."

"I'm sure you will," Elliott said smugly, confident Adam would never catch the rooster.

It was a busy hour for lookouts; Maddy soon noticed that *The Golden Gander* had altered course and was sailing towards them. It was Maddy who noticed this, but Tudor took the credit.

"Captain!" he called, "A ship!"

"*The Golden Gander*!" Maddy shouted over him, "It's coming for us!"

"Why do you have to be so negative?" Doyle said, "They aren't definitely 'after' us, maybe just realised we knew a quicker way."

"No, Doyle, they're after us."

"Alright, Elliott, I'm sorry for having an idea."

"I'm not having a go at you, Doyle, but why would *The Gander*, and only *The Gander*, be following? She has no cargo, so Thatch can risk sending it to fight."

"Don't fret, boys!" Glove said calmly, "She's far behind us still."

"Yes, but once we get to the river mouth, we're sailing upstream – and in a bigger boat."

"Then, Elliott, all I can say is 'load the cannons' — oh, for crying out loud, we have no cannonballs! Find whatever you can, even if it's in the Tin."

"The Tin?"

"Aye, Tin-o'-tetanus."

"Oh, Tin-o'-tetanus, it's disgusting! Any cannonballs in there will probably disintegrate!"

"We have no others."

"I'll take a look."

The brig

Elliott had little choice but to go downstairs. He, Tom, and Adam began searching for 'the Tin,' and soon Doyle and Noah had joined to observe. In the brig, near the chicken coop, was a pile of wooden boxes. Each person grabbed a box, opened it, and then was ordered to re-stack any incorrect boxes in an orderly fashion (by Elliott if I need say). There was an odd assortment of goods ranging from useless maps to stuffed ferrets in the boxes, but the box they were looking for contained an old metal tin. Doyle lifted a particularly heavy box that jingled when shaken. He dropped it because of the unexpected weight, and the lid fell off, revealing the rusty tin they had been looking for.

"Tin-o'-tetanus," Elliott announced, "we should have left its contents with the Devil himself."

They all stared at the tin, which was roughly a cube and about two feet in each dimension, as Elliott put on some old leather gloves and lifted the lid. The contents were sickly orange and rusted. All the items inside were metal, ranging from needles and thimbles to nails, spanners, and cannonballs. Elliott moved a spanner out of the way, and it snapped as soon as his heavy hands reached it. He then ordered the men to form a line and began passing cannonballs down the hall and up the ladder to the gun-deck.

"How come you get gloves?" Doyle complained to Elliott.

"I'm sorry, Doyle, but they are my gloves."

"Where are my gloves?"

"Sorry, did you bring gloves?"

"No."

"Well, I can't help you then, can I?"

The cannonballs, which were once about 10 pounds in weight, weighed now closer to 9 pounds because of the layer of rust that crumbled off of them. Elliott passed one to Adam, who passed it to Noah, who passed it to Tom – who was at the top of the ladder – who passed it to Doyle. Doyle placed it into a cannon. This repeated until four cannons were full – two on either side – and the rest were then placed to the side to be reloaded. There were about ten cannonballs in total.

"I'll stay down here," Elliott said before asking Adam, "Mind keeping me company?"

"A'ight," Adam replied, before placing himself carelessly onto a barrel to sit down, though the barrel almost tipped over.

Main-deck

"How many men do you see?" Glove asked Maddy.

Tudor replied, "Ten or more men, and one woman."

"How can you tell there's a woman?" Maddy wondered, as she slapped Tudor for answering for her.

"I dunno, one looks short."

"It could be a short man!" Maddy bickered, but the captain agreed with Tudor.

"If she's got brown hair, it'll be Miss Sings," Glove explained, "Thatch's favourite helmsman."

"Don't you mean helms-woman, captain?" Tudor emphasised the fact that he was in fact correct.

Doyle got back onto the main-deck and cleaned his hands, which were covered in rust, in a bucket of water. There was one issue with this: the water he had used was 'fresh' water, used for drinking. It was safe to say that Doyle Clementini was not the most popular man of the hour.

"Uh, Doyle?" Tom exclaimed, "what do you think you're doing?"

"Uh, washing my hands?"

"In the drinking water?"

"Uh-huh, they were literally more orange than my hair."

"Let me say that again. In the drinking water?"

"Yeah?"

"Are you trying to give us lockjaw? We can't drink that now. You touched something from the 'Tin-o'-tetanus' and thought you'd make us drink it? We'll get tetanus, it's called the 'Tin-o'-tetanus'!"

"I'm sorry, but how else do you expect me to clean them? I'd get tetanus if I didn't."

"In the saltwater, for God's sake!"

"Stupid, stupid Doyle!" Tudor boomed from the crow's-nest as a form of friendly banter.

"Shut up, Tudor! The saltwater stings my hands sometimes."

"Oh! Right then! I apologise!" Tom scolded Doyle, "I didn't know the saltwater 'stung your hands sometimes', or I wouldn't have minded you trying to kill us!"

Because of the change in direction, the wind, rather fortunately, blew so that it filled the square sails and propelled the vessel close to its top speed. The cool slate grey of the cliffs in the north had become more apparent as they approached the coastline that bordered the estuary. A series of grand stacks and arches of the same sedimentary rock reached out from the cliff to greet the crashing waves. The smell of the air was very clean; the aromatic scent of the pine trees had dwindled and been replaced by the reassuring scent of saltwater as the breeze lifted it. The crew was hopeful. Of course, they had a rival in pursuit of them, and had made a rather illicit agreement with an evil religious entity, but they had found something that they hadn't had for a long time: purpose.

Glove remained at the helm, steering the ship as he had five years before, in a sheer desire for what was once impossible. Tom and Doyle, despite their recent disagreement, stood together with Noah and did absolutely nothing but engage with their environment. There truly was something that generated a potent feeling about being finally in an ecosystem so familiar, and Tom could only imagine what this feeling would become when he reached home. Except, obviously, they weren't going home. Tudor climbed down from the crow's-nest and stood with the three men. Not one of them spoke a word.

Below deck

To be frank, the boat was completely silent. I suppose that isn't being frank, because it isn't true. As with any ship, let alone one of *The Lady*'s age and condition, the vessel's beams and slats groaned every so often due to the very nature of a large, wooden construction. The sails and flags too made some noise, and so did the other equipment. What I should have said, rather, is that there was no organic noise coming from *The Lady Mary*. That's right – not even a crowing rooster. Not even a talking Elliott Ethan. And not even a complaining Adam Lumberlodge.

The only reason Adam wasn't complaining was that he had nodded off.

The waves gave the boat no rest, so it shook occasionally, depriving the man of deep sleep. His eyes opened and shut again several times a minute. Silence, however, did not last long on *The Lady Mary*, even throughout the night. Elliott felt it was inappropriate for Adam to sleep, so, to keep him awake, he made conversation, making most of what I just said redundant.

"I know you don't think that you can change anything," he began as Adam looked up sleepily, "but would you? If you could."

"Why have we got to talk about it?"

"Because how else do we make the right decision?"

"We never talked about nicking the stone that brought us here. We never talked about stuff before. We did as the captain said. I sometimes thought it was bullshit, but you all did the same. I couldn't do anything about that then, and I can't really do much about this now."

"Did you try?"

"When we were boys. I soon realised it was no use."

"Even if it is of no use, what would you change?"

"Is there something you want me to change?"

"No, no, I just – I just wondered what you thought about it. I mean, are you thrilled about having only twelve years?"

"Give you twelve years or twelve hundred years, what difference does it make? The world will end at some point, and you'll probably be back here, anyway."

"I suppose so," Elliott stammered as he got up to look out of the window. *The Gander* was maybe an hour behind, further away from them than they were now to the north coast of the inland sea. Elliott then added another twenty minutes to this time, because they were sailing with the wind, while *The Gander* was sailing somewhat perpendicular to it as they were further west than the river mouth.

Main-deck

The silence had now also broken on deck, Doyle being the first to speak.

"You know, I'm actually looking forward to getting there."

"Do you not think you'll miss Earth?" Noah asked him.

"I've already been to Earth. Heaven is a place I was never too sure existed, something like that is where I want to be."

"Surely you could say that about Hell?"

"But there isn't anything good in Hell. I just know Heaven is going to be fantastic."

"I second that, Doyle," Tom decided, "though I do think I'd miss Earth, surely, we'd forever regret not taking the chance to experience Heaven."

Doyle took the time to retie his bandana around his forehead, then allowed his curtains to spill over it. This was a waste of time. Tom had whispered to the other two and arranged for them to distract 'Redtop' for a minute. In this minute, he lifted the now contaminated bucket of drinking water above his head and plonked it down over Doyle's. Instantly, the two dry pirates and cowboy burst out in laughter.

At first, he didn't even remove the bucket from his head; the bucket shook in disappointment as a faint groaning came from within. Then, removing the bucket cautiously, he spat out the slightly orange water. He followed this by placing the bucket down and picking up the wooden ladle, which had fallen from it. With complete accuracy, he threw it. Tom had retreated a few yards by now, but the utensil hit him right on the forehead, heavy end first.

"Don't hit Thomas, Doyle!" Tudor called.

"I think he deserved it, to be fair," Noah said.

"Yeah, yeah, we're even now, Doyle!"

Their captain, though he realised it was inappropriate because of the severity of the journey, just chuckled and overlooked this.

Chapter III

Oblitos: the river mouth

The Lady Mary

It did not take *The Lady* very long to traverse the inland sea, since Oblitos was so small. They were so close that Elliott could now see the layers of strata that made up the cliff. He observed that the rock was not just slate grey but composed of a variety of colours, from warm browns to lavender blue. Birds scurried past as they moved from stack to stump and out of sight once more. The waters below them behaved differently too. Blue ocean-water brushed coldly against the muddy water of the estuary and refused to unite with it. The river mouth was almost a mile across. Its stream was heavy and fast, resisting the advances of the pirates' ship.

"Elliott!" Glove called so that his voice was heard down below him, "How did you expect us to sail upstream again?"

Elliott appreciated *The Gander* was so far behind them that he needn't stay below deck. His greatest concern was getting the large ship down the river. The steep coast became level around the banks of the river, making the estuary rather open. Elliott came upstairs and suggested that Glove should just let the sails do the work. After all, the wind was blowing parallel to but in the opposite direction of the river. Now, all the water under *The Lady* was brown and slowed her down slightly as it ran against her.

"It shouldn't be too hard!" Elliott said, "It's just like sailing up the Thames!"

"I'm surprised you can remember the Thames, boy!" Glove smiled at the memory of sailing to London at night with a small boy as his first-mate.

Now, the race had truly begun, for Glove and Thatch were on their separate routes to the North Pole of Oblitos. To be precise, there were two races taking place: one between *The Lady* and the *Revenge*, and another between *The Lady* and *The Gander*. *The Gander* was still in full pursuit of Glove and his crew. She had gained little distance on them yet, but her sails were full as she weaved through the waves. *The Lady* was ahead of her, and it was Glove's aim to stay ahead of her.

Once the ship had crossed the boundary between the coast and inland, Elliott could observe another strange fact about Oblitos. The floodplains around the river were carpeted not with grass, but with ferns similar to those in the forest. They were lower than the ferns of the forest as their tips had been torn off as if they had been grazed upon. He then noticed what he thought was a drinking deer out of the corner of his eye. It fled at the sight of *The Lady* and was disguised by the ferns. All Elliott saw of it was a sign that it was not a deer, as a lizard-like tail could be seen just before it disappeared into the vegetation.

Glove nudged the wheel so that the ship sailed towards the riverbank. Here, the water was slower than in the centre of the channel and therefore gave less resistance to sailing. There were no trees, so the sails were not obstructed when the boat got very close to the banks. The keel churned up silt and made clouds in the water, which rushed against them, causing small fish to splash around out of the way. A large toad too, which wallowed in the mud by the bank, jumped once away and then continued with an awkward crawl.

The Golden Gander

"What's the agenda, Commander?" the quartermaster of *The Gander* asked Sings.

"Stop *The Lady*," she replied quietly.

"Why?"

"Do you want to get off and ask Thatch yourself?"

"Surely you have an idea."

"Clearly, Glove wants out. And that means he might get in our way. That makes him competition. We might well have to fight him, so we may as well get it done with while it's on our terms."

***The Lady Mary*: main-deck**

"I wish I had a ship like yours," Noah commented to Tom, "then I could sail wherever I like. Whenever I like, with no need to do any more than what I feel like."

"You're sailing where you want to go now, with us."

"Yes, but this is a one-way ticket."

"So?"

"It may sound nice, you know, but we're giving up our freedom, aren't we?"

"But it's still what we want."

"Is it what we want, or is it what he wants? You keep saying it's good for all of us, but is it what we want?"

"Why would we not want what is good for us?"

"For one, because we don't always know what actually is good for us. And for two, because we didn't earn it. I mean, do you really think you could sit in Heaven, amongst saints, and not feel out of place?"

"I feel like we pretty much have earned it if we go through all this trouble."

"Why spend so much effort trying to cheat it, when you could just earn it properly?"

"And what were you doing again to end up here? Trying to cheat, wasn't it?"

"I'm a hypocrite, I guess, but I still think you should think about it."

"If I may," Tudor asked, without getting an answer, "we were so clearly skilled to get here, I think I deserve to be in Heaven."

"You mean 'we' deserve," Doyle corrected him, "We deserve to get there, and who cares, anyway? We want it and we can have it, so why are we worried?"

"Do you not think there may be consequences?"

"We're pirates, we're used to taking what is not ours and facing no consequences."

"And look where that got you."

The ship was now faced with the first meander of the river. As the river was wide, the manoeuvre was not too precise, and the wind aided the first half of the turn. After the turn, however, the wind was against them. As soon as the breeze caught the square sails, the boat shook and came to a halt. With the second gust of wind, *The Lady* drifted backwards, and was only sped up by the river's own current.

"Boris!" Glove yelled, and Tudor knew exactly what to do. He lowered the anchor as quickly as he could. Doyle offered to help, but Tudor refused. Because of this, the ship lost a few more yards than necessary, coming to a stop at the turn of the meander. The river catchment had become more forested than it was closer to the shore, though as still certainly more of a grassland than woodland.

Below Deck

The ship shook, and this stopped Adam from nodding off once again. Elliott looked out the window to investigate.

"What happened?"

"We're sailing against the current, and against the wind," Elliott answered, "It's impossible."

"Are you stupid?" Adam asked, "Why didn't you tell us?"

"It was your idea!"

"I've never actually done it before!"

"I was only five when I did!"

"But you did do it!"

"Yes, we could because the tide was coming in."

"Well, make the tide come in!"

"How am I supposed to make the tide come in?"

"Do something!"

"Alright!"

Main-deck

Elliott dashed onto the deck and looked around for ideas. The faster currents at the outside bank had caused the ship to drift over and start rocking as it hit the shallower riverbed, the anchor planted firmly many yards in front of them. Elliott looked at the capstan, and then at some ropes.

"We need men on the ground!" He called to Glove.

"What?" Glove questioned, "No men should leave the ship alone, we don't know what is outside."

"We're going to have to risk it if we want to get up this river."

"I can do it, I guess," Noah stepped forward.

"Let me do it, I'll be quicker than you," Tudor said.

"I'll do it," Tom responded.

"Nay, the two volunteers will suffice!" Glove demanded.

"Tom, Maddy, can you two raise the sails, please!" Elliott suggested.

"Right," Elliott began talking to Tudor and Noah, "I need each of you to take a rope, the longest, strongest ropes we have, and belay it to a tree, either side of the river."

"I'm not taking orders from you," Tudor bickered.

"I'm first-mate, so you are," Elliott retorted.

"You're not quartermaster though, or captain."

"There is no quartermaster!"

"Boris!" Glove yelled, "Listen to him for God's sakes!"

"Aye-aye!"

"Tie the ropes good and firm around a strong-looking tree, and I will fasten them to the capstan. We on deck will turn the capstan once the ropes are secured, and the ship should be pulled forward."

"I'll take the inside," Tudor said, wanting the more arduous task of swimming across the river. In the meantime, Elliott searched for the most suitable ropes. He brought back with him four ropes, telling each man to bring two, just in case one should snap. Each rope, being spare rigging, was over one hundred feet long, but compared to the length of the river up to the lake, this was a tiny fraction. As a result, once they had reached their destination, the capstan would have to be left to spin the other way to lower the anchor, which would then provide enough line for the men at the bank to move forward and tie the rope again to a further tree. This sounded like a tedious task, and it was going to be. But once the time and effort had been put into 'sailing' up the river, they would be left with the much easier task of letting the current push them along and out to sea in the north. His information made the men more reluctant, but they knew it was the only option if they wanted to overtake Thatch now.

Tudor tied the ropes around his belt and jumped into the brown river water. It took a few minutes for him to reach the other side, and when he did, the strong current had pushed him thirty yards backwards. He got out enthusiastically and shook himself dry, immediately beginning to pace forwards until the rope allowed him to do so no more. Noah was slower about it, climbing down the side of the ship and swimming less strongly than Tudor. He then trod through the mud along the bank and finally got out, walking to the most suitable tree.

Once they arrived at their trees, both men tied their ropes around them several times and knotted them well. Tudor tied both ropes around the same tree, whereas Noah chose two different trees about twenty feet apart. Elliott put a pin through the four ropes and wrapped them around the barrel of the capstan. Observing that the two had both completed tying the ropes, he called to all on deck, besides Glove, who remained at the helm. He ordered them to the capstan and told them to turn it with him. The ship at first continued backwards as the anchor too had been raised by the capstan. Once the ropes were taut, the capstan turned against them. The beams of the capstan shoved all the crew backwards as they painfully resisted. Once they had forced it to stop turning, they could slowly push back. Finally, *The Lady* crept forward. Glove kept the wheel turned, so the ship straightened its path as it turned.

It was a strenuous task for the crew on deck: Elliott, Tom, Doyle and Maddy. Adam was below deck, not doing anything. I probably no longer need to specify his whereabouts anymore, unless he does something more remarkable. I wish I could describe it more exciting, but physically there is no quicker way to achieve what needed to be done. It took about ten minutes to move maybe fifty feet before the process had to be repeated. I could repeat this description as frequently as the action had to be repeated, but I fear that might just cause you to put the book down. So, you're lucky, I won't!

There were two more meanders before the river met the lake. Wide, long meanders, almost reaching back on each other as you would when losing a game of snake. This, you may know, is characteristic of a river's flow when so far from the source. However, it wasn't really all that far from the source; the continent was so tiny there was hardly enough distant for a river to behave like this. Though everyone failed to notice, Oblitos had a strange sense of artificiality, as if it had been made to be lived on, rather than naturally moulded like Earth. Everything seemed like a miniature (or sometimes less miniature) version of Earth, like a garden cultivated to resemble a greater, more wild environment.

Another example of this was how the men were able to walk as ably as they had on Earth or the similarly sized planet Hell, even though the planet was as minuscule as described. Perhaps the bedrock of Oblitos was vastly denser than that of the larger planets. However, it may just be easier to believe that physics behaves differently in the solar system of Hell.

Gun-deck

Adam was no longer asleep, nor was he trying to sleep. Nor could he sleep, for one thing was preventing this.

'Cock-a-doodle-doo!'

"Little fucker," Adam muttered in complete fury. He picked up his musket, which was kept close by, and marched to the brig.

The brig

The rooster was still crowing, though no other roosters were there to answer its call. The bird stared into Adam's eyes as it took a deep breath in. It paused for a second, then let out the strongest call it could produce. At once, Adam raised his gun and shot, not really aiming, but the target was both close enough and big enough. The shot did not hit the animal, however, but hit the wire, and bounced back and hit the wall. He ducked to dodge this, though it missed him by several feet. At the sound of the shot, all the chickens burst out in panic, flocking towards the coop and into it through the pop-hole. Adam reloaded his musket before entering the chicken pen. He struggled to undo the latch on the door, but finally got in and paced towards the coop. Opening the door to the chicken shed slowly, and only a crack, he poked through his head. The chickens had jumped onto the roosting bar on which they slept. Adam inspected each chicken. One was brown and had swollen, scaled legs; one was a gold-yellow colour, and rather plump; one was white, skinny, and had a large, red comb which flopped over to cover its left eye; and one was black and white, and particularly old looking. But he couldn't see the rooster. It wasn't on the floor, nor was it in a nest-box — for whatever reason a rooster would be in a nest-box.

Adam shut the shed door slowly and paused. He knew exactly where the rooster was – he could sense it. It stood proudly behind him, clucking menacingly, and he knew that as soon as he moved, or even turned his head, it would go for him. But he had to move because he was less patient than the bird was. He turned his head to face it. It flapped its powerful wings as an intimidation strategy, and then attacked. Covering the three yards between them in a second or so, it immediately kicked at Adam. He attempted to mirror the chicken's method and simply ran at it too, kicking out to push it back. While he did this, he recklessly tried to shoot it point-blank. However, the rooster was as close to him as his musket was long, so he couldn't really aim. The shot just marked the floor. Having given up shooting, he turned the musket around and used the thick end as a club, bashing away his aggressor.

After being bitten and kicked and flapped at for five minutes, Adam again made a 'strategic' retreat.

Main-deck

"I bet Blackbeard's not doing this!" Tom complained.

"Are you saying you'd rather be Thatch and not be doing this than be yourself and be doing this?" Elliott asked.

"That's not what I said!" Tom panted, straining from the effort of pushing the capstan, "but I'd like not to be doing this!"

"But it's the only way to overtake him."

Maddy gave the capstan a shove so that the beam almost hit Tom, "Did you think it would be easy?"

"No, I just wish it were."

"It was never going to be easy! Getting to Hell is one thing, that's easy – getting to Heaven, that's a different game."

"Well said," Elliott complimented.

"Look at you, you good Christians," Doyle added with tone.

"I'm simply saying," Maddy clarified, "not all that is good is easy."

With this, the crew gave one more push on the capstan and the boat turned around the last meander. The lake was now visible, a straight line ahead. *The Lady* dawdled towards it. When the two men untied the ropes, the ship drifted backwards until the anchor stopped it. The crew on the ship tossed the slack of the rope back into the water so that Tudor and Noah could easily walk it to the next tree. The anchor was raised for the last time; the ropes attached to trees on either side of the lake, which formed a sort of finishing line.

The force being applied by the ropes to the capstan was immense, the weight of the ship and the force of the river were too great to be overcome by the force the crew could apply themselves. Because of this, *The Lady* stopped progressing. Tudor, who was still on the shore, realised this. Without thinking much about it, he dived into the river and swam towards the boat. As if it were one motion, he climbed onboard, grabbed the capstan next to Tom and used the momentum to turn it. This achieved the desired effect; the ship was pulled a further ten yards forward with a few rotations of the capstan. But then, something less desirable happened. One of the ropes snapped.

Nevertheless, they all kept turning the capstan. There was no other choice, for they knew *The Golden Gander* was waiting for them should they slip back downstream. The single rope on Noah's side of the ship pulled tighter and tighter, and the boat moved away from that side of the river. The boat refused to surrender.

And alas, though it was marked by no other physical change, *The Lady Mary* made its way into the lake. The entire crew at the capstan dropped down at once when they had realised that the resistance from the river's flow had reduced. Tudor now shook himself dry as Doyle panted, and Tom wiped sweat from his brow. Far more trees surrounded the lake than the river. Glove ordered the men to lower the sails once again, as the wind continued to blow north. He realised, however, that a break might be appreciated, so allowed the crew to rest for a few minutes first.

As if he had planned it to avoid any hard work, Adam made his rare appearance on deck.

"He's a twat!" he yelled, only Elliott knowing what he was referring to, "You're a twat!"

"What?" Elliott questioned, "I kept my part of the bet."

"You knew! You knew what would happen, you, you menace."

"Okay, okay, Adam, I suppose he'll have to stay."

"No, no, I'll get him, I'll get him somehow!"

"Oh, I'm sure."

Small birds, most no larger than thrushes, scurried and dived above the ship, from one canopy to the other. The crew heard them chattering away in a series of chirps and whistles. The ship sailed so close to the bank that some branches reached out above it, and birds flew above as well. It was apparent that there were multiple types, for some were as large as a hawk.

"See, Adam?" Maddy asked, reminding Adam of their conversation earlier, "Birds."

"They're bloody bats! Bats, look at the bastards' wings! No feathers!"

"Oh, you can tell they have no feathers? They're flying too fast to see individual feathers."

Adam drew a loaded pistol, aimed for a second, and shot into the air. Something dropped onto the deck.

"Adam!"

"What?"

"You weren't supposed to shoot the poor thing!"

"Why not? If it's a bird, why can't I shoot it?"

"You're not gonna eat it, are you?"

Tudor butted in, "I dunno, could be pretty delicious. You never know. I could skin it if you want."

"No, no one's skinning anything! You shouldn't 'ave shot it, Adam."

"Yeah, Adam," Doyle added in an annoyingly patronising tone.

Tom and Elliott both walked over to observe the creature. The shot had gone only through its wing, so it was actually still breathing, though unconscious from the fall. It was a strange animal. When Maddy came over, she yelled, "Told you!", but as Adam walked over, he did the same. Its wings were not feathered like a bird's, instead, they were more like a bat's, though not exactly. The outer finger was extended backwards and from it a layer of leathery skin connected to the hip to form the wing. But unlike a bat, it lacked all the other fingers that support the middle parts of the wing. It was also fuzzy. Not furry — fuzzy, like a baby chicken. Its body was like a cat-sized, fluffy lizard, though its head was the same size as its torso and ended in a wedge-shaped, yellow beak. Its eyes were big and dark, and the neck that connected body to head was short but barely narrower than the round torso. Behind it hung two spindly legs and a long, ratty tail ending in a diamond-shaped fin, all connected by another sheet of the same skin which made the wings. Yes – a very strange creature indeed.

"Adam, it's not even dead!" Maddy continued to protest, "Think of all the pain!"

"I could snap its neck," Tudor suggested, strangely eager to do so, "and then I'll skin it and gut it. And Tom, you can cook it for the two of us."

"I shot the fucker!" Adam argued, "So why don't I get a try?"

"No one's eating it!" Tom decided, and he looked towards Elliott Ethan, who simply nodded in reply. Elliott picked the animal up by its wiry legs and placed it in his other large hand, where it lay limply. Next, he lifted its head up and raised it to his face. With one puff, he blew into its beak, and it began to pant and gasp for more air. Tom had already gone to fetch an old cage, which may have once contained a parrot or canary, and filled a glass with water. Both Elliott and Thomas helped clean up the wound and applied some alcohol to at as a disinfectant. Its large, round eyes, and a tuft of longer, orange fuzz which protruded from the back of its head, gave it an even more startled appearance. Around its eye was a red ring of scales, and this same red was striped down its yellow, puffin-like beak. Otherwise, it was covered mostly in a fluff of a cream colour with blotches of a darker brown. The scaled fingers in the middle of the wings and its lizard-like toes were also red, though the leathery skin between its wings and its legs was a dull beige.

The animal sat up on the deck, not yet in the cage, its hands on the ground and its legs bent at both knee and ankle. It was a bit like a dog, a bit like a frog, and a bit like a bird. To inspect its new environment, it flicked its head from side to side. It even preened itself like a bird. Tudor examined it, "Look at that, he's got ginger hair," he added, looking at Doyle.

"Like Doyle!" Maddy exclaimed.

"Yes, and it's even got a big old nose like him!" Tudor continued.

"Well, we all know what that means," Tom added, grinning.

"No!" Doyle insisted, "just no!"

"Oh yes, we're calling it Doyle!"

And so that became its name. Doyle, the bird, bat, frog, dog, lizard thing.

And Tudor Boris wasn't allowed to eat it.

Chapter IV

The Golden Gander

Now, do you want a repeat of the tale of all the effort put into getting up the river? I thought not. *The Gander* was, of course, a smaller, and therefore more agile ship. It also had twice the manpower. It may be lazy writing, but I am going to tell you they make it up the river and leave it at that. Sings claimed the idea of using ropes and the capstan as her own, but had actually just noticed *The Lady Mary* doing it too. The ship also had oars, unlike *The Lady*, which improved the process. They had not made it up the river yet, though, at the end of the last chapter. Just know they do, because it might be important later.

The Lady Mary

Elliott went and found a tin of cured beef from the larder. He opened it and brought it back to the deck, where the new creature named Doyle sat, dazed.

"There's only one explanation!" Tudor insisted, "It's a dragon!"

"Doyle the dragon!" Tom chuckled.

"It can't be a dragon," Doyle added, "and it's not called Doyle!"

"What else can it possibly be?" Tudor asked.

"Not a dragon, and not a Doyle!"

"Yeah, yeah, sure," Tudor said, not meaning it.

Elliott broke off a small piece of beef and tossed it to Doyle the dragon. The creature put its weight onto its hands and walked towards the food on all fours, its long, outer finger pointing backwards and upwards with the wing membrane folded against it. It sniffed the beef and picked it up with its beak, swallowing it whole. It then turned its head to the side and looked at Elliott, turning its head to the side to observe with each eye independently. As it scurried towards the man, he threw another piece of beef to it, which it caught in its beak with sharp instincts. When it opened its beak, Elliott noticed it had teeth. Longer, snatching needle-like teeth in the front, and wider, more robust ones at the back.

Tom then went and got the end of a stale loaf of bread. He too fed the 'dragon'. Doyle the dragon dashed and leapt across the deck to catch and devour the treats. The two got a little carried away, resulting in more food on the floor than the animal could clean up quickly. It was at that point that another 'dragon' of the same species as Doyle dived from the trees above and picked itself up some food. Swiftly, it flew back up and out of sight. Then another did the same. Then another, a smaller one, perhaps a different kind of dragon, or at least that's what Tudor thought. Soon a dozen or so miniature 'dragons' were either on deck or flying towards or away from it.

A swarm quickly gathered above the boat, but as the creatures were so fragile in build, they seemed to pose no threat to the folded-up sails. Also, because of their builds, they could not fly off with large pieces of food, such as an entire crust of bread, so devoured what they could before becoming airborne again. When they took off, they did so by lunging forwards and leaping over their own hands, which remained on the ground until the wing was unfolded to transfer this momentum into flight. At that point, Elliott brought out an entire unplucked chicken wing — of the hellish variety. He tossed it into the swarm, some of which darted at it, but it landed on the deck before any took a bite out of it. The tiny dragons pulled at the quills in an attempt to get to the skin, and eventually what was under the skin. Five or six, including Doyle (not the man), had covered it so that the wing was invisible, until the creatures had tugged a small pink chunk off and tossed into their gullets.

The dragon-like animals had increased further in number – and now in size. Some above, which did not come down yet, looked to be the size of buzzards, or even herons. They had the beak of a heron to match, but even larger relative to their bodies. These larger individuals circled high above, flapping little. It was likely the case that they could observe no carrion below worth the effort of collecting.

Tom threw small crumbs of bread high into the gathering of winged reptiles, which they could catch instinctively without altering their flight. The chicken wing had now been stripped of its waxy black feathers and the actual food exposed. This caused the dragons to fight each other, as they knocked each other out of the way to get to the revealed flesh or stole food from one another's mouths.

Elliott slid the other wing of the chicken towards the flock. He looked up. As if it were falling, one of the larger creatures dived vertically down, beak pointing down and wings up, folded tightly back. The smaller dragons dodged, though it wasn't hunting them. It landed heavily, revealing that its beak was banana-shaped, curving upwards at the tip, but not to make it an ineffective feeding instrument — or weapon. Standing four feet tall, despite its stubby legs, it turned its head from side to side to observe its new surroundings. Rather than paying attention to the new chicken wing, it bullied the much smaller creatures away from the now easier to handle first one. The wing, being from a Hell chicken, was two feet long when extended. The beast's beak was almost three feet. It speared the food with its upper bill, which was longer than the bottom jaw, and flicked its meal upwards before thrusting its head further towards it, and swallowing it whole. Maddy tossed a plank of wood at it, missing, but scaring it back into the sky. Another tried its luck, but she made such a visual fuss, it retreated.

Then came a noise that sounded like a foghorn, followed by a strange, shrill chuff. And then the sun was blocked for a second.

This caused some dragons to depart, though most remained. The sound was from above, from a silhouette so great it covered the entire sun when flying in line with it. It was an enormous creature, with the size and carriage of a giraffe, the accompanying neck fully extended and the beak of a stork at the end. The beak was clearly large enough to pick up, and possibly even swallow, a human, at least a skinny one. It flapped powerfully to create the effect of thunder. It too circled like a vulture, though vultures cannot kill their own food, whereas this brute presumably could.

"Sails!" Glove commanded, and quickly the crew lowered the sails as implied.

"We let one eat, now they all want food," Elliott said in reflection, before addressing the sinisterly large 'dragon' above him, "the swarm was only a beacon for the others to join, others like that."

"You started it!" Maddy cursed Elliott in both anger and fright.

"I know that!" Elliott reddened as he confessed.

"It's getting lower!"

"I can see that!"

Maddy waved her hands about and shooed the smallest creatures away from the chicken wing and picked it up. Not much later, came a clatter. Not a crash, may I make clear. You might likely expect an animal of such an immense size to land with a crash because of its weight. You'd be forgetting, however, that this animal, despite its size, can still fly, something a creature with the mass of a giraffe would fail to do. Birds have hollow, light bones filled with air sacs to minimise their weight and therefore become aloft. Judging by the sound of this beast as it landed, the same could be said about it.

It landed on all four feet. Like the smaller counterparts, it had two rather short back legs, though they were still as long as a person is tall, and hands on the wings, most of the wing being made from the elongated outside finger. Unlike the small, sharp claws on the digits of the small, tree-dwelling dragons, this one had blunt, hoof-like nails: three on each wing and four on each foot. The former hooves were larger than the latter, but obviously not so robust and cow-like that they would interfere with flight. It was covered in a mossy-green coloured, shaggy, dirty-looking coat of fuzz all over, except the most flexible parts of the wing and horn-covered beak. It had a rather short tail, like a bear or a docked sheep. The beak was at least six feet long, but narrow and spear-like. It was dull brown with black mottling, but paler in parts due to wear. The head made up around a third of its silhouette, giving it a ridiculous stature and making the idea that it could fly seem absurd. Connected to the beak with the same sheet of horn was a small, jagged crest, which ran down the centre of its head, from just in front of the eyes and towards the back of the skull. The crest had blotches of crimson red on it, circled by white. Its eyes too were red – and tiny.

Its eyes were also looking. Looking at Maddy.

"What have you done?" the woman yelled at Elliott, staring back at the fifteen-foot-tall creature in front of her.

At first, no one knew what to do, so they all froze. The dragon too seemed to freeze, looking stupid and aimless. Its appearance could have been subject to comedy rather than terror — if it had not been so large. It is often the stupidest creatures that you have to be careful about. They are thoughtless, and therefore unpredictable. Dragons are often thought of as wise beings. This one had such a vacant expression it was difficult to even consider it a being. It swung its colossal head around, its upper and lower jaws clicking as its beak shut. It walked slowly towards Adam in a manner that portrayed both grace and clumsiness. Its wings were tucked well into its arms, which were clearly as useful for terrestrial activity as they had been in the sky.

Adam knew he was in striking range of the great beak, but did not know when was appropriate to move. He slowly reached for a gun.

Not the musket, for that was too bulky, and he needed to be evasive. With his hand on a pistol, he looked over to the stairs and dashed towards them. But he was right. He was within striking range. The dragon struck down with its beak like a heron striking a fish. His arm stung, as if a cane had hit it, as the tip of the beak caught it. He was lifted off his feet and pulled toward the dragon. Without seeing his target, he fired the gun. This caused his captor to release him, but it did so by tossing him overboard.

"You twat!" he could be heard yelling just before he hit the water.

"Look what you've done!" Maddy yelled to Elliott, though he was very much aware of his folly. Her arms flailed around in frustration as she tried to shame Elliott. But Elliott was the least of her worries — at least he should have been. All this fuss redirected the dragon's attention onto her. It quickened its stride into a trot and approached. Maddy tossed the chicken wing off of the ship, so far that it reached the sandy bank on the right-hand side of the ship. It was on this sand that Noah, who had not yet returned to the ship, was now running to catch the moving ship. However, the chicken was not what the dragon was interested in. It was hunting, hunting her.

After seeing Adam being thrown overboard, Tom, despite the threat of the large aggressor, rushed to have a look into the water. Luckily for him, the animal had its eyes set on Maddy, so paid little attention to his movements. Adam was flapping around to orientate himself, but did not appear to be in much further distress. The boat quickly overtook him, but Tom could notice that Adam was pointing to the other side of the ship. Tom dashed up to the helm, where he looked over to the starboard side of the ship, finally realising that they had left Noah on the bank.

He tied a rope to a plank of wood, then he tossed it to Noah. In the panic, all his attention had been diverted away from Adam, who was swimming towards the shore. The wood landed a few yards ahead of Noah and dragged along the sand as the boat pulled it forward. The cowboy leant forward in his sprint to grab the rope. He overtook the chicken wing, which had been discarded.

Then again came the foghorn call. But it was not from the ship. The outline of the thirty-foot wings was cast as a shadow over the sprinting man. The tremendous flapping grew louder and louder. Noah reached out his arm and grabbed not the plank but the rope. He was almost pulled off of his feet but walked himself into the water by pulling the rope towards him. The plank trailed behind on the sand.

"Look out!" Tom yelled, pointing past Noah, though he was already indeed looking.

On the bank

Another dragon of the same hideous, large kind as on the boat was now gliding just above head-height, fifteen yards in front of him. When it was only six feet off of the ground, it swiftly folded its long finger into its wing and dropped all four limbs down vertically, trotting afterwards to continue the momentum it had gathered. It splashed in the water but did not make a direct path for Noah. Tom began to pull Noah in, getting himself tangled in the loose rope behind him in the rush. Noah saw himself getting closer and closer to the ship when he was able to lift his face out of the water to catch a breath. As far as he was aware, everything was going fine – he was going to make it.

But Tom knew something he didn't. He realised he could no longer pull the rope; something was at the other end. Indeed, the dragon had snatched the rope in its beak, the plank of wood hanging out the other side, lodging it firmly in its grasp. He looked at it disapprovingly, and it just stared back blankly. Then it stood up on its back legs, freeing its wings to flap. With this force, it swung back its head as its entire body took off the ground briefly. Noah was forced out of the water, landing five yards closer to the bank with a splash. Maybe the dragon was smarter than I gave it credit for. It then paced into the water in pursuit of the man.

Main-deck

Maddy drew a sword in time to swipe it against the beak of the dragon, just before it was to close around her head. But the animal's own head was larger than her, so it forcefully retaliated and grabbed her by the shoulder, but so that end of the beak was at her knee. The entire right side of her body was in its beak, with the other half only just poking out. It plucked her off of the deck, and she wrapped all her limbs around the bottom jaw so that she didn't fall either off the ship or into its gullet. It opened its beak and swung its head back to get the woman further towards its stomach. This achieved little except securing Maddy's head within its beak. Tudor swung his sabre at its throat, but to an unintended effect. It pivoted to face away from the ship, then leapt over the railing and flew off.

Maddy, still having her cutlass in her right hand, swung blindly. She could feel the disturbing touch of the dragon's warm, slimy tongue against her face. Noah could hear a muffled screaming as she was flown over him. Passing the sword to the freer left arm, she held it pointing towards her head, close to her body. Slotting the weapon in between the upper and lower jaws, which formed the pointed beak, she thrust it upwards until her arm was as extended as it could be. She quickly felt herself descending — and gaining speed. She then hit the water, still in the creature's beak.

On the bank

Adam had successfully swum to shore. He was in line with the ship, ahead of Noah and the predator. How he had achieved this was a mystery to him, as it meant he had accidentally swum in a diagonal path. Luckily, he was safer because of it.

"Musket!" he yelled, hoping someone on board could hear him, "Musket!"

"Musket!" Tudor unhelpfully called back.

"No, give me my musket!"

"I'm not coming down there!"

"Just lob it!"

"It will get wet!"

"Just lob it!"

Tudor rushed to Adam's room to find the musket and picked it up along with some ammunition he placed in a leather bag. He loaded the gun in advance, and when on deck, fired at the beast pursuing Noah. He missed. Giving up, he wrapped the strap of the fastened bag around it, braced himself and 'lobbed' the gun as far as he could. He chuckled as he was proven right, since it did in fact get wet. Adam dashed a few steps into the water to retrieve it, shook it dry and put the bag over his shoulder. He loaded it not from the bag but from ammunition kept in his pocket, which was sealed twice to remain dry. Then, he did something a little unexpected. He ran. He ran straight for the denser forest, away from the water and away from the ship. Of course, this was also away from the dragons, but it still felt odd, because the ship was the only long-term escape route.

In the water

The water turned red around the dragon after it hit the water. Maddy kicked and squirmed around to free herself from the beak. She had to pull the sword out of the back of its head, just between the neck and skull. This (rather lucky) blow had killed her aggressor. I's toes and wings twitched, but it was clearly dead. It floated easily on the surface of the water, its wings spread out. The ordeal had coated in the dragon's saliva, so she washed herself down in the water before swimming to shore, which was closer than the boat.

"Adam!" she called, "What are you doing?"

Adam seemed reluctant to interact, but yelled back, "The trees! They can't fly through the trees!"

Maddy approved of this idea, and dashed after Adam into the forest, leaving only Noah in danger of the large, winged reptile.

The dragon let go of the rope as it waded into the water, which turned cloudy as it churned the sediment below with its feet. It seemed to be deliberately splashing its way towards Noah, with a bounce in its stride. It speared him with its beak, catching him by the leg. He held onto the rope to evade consumption, to Tom's dismay, for the beast took flight. The rope, which was wrapped loosely around Tom's arm, was pulled tight as the man at the other end was lifted above the water and back towards the shore. The dragon wasn't able to gain much height, causing its head to drag Noah across the surface of the water. After it had flown five yards, the rope was entirely taut, and Tom had failed to free himself. He was flipped over the railing and splashed into the water, too skimming across the water as they continued towards the sand.

The two men splashed and splashed and flailed about, but their speed decreased as the weight of the both of them slowed the beast down. As they reached the edge of the lake, Noah could sink his foot into the sand below. This caused the animal's head, which still had a firm hold of his leg, to remain where it was. But of course, the flying body of the five-hundred-pound reptile did not stop so quickly. It flipped over its head, forcing it to release its prey. Noah skidded across the water and landed in the sand, which coated his sodden clothes. Tom too almost caught up with him, landing in the shallow water just before the bank.

The dragon remained airborne for a few seconds while it corrected its flight. The two men, realising the risk of swimming back to *The Lady Mary*, rushed to their feet and drew their weapons. Tom held out his cutlass, while Noah revealed his weapon for the first time: a revolver. He checked the gun for bullets, and all six slots were filled. From the corner of his eye, Tom noticed Adam running towards the forest.

"Adam!" he yelled through gritted teeth as he freed himself from the rope, "Where are you going?"

After turning around, the dragon flew towards them. Noah looked at its thirty-foot wingspan, and then at the forest.

"Follow them!" he called to Tom, "They can't get to us in the forest!"

He fired his revolver, missing two shots and landing a third on the dragon's beak. The bullet marked its keratin bill but did not cut through it. It shook its head and flicked the small metal irritant away and flapped to maintain its height rather than landing, still approaching the two men. From behind it, a second one showed its ugly face. It was several yards above and many more behind the first, but obviously planned to join it for dinner.

"Go! Go!" they called simultaneously as they turned to dash towards the forest. Somehow, the colossal animal was able to fly faster than the men could run, gaining distance on them every second. In the shiny metal surface of Tom's cutlass, he could see the reflection of the long, mottled beak. Without looking, he held his sword high behind him and swung it strongly but continuously. The dragon attempted to spear its head towards him but retracted it in evasion of the sword. It lingered unintelligently, failing to compute its next phase of attack.

The following dragon took a different method of attack. It landed. It landed and galloped towards them; its neck held out to bring its head to their level. Without the risk of plummeting into the ground, the running dragon travelled faster than the flying counterpart. They were twenty-five yards away from the dense part of the forest before it caught up to them. Noah felt a humid breath on his shoulder, accompanied by the stench of death. As if by instinct, he turned and shot over his shoulder, skimming the small red eye of the dragon. Locking its wrists and elbows, it skidded in the sand to come to a stop. It shook its head madly, now blind in its left eye. This removed the person who fired the bullet from the beast's vision. Out of its right eye, it could still see Thomas.

It ran again, this time rocking its head back and forth like a rocking horse as it did. With each stride, its head swung towards and away from the pirate's shoulder, each time approaching slightly closer. The lower jaw slid under a belt, which fastened across Tom's left shoulder over his coat. It failed to keep hold of the leather strap, so bit again, catching this shoulder. With reflexes even sharper than Noah's, he struck the end of the beak with his steel blade. Both he and the predator stopped. The former faced towards his aggressor and held out his sword. The dragon reared before tossing up sand as its front hooves returned to the ground. It made its foghorn call as snapped at the man, who blocked with his sword. With either courage or stupidity, he jumped and swung his cutlass again. The animal was too tall for Tom to reach its throat, but it jumped backwards.

The flying dragon flew straight past the other and continued in pursuit of Noah, who dived into the brush of ferns, which were surrounded by the tall conifers. Knowing that its wingspan was too great to manoeuvre itself within the forest, it turned away and circled.

It had now dawned on Tom that fighting the giraffe-sized carnivore was not the ideal solution. His sword served an obvious function, but the dragon's beak had two. It could fight like a sword against the cutlass, but also grab. And grab it did. It grabbed the cutlass and lifted Tom a few feet off the ground until he let go in fright. He landed on his feet, now defenceless. But then the dragon's brains were blown out. Blown out by Adam's musket.

The sword landed point down in the dirt, while the creature's spine curled backwards before toppling over. Seeing the other circling, Tom picked up his cutlass and sprinted towards the trees from where Adam had fired the shot. As he turned back, he noticed yet another flying towards him.

"Adam!" he said, trying to glimpse at his friend, "Adam, where are you?"

He made it to the forest and immediately found himself surrounded by green, and kept calling for Adam. When he found him, Adam was leaning against a mossy tree stump, his brown eyes closed and his face frustrated.

"Adam!" Tom said again, "Why didn't you go back to the ship?"

"I'm done!" he replied bluntly.

"What?"

"I said I'm done!"

"Done with what?"

"Done with your stupid escape plan, I'm done," Adam flapped his arms in the air in discomfort, "I was good and safe as I was, in Hell, nothing to worry about. Now, I just, I just almost got eaten by a bloody, eh, a bloody, a bloody thing!"

"It's the risk we take for something better."

"What? My life?"

"You're supposed to be immortal!"

"Supposed to be! Evidently not though."

"You're dead! We died! Don't you remember?"

"So, if I let that bastard eat me, I'd be completely fine?"

"Well, maybe not."

"Look out!" Maddy shrieked, pointing between two trees. A tall, green, mossy shape branched out from the ground. But this was not another tree. It had wings. And a beak. And it was walking towards them. The dragons could not fly into the forest with their wingspans. But they could walk through it. Making itself as slender as possible, with its bill tucked up against its neck and its wings as tightly folded as they could be, it stalked through the ferns slowly, somehow without drawing much attention to itself. But now, it had their attention.

"Run!" Tom said.

"No, run north!" Adam added, "We can overtake *the Lady* if we go north."

"Which way is north?" Maddy panicked.

"I don't know!" Adam realised he had lost his sense of direction in the endless canvas of green, "Which way is the lake?"

"Erm, that way!" Noah unconfidently suggested.

"The sun!" Adam yelled, getting annoyed, "Look at the sun!"

"North's this way!" Noah inferred from the sun's direction, so they all started running, but he added, "If it's morning!"

"For God's sake, it's afternoon!" Adam corrected, "It was noon when we arrived!"

The four of them pivoted in their places and ran in the opposite direction. A second dragon poked its foul head from behind a tree in an attempt to view the pirates.

"Keep running!" Tom called, "Don't look at them, just keep running!"

The first dragon had given up stealth and sped up its pace towards them. It kept itself small to avoid hitting any branches. It stopped in front of Tom, just as the other three had run past. He knew he had to go north, but there were two dragons in front of him, giving him no way to run sideways.

Stopping stunned, Tom's eyes glanced around the trees for an alternative route. He looked to the second dragon, which was peering around the tree, and realised that it couldn't snap at him with the trunk in the way. So, he ran around the tree. As predicted, the dragon struck its beak towards him but got obstructed by the same tree. While he was behind it, Tom just dashed in a straight line in pursuit of the others. And he just kept running. He could hear footsteps behind him. In fact, there were two sets of footsteps.

The dragons were even less conspicuous now, snapping off branches in their view and randomly tossing them. This caused the two dragons to sound like five. The first gave out its foghorn call, only giving the four people more of a reason to keep running. They couldn't help but look behind them at their predators, noting the absurd creatures' obscure hunting strategy. Their efforts seemed to resemble a more frightening, vicious form of a game-shoot beater's. The first dragon, which was on the side furthest away from the lake, overtook the others, running at the crew on their right-hand side. The two dragons formed a diagonal line, encouraging the people to run outwards towards the open. Maybe the dragons were smarter than they looked.

Noah realised they were veering off to the beach, where they were more vulnerable from aerial attack. "Keep running straight!" he reminded, "Don't let them push you into the opening."

"That's easy for you to say!" Adam replied, being much closer to the first dragon, which was approaching almost perpendicular to his path.

He couldn't help moving away from it, though he knew very well that he shouldn't. Correcting his instinct, he straightened his path and sprinted as fast as his legs would allow. A branch reached out sideways five feet above the ground, about fifteen yards ahead of him. He had a plan. He didn't even process the plan in his mind, not consciously, nor verbally. But he had a plan.

I just said he sprinted as fast as his legs would allow. Apparently, his legs changed their minds. They could run twice as fast. So now he ran as fast as his legs would allow and ducked under the branch. As he did, he grabbed the end of the branch, letting go so that it snapped back. His plan worked as he'd hoped; the branch caught the dragon on its wrist. Being a top-heavy animal, its body didn't take too kindly to this blow to its wing. Its front feet stumbled over the branch, but its head travelled further than its body. In a lever motion, its neck swung to the floor. Adam didn't look behind him but gathered from the crashing sound that his plan was successful.

Since it was harder to herd four people single-handedly, this gave the second dragon a harder time with its own plan. It galloped a few more paces, a foam beginning to form at the back of its beak and its beady red eye unblinking. Then it thrashed its head against a branch to remove it from its sight, and came to a stop. Its hooves scraped in the leaf-litter below, but it was clear that the creature had surrendered. The four people, however, had not, so ran and ran until they were in the thickest part of the forest where they could stop for a rest.

The Lady Mary

"Ought we to lower the anchor, captain?" Elliott asked.

"Nay, they'll find us, they have a straight path."

"But they don't have a map."

"They have Lumberlodge, and he's seen the map. You know how he is, and that's all they need."

In the jungle

Branches snapped under their feet until their stamina was depleted, and they finally stopped to take a breath. The great mossy trunks of the trees formed the pillars and walls of a furrowed refuge against the dragons from the beach. In fact, the trees were so close together that the buttress roots of some were conjoined. Luckily, there was no way for a dragon to find its way in, unless it was seeking them out.

Adam dropped himself onto the floor and lay face up and his arms spread out. He huffed, his face red. Realising that everyone else was as exhausted as himself, Tom ordered everyone to take a break.

"Why are we going north?" Maddy asked.

"That's a good point, Adam, why did we just follow you?"

"You don't even want to be here," Tom added, "Have you even brought us the right way?"

"Calm down, calm down," Adam assured, "the river meanders up north, and *The Lady* has to follow all those curves. If we make it to the river again, the ship should be just upstream."

"Brilliant, we'll set off when you're all ready," Tom said, being both polite and encouraging, before Adam interrupted.

"But I won't be coming with you."

"What do you mean?" Tom frowned, "Of course you're coming with us. Why wouldn't you be coming with us?"

"Were you not listening to me?"

"Yes, but you weren't being serious. How could you be serious?"

"Because I said I'm done!"

"But you're not done!"

"But I am done!"

"No, you're not!"

"Yes, I am! I'm done! I'm done!"

"Why?"

"You know why! I was fine how I was; I have no reason to go any further."

"Well, don't do it for yourself then, do it for us lot, do it for me!" Tom raised his voice and panted after as the two settle down, "And besides, what else do you have that musket for?"

"Come on then, knob-heads," Adam sat up and stretched.

"So it's a yes?"

"I may be done, but I'm not a dick," he smiled, and got to his feet.

They all stood up, a great breeze woodshed through the canopy. The sky above became dark, and the air became humid. Pine needles fell down like rain, accompanied by the odd pinecone, which hit the ground and bounced. The rustling of the trees sped up, and something else joined the organic matter falling to the ground. The canopy was reasonably dense, but a patter of rain broke through and landed on foreheads and bare hands, announcing the storm to come. This rain was light for now, but all had a feeling that it did not plan to go away very soon.

Their method of traversal now was a mixture of stealth and vigilance. They had had a taste of the terrible creatures who inhabit Oblitos and had no plans of having another run-in with them if they could help it. Adam tried to mask his feeling of being out of breath by intentionally slowing his breathing, which was, as a result, patient, but deep and irregular. The wind, which was chillingly cool, had already blown the sweat from his skin, which he appreciated. But the rain was too cool, which he did not appreciate. It was a frustrating feeling, knowing that you were in a warm environment, but feeling cold, even though you just felt warm.

What felt like light rain was presumably heavy, indicated by the sound it made on the trees above. A singular bird, or maybe one of those small dragons, whistled in the canopy, but received a reply only from the wind as it blew through conifers. Adam's footsteps were by far the loudest of all four of them, because of the way he walked. His head bobbed, his eyes down as each boot pushed all force directly into the ground. Maybe because they had quite a trek ahead, no one talked. Tom whistled occasionally, which the others found irritating, though they didn't want to say anything about it.

All four pirates (or rather all three and the cowboy) could not help but be overcome by the sense of what I can only call nostalgia. The combination of the gentle white noise around them, the petrichor from the weather, and the chill which kept their senses heightened, all combined to create the warming sense of contempt one gets on an autumnal walk. Not that they didn't have a hint of dread. Of course, they were still concerned for their own wellbeing; it was hard to forget being hunted by ridiculous-looking giraffe-stork-dragons. But they weren't being hunted anymore, so they could rest for the meantime, even if they had to remain aware of all the sounds and sights around them.

The Lady Mary

"We'll meet them at this meander," Glove pointed to the map, at the exact point which Adam had been talking about, "We're travelling faster, but they have the straight path. It will take us an hour or more to reach it. Plain sailing, of course, if you can call it sailing, but it shan't take them much longer than an hour, if we're right about the scale of this map."

"Time isn't their only opponent, though," Elliott worried, more concerned than his captain appeared.

"I know that," Glove chuckled, "but that should only make them all the faster!"

Eventually, the entire swarm of small dragons had dispersed, and Doyle the dragon was contained in the birdcage. His hind-limbs and hands all grasped the bar of the small swing, and he rocked back and forth and even swung upside down like a gymnast. He frustratedly bashed himself against the side of the cage at first but gave up pretty soon to proceed with his swinging.

"Doyle!" Tudor said, one hand against the cage.

"What?" Doyle (the person) said back.

"Not you, I mean Doyle, Doyle!"

"I'm sorry, I thought I was Doyle!"

"You can be Doyle two."

"I'm Doyle two, so that thing is Doyle one?"

"Precisely."

"No, not precisely, thank you."

"Alright, you can be Doyle the second then."

"No, just no."

"Anyway," Tudor continued, quieter and directly to the reptile in the cage. He kept calling its name, watching closely for a response. He clicked his tongue, then his fingers, then tapped on the bars of the cage. The creature would jerk its head to see where the sounds came from, but never responded to the name alone.

"He's not a dog, Tudor," Elliott tutted as he walked past him, "Now, take him below deck, keep him warm."

"I know he's not a dog." Tudor laughed, "I think I'll take him downstairs."

Elliott looked over to the forest on his right and tried to glimpse the crew on the ground. He saw nothing. All creatures had retreated further into the trees. A sense of life buzzed from the jungle, but none of it was willing to present itself.

The Lady sailed on at a steady pace through the lake. In the north, the river that drained the lake could be seen clearly. It was worrying narrow with steep banks, which were no longer sandy. The treeline followed the river tightly, funnelling the boat towards its flowing waters. Helped not just by the wind, but the force of gravity, the lake water drifted north towards the river, pulling the ship along with it and causing it to pick up speed. The course of *The Lady* was altered towards the river's opening without human intervention, as if it were in pursuit of its destination. Ultimately, it did reach the river, which it could just fit down. The only issue was that the grasping branches of the trees reached out towards the sails. So, the anchor was dropped; the sails folded up, and then they were off again.

Chapter V

In the Jungle

It was almost half an hour before the four of them had caught their breath. Well, it was fifteen minutes for three of them, Adam took longer. When he had got out of his hammock, he hadn't expected to go on a trek. At least, that was his excuse. Tom had assumed a position at the front of the group, though Noah had to keep pointing him to the north.

Knock!

From fifty yards ahead, off to the right, came a knock. A knock against the trunk of a hollow tree, followed by another knock. At first, it seemed like it could have been a pinecone hitting the log. But the second time seemed to come from the same location. And a third time confirmed this. So unless a pinecone fell down on the same spot three times in a row, it seemed that the sound was man-made. But made by whom? This question made them all stop in their tracks. Except Adam, who thought nothing of it. He heard it, but he didn't much care.

Tom called to him and grabbed him by the shoulder. There was another knock, followed soon by another. This series was repeated twice again, and then escalated to three knocks. Without moving, Tom asked Adam, "Pick up that branch," pointing to a branch about the size of a rounders bat.

"What?"

"That branch there — pass it to me."

"Why?"

"Just do it!" Tom said in a piercing whisper, and so Adam passed the stick to him. He hit it against the nearest tree. His own knock was higher pitched but elicited a reply a few seconds later. So, he knocked twice. Two knocks came back. Adam took the stick back from his friend and soon hit the log five times rhythmically. Rather than repeat, the mystery person concluded the pattern with two firm knocks. Adam waited a second and thought to himself. As if by second nature, he proceeded with a complex and obscure tune. While Tom looked on dumbfounded, the other knocker joined in and matched the timing almost perfectly.

"Lewis!" Adam yelled.

"Adam!" the unknown person, who was apparently called Lewis but was not yet visible, called back.

Adam walked towards the area the knocking had come from and could hear Lewis' footsteps. There was still a thick line of trees between them. One of them tripped and stumbled through the brush, or perhaps it was both of them. Whoever it was that fell, they crashed straight into the other. They each took a step back and looked each other up and down before Lewis called to his evident friend by name, "Adam!"

"Lewis bloody Plaque!" Adam replied with delight at the sight of a man with a remarkable but practical build.

"What are you doing here?"

"We're trying to get out of Hell!"

"Sound, sound," Lewis spoke in a way that was not dull but not very lively either, "you going to Fractaige?"

"What the fuck's 'Fractaige'?" Adam asked.

"The next planet. You are going there, aren't you — on the way to the Gate of Ubyvis?"

"Yes, I think. That is right, isn't it, Tom?"

Thomas, who looked awfully confused, eventually replied, "Are you telling me you weren't listening to us?"

"I try not to," Adam shrugged, "but you're all gob-shites so it's difficult not to. Yeah, you're right, I'm right. Yes, Lewis, we are."

"Good, I wouldn't have been pleased to find there had been an easier way to get out all this time."

"So, you have got out before?" Maddy took the opportunity to validity Adam's story about Lewis and his homicidal donkey.

"No, of course not, too hard to reach the Gate, especially without a boat."

"But Adam said…"

"Oh, I was making that up!"

"Why the Hell would you make that up?"

"Why the Hell would you believe it?"

"You swore!"

"I swear all the bastard time!"

"So, you're going?" Lewis interrupted.

"Yes."

"Let me come with you, I need to reach the bazaar on Fractaige. Please tell me you have a boat."

"Why don't you have a boat?"

"Fucking donkey."

"Alright," Tom said, pausing to chuckle, "what do you mean, 'Bazaar'?"

"A bazaar, like a market, on Fractaige. You can get anything there. It's how most people stay alive around here."

"And you could help us get there?"

"Of course."

"Come on then, and yes, we have a boat. We'll catch up with it in a while, just keep walking north with us."

Again, they set off, Adam walking ahead with Lewis. They chatted as two friends who haven't seen each other for a while might, and the others tried their best to eavesdrop, just for some entertainment. While his donkey may not have killed him, it was apparent that it was rather misbehaved. An obnoxious braying laughter soon proved this assumption. Through the dense undergrowth, a miniature donkey came bounding towards the crew and bowled its round body through the huddle of people. The equine assailant then shook his head so that his oversized ears flopped up and down as he slowed down to a trot alongside Lewis.

"Here's the little sod," Lewis announced, patting the donkey on the withers. It was only at that point that the animal stopped calling for attention.

"He's alive?" Maddy laughed, "You said you –"

"I was making it up, Maddy!" Adam decided Lewis didn't need to hear the end of that story. He stroked the donkey too, but it snorted and moved away from him.

"Oliver, be nice," Lewis ordered the creature, revealing its name.

The Lady Mary

The trees that lined either bank of the river came close to the water and grew thick. They funnelled the wind, the view, and the ship down the river on a one-way trip. The vibrant songs of the small dragons came from the canopy, and thankfully only creatures smaller than Doyle (the dragon) could be seen. Elliott could not help but sense that they hadn't seen even a fraction of the life on this planet. For one, he hadn't seen a being to which the feather he had found could belong. The dragons all had fuzzy feathers, a bit like hair. They weren't complex and bird-like, which the one he had found was. So presumably, there was at least one enormous bird somewhere.

Rather unfortunately, the sun was already setting. Maybe it wasn't unfortunate, as they didn't really have much to do. The river's current was causing the ship to move, so all Glove had to do was steer away from the banks at fast corners, and hope the river was wide enough throughout its course. This left the others with the opportunity to admire the first non-hellish sunset they had seen in five years. Blue, orange, deep purples and reds. All these colours and more were refracted by the atmosphere and shone upon the land. The formerly green trees glowed amber as insects hovered above the water, sunlight catching their transparent wings. The sun itself was so low now, it was only visible through cracks in between the trees, appearing to flicker as it moved in and out of sight.

All aboard *The Lady* sat on barrels, besides Glove, who was at the helm, to take in the view. The golden glow of the brilliant star gave them hope, relief, but also warned of the chilly night ahead. The temperature didn't fall especially low, but the night would be unfamiliar, and proved that time was still working against them. These factors are what would make the night cold. But for now, they just watched the sunset.

The sunset also reminded them of something else; it had been a very long day for them all. Tudor yawned loudly, struggling to keep his eyes open. Elliott rejoined his captain at the helm, taking his barrel with him. He looked at Glove briefly, but didn't say a word. Instead, he observed the map, turning his head to better imagine where on it he was. He figured it wouldn't be long until they met up with the others. There was just one more meander until they would have to anchor the ship either to meet or wait for the rest of the crew.

In the Jungle

"Who's your captain, anyroad?" Lewis asked Adam.

"You know Glove, Tom's old man!" Adam assured.

"Do I?"

"Yeah, yeah, you'll remember when you see him."

"Are you sure?" Tom asked, not recalling a time when he nor his father had met Lewis.

"Yeah, you know each other!" Adam insisted, though no one was really that convinced.

"So, he'll be alright with me joining you?"

"No problem," Tom added, despite the fact he didn't recognise Lewis.

"I don't know," Maddy, who felt left out of the conversation, inputted.

"What do you mean?" Tom frowned.

"Well, you have already let one person join the crew, and now another. It's just, well, you know."

"I know what?"

"You know, it's not like he's the most trusting person in the world. There were seven people in our crew, two strangers is quite a change."

"Who're strangers?" Tom questioned as he looked at Maddy and then at Noah.

"I'm just saying."

Adam heard the sound of flowing water, though the others talked over it. He knew they were close to the river again. He noticed it was a slight way off to the left, so directed everyone towards it. Horizontal streaks of brown broke through the vertical green of the strokes of tree trunks. When they were about thirty yards away, writing could be read: '*The Lady Mary*'. The ship was tugging on its anchor, which sat on the riverbed and churned up clay.

Tudor, of all people, called down to them all, even referring to Lewis Plaque by name. He slid down the ladder, which was easier to ascend than the ladder that was actually attached to the side of the ship. He had informed them they had been anchored for half an hour, suggesting that either someone's calculations were incorrect, or they had been dawdling. Lewis had to carry the donkey under one arm to get up the ladder, which the animal verbally disagreed with. Before he left to make dinner, Tom introduced Lewis to Glove, who was adamant that he had never met him, even though Adam, and now Tudor, were insistent on the contrary. Glove stared down Lewis for a while, but eventually agreed that he could stay aboard for a ride to the Bazaar, in exchange for all the useful information he had along the way.

Elliott offered to man the helm for a bit, allowing Glove to rest in his cabin, an offer the captain gladly accepted. He was tired from the day before, and was usually the first to sleep, after Adam at least, depending on Adam's sleep-schedule. Speaking of Adam, he, despite being reunited with a long-lost friend, decided too to drift off in his hammock with his door closed on the world above-deck. He didn't even say as much as 'goodnight' to anyone.

On behalf of his captain, the first-mate ordered Tudor to lift the anchor. Tudor often loved to lift the anchor, mostly to seem strong, but complained when Elliott asked him. The ship sighed in relief as it was released from the riverbed and hurried through the water, between the constricting trees. Branches now grabbed at the flagpoles, but the pushing of the boat by the powerful river forced it straight through. Pine needles, twigs, and cones dropped from the sky and bounced on the deck below. This alarmed the dragons in the treetops, and they sounded in panic.

But soon the dragons fell silent. Just as they did, Oliver the miniature donkey did quite the opposite. Whinnying like a hysterical child, he called out incessantly. He wouldn't stop, even with Lewis placing his hand around his mouth. He shook his head, and his ears flapped against it. They left the donkey on deck when, to their relief, Tom called them for dinner, as the scent of roasting chicken drifted from the chimney. Elliott remained at the wheel.

Below deck

Still being a popular choice, Tom had cooked chicken and bread, placing them in the centre of the table for people to help themselves. Noah introduced the concept of a sandwich to the crew, and they all copied him. Lewis agreed sandwiches were a real and popular foodstuff, though it was rather unclear how he would know the truth. The final faint beams of sunlight, which broke through the trees, shone through the small dining-room window and marched across the back wall. Tom took a sandwich for his father and for Adam, delivering each to their respective quarters.

The helm

When Tom walked back towards the dining room, he could hear better that Oliver was still braying uncontrollably. He went above deck to stop the donkey but noticed that Elliott was no longer there. There was no one steering the ship. *The Lady* was moving through the flower moving waters at the bank of the river, hitting the side once or twice. Taking the wheel, he looked around for the donkey. Oliver had trotted over to the stairs and stumbled down them to the dining room, crossing paths with Elliott on his way up. The man chuckled as the donkey brushed past him, a sandwich in one hand, the crust of which he tossed to the animal.

"Elliott!" Tom called harshly, "What are you doing?"

"I need food too!" Elliott laughed innocently, "That donkey is a chatty fellow."

Tom looked slightly guilty, as he knew he had forgotten to bring Elliott a sandwich, despite giving one to Glove and Adam. Not that this offended Elliott, but Tom realised he couldn't blame him for having to get one himself. To make up for it, Tom remained at the wheel and allowed his friend to eat.

The Golden Gander

Amber stood, leaning over the wheel, using her shoulders to steer more than her arms, unless *The Gander* reached a sharper turn in the river. Being a smaller, more gracile ship than *The Lady*, *The Gander* was better at dodging the branches of the trees above. Even so, the conifers clung tightly to the river, strangling the ship like a noose. The crew was tense. Amber stared through her telescope and into the forest to attempt to view *The Lady* as it too turned on a meander. She thought she had caught a glimpse but wasn't entirely sure. Subconsciously, she leant even further forward, not that it actually increased the speed of the boat. She knew that there was no way to increase speed at this point, but that was the frustrating part.

But there was a way to go faster. *The Gander* had never, to this point, used its oars, but it had a dozen of them nonetheless. The twelve lowest-ranking members of the crew, to whom Amber did not speak directly nor audibly, were commanded to each collect an oar and row the ship down the river to gain distance on *The Lady*. They all, of course, did. Each slid their oars through the oarlocks and began rowing in sync. Since the deck of *The Gander* was spotless, there was no barrel or chair for any man to rest on. An elderly crewmember leant against the railing but made the mistake of turning to look guiltily at his commander. Silently and slowly, she shook her head. He stood up straight after that.

Then, the boat tipped to one side; the mast knocking against branches. The awful splintering sound of a ruined saw against wet wood dragged down the deck. When this ended, the ship rocked backwards, as if it had been released from a terrible grip. This was followed by what could only be described as the sound of a reptilian chainsaw. By this I mean some combination between the drumming growl of a crocodile and the revving of an engine, but much louder than either. The horizontal back of a large animal, which was lined with spines like an iguana's on the top, rose into view of the rowers, who stopped immediately. An officer ordered them to return to rowing, and quicker than before. They did — at the sight of the whip.

Amber couldn't see the aggressor very well, but assumed that out-speeding such a large beast was the optimal strategy. Though she couldn't determine the shape of the creature, it was clearly a combination of an enormous head, torso and lizard-ish tail reaching just short of fifty feet in length, the tail making up half of this. Again, it rocked the boat, this time as if it had simply pushed its weight into the side. The reptile gurgled a second time when the ship swung back towards it. Then, it grabbed an oar, flipping the rower over and pulling his arm through the oarlock. A splash was heard as the oar hit the water.

"Cannons!" an officer called before seeing Amber's discontent and contradicting himself, "Keep rowing!"

A scaled, five-foot head, tall and long but narrow, and roughly the shape of a golfing iron, opened its jaw. The mouth ran the full length of its skull with narrow lips and little in the way of cheeks. Several dozen visibly serrated teeth, about the size of a small butcher's knife, lined either side of both the top and bottom jaws. The tooth row was rather flat, the teeth sitting neatly like a saw-blade. Opening its mouth to a right-angle, it swung down its top jaw like an axe and immediately crumpled the oarlock and one of the rowers with it. Its teeth sunk into the deck and smeared it with blood as it withdrew its skull. Rather than lifting its head, it pulled its teeth across the wood and, with some effort, sawed through it. Bone splintered from the unfortunate man as his mutilated body was dragged off of the ship, the beast catching him midair and swallowing him without chewing.

This animal was not a dragon, for it had no wings, but had legs which were far too great to classify it as a serpent. It had left a single tooth, which had come out of its gums, embedded in the deck, just by the new bloodstain. Fresh red blood dripped through the punctures the animal had made and onto the gun-deck below. As you could imagine, the other rowers had failed to keep still at this point, all jumping up and away from the side which the reptile had struck. Some retreated below deck, taking up a position at the cannon despite the order not to. Others remained on deck, but as far away as they could from it.

The beast wrestled the ship, pushing it towards the far bank, which caused the keel to haul through the mud on the riverbed and come to a stop.

"Keep rowing," Amber breathed. The sailors looked blankly at her, then back at the scaled brute. "Keep rowing!" The commander stomped her foot. But even if she raised her voice, she was not a fifty-foot reptile with a hacksaw for a skull. Their aggressor was on the right side of the river, so they could jump to the left side.

"Keep rowing!" Amber Sings scowled at the officer holding the cat-o'-nine-tails. At the sight of the creature raising its head and again opening its mouth, the officer muttered, "Abandon ship."

With this, half a dozen men jumped, with no thought to their landing. When they found their footing, they ran. Ran away from the huge, scaled monster, and away from their commander, who was flustered and red. The infuriated sight that was Amber Sings convinced the last remaining men on deck to abandon as well.

On the bright side, the loss of weight on one side of the vessel caused *The Gander* to push back against its reptilian predator. Instead of attacking the deck of the ship, the animal bit the side of it. Only the teeth on one side of its head scraped on the carpentry and closed around a cannon. The cannon fired, with no chance of hitting its target because of the way it had hold of it. The shock and noise, however, caused the attacker to pull away, tearing the cannon out of the ship as it did. Focussing on the wound it had just made to the boat; it enlarged the gap in the wood. This put it in full view of the pirates, who gave up all hope of shooing it. Instead, they did as their companions had; they ran to the deck and jumped straight off the other side.

With little hope of moving the ship, Amber took a flaming torch and tossed it onto the scaled hide of the hunter. It snarled and shook itself around. Then, it froze, and *The Gander* was free to let the current take it further down the river. A distant sound could be heard — that which a donkey makes.

The Lady Mary: below deck

The rest of the crew in the dining room lay back in their chairs and yawned. Tudor put his feet up on the table, to the discontent of many. The babbling of the river calmed the room and encouraged some men to drift off to sleep. These men, however, were woken up abruptly when Oliver the donkey burst into the room. His call had become wheezy and sounded like a croak; likely because of the strain he had put on his larynx. He stopped immediately when he looked out the window.

Noah sat next to Tudor and muttered to him, "If we got to Earth, rather than Heaven, do you think you'll be able to say you're better than your brother?"

"I'll be able to say it if we go to Heaven, too."

"But he won't know."

"It's not about him knowing," Tudor explained, looking down the edge of his sabre, "It's simple. It's about being the best. Whatever that takes."

"Just don't die trying to prove that," Noah cautioned.

"Depends on the cause."

A single dark orange eye, sitting on the side of a head which blocked the rest of the window, looked plainly through the small glass panel. Whatever was outside gave a drumming bellow. The eye blinked using the transparent third eyelid, which a bird has; the one that closes from the inside corner to the outside. The other two eyelids closed, however, when the being outside the window pushed its head against the window. Its weight rocked the ship away from it, and its rough manner put a crack in the glass.

All stood to attention. They left their plates and glasses in their places, one smashing against the floor, and ran to the main-deck. To everyone's disappointment, the donkey started braying again. The reptile raised its foul face, making it eye level with the pirates. A pitted ridge of horn ran from the tip of its nose to above its eyes, splitting in two above each eye to form a pair of small, upturned horns. The keratin sheet then continued back and down around the eye, framing it. It had red, fleshy skin, free of large scales, around its eye as well.

"What the Hell is that!" Noah screeched.

"I call her 'Queen Anne', she's the second largest predator on this planet!" Lewis called.

"You've got to be kidding me," Tudor muttered, his sabre already in his hand, "'Queen Anne'?"

"You're saying there's something bigger than this!" Maddy shouted over him.

Queen Anne tilted her head sideways to look at the boat with a single eye on the side of her face. She opened her mouth as flies buzzed around her teeth, which were bloodstained. She bit down on the deck, obliterating the railing and sinking her serrated teeth into the planks. Having two very powerful legs, which looked somewhat like those of a bird but stockier, the reptile stepped back, pulling *The Lady Mary* with her. Glove dashed out of his quarters, took the wheel from his first-mate and ordered him and Doyle to man the cannons.

"Musket, man!" the captain called, though Adam remained in his slumber. Glove steered ferociously to stay on track, but the ship did not escape the bite of Queen Anne. "Someone shoot the bugger!" he called in a second effort.

Maddy drew a small pistol and fired at Queen Anne's face. At first, her teeth remained caught in the timber, so as she flinched the boat rocked too. With a second movement, she got free and back-stepped away from *The Lady*. Tudor marched towards the right-hand side of the ship. Getting a better view of their attacker, he saw she had a rectangular body covered in a pavement of tiny scales, which were a murky brown-green and varied in shade. She gave the impression of having the same skeletal arrangement as a bird; the spine running parallel to the ground despite being a biped, but having in another sense a grossly different morphology to the likes of a chicken. Her torso was taller than it was wide, as her head was, and the tip of her spine raised to a peak. From the front, the body was a diamond shape, widest at the middle, with two stubby arms with three sharp claws being tucked into the belly. The tail was striped and used mostly for balancing the huge body and head.

The bullet drew blood but didn't seem to cause too much of an effect.

Gun-deck

Elliott and Doyle both lit torches ready to fire the cannons, which were still loaded with the contents of 'Tin-o-Tetanus'. Queen Anne bit the side of the ship. Her teeth left indents through the wall and caused Elliott to light a cannon on impulse. The cannonball disintegrated as it was shot, due to the rusty state, projecting a red cloud of dust towards Queen Anne, rather than an effective projectile. Just as she had *The Gander*, the huge reptile put a laceration into the side of *The Lady*. She shook her head to remove the planks of wood from her teeth, her arms came forward to remove the obstruction but failed to reach. Feeling exposed to the beast's wrath, Elliott fired more cannons, putting a visibility barrier between it and them because of the cloud of rust. Queen Anne continued to swing her head back and forth, then gave out a gruff sneeze.

Blindly, she lunged through the dust cloud, and the ridge of horn on her skull collided with the already weakened exterior of *The Lady*. Hungry, butchering jaws snapped around in the gun-deck, until Doyle caught the tip of her nose with a sword, and she slithered back.

Main-deck

As Queen Anne grew accustomed to the dust cloud, she peered over it and focussed on Tudor, who was standing sword in hand. The ship continued at a steady pace down the river, but the reptile pursued as any predator would. Arching her neck, she raised her head to the level of the deck and once again sawed at it, this time with the side of her mouth. The force pushed the keel of *The Lady* to the bottom of the river, causing the entire boat to quake as it dragged against the clay. Tom drew his sword at the sight of the great head and marched towards it. Tudor stood in front of him, put his hand on his shoulder, and said, "Let me do it — I'm — just let me do it."

Rather boldly, to give him credit, Tudor approached her and struck the side of her face with his sabre. Queen Anne withdrew her teeth from the deck and snapped at Tudor, her weight leaning against the ship to reach to him. Maddy shot at her again, but the tilted mast caught a branch, shaking the ship and throwing off her aim. Tom grabbed a barrel that had been rolling around on deck and used both arms to toss it at Queen Anne's face. The barrel didn't break but caused her to pivot and follow *The Lady* from a greater distance.

Glove steered the ship as far away as he could in the narrow river, but they were still left in biting range.

Gun-deck

"Pass me one! Pass me a cannonball from one of those guns!" Elliott requested, but when he turned around, Doyle had rushed away. Instead, he pulled the last two oxidised cannonballs from the port-side cannons and trucked them under his arms. In haste, he dropped one on the floor and failed to keep up with it as it rolled away from him and out of the lesion that Queen Anne had caused the boat. "Bugger!" he screamed, forcing the final cannonball into the gun closest to the scaled beast and fired, again to no avail, "You big bugger – you second biggest bugger!"

This remark gave him an idea, so he rushed to the main-deck, grabbing what seemed to be the last tin of cured beef in the cupboards. He noticed an old boarding pike in the corner of the hallway, so picked that up too.

Main-deck

When Tudor saw the spear that Elliott had retrieved and asked for it. Elliott agreed and tossed the pike to him. This weapon gave weight and range, something that may keep Queen Anne at bay. Elliott, regardless of the danger, began tossing chunks of beef around the deck.

"What are you doing?" Noah asked him.

"That," Elliott replied as a small dragon swooped down to consume the meat.

"What's 'that'?"

"Lewis said she's the second biggest predator on Oblitos."

"Yeah?"

"So that means there's something bigger than she is!"

"So what?"

"Remember when we fed the dragons earlier? They flocked until bigger and bigger ones came."

"You want to bring the bigger one here?"

"It might scare her away!"

"But – but," Noah failed to explain his criticism of this plan and just stared in confusion as Elliott attracted a larger swarm of flying animals.

When Queen Anne pounced again, Tudor used the pike to keep her away. She tried again, and the spear cut her face, in between the nostrils at the front of her skull and eyes at the back. Groaning with anger, she shrugged, Tudor keeping grasp of the pike to hold her off. Using the top of her head, she pushed the spear away and reached up again to the deck. Her nose caught Maddy and knocked her over. Queen Anne got hold of the tip of her coat and pulled the woman closer, as she kicked and writhed to escape.

"How have you survived with this thing?" Elliott yelled to Lewis.

"It doesn't hunt individual people, that's a waste of time. There are animals here with legs like tree trunks. The prey she hunts is as big as a ship. The prey nothing else can kill."

"Nothing else? Tell me about this even bigger beast."

"Well, I call him Scotty. He's a bit like Queen Anne, but plumper. He doesn't bother with the biggest prey, but his bite shatters the bones of his victims before they can fight back."

This conversation was ended by Maddy's scream. Lewis tried to assist her, while Elliott went on feeding dragons, even tossing some food off to the bank. Queen Anne had pulled Maddy by her coat so that her legs were hanging off the side of the ship. The serrations of the teeth cut the coat, losing grip when they reached the edge. This gave Queen Anne an attempt to get a better hold of the pirate. But then Tudor's boarding pike impaled her face, behind her nostril, and came out the other side as if it hadn't been obstructed by a bone. The man holding the weapon, strangely, opted to jump onto Queen Anne's head, keeping hold of the pike with one hand and trashing his sabre with the other. He cut the hide of her neck but couldn't get through to the jugular vein as he had intended.

The reptile tilted its head and bashed it against the ship to free the spike from its sinuses. Tudor dropped the weapons and grabbed hold of a line from the rigging. Queen Anne bucked and flipped him from her nose, leaving him to dangle from the rope down the side of *The Lady*. Tudor screamed in terror, but managed to tie the rope around his belt to climb up it securely.

But Queen Anne hadn't diverted her attention. Her heavy jaws clamped below his knee, and the rope alone kept him from being swallowed. The front teeth were smaller but sharper than the others; they unseamed the skin of Tudor's leg from the knee to the ankle as the ship pulled him away from the reptile. The flesh of the calf was also filleted cleanly, as if a butcher had done it with a new cleaver. Red blood immediately coated his entire leg. With a gasping breath he screamed, but no sound came out, as the sinews of his ankle split like a snapped rubber band.

The Lady tilted as she was pulled towards the bank, all the force running through Tudor's body. When Queen Anne's teeth had sliced down to his shoes, which were cut in half at the heel, Tudor was released and the ship sprung back because of the elasticity of the rope. He managed to produce a sound and cried for assistance. Tom located the rope he was tied to and pulled it in, so that Tudor reached the top deck and spilt blood all over it.

Gun-deck

Doyle ran back to the gun-deck from the sleeping quarters with a wooden box. In it were various items, including some tinned beef, but more importantly, two small cannonballs.

"Elliott, I've…" he announced, stopping when he observed Elliott had vacated the gun-deck. He fell back as the ship was pulled by the Beast outside. He heard a scream too, so decided to load a cannon and aim, ready for a good shot.

Main-deck

Queen Anne, still determined, reached for his mauled leg, and bit it with a greater length of her jaw. The longer teeth in the middle of her upper tooth-row bypassed the fresh wound and sank straight into his shinbone, which did not snap but crunched as the teeth pushed through to the marrow. In great pain, Tudor clenched the cross on his necklace so hard that the chain snapped from his neck. Tom, now with help from all but Elliott and the captain, struggled tirelessly to reel their friend back to them, but the predator fought back. Tudor reached both arms towards the others, grabbing the rope with both and dropping his cross in his blood on the deck.

The Lady was now dredging its keel through hard gravel in the riverbed, and the mast collided with the trunks of trees at a forty-five-degree angle. Small dragons of many varieties swarmed above it, circling as they expected a meal. Glove battled the strain with might, but his ship only stumbled further to the side.

"I need help!" Tudor called, tears falling down his face in a way no one had ever seen. "Help me, please!" Glove looked at Tudor and then his crew, who were so desperately trying to help him. He then looked at his ship, his only way to his wife, which was one sudden movement away from pummelling straight into the riverbank. Tudor, Queen Anne, the crew, and even the ship all cried in their efforts. "Help me!" Tudor called once again, but then, Glove shot the rope.

Instantly, the rope frayed and snapped. *The Lady* was released; the crew falling back as she swung back upright. There was a scream, and Queen Anne's blood-coated jaws snapped shut. Tudor Boris was dead.

Chapter VI

The Lady Mary: Main-deck

But Tudor was not a full meal for Queen Anne. As a result, the crew didn't exactly have time to process his death at first. Having stopped briefly, Queen Anne sniffed a puddle of blood by her feet. Seeing her prey floating further down the river, and the flock of dragons above it, she moved forward in what was presumably the large biped's attempt at running. She was a slow animal but could still catch up to *The Lady* as it had only the current to propel it. Preparing her attack, Queen Anne held her mouth open during the final strides towards the ship. But then, she stopped, and her three-toed feet slid through the mud.

A single booming tone seemed to come from the ground itself and shook the air. Queen Anne chuffed curiously and tiptoed around *The Lady* to face ahead to the opposite bank. The red eye-shine of two forward-facing eyes, about the height of Queen Anne's, blinked in between the trees. The trunks of thinner trees bent out of the way as a bulky creature slowly stepped towards the river. It was of a similar structure to Queen Anne, but its chest was barrel-like and wide, having a smooth back and full belly. While Queen Anne appeared to stand maybe a foot taller and a few feet longer (which is little difference when comparing two creatures of such size), this newcomer clearly had the weight advantage.

"There he is!" Lewis called, tapping Elliott, "There's old Scotty!"

Elliott's face turned white as he observed the very thing he had summoned. Scotty's hide was a cool brown and mottled, with a sparse hairy down along his back and tail. Rather than having a narrow head with eyes facing sideways, his faced forward, sitting in the back of the head, which was wider than the snout. He called without opening his mouth, a ghostly drone of a bellow.

Though a river separated them, the two reptilian behemoths paced towards each other, stopping before the boat to lower their heads and bodies above the water, their noses five feet apart. Both set their feet firmly in the clay of the bank, and did not flinch. Scotty had two round bosses above his eyes, and rough skin, crumpled like that of a turkey, covered the top of his snout. It was clear that they intended to fight, obviously by biting, as it was less clear to who had the more useless pair of arms. Scotty's arms were even shorter than Queen Anne's and had one less finger, but appeared more muscular and had two strong, hooked claws. The animals remained rooted in their stance, but *The Lady* kept drifting closer to them. It was only a few feet away now, but neither wanted to be the first to react to it. Being the stockier of the two, the bow of the ship brushed Scotty's side first, so he turned his head to snap at it. Queen Anne took this opportunity to bite him on the nose, and she dragged him into the river.

Scotty, who weighed perhaps ten tons, hit the water back first with a great splash. His powerful legs kicked about to orient himself before *The Lady* barged into him. The river's water turned murkier as he then swam to the other bank towards Queen Anne. First, shaking like a wet dog, he rumbled the front of his thick, s-curved neck and attempted to intimidate his rival with his size. Queen Anne angled her body to the side to allow her high back to give more area to her silhouette.

Both creatures paced diagonally, beginning to circle around each other in a way that made each look as fearsome as possible. The two carnivores were distracted, and *The Lady* slipped past them further down the river. Understanding that Queen Anne had no intention of backing down, Scotty lunged for her neck. He missed the bones of her spine, but his teeth, which were more robust but blunter than hers, grabbed the pouch of skin which formed a dewlap under her throat. His lips were thick and protected with large scales. His cheek muscles were also more substantial than Queen Anne's, giving his mouth an appearance matching a Staffordshire bull terrier's (or as close as a reptile could come to it). The largest of Scotty's teeth were in the middle of the tooth row, which was convex on the top jaw and concave on the bottom to form a point of highest pressure at these teeth.

Queen Anne's breath became a struggled hiss, which grew less frequent but louder each time. The heavier animal's bite was evidently so strong that pulling away from it would injure Anne more than staying close would, so instead she leant into Scotty and pushed him against a tree. She got free and evaded a subsequent bite. Their new stance gave Anne the opportunity to use her saw of a skull against her rival. With a clear swing at Scotty's side, she grated skin from his back and opened the hide around his ribs. She then got a firmer hold around the top of his back and tried to push his weight to the ground. She lacked a ton or more of his weight, and consequently the strength to easily push this much mass.

Neither had a great degree of flexibility, but Scotty still managed to curve his spine to aim his head back towards Queen Anne, at least enough to bite her arm. Straight away she released him at the sound of a snap, but Scotty used his might to tear her arm away from her body like you would the wing of a cooked chicken. Half of the humerus remained in the socket, but the other was torn off at a splintered break, as tendons and sinews broke away one by one. Scotty swallowed her arm, Queen Anne submitted, and promptly made her way into the forest to be seen of no longer. Her drumming sigh faded away.

The Lady had made little distance from the even larger animal, who looked straight at the moving vessel and walked after it patiently. He seemed very aware of the people aboard, keeping both his eyes fixed on them. When he got to the ship, he nudged his boxy face against it and tried to snap at the side. His lips, however, blocked his teeth from scraping the wood, even at the most curved part of the outer plating. He tried again, but even his front teeth couldn't grasp the timbers. Elliott, who clung onto the mast in dread, sighed in relief when Scotty gave up and walked idly away.

The Golden Gander

Amber Sings stood at the helm as she had before, dumbfounded. She was used to her crew fearing her as much as God, and being equally as faithful towards her. Oars dragged in the water, wedged in their oarlocks, but fell out into the water one by one. These floated down the river faster Han the ship did, soon running away from Amber as her crew had. She revelled in the fact that their souls were, at least presumably, soon to be in possession of Satan.

The Gander, though beaten, was still perfectly able to float down the river, with its commander at the wheel. So, she leant against the wheel, depressed, and guided the injured vessel along the channel. In theory, she could still reach *The Lady Mary*, but with no men to fire the cannons while she steered, any efforts of sinking it were unlikely. But the river was the only way forward and restricted any way backwards, so all she could do was steer *The Golden Gander*, and wait.

The Lady Mary

"See to the damage, Boris!" Glove yelled, as it was typically Tudor to do the handiwork on *The Lady*. The deck remained silent.

"I'll do it, cap'n," Elliott huffed, his head low. As he walked down from the helm, he passed the puddle of Tudor's blood, bending over to carefully pick up his cross. He wiped the red from its silver surface and put it in his pocket.

"He may just be the bravest man I've ever met," said Noah with sincerity. Neither Tom nor Maddy commented on this statement, though tears dripped from the ends of their noses.

"Don't let his death get you down," Glove said from the helm, "Use it as a lesson, and as a reason to stay strong. He was a brave man; let's honour his memory by achieving the very best."

Gun-deck

"Where did you go?" Doyle asked Elliott accusatorially.

"Tudor's dead," Elliott told him, causing the harsh look to fall from his friend's face, "that – that thing killed him."

"But we're immortal."

"Clearly not."

Doyle looked inside the box he had retrieved and picked up a shiny cannonball.

"What's that?" Elliott asked.

"I've been saving them — for an emergency," Doyle explained, but this made Elliott frown.

"This was an emergency, Doyle."

"That's why I got them."

"I can't believe this!" Elliott raised his voice, which was unusual.

"What, it's a sensible plan!"

"We could have used them!"

"I know, but you weren't there when I got back!"

"Because I had to make a new plan! Can't you see? Tudor died because you were hiding these away!"

Tom came down with some slats of wood to help repair the side of the ship, which Queen Anne had torn open. Elliott deliberately took an excessive handful of nails out of Doyle's case, which Doyle then closed and stormed out with.

"I can't believe him," Elliott was quick to grass on Doyle.

"What?" Tom asked, anticipating trouble due to Doyle's moody disappearance.

"He's been hiding cannonballs away from us all this time — all this time when we could have used them to fight terrible beasts like Queen Anne! In fact, there's all sorts in that case of his, I bet we could benefit a lot if it weren't for him. Him and his – his greed," Elliott grew redder as Tom tried to comfort him, "I thought I had used all the cannonballs, and doomed us, but he was simply keeping them for himself!"

Tom took the hammer from Elliott and nailed a plank of wood across the gap in the wall, holding the now snapped beam back together. He then fixed overlapping horizontal slats to the beam to fill in the wound. The ship certainly had taken a toll from Queen Anne's bite, but at least it wouldn't be so easily flooded. Elliott got up and aided him but holding the wood in place while Tom hammered.

With hesitation, Tom asked Elliott, "When did we run out of cannonballs?"

"When we first fought Thatch," Elliott said softly, "it didn't seem important to use them sustainably at the time, we just had to fight him. We just had to stay alive."

"But you must have noticed them running out?"

"What, did you expect me to think, 'Oh, I mustn't waste the last cannonball on Thatch, we may have to fight the creatures of Hell later'?"

"Touche," Tom thought it would be best to leave this conversation there.

Main-deck

While the gun-deck had become enclosed once again, the crew above deck had a different experience. The thick fog of trees had lifted to reveal a more open environment. There were still trees, but they sat many yards apart, and gave way to shrubs and scarce grasses. It was the middle of the night, but light glared over the water and on the dew from a bright white moon on the horizon. This moon appeared to have a face made from craters, as many say ours has, but the face of this satellite was cruller and more unhappy looking.

Large silhouettes crept across the landscape. These were four-legged creatures, who grazed peacefully and did not give the crew reason for alarm. They were quite far away from the water's edge anyway, occasionally raising their heads to view the ship or the forest edge, then continuing their feasting. Some had large, narrow bodies and long tails like Queen Anne, with their front limbs being longer and hoofed so touched the ground, and heads which were horselike but beaked. Others were shorter but much rounder, with smaller tails, and huge, horned heads. These creatures lowed and honked back and forth at each other.

These distant animals have no impact on the plot, although they reveal exactly why there was such a sense of life from Oblitos. While they were unrecognisable to the pirates, they had some familiarity about them, sharing features with the creatures of Earth. Like cattle, they spent all their time taking in greenery or chewing it, often both simultaneously. Like the wildebeest and zebra of Africa, they herded in masses across the plains. But they weren't mammals like our modern grazers; they had scales, making them reptiles. But like I said, they weren't important for the plot, other than the fact that the crew enjoyed watching them, feeling humbled by the vast majesty of creatures far bigger than they had ever seen (unless any of them had been lucky enough to see a whale).

Glove didn't feel the need to go back to sleep, so remained at the wheel. Once the ship was repaired to the best of Tom and Elliott's abilities, they came up from the gun-deck. Doyle was on deck, sitting away on a barrel. The others had tried to speak to him, but he wasn't willing to entertain their company. Deciding only now to get up, Adam finally returned from his hammock. He didn't notice that the others were glum.

"Something was making a lot of noise!" he shouted, not even ashamed of having been unhelpful.

"Queen Anne attacked," Tom said vaguely.

"The fucking queen?"

"No, Adam, a big, scaly thing with an enormous mouth."

"Morris is dead," Glove said solemnly.

"Fuck off," Adam smiled, assuming it was a joke.

Elliott, feeling strangely angry, muttered, "And it's Doyle's fault."

"You what?"

"Doyle hid some cannonballs when we should have been using them."

Adam, for once, couldn't speak. Maddy, new to this information also, could.

"Doyle, you selfish bastard!" she said as she walked towards him.

Doyle stood up immediately, his face red, "Why would I keep cannonballs to be selfish?"

"Cos you're a greedy prick!" Adam soon found the words to say, as Maddy smacked Doyle on the shoulder (and not in a friendly way), "And now Tudor's dead, you dickhead!"

"For God's sake, I didn't kill him, did I!" Doyle pushed Maddy back and stomped away.

"We're still here though," Tom began, "We're almost off this deadly planet, anyway."

They wouldn't see the sun rise on Oblitos before they reached its own stone table. Just as the forest had thinned out into grassland, the grassland dissipated into desert, on which fewer creatures grazed. And the desert, as they approached the coast, became a salt-marsh. Drifting southeast now, the wind blew with it the mist of the waves, accompanied by the scent of sea-salt. What looked like turkey-sized, snouted and long-tailed birds waded through the marsh, stalking small schools of fish, which weaved through the knotted web of streams. Small dragons flew close to the water's surface, and skimmed the fish from the water with long, curved bills. A mosquito buzzed around and bit Noah's arm, getting away before he had realised.

Most of the crew continued to revile Doyle, each working the others up more, until the next made it even worse. They were certainly frustrated with their friend. As far as Elliott, and all he had convinced, were concerned, Doyle had rapaciously hoarded goods and consequently caused Tudor's death. They were certainly filling the story with more malice than was perhaps warranted, as is often the case in such a discussion. Doyle, below deck, went to bed, which would have been a wise decision for all, though they chose against it.

Tom looked up to see what must have been stars – except they weren't. Within the endless darkness of the night sky, the shadow of a large, round planet loomed in the sky. Small, lonely specks of light — lights of all colours — shone from the surface of this planet. As they had on Hell, lights and bright wisps leapt to and back from Oblitos. On the horizon now, from where these lights were heading, the figure of stone slabs stood on a distant island.

The wind was not blowing in the ideal direction, but they were going to need wind in the sails.

"Sails, men," Glove said quietly, though loud enough that all assisted the process as soon as they were out of the estuary. The sails were pulled down, grabbing the breeze now that they were unobstructed by branches. They were angled so that they pulled the ship northeast, as going straight north would have been impossible. After a quarter of a mile, Glove turned *The Lady* sharply, and insisted that the sails be turned to face the other way from the way they had. This allowed the ship to sail this time northwest. In a series of zig-zags, *The Lady* battled the opposing wind and made way to the island, and the Stonehenge on it.

Once they were there, the ship's keel left the water, the donkey started braying again, and *The Lady* escaped Oblitos.

The Golden Gander

Miserable, Amber attempted to pull down the sails of *The Golden Gander* by herself. She managed, with great strain and discontent, to make the ship suitable for sailing on open water. She lifted her telescope and viewed *The Lady Mary* just before it disappeared from the horizon. Though Glove may have never admitted it, Commander Amber Sings was a better sailor than he, at least when it came to steering. She made a better effort at fighting the oncoming wind, and made some distance; though of course, *The Lady* was just under an hour ahead by the time she had reached the stone table.

She did not wish to wait for *Queen Anne's Revenge*, so proceeded at once.

Queen Anne's Revenge

Blackbeard's own significance to the story had become second-thought. *Queen Anne's Revenge* and *The Bristol Dragon* finally weaved around arches and stacks and stumps; the coastal landforms found on the east side of the continent. Two additional hours behind, they made their way to the Stonehenge.

"She's not here, Captain," Israel Hands noted to Thatch.

Blackbeard's face was red, but that was typical. He remained calm and replied, "That means she hasn't got them yet, but we can leave it to her. They must be hours ahead of us, Sings waiting would only waste the opportunity to take Glove out of this race."

Thatch observed the next map of the pile, "We have a clear run at them," he remarked.

Act 3: Welcome to the Jungle

Chapter I

Fractaige: *The Lady Mary*

The Lady landed in the waters of the next planet in a smooth motion; the wind blew it along as if it had been sailing continuously. The water was blue, which I know shouldn't be a surprise, but as of this point, the ratio of planets with red to blue water was 1:1. As Lewis had mentioned, the name of the third planet was Fractaige.

The map depicted the landmasses of Fractaige as being split down the middle. While Oblitos had had only one major continent, Fractaige had two. Conveniently, they found themselves right in the middle of the wide, dividing sea, with the stone-henge being in the south. As is the case when arriving in a new destination, the first step was figuring out way was north, and east and west, and particularly, in this case, south.

Glove gave the map to Elliott, whose compass was again spinning. He could work the direction out himself, but being smart enough to do so, he handed it to Adam. At first, Adam questioned why, but Elliott explained the need for orientation. Since the sun was directly above at this point in time, he scanned the horizon, where two stretches of forested continent blocked the site where sea met sky, on both his left and right. Beaches, spits, islands, tombolos, bays, lagoons, caves, arches, stacks, stumps, cliffs, hills, mountains, and, most notably, buildings decorated the landscape. The pattern of these features was repetitive across the long stretch of land, but unique to each coastline. Adam and Elliott both looked at the map, then the coast, then the map, then the coast.

"South!" Adam called, pointing south, the direction *The Lady* was already sailing in.

Lewis took hold of the map, looked for a second and said, "We need to go north first."

"What are you on about?" Noah said, "We need to hurry, we need to go south."

"You lot need to go to the bazaar as much as I do, and to get there, you need some air!"

"Air!" Tom chuckled, pointing his arm around to the surrounding air, "We've got air, lots of air, it's pretty useless stuff!"

"We need the air to breathe!"

"We need the air to breathe!" Adam echoed.

"I know we need the air to breathe!" Tom insisted, "But what's that got to do with a detour!"

"Because," Lewis said, "if you wouldn't interrupt me, the bazaar is underwater! We need some gear, and I know a guy. And we need some air; I know I guy for that, too!"

"Let me get this straight," Elliott brought himself into the discussion, "we need to get some air, and what, diving gear? Just to get into the market?"

"That's right."

"But we only promised to drop you off, nothing about changing our schedule."

"But you aren't listening."

"I assure you I am."

"We need to go to the bazaar as much as he does!" Glove interrupted, "We don't have any cannonballs, yet need to fight Thatch for the stone."

This made everyone silent, as they hadn't really thought about having to fight Blackbeard. Tom, however, at this point realised that they didn't have to fight him, for in his pocket was still the stone which Noah had given to him.

"Father!" he called, laughing to show that his keeping of the item was accidental,

"We have a stone, Noah brought one!"

"Let me see that," Glove snatched the shining stone from his son's hand, laughing when he realised what this meant, "You could have told me before now, son! We do not need to make a detour, we just need to get there as quickly as possible!"

Noah frowned and added, "But we need to fight him, for Earth's sake."

"Let it burn," Glove interrupted, "let it burn."

"What, Captain?" Elliott asked hesitantly.

"We are going to Heaven. What happens to Earth is not the business of you, nor I."

"So you wouldn't save it out of goodness?" Noah persisted.

"I lost all goodness when Thatch took Mary from me."

"Then avenge her death!" Tom called impressively, "That's what you said before, that's what we're here for! Blackbeard is an evil man, so let's kill him! And we can't do that without resupplying."

Glove though one and hard, his brow furrowed and pink. He acknowledged that it had been he who had set out to kill Thatch, and pondered the reasons why. For one, he was furious at the man, and would indeed love to see him dead. But he had a different priority. Before, killing Thatch and reaching Heaven were achievable simultaneously. Now, they were ahead of him, making the first part of that plan less attainable, if he did in fact prioritise the second part. But giving his crew an enemy is a good way to keep them motivated.

"How long of a detour is it?" Glove asked Lewis impatiently.

"A couple of hours," the guest replied, though to call him a guest may be inaccurate, as any guest on a pirate ship was as much a member of the crew as the next man, at least on most pirate ships.

"And we can get cannonballs and gunpowder and bullets and guns and swords and rope…"

"Let me stop you there," Lewis cut in, "You can get anything at the bazaar, anything."

"Oh, get the sails then!" Glove gave in, but with a smile, knowing he may again get the chance to battle Thatch. He turned the wheel to lock, and *The Lady Mary* swung clockwise, sailing north. The wind, while it blew south, was not blowing completely parallel to the ship's course, so the ship, with correct sails, was able to sail in its intended direction. Lewis pointed out a series of shapes denoting buildings on the map, saying this was where they needed to be. So, that's where they sailed, and they arrived simply, so as not to waste your time, and for the sake of easy writing.

The Golden Gander

The Gander drifted sadly south in the sea that separated the continents of Fractaige. Amber spotted *The Lady* sailing north, so, having no map to tell her the right direction, she followed, grumbling as she had to alter the sails alone. There were a great number of inconveniences and setbacks, but she kept the ship on track, remaining an hour behind *The Lady Mary*. She tensed when the ship rocked, allowing the waves to leap into the hole left in the side. But despite this, *The Gander* remained buoyant, even if not as shipshape as it formerly was.

It would be a while yet until *Queen Anne's Revenge* and *The Bristol Dragon* would reach Fractaige. Amber followed *The Lady* as to follow the orders of her captain. What she could actually do when she got there, she didn't know, but she didn't know what she would do if she returned to Blackbeard unsuccessfully either.

Chuck's Cabin

Chuck was the man they had to see; he was a diver and instructor, so Lewis knew that he would have spare diving gear. To call his house a cabin describes the nature of its construction but is perhaps a bit too grand a word. Instead, the word 'shed' comes to mind. It had a porch that extended into a small pier, where a rowboat was tied. On it sat a lounger of animal hide, where a short man lay asleep.

Lewis called his name, "Chuck," and he shook himself awake. *The Lady* anchored, and Chuck gestured for a rope. Tom threw the rope down, so his host pulled it and tied it to the pier. Glove ordered the ladder to be lowered, and he, Tom, Maddy, Noah and Lewis disembarked. Adam, who was sleeping still, Elliott, who guarded the helm, and Doyle, who was sulking, remained on board.

Chuck was a stout but muscular man, with tanned skin like leather. The bone of his brow was prominent and shaded his brown eyes. His hair was shaved short, and he had a big grin, revealing square, once white teeth. Speaking with a high and nasal voice, which was soft but not quiet, Chuck replied in rather clear English, "Lewis, my friend! What brings you here on this day?"

"We're going to the Bazaar! And you know what that means," Lewis responded, before introducing, "Tom, er, Noah, Maddy, and Captain Glove."

"So, you, Tom, er, Noah, Maddy and Captain Glove all need some diving equipment?"

"Yes, so I said to them: Chuck – he's the man you want."

"Have you dived before, Captain Glove?"

Glove looked slightly confused. He understood the general idea of diving, but not in a sense that required the equipment spoken of. "Yes," he answered, "well…"

"No, he hasn't," Lewis interrupted helpfully.

"Don't worry, my friend, I will teach you, and then you will be all good to go to the bazaar." Chuck said increasingly loudly as he walked down his pier and porch and then down and around the side of his house. Lewis followed closely, then the others caught on and followed him. There was an even smaller building behind the house that Chuck opened and brought out a large canister, which looked to hold just short of three gallons. He then opened the door to an identical shed next to it and took out some hoses and belts and a jacket and a one or two other things.

"You're not in a rush, no?" he asked with a smile.

"Sort of," Tom said.

"Yes," said Glove.

"Alright, no worries, we can skip the training, just follow carefully with my demonstration," Chuck said, then he took four identical sets of equipment out of the second shed and passed them on to Glove, Tom, Maddy and Noah. The group wrestled with the tangle of hoses and observed with confusion. Their host then plonked a steel canister at their feet. He took back his own apparatus and began to talk the pirates through it all. He gave the impression that he had given such a demonstration before, but was just as delighted to do it again. Showing them how to attach the hoses to the tank, the tank to the jacket, and then the jacket to the hoses, he soon had each of them setting up their own diving gear. He then handed them a mask, showed them how to wear it and their entire set-up, and then how to take it off again.

Knowing that there would be help at the bazaar in the situation of anyone struggling, Chuck spoke only of the most vital of safety precautions. These included a slow, gradual descent, with frequent 'equalisation' of pressure (which means holding your nose and mouth shut and blowing, so the pressure in your ears is altered), and the procedure should the mouthpiece come away from you.

"You can take the equipment, as long as you promise to bring it back at some point, Lewis," Chuck said, handing the set he had demonstrated with to Lewis.

"Thank you, kind sir," Glove nodded, lifting his equipment eagerly to set off, then remembering, "but we could do with three more."

"Say no more," Chuck said, still smiling, going to his second shed and tossing the crew three more jackets and three more sets of hoses and three more belts and three more of the one or two other things. He then opened the first shed and tutted. "There's not enough air!"

"What?"

"There aren't enough full air canisters, you'll have to pick some up."

"Where can we pick some up?" Glove asked.

"On your boat, about an hour north of here."

"Anywhere to get it south of here?"

"Hmm, no, nowhere reputable."

"What do you mean by 'reputable'? How can air be reputable?" Maddy questioned.

"Safely checked by professionals."

"Why should our air have to be checked by professionals?" Glove scowled.

"Do you want to meet God?"

"Well, we want to go to Heaven."

"Then use reputable air! If you don't, it's straight back to Hell with you, and you can meet Satan and his elves and my cousin Shane!"

The pirates thanked the man, so subtly confused they didn't question a word. Chuck quickly ran back to the shed and tossed the crew a handful of rubber flippers in various sizes. There were more pairs than people, just to make sure each person could find an ideal pair. Lewis waved his friend goodbye, then they all boarded *The Lady Mary*.

The Lady Mary: main-deck

"I suppose you know how to reach this source of 'reputable air', Mr Plaque," Glove suggested.

"Do you have any money to buy it?"

"We have a little gold, will that do?"

"You have to understand that professionally certified air comes with quite the fee. Here's an idea, okay? Forget about what he said about reputable air; air's air."

"Right?"

"I know where we can get some cheaper air, and it's on the way to the stone-henge."

While this conversation took place, Tom and Noah explained to Elliott the ins and outs of the operation, and tried to demonstrate how the equipment worked. He caught on quickly, but struggled to arrange it all correctly. But he understood, and that was the main thing. At the proposal of a compromise of safety, he objected, "I don't think it's worth the risk, really. And besides, do we even need to go to the bazaar?"

"You won't regret it," Lewis insisted.

"We've taken the detour now," Glove added, "we've given Thatch a chance to gain on us. Of course, he has no real reason to attack us, but we need resources in case we have to fight him."

"We do have to fight him!" said Tom, "or else he'll destroy Earth!"

"Forget..." Glove interrupted before being himself interrupted.

"Okay then, we need to fight him to avenge her death!" Tom argued, not specifying who he meant by 'her', as it would only anger his father more.

"We need to get to her!"

Finding this exchange rather awkward, Lewis redirected the conversation towards the matter of air. Though Elliott was against the idea, the rest of the crew reached the consensus that they were to sail South, to meet 'Arnold' and buy some not so reputable air.

Arnold's Farm

Lewis had directed Glove to the Landmass on the other side of the sea, in which there was little architecture and mostly forest. He watched the trees intently for whatever sign that suggested that he was at his destination. When such an indication had presented itself, he told Glove to "anchor just here," so he ordered the anchor to be lowered, and it was.

Elliott brought to Glove a small pouch of gold coins.

"What happened to the rest of it?" the captain asked.

"We spent it on dinner, and then the rest on rum," Elliott reminded him.

"When? Oh, never mind when, just tell me, is this enough?"

"For two tanks, yes, maybe not three, unless you barter well."

"We are pirates."

"Yes, but Arnold is a strange sort of fella, which reminds me, only a few of you should come with me."

So, Lewis disembarked, Tom and Elliott with him. Elliott kept hold of the money, which he placed in his pocket. They used swords to cut through vines to make their way into the forest. They crossed paths with a pair of short, stout men, who appeared to be doing their best to remain hidden in these forests. Quietly, they beckoned the three pirates, who stumbled towards them. The first man swiftly drew a sword – a cutlass. With the press of a button on the sword's handle, the blade caught alight.

Threatened by this, the pirates stepped back, Tom drawing his own sword. At this, the two strangers looked surprised. In a Yorkshire accent, for some reason, the second man whispered, "No, you pillock, it's not a threat, it's for sale!"

Tom didn't actually respond to this; he just stared longingly at the weapon, brought back to the fun of yielding a flaming cutlass himself. Appreciating his desire for the sword, Elliott asked cautiously, "How much?"

"What you got?" the man with the sword asked, so Elliott turned away to hide the pouch of money as he took a single gold coin from it.

"How about some gold?" he offered, revealing the coin.

"That will get you an 'andle," the man responded, dropping his 'h'. Elliott turned around again and took a second coin from the purse, but the two men again rejected this offer. So Elliott looked at Tom again, who wanted to pretend that it wasn't a big deal.

"It's alright, Elliott, we need the gold anyway," Tom insisted, but hesitated, "well, erm."

And with that, Elliott took another coin from the money pouch, a larger, silver one, before announcing it was his "final offer." The man turned off the flame of the cutlass and handed it to Elliott in exchange for the coins, along with its scabbard. Then they snuck away, and the three pirates progressed onward.

Elliott smiled, grasped the cutlass within the scabbard and fastened the scabbard to his belt but immediately drew the sword from it, admiring the steel blade for a second, but ultimately being most impressed by the flame. The grin on his face gave an even larger smile to Tom, though this smile soon turned to a face of jealousy. The pair decided it was a worthwhile purchase.

It seemed that Lewis knew the way by the trees alone, for there was no sign of any man-made structure or modification to the landscape. That was until the trees thinned out and they saw before them a field. Stout stalks with broad leaves grew from purple, bulbous roots. Lewis pulled one from the ground: it was a turnip. He then bit the turnip. He then remembered that turnips aren't the kind of vegetable you eat raw. He then spat out the turnip.

"Welcome to Arnold's farm," he said, directing the other two to a small farmhouse in the middle of the field.

Arnold's farmhouse was basic and made of old logs. It smelt fusty as the door was opened, and no lights were on inside. There was a staircase on the landing that led upstairs, but Lewis walked past this and opened the cupboard under them. The cupboard under the stairs contained a second flight of stairs, which led down. Elliott brushed a cobweb from his face on his way down the stairs, which distracted him from a faint buzzing. The basement they found themselves in had concrete walls and a concrete floor. It had the same square footage as the ground floor of the farmhouse.

And in the middle of it, sat on his backside, was Arnold. It was clear that Arnold was not a human, but he had some human features. He could be described as an ape, but only in the same way in which an anthropoid alien can be described as a man, for he was no chimp, gorilla nor orang-utan, nor any extinct ape of Earth. But he had a large, round torso, with short legs and long arms, he was covered in amber fur, which was thickest on his head. His face was pale blue, and he had bright eyes, big cheeks and somewhat of a snout.

It took a few seconds for Arnold to register his visitors, but when he did, he recognised Lewis.

"Ah, it's you, John," he said in English, though it was unclear why he could speak it.

"No, I'm not John," Lewis corrected.

"Saul!"

"No."

"Simon?"

"No."

"Elliott?"

"I'm Elliott," Elliott said, waving.

"Ah, Elliott, I haven't seen you in ages!"

"You haven't seen him ever!" Lewis shouted.

"Right, Louise!"

"Louise? It's Lewis!"

"That's what I said!" Arnold yelled excitedly, revealing pointed but blunt canine teeth, "anyway, Louise."

"Lewis."

"What brings you here?"

Tom had lost his temper, so got to the point.

"We need air, and Lewis says you have some," he said, as Arnold got up and hauled himself using his long arms towards two big tanks at the back of the room. He slapped the tanks approvingly.

"Only the finest quality air, fermented straight from turnips."

"I'm not sure if fermented air is quite what we're after," Elliott tutted,

"Why, of course it is!" Arnold insisted, this is the finest air in Fractaige, has all the right gases in.

Tom took the pouch of gold from Elliott and asked, "Could we get three tanks for this?"

Arnold took the coins in his large, calloused, blue hands and observed them, turning each one over. He announced, "You can have one for this."

"One tank of air for a handful of gold?" Elliott protested, "It's flipping air! Air! For gold!"

"Come on, Arnold, for your old friend," Lewis tried to barter.

"Alright, Louie," he began.

"Lewis," Lewis corrected once more.

"Lewis, for you, two tanks."

"But –" Tom burst out, but Elliott consoled him.

"If you think about it, we don't all need to go to the bazaar. I, for one, am not too fussed abut diving down there."

"Alright, we'll take two tanks."

Arnold stood up on his crooked, stumpy legs and reached for two cylinders, a tad smaller than the ones Chuck had given them. He hooked them up to a pipe from a tap in the large tanks and let air flow into them. As air rushed past him, his long fur blew around, with flies buzzing out of it. The air leaking from the pipes smelt of rotten vegetables, making Elliott suspicious. There were two other suspicious sights that stood out in Arnold's basement. One was what looked to be a ton pile of turnips – all with their round bottoms sharpened to a point. The other was a row of plants under UV lights, with long stalks and almond-shaped leaves.

Tom addressed the former sight first, asking, "What are you doing with all those turnips?"

"I like turnips," Arnold said heartily and innocently, in a suspicious way.

"Yes, but why are they sharp?" Tom pried, but Arnold just whistled to himself and smiled. With no answer to this question, Elliott brought up the UV lights.

"What are those plants under those lights?"

"Wouldn't you like to know," their host laughed.

"That – that's why I asked."

"They're, erm, turnips."

"They don't look like turnips to me."

"They're a special kind of turnip, one I'm developing."

Elliott didn't believe this, so began with an "erm," before Arnold interrupted.

"I'm not being paid to answer questions, am I?"

Once the tanks were full, Arnold roughly passed them to Tom and Elliott, and neither of them was dying to stay much longer. So, they thanked Arnold, who then gifted them each a turnip, walked up the stairs and back through the turnip field. It felt to take less time to walk back to *The Lady* Marry than it had to walk from it.

Chapter II

The Lady Mary

Once the three men returned, they placed the two tanks of air with the others. These two tanks stuck out from the rest due to their battered state and smaller size. They also lack a series of stamps that were marked out on the others. Elliott explained to Glove that he'd watch the ship when they all went to the bazaar, so the lack of one tank was not an issue. Glove had already thought of this but thought it would be him to stay behind. They didn't reach a clarification of who would be the one to stay, but both were happy to do so.

The ship, now pointing in the correct direction, faced a horizon on which the sun was sat high in. The sea ahead of them lay straight and deep into this horizon, until it was interrupted by the bold, blue sky. A single dark ship could be seen on the sea. Its sails were full, yet it seemed sluggish and sad. And that it was, and so was its commander, for it was *The Golden Gander*.

The Golden Gander

Sings had kept *The Lady Mary* in her sights the entire time on Fractaige, but regretted doing so when she noticed that it had turned around; it was now sailing towards her. She knew she couldn't fight it with an unmanned, slowly sinking ship. But the same unmanned, slowly sinking ship had no chance of outrunning *The Lady* either. She huffed, then left the helm and opened the box of flags.

Drawing down the back Jolly-Rodger flag, she replaced it with the inverted version – a white flag with a black skull and crossbones. This flag denoted a conference between opposing parties – a parley. She looked again at the larger ship and tossed this flag back, taking a different flag out. This flag was entirely white. Shamefully, but decidedly, she raised the white flag of surrender, and waited for *The Lady* to respond.

The Lady Mary

"It's *The Gander*," Glove observed through his telescope.

"But no *Revenge*," Elliott noticed.

"The *Revenge* shouldn't be here yet," Glove said.

"Then neither should *The Gander*."

"Unless she followed us."

"Why would it follow us?"

"Same reason it's heading towards us now," Glove suggested, implying that it was there to attack, but then he noticed the white flag rise on the mast.

"It's just Sings," Elliott noted, "It's just her."

"Nonsense, it's got to be a trap."

"Look, I think the ship was attacked, she's on her own, and in trouble."

Glove looked at the gaping gap in the side of *The Gander* and saw the water spilling into it. "You think it was that Queen Anne beast?"

"I think you might be right, Captain."

"But she will have cannonballs, we don't."

"I have a feeling she won't use them."

"I hope you're right."

The two ships continued on their paths towards each other, Glove, Elliott and Sings looking down their telescopes. Maddy and Tom went to the gun-deck to man the cannons, which held the handful of cannonballs retrieved from Doyle's chest. Elliott, who had for some time felt guilty about using up the cannonballs, suggested that the crew could take the cannonballs from *The Gander* so that they didn't have to worry about being short on them anymore. He also suggested that the crew, which was already rather small for a ship of their size, would benefit from the skill and experience of Commander Amber Sings. Glove, being the way he was, refused at first, despite agreeing to take the cannonballs.

"Captain, you don't mean to say that we should board her ship, restrain her efforts and steal her cargo, only to leave her on the sinking ship to die, while we sail off."

Glove was tiring, and didn't want a moral argument, "She came to kill us, son."

"Shouldn't she get to confirm that at least?"

By now, there was only a ship's length between *The Lady Mary* and *The Golden Gander*. Telescopes were unnecessary, for they were close enough to hear each other. Despite this, Sings did not speak. She stood frozen on the side of the deck and waited without agency. Doyle, who had cheered up slightly, tossed grasping hooks over the flagpoles of *The Gander* and tied them down on his own vessel. Noah lowered the anchor, with the help of Doyle. Once the ships were secured to each other, Elliott slid a plank from one deck to the other. He and Doyle boarded *The Gander*, though neither communicated.

The Golden Gander

"We mean you no harm, Miss Sings," Elliott announced, "but we believe we're obliged to your ammunition under the conditions of your surrender."

Both men went to the gun-deck while Amber remained still, as if she were in a trance.

The Lady Mary: gun-deck

"Well, it doesn't seem like we're under attack," Tom noted.

"Maybe we should be the ones attacking," Maddy suggested, "After all, it won't take much to sink it."

"We don't need to sink it," Tom argued.

"Tom, these bastards have come after us! For God's sake, they work for the man who killed your mother!"

"But they're not he," Tom attempted to remain sensible, but it was Maddy, not him, who held the torch.

In a fit of un-sourced anger, Maddy lit both cannons. Within a second of each other, the two rounds fractured the wall of *The Gander* and, due to its previous injuries, large parts of its side gave way. A wave leapt in like a scavenger eager to feast on a not quite dead beast. But most scavengers, provided the correct number of pack-members and weakened state of their meal, are capable of hunting. This is as true of waves as it is of hyenas or crows. So, through the wound in the ship's side, subsequent gushes of water spilt into it.

The Golden Gander

The shots that had been fired rocked the ship, snapping one rope that bound it to *The Lady*. For *The Gander*'s anchor was not down, the back portion of the ship, now being free, attempted to drift forward. As the front was still tied to its adversary, *The Gander* pivoted around like a car going around a corner too quickly. The plank on which the men had boarded fell into the sea below.

Not only was the ship rotating, but it was quickly sinking. This pulled down on the second grappling rope, threatening to snap this one as well. The shaking and rocking had caused both Elliott and Doyle to drop their handfuls of cannonballs on their way up the stairs. Panicking, they ignored the cannonballs and rushed to the main-deck. Observing the worsening situation, Elliott broke his silence with Doyle and ordered him to make a run for *The Lady Mary*. So, he did, and he managed to find a ladder to help them all over. For some reason, he waited for Elliott to catch up before he crossed.

Elliott made his way towards Doyle, but first, he called to Amber, "Miss Sings!" he called to her.

The chaos had shaken Amber out of her daze, so she was conscious enough to correct her title to, "Commander Sings!"

"I fear you won't be the commander of anything for much longer!" Elliott ordered her priorities, "so, come on."

Elliott directed Amber to the crossing point and helped her over. Doyle told Elliott to go first and ran back to scoop up as many cannonballs as he could. Elliott didn't realise this but was about to cross himself when he clumsily stood on a broken rung of the ladder, and it snapped. He fell onto his hands, suspended above the air on the ladder, but Amber grabbed his arm, helping him reach the deck. But the ladder wasn't the worst thing to snap, for at the same time, the rope did, and *The Gander* slipped away from *The Lady*, Doyle still on it.

Rather instinctively, Elliott grabbed a rope and threw it over to Doyle, who grabbed it in his one free hand but had little way to actually get across. The rope between the two men became taut, and both realised that Doyle would have to jump, so he did with brief hesitation. He hit the water very close to *The Lady* and was glad the rope hadn't been a foot shorter than he would have been swung into the side of the ship. Elliott tied the rope to a hook when Doyle announced he was about to ascend and offered a hand when he reached the top.

The Golden Gander struggled to stay above the waterline, and the surrounding sea bubbled as air was released from its corpse. Amber swore under her breath at the sight. Before she even got another word in, Glove ordered that she be taken to the brig, and so Doyle and Tom escorted her there. With the nonchalance you may have come to expect from her, she went silently with them. Glove and Elliott watched *The Golden Gander* disappear into the waves when they noticed another ship.

It was half the size of *The Lady*, and despite the distance away it was, it was clearly a much more modern ship. It had sails, but these were crisp, bright white, not the stained and yellowed canvas of *The Lady*. Its body was constructed from a combination of steely blue metal and pale wood, with no sign of wear or damage on a spotless exterior. There was a group of sailors on it. Most of them wore white or blue shirts with dark trousers and body warmers you could have guessed they insisted on calling gilets. The closest, however, wore a grey worsted suit.

As they approached, it was noticed that the ship had no cannons, so, while still hesitant, Glove did not order a response to the approaching vessel. Another, smaller ship became visible from behind the first, again unarmed and manned only by one sailor. This ship had no sails but appeared to run by motor. The suited man appeared to prepare to engage with the crew of *The Lady*.

"Good day, good sir!" the man greeted brightly. To this, Glove tipped his hat and nodded.

"May we interest you in this fine Berkshire 3000 S model sailboat?" the man asked in an attempt to sell the ship he was sailing on.

"No thanks," Glove forced a smile and looked away from the salesman.

"How much?" Tom asked as he returned from the brig.

"We don't have any gold, son," Glove said through gritted teeth. This didn't stop Tom from admiring the refined and sleek nature of the new ship.

"How much?" Tom asked again, but was cut off.

"We won't be purchasing any boats today, good day to the lot of you!"

"But Blackbeard has three — I mean, two — ships, so why shouldn't we?"

"We don't have the crew for two ships! If we aren't all on the same ship, we'll face so many unnecessary problems – leave off it, boy!"

Getting the message, Tom stopped asking, and the salesmen left.

"They rip you off anyway, that lot," Lewis muttered to Tom, adding, before he snook away, "my guys will give you a better deal."

Despite his father's stubbornness, Tom thought of the joys of sailing on a new and fancy ship like the one he had just seen. He also remembered the brief time which he was a captain himself. He had actually been captain for five whole years, but as there was little to do in this time, it didn't feel as long as this. The longing encouraged him to counter Glove's statement.

"You know, we have other things I bet we could sell for a ship."

Glove frowned before replying, "What did I say?"

"You said we couldn't afford it, and that it would cause problems, but I bet since it looked to be in such nick, it wouldn't take much manning."

"I don't care; I'm not allowing it."

"Why?"

"Because you're acting out of envy, not sense! We don't even have any money to buy cannonballs in the bazaar, and you want to spend more on a ship we don't need just to feel important again!"

"If I may, captain," Elliott tried to help, but Glove, in his fury, refused.

"No, you may not! It's your fault we don't have cannonballs; it's your fault we don't have any money left!"

Glove had lost his temper entirely, so turned to each member of his crew, ignoring any newcomers, and took his anger out on them.

"And Miss Casserole: we had a ship right in front of us, and you had to go and shoot at it, for no reason! You want a ship; that was the chance! But that's not all, no! Lumberlodge is too lazy to even show his face, Doyle's so greedy he got Tudor killed, and on that matter, Mr Boris was so full of himself he thought he could fight a fifty bloody foot long lizard!" Glove panted after this, but began again before anyone could argue with him, "I've looked after you lot, raised you, fed you, trained you, and this is all the payoff I get! I'm gonna get theological here, but Envy, Gluttony, Wrath, Sloth, Greed and Pride, do you lot know what that means? Sin! That's all I get from you, is it?"

In Tom's entire life, he had never seen his father as furious as he was now, and being in that kind of shock which you can only respond to with humour, he chuckled, "There's seven sins, father, you forgot one."

This only fuelled the fire, causing Glove's face to burn red. Tom bit his lip, but sighed in relief when Elliott intervened. Despite the volatile state of his captain, Elliott got a word in to remind him of the prisoner downstairs. This didn't calm him, but distracted him.

"Come on, Elliott, let's go and pay Miss Sings a visit."

The brig

Only one cell of the brig had not been repurposed into Elliott's chicken coop. So, it was this cell, which received far less torchlight, in which Amber stood. She leant against the bars that enclosed her and sulked silently. Some pirates, she included, wore dark makeup under their eyes – this was to shield the eyes from the bright sun's rays (she profusely denied the notion that it was simply an aesthetic choice). Regardless of its purpose, this makeup now ran down her face, though it was unclear whether tears, sweat or seawater was the driving force behind this.

She heard her captors' approaching footsteps but acted as if she were unaware of their presence. Glove had not yet calmed down entirely

"Miss Sings, I've heard much about your skill as a helmsman," Glove attempted to get her to engage.

"Helmswoman," Elliott corrected with a chuckle, not much to the amusement of Glove nor Amber.

Glove continued with, "We saved your life, the least you can do is talk."

"What is there to talk about?" she mumbled, her eyes on the ground.

"Why were you sailing towards us? The stone-henge is in the south, but you were sailing towards us."

"I don't have a map," she replied, allowing Glove to infer the rest of her point.

"Why weren't you with your flagship?"

"He told me to follow you."

"And what were you going to do when you reached us?"

"I don't know."

"You don't know!"

"Kill you, I guess," she said a little more boldly, this increase in volume mostly because of panic.

"Kill us?"

"He told me to!" Amber flustered and stepped away from the bars of her cell.

Chapter III

The Lady Mary: **main-deck**

It took little more sailing until the sea widened, and Lewis instructed the crew to look out for signs of the bazaar. Glove, who had calmed down slightly due to this greater distraction, suggested that the crew should assemble their diving kit. And so they did — Maddy, then Noah, then Doyle, then Lewis, then the captain himself. Each took air canisters from the back, taking the certified air and avoiding the more dubious, uncertified equivalent, though this may have been subconscious for many of them.

"We don't have any gold, lad," Glove told Lewis, asking, "so what do you reckon should be our substitute for this ol' bazaar?"

"You don't need gold, you'd be no good with gold down there, anyway. All them daft aquatic sods value as currency is good old humble rust. Any metal too, but the rustier, the better."

"I beg your pardon?"

"Rust! Don't tell me you don't have rust!"

"Oh, we have rust," Tom laughed, "If they want rust, we'll give them rust!"

Tom then put his hand on Doyle's shoulder and asked him to "get the Tin."

"What tin?" Doyle asked blankly, clearly not listening to the others.

Tom pressed his hands against his eyes and took a second to answer, "What do you mean 'what tin'? What other tin could I be talking about?"

"Depends on what you wanted — a tin of beef? A tin of beans?"

"Rust! A tin of rust! Listen, man!"

"Alright! What, you want, the tin?"

"Yes, I want the tin! I asked for the tin!"

"Well, if you want the tin, I'll go and get the tin," Doyle said nonchalantly, before Maddy interrupted him.

"Go and get the tin!" she said, smacking him on the back and encouraging him to get on with it.

Elliott, who had nipped down to see if Adam wished to join them at the bazaar, told Glove, "Adam won't be joining you, though he has asked that we bring him something back."

"I'll have a see what I can find for him," Lewis suggested, knowing the bazaar better than the rest.

"Well then," said the captain, who had noticed neither Tom nor Elliott had set equipment up, "we don't need two of you to stay also – in fact, we need as many feet in the ground down there to ensure we get what we need."

"Be my guest," Elliott said to Tom, being hesitant about going diving himself.

"No, Elliott, why don't you go and enjoy yourself?"

"No, I insist."

"No, I insist!"

"Oh, flip a coin, boys!" Glove commanded to hurry the decision.

"We don't have any," Elliott muttered, so Tom made his own suggestion.

"Rock, paper, scissors?" He said, and so they did just that. Best of three, they declared before it began. Elliott first chose rock, Thomas choosing scissors. One - nil to Elliott. Again, Elliott picked rock, Tom doing the same, and therefore this match was a draw. The next two matches were identical: Elliott remained steadfast to his hand gesture of choice, while Tom bested it with paper.

"You win," Elliott said, partly relieved until Tom suggested that, as victor, he got to choose who went to the bazaar. He chose Elliott, not because he didn't want to go himself, but that he wanted his friend to more. He did, however, set up the diving equipment for him since it was he who had received professional instruction, as insisted by Elliott.

The sea above the Bazaar

There were many vessels of all sizes and technological ability sitting anchored in rows just ahead of a large bay on the continent to their left. Men on speedboats had glowing sticks like those who direct pilots at airports have. In the same fashion as such people, they guided boats into parking spaces denoted by buoys, with smaller boats in one area closer to the shore, and larger ones like *The Lady* further out. Glove steered his ship carefully, ordering the crew to take in the sails. He didn't much listen to the men with the glowing sticks, who surrounded *The Lady* and called to him in a plea to co-operate. Yet eventually, the ship was parked; its canvasses folded up in their entirety, and the anchor lowered.

Once each person had aided the next in getting into their diving vests, with the canisters of air attached, they placed their masks on and prepared for their first ever experience diving. They then stumbled around the rocking ship to put on their fins. Two small boats with electric motors chugged their way towards *The Lady*, stopping at its ladder, so that the crew might climb down and board them.

Before they had noticed these ships, the contents of the Tin-o-tetanus had been shared somewhat evenly between the members, though when Doyle attempted to take slightly more, Glove took this from him and kept it himself. They fitted the rusty scraps into pockets and belts, which had little space in since they had all removed their large coats and jackets. Glove handed his son the stone, which he had placed in a smaller, silver locket than he had handed to Thatch.

"Take care of it, son," he ordered, "It's our surest way to her."

In each ship was a driver, though of the last sort of people you would expect to be in a boat. By this, I mean mermaids. They immediately began talking cordially upon their arrival. The mermaid in the closest boat was clearly the taller of the pair. Not that she was tall, more that her company was rather short. With a smile, the first mermaid announced herself as Charlie and asked for no more than four people to climb down to her boat.

No one was fast to volunteer, but ultimately, out of awkwardness, Elliott stepped forward. He considered himself the clumsiest crewmember at the best of times, never mind when he had two ridiculous rubber flippers on his feet. When he got to the first rung of the ladder, which ran down the side of the boat, he slowly turned around to put his back to the water below him. When he tried to take a step, the flipper caught the side of the deck, and flicked back like elastic when Elliott forced it down. This force struck a barnacle from the wood, which splashed fifteen feet under him.

Charlie looked at the second mermaid, who was named Neve, and the two laughed with each other. When Elliott heard this, his face became rubescent. "Is this your first time diving, perchance?" Charlie smiled. Elliott laughed and replied, trying to hide his embarrassment.

"What makes you say that?"

"You've got your fins on!" Neve said in a less calm tone, "You could have waited until you got there!"

Doyle swiftly kicked his flippers off so he could justify saying, "Yeah, Elliott — and you're supposed to be the smart one!"

The rest of the pirates looked at each other in realisation and laughed at their mistake. Elliott would have claimed that Doyle's comment didn't have any meaning to him, and this was true, for he was able to take a joke. But this doesn't mean it didn't have an effect on him, as it caused him to subconsciously rush his descent. He thought, in misjudgment, that he could remove his flippers while on the ladder. Keeping his left arm and leg firmly planted, he raised his right leg so that he could grab the end of the fin. But he couldn't reach the bottom, and this is where it attached to his foot.

As he tugged on the end of the flipper, he forced his leg up to an unnatural angle, causing his left leg to give way to relieve the tension. And the side of *The Lady* was slippery, so his hand alone could not hold him to the ladder. So, with much kicking and splashing, Elliott landed in the water by Charlie's boat. In distress, he didn't think to inflate his diving vest or put his mask over his face, but just reached around until he could grab the side of the boat and haul himself onto it, his air tank clanking behind him. "I made I pig's-ear of that!" he said heartily as he recollected his thoughts.

The rest of the crew, learning from their unfortunate friend's mistakes, boarded the two ships with relative ease, factoring in the unfamiliar weight of the equipment on their backs. Elliott, Glove, Doyle and Lewis sat in two rows of two in the first ship, leaving room in the middle of its length for the driver's tail, which they thought it would be rude to ask about. But it was a sight unlike anything the pirates had seen. It was no longer than a typical pair of legs, but coated in a skin of smooth, opalescent scales, which made the sunlit boat even brighter. Her tail was fluked, which increased the total length by a few feet. Each fluke was intricately patterned with subtly different sized and shaded scales, as was as having tidy folds in its resting state.

Despite being out of the water, neither the mermaids' tails nor skin appeared at all dry or out of place. While many mermaids are traditionally described in a state of nature, the context of a public gathering socially mandated at least some level of clothing, which was coordinated with the colour of their scales.

The remaining pirate and cowboy, Noah and Maddy, boarded Neve's ship, but the smaller number of people, combined with this mermaid's shorter tail, made the ordeal less precarious. While Charlie's fawn skin made her tail look lighter, Neve's skin would lead you to believe that Irish mermaids exist. While the scales on her tail were likely no different in tone from her friend's, they appeared to warmer and easier on the eye when contrasted to white, freckled skin. In fact, the only difference in the scales of either mermaid's tail was the slightest difference in hue: Neve's being bluer while Charlie's was pinkish white.

I appreciate this is a lot of rambling about mermaids' tails, but I just want to paint the picture of what sort of mermaids we're dealing with. Not reptilian, hardly human sirens, but the more elegant interpretation of a woman who happens to have a tail (and it is a dysphemism to compare this to a fish's).

Once they were all in, the mermaids switched on the boats' engines and the two groups floated along, through and in-between rows of neatly parked ships. They could hear the sound of waves crashing on the distant shore and even the sound of gulls, as well as the unclear talking and moving about of people. Within the centre of the large bay, where there were no boats parked, it was clear that the water was quite deep. A dock floated on the border between the parking area and clear waters, and on it sat a large, bright sign, reading 'The Underwater Bazaar of Fractaige'.

"That's a lovely ship you have there," Neve commented, "looks very, erm, vintage."

"Are you pirates?" Charlie asked with curiosity.

"Yes, we are, and you're a, you're a, a…" Glove stammered in disbelief.

"A mermaid? Yes."

"I can't believe we're meeting real pirates!" Neve called to her friend in delight.

"You can't believe it?" Elliott laughed, finally over his previous embarrassment.

"Since this is your first time diving," Neve said, "I take it you have never visited the bazaar before."

"I have," Lewis said smugly, "but these lot haven't."

"Not to worry," Charlie replied, "It's our job to talk you through it."

"So, the bazaar sits forty feet down in this bay. Many currencies or materials are accepted as payment. We're going to take you over to the diving point, where you will jump off this boat and descend to the market square."

"It is very important, you must understand, that when you return up, you must ascend from the market square again, or else you might become too personal with the keel of a ship."

"Or worse: the propellers!"

The boats continued towards the floating structure, where they stopped at a gate controlled by a security guard. The security guard, who was also a mermaid, sat in a chair, who was paying no attention. Charlie called to get this mermaid's attention, presumably using a personal nickname, "Fernypie!"

The security guard, who was called Fern, not Fernypie, shook themself to attention.

"We've got ourselves some real pirates!" Charlie announced proudly, as if she had had any actual effect on this occurrence.

"Oh, my golly-gosh," Fern said, ironically, but still impressed, proceeding to lift the barrier.

The boats slowly drifted to the other side of the barrier, Elliott said, "I don't know why you're so amazed by us. You know, it's us who should be impressed by you, we're just people."

"But we don't get many Earth people here, that's the point," Charlie insisted.

"Enough of that, we're here," Neve cut in, ordering all the crew to prepare for descent. So now, they all returned their flippers to their feet, checked their air tanks, sand strapped on their masks. Finally, one by one, they sat on the side of the boat, placed their mouthpieces in, and allowed themselves to fall backwards into the sea below. Each person took a different amount of time to do this, but eventually, they were all treading water and trying to avoid collisions with each other. "Remember to ascend at the market square, I hope you find what you are here for," Charlie smiled as the two boats left the pirates in the water.

The sea was warm, making their lack of wetsuits a forgettable mistake. One by one, the crew remembered how to inflate their vests, which they did by pressing a button on a device attached. Elliott, though he was alone in this, believed he could taste the aroma of boiled vegetables through his mouthpiece, though he was unsure since he wasn't able to smell it. Glove removed the mouthpiece from his own mouth and said, "Remember what he told us?"

"Yes, we need to deflate our vests," Doyle replied.

"But we just inflated them," Maddy said in response.

"He's right, though," Lewis ensured.

So, they held the device that controlled the air, which was connected to the vest via a tube, above their heads, and held down a button to release gas. The jackets hissed as they shrivelled down, and the crew sank slowly, their bodies vertical. After about five feet, Lewis reminded them to equalise by pointing to his nose, so all remembered to hold their noses and mouths while forcing a breath, causing their ears to receive this pressure. Lewis then also kicked slowly to orient his body horizontally, so everyone else mimicked, then followed as he swam towards the market.

As they swam slowly downwards, occasionally deflating their vests further and equalising their ears, the light of the distant bazaar penetrated the green, only slightly murky, water. Elliott thought to mention this, though was bitterly disappointed when he came to the realisation that he couldn't speak while wearing the diving gear. When he tried, salty water entered his mouth, distracting him for a while, making him bump into Doyle's flipper. Doyle, not realising that it wasn't himself at fault, turned round and waved in apology.

When they were twenty feet from the floor of the market square, dim, blue lampposts lit the stone slabs which lined it and had turned green with algae. The crew stopped swimming to orient themselves vertically again as they let the last pockets of air out of their vests. Slowly, though some faster than others, their feet met the ground. When they did, Elliott and Doyle both slipped around as they heavily placed their feet on slimy tiles. Lewis showed them that their flippers, which had small studs on their top, folded in on themselves to point these studs down, and reduce their drag. The crew all did this to their flippers and found their footing on the paved seabed.

The Lady Mary

Thomas sat on the deck of *The Lady*, slightly bored and wishing he had chosen to go below the sea. He thought he could pass the time by going to his and Adam's room and lying in his hammock. His friend's eyes were closed, but Tom had the feeling he was awake. And he didn't need to ask to confirm this when Adam asked, "So he's really dead?"

Tom sighed, as he hadn't himself given it enough thought, "Yes, he is, he's dead."

"So, it was all bullshit?"

"What?"

"'The key to everlasting life,' that's what we were told. That was the promise, and that's why we all went along with it. But it was bullshit."

"Maybe that changed when we made the deal."

"I said we never should have done that. We never should have done any of it."

"We never knew this would happen."

"That's the point! We didn't know, so why did we bother?"

"Because no one would achieve anything if we only did the things we know the ending of. Other than dying, what can we ever know?"

"I know that if I lie in bed, I'll eventually fall asleep."

"And I suppose that's why you do it so much," Tom joked, though the answer he received was no joke.

"Exactly."

"But it's no life, is it?"

The locket, which had been shut firmly to enclose the magical piece of geology, for some reason chose to be shut no longer. The stone itself had gone a while with no ghostly apparitions, but this streak was about to end. It was only the light from the cloud that the stone created that caused Adam to open his eyes.

On a black night, a starving black stallion hung its head over a stable door, neglecting to repel the flies which crawled over its hide. A man, once stout but left only short and frail by his own hunger, woke the animal and slid on loose tack, though it responded to none of this. The cart the skinny horse had to pull held three coffins, stacked vertically. Moving slowly and on a split hoof, the horse complied with its duties and pulled the cart and coffins to a churchyard. It walked straight through fields, which mothered no crop but withered, white leaves and the chaff from grain harvested too early.

Once the horse and its master had reached the cemetery, the three coffins met only one, six-foot grave. Silently and solemnly, by two men who looked no better off than those inside, the coffins were lowered into the hole, the next being stacked onto the one below. Hardly a foot of soil was laid over the final coffin lid. Row by row, the bodies in coffins were laid to rest in the same fashion, filling the churchyard and leaving great piles of soil which had been replaced with the dead.

It wasn't this sight, however grim, that made Thomas sit up. It was instead a sight from within a larger, grand house of brick and wood. In the dining room of this building sat dozens of men in black dinner jackets and grey striped trousers. Each was accompanied by a woman wearing a grand dress with a magnificent skirt. As expected from their location within the house, they were dining. Their meal was as splendid as their tailoring, comprising great joints of roasted meats and whole, fat birds and plates of roasted vegetables and bread to soak up the juices. Then came wines, then cheeses, then ports.

"Would you look at that food, Adam," Tom remarked, though he may as well have been talking to himself, "I bet I could get us some good food in the bazaar."

Eventually, Adam registered what his friend had said, and asked, "Then why aren't you there?"

"Because I need to guard the ship," Tom said drearily, adding after, "but."

"But what?" Adam failed to sense the direction of the conversation.

"Since you're up, you could watch the ship, and I could go."

"Bring us some food back then," Adam was more than welcoming to the idea of more food variety.

The two left their room, Adam taking longer to get up than Tom, and made their way to the deck to sort out the remaining set of diving equipment. Tom then realised that he had no currency; no rust to purchase anything at all.

"They get to go down there and spend the loot of Tin-o-tetanus, and I get left with bugger all!" he laughed in an unappreciative way.

"What do you want that rusty old shite for?" Adam asked, not entirely caught up with the situation.

"It's the going money down there, apparently. At least according to Lewis."

"Well, there's got to be some rust still lying about on a pirate ship," Adam suggested.

"Doyle, the greedy sod," Tom remarked, "I bet he's got something in that old box he has been keeping away from us."

So, that was what Tom was looking for. Under beds and benches, in cupboards, beneath floorboards and within walls, he searched until he found Doyle's wooden box. He couldn't resist eating a single slice of beef from an unopened tin, then turned bits of steel, iron, lead and brass around to find the most oxidised pieces. These included a handful of the rustiest nails, an aged compass and a thimble. Placing them in his trouser pocket, he put together the diving equipment, his tank being the remaining tank bought from Arnold.

Acknowledging that he would likely require a boat to come and retrieve him, he held his fins under his arm and looked out in search of one. He used the flippers to wave when he saw Charlie in her boat about a quarter of a mile away.

"Hello!" he called. However loud he was, and he was loud, the waves and wood absorbed his voice. Charlie had no passengers in her boat but was not on the lookout for distant travellers wishing to board. What eventually grabbed her attention was gunfire. Adam's gunfire.

This caused the mermaid to turn and view *The Lady* and finally notice Thomas waving his fins in an exaggerated fashion. After turning around, the small electric boat weaved its way through the formation of anchored ships and made its way to this signal. Charlie approached with a comically uncertain look on her face, but this turned to a smile when she looked Tom in the eye. When Tom asked to be taken to the bazaar, she welcomed him aboard. Rather than climbing down the ladder, he leapt right off of *The Lady* and splashed in the water, sunk, allowed himself to float back up, and carried this momentum to lift himself onto the small boat.

Like a wet dog, he shook himself dry and grinned at his host.

"Hello," he said, trying not to laugh. This was a disguise that Charlie saw straight through.

"What's so funny?" she smiled back.

"I'm sorry," Tom smirked, "I just don't know what the acceptable way to react to a woman with a fishtail is."

Charlie whacked Tom with the fluke of her tail at this comment, he being relieved that it wasn't as slimy as a fish's.

"I'd love to live on a pirate ship like yours," Charlie changed the subject, shamelessly fishing for an invitation, though Tom changed it a second time.

"How good is the food down there?"

"Do you like seafood?"

"Of course, I do live on a boat."

"Ah, clever point," Charlie laughed, as she thought, "I could tell you about it all, but maybe it would be easier for me to come and help you pick it out."

The bazaar: in the water

Elliott couldn't help but feel queasy. Which he thought was odd, as he didn't feel as stressed as he'd imagined he would, and his heart rate was steady. In fact, he didn't feel stressed at all; he felt rather confident, smiling through his breathing apparatus. When the captain had figured out how to effectively sign 'cannonballs', Elliott took up the task apply and paced confidently away in search of an appropriate vendor. He couldn't see very far, as a tall forest of kelp lined the view, but lines of market stalls sat nestled within this underwater jungle. The pale lights seemed to have within them colonies of tiny, luminescent creatures, which made Elliott laugh at an unwarranted level.

But he composed himself to focus on the task at hand, which was replenishing the cannonballs he had himself used up. As he walked towards the market stalls, his movements were slow and exaggerated in order to combat water resistance. He could make out the shapes of other people, some in gear more advanced than his, who too were shopping at the bazaar. In fact, the stalls were rather crowded, people pushing their way through to the front, where they were greeted by a menagerie of water-dwelling beings of various forms.

Charlie's boat

When they arrived at the diving point, Tom agreed to let Charlie guide him to the best seafood stalls. As he sat himself up on the edge of the boat, Charlie tied her braided hair behind her head, revealing to Tom what appeared to be gills underneath the bottom corners of her jawbone. He didn't want to make a fuss, for he hardly knew her, nor anything about mermaid anatomy, but couldn't help but stare at this feature. Her gills were not particularly grotesque, rather, they were subtle, but the idea of breathing through the side of your neck confused the pirate. Charlie noticed his curious expression, so laughed, but pushed him off of the boat with both hands.

"You bugger!" Tom spat water from his mouth. He wasted no time, so grabbed the mermaid by her hands and pulled her into the water. He then realised two things: maybe that wasn't an appropriate way to treat a stranger; and that forcing a mermaid into water wasn't an effective form of revenge.

"Are you ready to submerge?" Charlie asked Tom in a way that suggested she doubted his competence.

"Alright then," Tom said with zero sense of uncertainty.

"You sure?"

"Yes," Tom grumbled, "I just have to do this."

By this, he meant he had to deflate his jacket. When he tried this, he noticed nothing happened (because he was still kicking). The mermaid took the device from him and pressed the 'inflate' button, making Tom go "ah-ha" as he realised he had been kicking frantically to stay afloat, when he could have been buoyant effortlessly. She made sure he refrained from kicking, then told him to deflate as he had attempted previously. "Follow me," she said, placing the mouthpiece, which Tom should have put on already, in his mouth forcefully, then diving gracefully forwards below the surface.

The Lady Mary

Adam had stood gasping out to sea for a while, so contemplated going back to bed, deciding quickly. He was strongly in favour of that idea, but as he was about to, someone called his name. He recognised the voice; it was Lewis's. "Come and see what I got you!" he called, bobbing up and down in the calmly rocking water.

"You come here," Adam replied quickly. Lewis folded down his flippers and walked carefully up the ladder, making sure he didn't slip with the heavy steel air canisters on his back.

He deflated his vest when he boarded the ship, water dripping from his body and his gear.

"What is it, then" Adam was eager to find out.

"Three words," Lewis said, placing eight balls of metal in his hand, "anti-gravity bullets."

The bullets, which were round as to be fired from a musket, were standard with the exception that they were heavier for their size than lead, and had small, almost unnoticeable engraved patterns.

Adam did not look amused. He dropped one on the floor.

"Looks like gravity to me, not that I've read anything written by Isaac Newborn."

"Newton," Lewis corrected, before remembering, "wait, no. That was it; they were 'gravity bullets.' They increase gravity when you shoot with them. Supposed to implode the victim or something. I'm only going off diagrams, they didn't have a demo."

Adam was not convinced but grabbed his musket and loaded one into it. Unfortunately for it, a poorly timed seagull flew overhead. He shot it, and it fell promptly to the ground.

"'Gravity bullets,' yeah right," Adam scoffed.

"It fell down, didn't it?" Lewis pointed out, "That's gravity, isn't it?"

"That happens when you shoot any bird with any bullet, nothing special. I hope you know you have been scammed."

The Bazaar

Elliott was on his way to buy cannonballs when a strange creature swam past his face. It had the smooth body of a shark, but was the size of an average carp. But more notably, it had two projecting, forward-facing, comically large and ridiculous-looking eyes. It also opened and shut its mouth like a goldfish as it swam.

In line with his character, though with a greater degree of distraction than typical, Elliott burst out in laughter. There was no one he knew around him to share this comedy with. In fact, no one around him could hear his laugh, as it was inhibited by the mouthpiece, which was supplying him with air, which he was now certain tasted like sweet vegetables. Perhaps less in line with his character, he felt compelled to follow it, forgetting remarkably quickly the job expected of him.

So, he speed-walked through the bazaar, which was becoming more crowded and labyrinthine, chuckling to himself, then gasping for air to compensate. Doyle caught a glimpse of these antics, but lost track of him before he could intervene.

Queen Anne's Revenge

Thatch was ruthless, but he was patient. The stops made by Glove and his crew had, as Glove had feared, given Blackbeard time to catch up. He steered his ship one-handed, his other plaiting his beard thoughtlessly. Through his telescope, he saw, about three miles away, the parked ships waiting above the bazaar.

There were ships of all sizes, but by far the tallest, due to its main mast, sails and flags, was *The Lady Mary*. Its coloured flag featured the typical Jolly-Roger, but also a man with a green feathered hat that looked like Peter Pan. The bow this figure was carrying, however, clarified that the design was going for Robin Hood.

"There she is!" Thatch said with sinister delight, "He's blundered! We can take him out now! There can only be one man to take all."

"What is he thinking?" Israel Hands remarked.

"Whatever the rest of them are, whatever that may be. But that makes no difference to us."

"You reckon Glove's on board?"

"One of them will be: Glove, his young first-mate, or his lad Thomas, or maybe the brother. One of them, anyway."

"I suppose that makes no difference either. They'll sink just the same."

"If we decide to sink them," Blackbeard said.

"Why wouldn't we sink them?" the quartermaster queried.

"Where's the fun in that?" the captain grinned, lighting a cigar that had been brought to him with the flame of a lamp.

The Lady Mary

"Come on, Adam," Lewis insisted, "try again, just one more!"

"Alright then, you mad bastard," Adam laughed as he loaded another bullet and round of gunpowder into his gun. Lewis placed a glass on top of the railing along the side of the deck and suggested Adam use it as a grounded target. So he did, standing fifteen feet away from it. He hit the target, but the glass shattered and spread outwards as expected, not imploding as suggested.

"I'm getting my money back!" Lewis huffed, heading straight back for the water. He didn't wait for a lift, but he believed he knew the area well enough to descend early. Adam placed the 'gravity bullets' into an empty pocket on his belt and buttoned it shut with no intent of opening it soon.

Before the Bazaar

Charlie swam, as you may expect from her species, with fluency and grace. Having gills, she did not exhale such a noticeable trail of bubbles as Tom was doing as he breathed through his mouthpiece. The mermaid was considerate of her company's terrestrial nature, so moved patiently and watched behind her to make sure there were no technical difficulties. Tom had at some point forgotten to equalise his ears, being reminded by a painful ache.

The Bazaar

People stepped out of the way of Elliott, who was running, fixated on the fish he was chasing. His breathing had become even more eccentric, and his laughter stronger. He wasn't paying any attention, but the meter that showed him his air levels was swiftly falling. He also paid no attention to any of his friends who tried to confront him, the impossibility of verbal communication amplifying this issue.

The strange fish had avoided capture but remained only a few yards ahead of its pursuer. Despite his comical feeling, Elliott kept his eyes locked on his target, and his pace matched it. He completed circuits around the bazaar, though oblivious to this, even passing arms-dealers from whom he could certainly have purchased cannonballs. It was even apparent to himself that he was in a dangerously unserious mood, but the thought itself did nothing to change that.

Queen Anne's Revenge

Timber and steel groaned and whistled as the *Revenge* shoved its way through the blanket of anchored ships at the bazaar, its great sails casting them in darkness. She was, of course, heading towards *The Lady Mary,* making no attempt to do so subtly or carefully. The few people aboard their vessels called and yelled, but little could be done.

The Lady Mary

Adam was, perhaps surpassingly, on deck, but he was sitting down, his eyes closed. Adam was very aware of his surroundings, but not always responsive to them. This gave Blackbeard the perfect opportunity to line his ship up with *The Lady* to prepare for an invasion. Israel Hands slid a board quietly to the deck of the other ship after the *Revenge* was anchored firmly in the parking space of a small boat, which had been pushed rudely aside. He then stepped aside for his captain to board first, five of their best men behind him.

Adam, though he wasn't conscious, faced the incoming crew of the *Revenge*, armed with no other weapon but his unloaded musket beside him. Thatch did not yet advance, but pressed his foot on the plank to make it creek, to test the awareness of his rival. Adam did wake, loading his musket instinctively, and it's his new 'gravity bullets.' While a musket takes maybe thirty seconds to reload, fifteen for Adam, Thatch knew he could not reach Adam in the time remaining.

He knew from the look on his face that Adam was about to shoot, so he did something rather cruel. He stepped to the side, as if he knew exactly when Adam would fire his gun, exposing Hands, whose vision had been obstructed by the captain's hat. Though it had no effect in defying any of Newton's laws, it hit the quartermaster in the mouth, and he dropped dead.

Thatch drew his own pistol, which was loaded, pointed it at Adam, and boarded *The Lady*.

The Bazaar

When Tom had reached the bazaar, he found himself in the sort of trance often compared to a boy in a sweet shop. While he was a bit too old fit be considered a child, and the stalls in front of him sold fish, the reaction remained the same. He stared at fish being removed from ovens, which spat out the water when they opened and closed, people trying small samples by removing their masks. He only wished he could have smelt it all, for he imagined all the unfamiliar herbs and spices that could have been present. Being underwater, he couldn't.

Tom wanted to get closer to try some of the food. He pushed his way to the front as respectfully as was possible, Charlie floating above him. When handed a small sliver of some sort of cooked flesh by a green and amphibious-looking figure, he took a deep breath before removing his mouthpiece. By the time the food reached his tongue, seawater had rushed in as well. He spat but struggled to dry his mouth while retaining his sample of food. When Charlie had finished her own, unfazed by the salty water, she pointed to Tom's mouthpiece, made him put it on, then blew bubbles. He copied, pushing the water successfully out of his mouth and replacing it with air. However, he then had to remove it again from his jaws in order to chew.

Rather disappointingly, Tom tasted only two things. The first was more obvious and expected: salt. The second, the flavour that he could just decipher, was turnip. He thought of the air he had purchased from Arnold and the enormous pile of turnips. This memory had two effects on the pirate. The first was the realisation of the origin of the taste of turnip. The second was the infliction of laughter at the thought of an imperial ton of sharpened root vegetables.

This did not alter his ambitions, however. He saw that the many visitors of the bazaar were cheerfully enjoying the various types of seafood and wanted in on the experience. So, one by one, he moved down to the next market stall in search of free samples, with some vendors more willing to hand them out than others. The two of them had consumed maybe a dozen samples, Charlie tapping Tom on the shoulder when she enjoyed one, all while Tom grumbled to himself that he could taste only salty turnips. Deciding that he might be better off tasting the food above the water, he rashly purchased a large net full of seafood from the smiliest-looking fishmonger available.

He spent all the rusty trinkets he had on him, exchanging them for handfuls of shellfish, prawns and small jars of pickled fish. What he was most happy about was two larger fish, which he could not fit in the net, so sat on top of it, carrying the entire purchase in both his arms. Onlookers could tell that he was chuffed with this trade, regardless of the fact that he had no sense of the exchange rates between rust and fish.

Tom stepped out of the crowd, still smiling to himself. When he looked ahead of him, he saw something that turned that smile into another bout of laughter. The sight that had made him laugh was a fish, the kind he had just bought, swimming towards him. After it was Elliott Ethan.

To avoid swimming into Tom, the fish altered its trajectory and swam out of reach of the men standing on the seabed. Elliott, whose folded flippers limited him to two-dimensional travel only, failed to slow himself despite having ample time, and ran straight into his friend. Slowly, because of water resistance, the two of them fell and landed on their backsides.

When Elliott saw the pile of seafood Tom had now dropped, he pointed to the bizarre-looking fish and laughed uncontrollably. Fr no reason at all, Tom joined in. As people weaved their way around the historical men, bubbles burst from their breathing equipment in large flusters when they needed to ventilate from laughing too much. Elliott pointed to the fish, which was ten yards above them, he unfolded his fins and kicked away after it. Leaving his purchase floating around in the sand, Tom followed.

"What are you doing?" Charlie called, frustrated, before she picked up the forgotten pile of seafood and swam laboriously after them. The pirates had not stopped laughing, which slowed their pursuit of the creature, and they eventually lost it in a jungle of kelp. Elliott's chest hurt, and so did Tom's ears, but they thought nothing of it and enjoyed the weightlessness of being underwater.

The enjoyment ended for Elliott abruptly when he heard a ringing in his ears. He then heard what may have been a memory, or a hallucination. A voice — a woman's voice — called in the back of his awareness, "Have you forgotten who you are too?" and was followed by a gunshot. This line kept repeating in his mind, and worried him, making him throw up in his mask.

A similar reality check came for Tom when he bumped his head on the wooden keel of a small sailboat, which was, thankfully, static. He felt no pain, though the sound of the collision could be heard through the water. His head rang, making whatever Charlie was saying to him indecipherable. Then, he passed out.

The Lady Mary

"Put down the gun, son," Thatch commanded Adam, who looked at him stubbornly before yielding.

"Bugger," Adam muttered to himself, noticing how the bullet had failed again to have any effect on Israel Hands that wasn't expected of a standard musket round.

"Where's your captain, son?"

"Down there, in that bazaar thing, with the rest of them."

"It's just you?"

"Yep."

"What could be so important they need to leave the ship?"

"Cannonballs, and food I think, but mostly cannonballs."

"Cannonballs for what cause?" Thatch asked gruffly.

"Fighting you, sir," Adam said without thought or hesitation.

"We should destroy them here and now, cap'n," a crewmember of the *Revenge* remarked, "They're clearly wanting the same for us."

"No, no, no, you daft bastard," Adam said rudely but casually, "They only want them to defend themselves in a situation such as this. The irony, of course, is that in the process of achieving this, the very thing they were avoiding has happened."

"Why would you need to defend yourself, is that you admitting that we are in competition?" Thatch though he had cornered Adam to an admission of guilt.

"We didn't think we were, we have different goals."

"And what are these goals?"

"They want to get to bloody Heaven."

At this revelation, Thatch smiled both sincerely and sinisterly. He even laughed out loud, though only with one exhale.

"Of course he wants to go to Heaven," he breathed, realising that it was he who had misinterpreted the situation, "I told him the Gate of

Ubyvis can take you anywhere. Or, as I suppose ol' Glove would have heard it, take you to anyone."

"His wife," Adam said to confirm Thatch's suspicions.

"I suppose the lot of you do, too?"

"I don't reckon much of it," Adam said honestly, "but the rest are onboard."

"You disagree with your captain?"

"I think it's a load of rubbish."

"I like your spirit, son," Blackbeard smiled and thought. He laughed again, harder this time, and even more wickedly.

"Here's what I'll do," he continued, talking over Adam, "I'll leave this ship unharmed, but you're coming with us."

Adam would have said, 'No, I'm bloody not,' or something of the sort, but realised that there were five men about to restrain him. His musket was pushed out of his grasp, falling to the deck of *The Lady* as he was escorted away from it. He was forced to board the *Revenge*, Thatch not revealing his reasoning for his hostage. Adam was taken to a cupboard, for the brig was filled with cattle, and left alone while the captain sailed away in the same entitled fashion as he had arrived. He was a mile away before the crew of *The Lady* had returned.

The Lady Mary: the brig

Amber had a sense that something was wrong before she heard anything. The sound of gunshot intensified this. When she heard the firm footsteps, they had been made soft through the many levels of floor and ceiling between the deck and her. But she knew whose footprints they were immediately. She felt sick before the conscious thought entered her head. It was he, her captain, Blackbeard.

She froze, tense, as she heard the muffled sound of his voice and Adam's above her. She couldn't quite work out what was being said, building both suspense and dread.

Chapter IV

The Lady Mary

The next thing Tom could remember was being sat on the floor on the main-deck. Standing around him was the entire crew, besides Elliott, who was sitting away on a barrel. There also was Charlie, standing on the flukes of her tail as if they were feet, as was the other mermaid, Neve.

"You silly sod," Neve scolded as soon as Tom had cracked open his eyes. The taste of turnip still lingered on his palate. The mermaid then poked him in the eye to watch his reaction. He reacted as any conscious person would to this — by closing it in pain. Charlie then tossed him a rag to dry his hair with.

"What did I do?" Tom said, genuinely confused at the situation.

"You used un-reputable air! Weren't you warned about un-reputable air?"

"It was his fault!" Tom deflected the blame by pointing at Lewis, who hadn't got his money back for the bullets.

"It was only a suggestion!" Lewis insisted, though his voice sounded more guilty than he thought it should.

"It doesn't matter whose fault it is," Neve interrupted the pirates' argument, "it poisoned you, and it poisoned your friend."

"You're safe now, just take it easy," Charlie spoke more softy than her friend, "I made sure you got back safely, your food is downstairs, by the way."

Tom remembered at this point the events that had occurred. He felt rather embarrassed and could tell Elliott did too by the colour of his cheeks. "I owe you a 'thank you,' I suppose," Tom said to Charlie, avoiding Neve's harsher stare. Glove had remained silent, obviously shaken by something.

"How can we possibly repay you ladies?" he said with gratitude, "I am certainly in your debt, you have done well to keep this child of mine alive."

The two mermaids looked each other in the eye and grinned, for they both had the same idea. "Let us join your crew," they said at the same time.

"What?" Doyle asked, "Why would you want to be on our ship, isn't being a mermaid better?"

"It seems you can be free on a ship," Neve answered, "Free from work, and bills, and people you don't like."

"She's got a point," Noah agreed.

"Do you not have better, more mermaid-ly things to be doing?" Tom said.

"We'll just tell everyone we were kidnapped by pirates," Charlie explained, "Everyone will be so jealous of us."

Glove was hesitant, so Tom added, "I think that would be lovely." So that was that; the crew of seven pirates (eight including Amber) and one cowboy gained two mermaids.

They then set off, being instructed out of the parking spaces by two men giving contradicting signals, oblivious to Adam's hostage situation, nor that Thatch was ahead of them.

Queen Anne's Revenge

Adam was surprised to find that within an hour of his placement within a cell of the *Revenge*, Thatch personally escorted him out of it.

"Come on, son," Blackbeard said unthreateningly, opening the door and guiding him to the captain's quarters, "we've got a lot to talk about."

When the pair reached Thatch's cabin, two guards stood at their posts outside the doors. The room was full of furniture plated with gold, and extravagant clothes hung from exposed rails and hooks. Incense burned in the corner, producing a smell that caused Adam to turn up his nose. Blackbeard sat down at his deck, which was covered in maps, artefacts, and, most obviously to Adam, the stone within the locket which Glove had surrendered to him. He was expecting a threat, a warning, a message to deliver. The last thing he was expecting was hospitality. But hospitality was what he got.

"That's a scruffy old coat you've got there, son." Thatch gestured to Adam, "Go on, take one of those, those ones over there."

Adam was hesitant, but he didn't want to pass up the opportunity. He wasn't sure if he'd even wear a new coat; he liked the one he had, but it was free. He picked coats, one by one, finding even more on the hooks revealed by the removal of the last. When he had too many to hold, he tossed them onto the desk. He took from its hook a smart looking, navy blue woollen overcoat with large rams'-horn buttons and slung it over the shoulder of his own faded blue cotton coat. He then hung the discarded options back up.

"Funny thing is, son," Thatch continued to talk, "when I was not much younger than yourself, I'd have killed for a scruffy old coat like that. I'd have killed for any sort of coat."

"You'd kill for a coat?"

"I don't have to now. When you're good at stealing, you don't have to kill for necessities. Why do you think I became so good at stealing?

If I'd have killed for everything I needed, I wouldn't have got very far."

"Are you familiar with the concept of money?"

"I'm glad to see you have wit, boy, but then again, children in your position often do. But I had no money growing up, that's why killing and stealing were the two options. I lived in the fear of having nothing, and so I made it my mission to take everything. And soon, I'll have that chance: to take everything."

Adam wasn't particularly in the mood to listen to Thatch's monologues, but he also enjoyed arguing, so inquired, "And I suppose I'm just part of that plan to take everything?"

"In a way, but mine and Glove's rivalry goes deeper than that."

"So, do you not think kidnapping me will evoke a retaliation?"

"Glove is many things, but he's not entirely stupid," Thatch spoke, "He knows he's overpowered by my fleet."

"I'm sure you know he has a temper," Adam reminded.

"I know that alright," Thatch said, grinning, "but he's likely got his mind set on one thing alone. Her."

"What? His wife? Who you killed?"

"What?" Thatch interrupted, "What has that man been telling you? I did a lot of things to Mary Glove, but I never killed her."

The Lady Mary

The crew, between them, bought an awful lot at the bazaar. The range of stock was as comprehensive as Lewis had promised. Tom had bought all the seafood he could afford. Lewis had bought himself various guns and ammunition, the quality of which he was starting to question. Maddy purchased a leather hat, just because she liked it, but also some sort of assault rifle. Noah got a sword, since he was the only one without one at all, leaving him with spare money to buy some sort of explosive device. The lack of clarity regarding the specifications of the purchases was mostly down to the lack of verbal communication between anyone underwater, but also because the crew had made rather rushed purchases.

Elliott, after all his shenanigans, bought nothing, returning with the same handful of rusty bits and pieces. Glove bought himself, quite unexpectedly, a series of bulletproof armour and clothing, which he changed into while letting Elliott, who had calmed down from his hysteria, steer. Finally, Doyle bought a pair of knives that sat within elbow guards. He immediately envisioned performing a spinning elbow with blades on his arms and fell in love with the idea.

Responsibly, he purchased these only after buying three dozen cannonballs. Although this form of ammunition was the sole purpose of the trip, yet no one else had actually got any, Doyle was given no credit.

Glove had spent a while in his cabin, so Elliott went to visit him, leaving Doyle at the helm. It was soon noticed that the first crew of salesmen seen before the bazaar were not alone in this stretch of sea. The two continents reached closer to each other here than they did at any other point, and from each side sailboats of all sizes and quality were accompanied by the smaller motor-powered boats which their crew kept paperwork on. They crowed and pestered and bartered with any vessel that drifted through these waters.

A couple of such vendors approached *The Lady Mary* while its captain was below deck. Tom, who manned the helm, resisted them at first, but the third ship to arrive caught his eye from half a mile away. He handed the wheel to Doyle when the salesman said, "Hello, good sir! I see you have your eye on this top of the range, class-one Jacquerie sailboat!"

Without hesitation, he asked, "How much?"

"Would you be interested in our part-exchange scheme?"

Tom thought for a second, but Maddy butted in before he traded the entire *Lady Mary* and its contents for this new ship. But Tom still wanted it. The ship was rather classic in design; it was made from dark, well-varnished wood, but its top section was painted matte white. The metal trimmings were glossy and black, and the deck was mahogany red.

"How about," Tom looked around for anything to swap for a sailboat, "how about a donkey?"

"A what?" the main salesman asked. He had no hair, and his skin was mottled yellow. Presumably, he was an alien with no knowledge of donkeys. The fact that Tom failed to notice his unusual appearance was a show of his transfixion on the ship. Tom walked over to the miniature donkey, who, to his surprise, did not bray, and picked him up in both arms.

"A donkey, this fella."

"He's like the one in Shrek!" a different salesman, who was likely from Earth, couldn't help but notice. Tom, being an 18th-century pirate, knew not who Shrek was nor his asinine accomplice. But he saw an opportunity in the man's delight.

"Yes, that is correct," he said. He spoke in a way that was robotic so as not to reveal his confusion.

"Please tell me he talks like him," the salesman said, though while this was optimistic, he spoke with the conviction that suggested he thought it was a possibility.

"You bet he talks," Tom couldn't help but smile as he said this, but backed it with, "Come on, Oliver, say hello. Aw, he's a shy boy, aren't you?"

Tom rocked the donkey, so it appeared to nod its head at this question. "I know he seems quiet now, boys, but trust me, you'll be wishing he didn't talk when he gets used to you."

"Deal," the second salesman said, to the disappointment of his senior. Tom was next ordered to the ship he had just acquired to sign some paperwork handed to him from the small boat which accompanied it. He whispered, "I'll pay you back," to Lewis, feeling slightly guilty that he had so quickly given away another man's pet.

The sales crew disembarked the ship, and all squeezed into the small boat, Tom then handing Oliver the donkey down to them. As soon as they were done, the salesmen floated away into the crowd of ships along the coast.

The new ship

Thomas Glove, now Commander Thomas Glove (by his own appointment), stood on his new ship and made way for the helm to keep in on its path. It was very responsive and didn't even creak like any wooden ship of its size would be expected to. Tom called to Maddy, and then to Noah. The two embarked on the new vessel, though they realised that the crew of *The Lady* was now as minimal as it practically could be, so no more people joined, the two mermaids more content on the older, more 'vintage' ship, anyway.

Maddy leant over the front of the ship and admired the gold plating that decorated the bow and bowsprit. This was a feature that Tom had failed to recognise initially, but pleased him once it was pointed out. Further joy was brought to him when he realised the sails could be lowered, raised and turned by a series of levers and buttons by the wheel. This brought relief also, as it was a rather helpful convenience given the reduced size of his crew.

The Lady Mary

Glove came back onto the main-deck with haste, ignoring the fact that he almost tripped over his boot-string. His face was instantly red with anger. Shock too played into the change in his attitude.

"You just had to, didn't you?" he said to his son, less than amused by his actions. Tom replied to this, but Glove wasn't listening. All he did was grab a couple of ropes and throw them to the crew on the new ship. The two boats were so close that the board that had been used to move people across remained in its position, despite them being in motion. Tom questioned the purpose of the ropes, which Glove answered by ordering them to be tied down so that Tom's ship remained close to *The Lady* at all times. He followed this with a reminder: "I'm still captain, you know, and all you my crew still."

He then dismissed Doyle from the wheel and took control. "Sail with me, boy," he said, then kept his mouth shut to avoid escalating his frustration.

The new ship

Elliott called to his friend, stumbling onto the ship temporarily, "What's she called?"

Tom smiled as he thought but couldn't decide on a name. Elliott then unfastened the flaming cutlass from his belt, and tossed it to Tom, who caught it. He took it out of the scabbard and watched the blade light. The two locked eyes and grinned; they both knew what the ship had to be called: *The Flaming Cutlass*.

Chapter V

The Flaming Cutlass

The Flaming Cutlass sailed close to and in the direct influence of *The Lady Mary*. This reduced the rush of freedom that Tom would otherwise have experienced due to being in control of a new vessel. Thanks to the revolutionary (to the 18th century crew) mechanisms of this more modern ship, Noah and Maddy sat on barrels beside Tom, who also sat on one beside the wheel, steering it gently when required. They spoke softly so that Glove couldn't hear it and react to it in his typical, hidebound fashion.

"We've come all this way," Noah began cautiously, "but we haven't really talked about it."

"Talked about what?" Maddy asked.

"Well, the captain wants to get to Heaven, but that's not our only option. That gate can take us anywhere we want, not just anywhere he wants."

"But what he wants is what we want," Maddy replied without thought.

"Is it what you want, or just what was convenient? I mean, we have our own ship now, we aren't bound to his decisions anymore."

Tom laughed and reminded Noah of the ropes tying *The Cutlass* to *The Lady*. "We are bound, physically."

"Then cut the rope," Noah responded quickly.

"If he hears you say that, he'll bind us tighter to them," Maddy said gravely, for she acknowledged her captain's domineering side.

"Then cut the rope before he can tighten it," Noah argued as if he had already planned this answer.

"But things will never be the same if that happens, it will be us against them," said Tom.

"From where I'm standing, it always has been," Noah countered every hesitation Thomas had.

"But I do want to go to Heaven, it's where my mother is."

"Do you even remember what she looked like?"

"What's that got to do with it?"

"You've been told to miss something you don't remember."

"I do miss her."

"Do you miss her, or do you feel you were missing something? Because they are two different things. Think about it – she'd basically be a stranger to you."

"Well, I'd have forever to change that."

Seeing that Tom had got uncomfortable, Maddy added, "I also want to go to Heaven."

"Why?"

"Because it's the best you can get, forever."

"But it isn't going to be forever! Twelve years — that's all. You know it's going to go up in flames, yet you still want it to happen. Also, you don't even know what it's going to be like, you've never been."

The Lady Mary

Glove stood on deck and called out to his crew across both ships. "Before we reached the bazaar, I was informed that the sly dog Thatch sent *The Golden Gander* to kill us! Mark my words – the truce between our own flag and his has been ended. He is a threat, so you should all listen, obey, and be prepared for an encounter!"

Despite this claim, Glove had no intention of fighting Blackbeard. He was entirely unaware that he had been aboard his ship and kidnapped a member of the crew. It's not that nobody cared for Adam, but they merely assumed that he was asleep, as usual. The ships had cleared the busier section of the inland sea and saw before nor behind them another vessel for many miles. *Queen Anne's Revenge* was visible in the distance, but not one of them had realised this, still thinking it was behind them. The sky was darkening to become an amber-red, and the crew had food on their minds rather than Blackbeard.

The brig

Elliott tried not to make a fuss as he walked down to the brig to see Amber, who had stood still since their last encounter.

"You look awfully fed up," Elliott said kindly, "We're having food soon, if that will cheer you up."

"No," Amber replied with a whisper.

"No? Can I at least bring you a drink?"

"I'm fine," she said with a huff.

"Be like that, then, you stupid woman," Elliott replied in a way which he had intended to sound like a joke, but noticed as soon as the words left his mouth how it instead sounded plainly offensive, "sorry."

He went back upstairs to ask about the meal.

The Flaming Cutlass: below deck

Tom had left Noah and Maddy to sort out the task of steering between themselves when he took himself on a tour of his new ship. He thought to himself that it perhaps would have been ideal if he'd have asked for a tour before he had purchased the ship. However, he was not at all disappointed with all the fittings and commodities he found below deck. Particularly, the kitchen gave him the most excitement.

A large, spacious marble worktop and island reflected bright, crisp, white electric lights. Though he didn't notice it at first, a huge fridge-freezer stood in the corner emitting a quiet, cheerful buzz. The cupboards, both high and low, were mahogany red like the deck and had black steel handles. But the centre of Tom's attention was two big electric ovens with a gas stove above them.

The Lady Mary

Glove watched Noah and Maddy talking, though he couldn't hear more than the sibilance, which is often emphasised by whispering. He asked Elliott, who had returned from the brig, "Go and see what they're talking about."

"How come?" Elliott couldn't hide his frown.

"We're almost there, boy, we don't need any complications."

"Are you saying they're not allowed to talk?"

"It depends on what they're talking about. It could be something dangerous."

"Talking wasn't dangerous before."

"What? They didn't have their own ship before, they were on my ship before, so I still had control. We can't let them come up with plans of their own, or I won't have control anymore."

"Why…"

"What's gotten into you? Just go and see what they are talking about!"

The Flaming Cutlass: the helm

Elliott climbed onto *The Flaming Cutlass* after he secured the plank between the two ships with rope. Neither Maddy nor Noah stopped talking when they noticed him; if anything, it seemed like Noah spoke louder on purpose.

"It just feels wrong, you know, cheating your way to Heaven."

"But we're cheating either way, if at look at it like that," Maddy replied.

"But if you think about it, if we stopped Blackbeard from destroying Earth, I feel like we've earned a place back on Earth."

"But if we save Earth, do you not think we deserve a place in Heaven?"

"How do you plan to save Earth?" Elliott entered the conversation.

"We have ammunition now, so use it. Use it and blow the side off of Blackbeard's ships. He can't deliver no herd of apocalyptic cattle if he don't have any."

"That's a plan I'm on board with," Maddy added, "We could even wait for him to catch us, then do it. We have two ships too now."

"It's a noble goal, but you haven't thought it all through," Elliott whispered.

"Oh, here it comes," Maddy complained.

"No, no, I'm not discouraging it, but don't let Glove catch wind quite yet. But my point is: this planet is full of life, just as the Earth is. It's no more heroic to let this planet be destroyed by those beasts than to let the same happen to your own planet, if anything, it's less heroic."

"It's not about being heroic!"

"Yes, but it's about being good. Of course it's about being good, we're talking about Heaven. If that's where you truly want to go, that is."

"Even if it isn't," Noah said, "I think you raise a good point. So, hopefully, we wait for one of the next two planets to be more desolate, then we get him."

"If we can, you have my support, but hold off telling the captain, I'll have to hint at it myself."

The kitchen

The concept of electricity was alien to Tom, so he pressed buttons on it as the display flashed with rods and symbols. Due to its location and dimensions, he understood it was indeed an oven, but struggled to figure out how to operate it. When he opened its spotless glass door, he found a small instruction manual. It wasn't that he couldn't read, but that he had got into the habit of passing on all literary tasks to Elliott. Because of this, he went back to the main-deck and called Elliott over.

Once in the kitchen, he found the English section of the book, and read its tiny writing. He commented on how he found the technology presented before him, "simply remarkable," though this didn't exactly help him understand it. He then pointed out that, "It's an oven, I believe," though Tom had figured this out himself. After prodding buttons and twisting knobs and opening and closing doors unnecessarily, the pair of them finally got the display to read 'preheating', and with little help from the little instruction book.

"It's a good thing you bought some fish at that market, because we fed all the chicken to the dragons," Elliott laughed, walking away tom's retrieve his purchase from *The Lady*, "actually, I ought to check on that little dragon of ours."

It was apparent that he hadn't checked on Doyle the dragon when he returned two minutes later with an armful of fish. Tom seasoned one of them and placed it on the clean rack of the electric oven, the others ending up in the fridge when it was eventually discovered. He got a shock to find that the oven had reached a high temperature, with no sight of a flame. He was delighted that a light allowed him to watch his food cook while the door remained closed.

"I'm sure you've had a think about it yourself," Elliott said quietly and with hesitation.

"About what?" Tom asked, not entirely sure of the kind of opinion Elliott would have about his conflicting ideas.

"This ship of yours gives you a great deal of independence from your father. An independence that has put your father on edge — I hope you won't repeat this. What I'm saying is that despite any reluctance your father may have, you have it in your power to take a path of your own. In fact, I very well remember that the contract he signed referred to 'the crew of *The Lady Mary*', and this ship is not she. As a result, I don't believe that you are contractually bound to such destruction as our ship, nor the *Revenge*. So, you could stop Thatch if you saw fit and return to Earth — if you wanted."

"Have you come here to persuade me otherwise?" Tom said gruffly.

"Not at all. While I will remain loyal to your father, I have no issue promoting and enabling less self-interested action if you took it upon yourself."

"I don't know," Tom said, "I feel like everyone's expecting me to go against the plan, to disobey."

"Disobey for the greater good."

"But maybe I like the plan we have, maybe I want to go to Heaven."

"Do you?"

"Well, maybe it's the best thing I can get. My father is right, we're all sinners, so what good are we on Earth, or anywhere?"

"If I may correct your definition of sin," Elliott said, thinking hard about what he wanted to say, "you've it too clear cut, you put sin and success in two separate boxes. But they're not. Sin is a threshold you have to exceed on the way to success. It's when you fail to achieve the best you can, the best you should: that's sin."

"What difference does the definition make? I'm no better off under your new rules."

"You're wrong there, you're much better off. Because you can change."

"How can I change? Why should I change? I have a free ticket to Heaven by following the plan!"

"You have to accept that you have fallen short of your attempt at being the best, most truly good version of yourself, which you have. But you've still got to accept what it is that caused you to fail at that, and change. The very idea that sin is on the path to reaching that goal shows you something important. You've tried, and not gone far enough, you stopped short and so live in sin. But all you have to do is keep going. You're already on the way, but something stopped you. You just have to dispel whatever it is within yourself that has slowed you down and then, only then, you will be free of the sin."

"But what is that? What is it I must dispel?"

"That — that is something you have to figure out. Just have a think about it," Elliott muttered as he left the room.

The Lady Mary: the dining room

Glove had insisted that the crew were to eat in the dining room of his own ship, himself at the helm and his son at the wheel of *The Flaming Cutlass*. The two mermaid guests waddled awkwardly down the stairs, their tail flukes acting like the webbed feet of a penguin. "Is there anything I can do to help?" Doyle asked inquisitively.

"If you have some spare human legs, we could cast a spell to give us legs!" Charlie said, Doyle not sure if this was a joke.

"You can have Doyle's legs, if you want," Maddy joked.

"I think you'd be better with Adam's legs," Doyle decided, "He hardly uses them, anyway."

The crew enjoyed the fish bought at the market, though it tasted just as fishy as Earth fish. One of the comical, shark-looking fish served all the crew with leftovers for breakfast. Thomas had also boiled up the turnips that Arnold had given him. To his credit, Arnold's turnips were the most delightful turnips any of them had ever tasted.

The absence of both Glove and his son had seemed to prevent any conversation about changing plans, in any direction. But the topic sat on Elliott's mind, and also Noah's, and both could tell this about each other. The silence was heavy, so Charlie broke it by informing Elliott, "It was nitrous oxide that poisoned you, as well as alcohol vapour."

"How did that get in the tank?" Elliott asked out of politeness, though he didn't really want to talk about it.

"It's what you get when the air isn't produced properly. That's why you should always buy —"

"Certified air," Elliott finished the sentence, "I know, I know."

"If you knew, then why didn't you buy it?" Neve said, laughing loudly.

"Because we didn't have time!" Elliott shouted back, trying to match the tone.

"Didn't have time for safety?" Charlie said with one eyebrow raised.

"I know, I know, I'm an arse," Elliott smiled as he took a plate of food each for Adam and Amber.

When he opened the door to Adam's room, he noticed it was empty, but thought little of it, assuming Adam had just woken up. He continued on his way to the brig to find Amber there, still tense.

The brig

Amber ignored the plate of food that Elliott had slid to her. She was still and quiet. "Here you go — some fresh fish, some bread, and some turnip," Elliott described the meal despite its simple nature.

"Is he gone?" Amber whispered.

"Is who gone?" Elliott said, confused.

"Him. Is he gone?"

"Miss Sings, you're going to have to be more helpful than that."

"The captain," she said un-specifically.

"Captain Glove? Why, he's at the helm now."

"No, my captain. He was here — when you were gone."

Elliott dropped the plate of food intended for Adam Lumberlodge and froze. He then spoke gravely and quietly. "He was here?"

Amber nodded.

"He was here? On this ship?"

She nodded again.

"Did you see him?"

Amber shook her head, "No, but I heard him, and gunfire."

"What kind of gunfire?"

"I don't know, probably a musket."

Elliott stared at her and shock and horror, waiting for what seemed like a minute, saying, before leaving, "You could have mentioned it sooner."

The helm

"Captain, he's ahead of us, and he's got him, he's got Adam!" Elliott called in distress before he had reached the helm. He then held up his telescope and realised that one of the distant ships was the great, dark silhouette of *Queen Anne's Revenge*. He then spotted Adam's musket, discarded on the floor. Glove did not speak for a while, Elliott having time to retrieve the gun and place it somewhere safer.

Tom, from the helm of his own vessel, listened intently, not sure if he had heard correctly.

"Then he is the latest victim of this cursed quest, and the latest victim of Edward Thatch, we shall mourn him and celebrate all he has done to get us here."

Tom had not much temper left for his father, and could not help but release his anger, "Bullshit!"

"What, son?"

"Bull-shit, you don't even know he's dead!"

"He's as good as dead!" Glove argued.

"No, he isn't! Not if we actually go and get him. You know we can catch up to them, you know this ship is faster than the *Revenge*."

"It's not happening! I'm not risking it! You just want to be the hero, you don't care if you get us killed doing it!"

The approach of a small electric boat interrupted this discourse. In it were the salesmen who had sold *The Flaming Cutlass* to Thomas, and they were hollering furiously.

"You scoundrel!" one called.

"Bloody pirates!" said another.

Oliver the donkey was with them, braying with his usual commitment.

"Take him back!" the senior salesman called.

"No refunds!" Tom said bluntly but with a smile.

"Just take him back!" the man called again, as the crew cruelly hoisted up the donkey and threw it onto the deck of *The Cutlass*. The ungulate landed on its feet and trotted around the deck unscathed. The salesmen left as swiftly as they had arrived, still muttering, "pirate scum," and similar insults.

The dining room

Elliott had snook downstairs and gathered Maddy, Lewis and Noah. He would also have got Doyle, but he had wandered off.

"Listen carefully," he began seriously, "Adam has been kidnapped by Thatch, but the captain isn't willing to go after the *Revenge*."

"What?" Maddy interrupted loudly, before Elliott shushed her.

"Listen, listen. But Tom is, I think he's ready. These two ships can remain bound no more. So, go. Go and help him, go and do what you know is right. If you want to go to Earth, and cannot get Thatch's stone, I'll see what I can do. I'll be in touch, just go."

Main-deck

All but Doyle, who was somewhere, but no one knew where, ran to the deck. The mermaids joined them, excited for 'a genuine pirate adventure'. Maddy ran straight to *The Cutlass* and took the wheel, pointing Tom to Elliott. Noah and both mermaids followed.

"What's going on," he asked.

"It's time, Captain Thomas Glove, to do what you have been waiting to do, even. If you didn't realise."

"What's that?"

"The right thing to do."

"Maybe I've ruined that by doing the wrong thing, by leaving him by himself. I just wish I could undo it all."

"It's a rather misleading word, 'undo'," Elliott thought.

"What?"

"'Undo,' there's a problem with that word. It can't be done. You can't change the past, it's done, already written. So go and fix it."

"What is the meaning of this?" Glove called from the helm.

To appeal to his humanity, Tom begged, "Come on, father, help us bring him home. Help us give Blackbeard what he deserves. You tell us all the time of what he did, why won't you come and avenge it?"

"You wouldn't understand, son," Glove said under his breath. Tom was on his own ship, but close enough to hear this.

"What wouldn't I understand? What is there to understand?" Tom cried as Glove left the helm and walked towards where his son and first-mate were standing, on opposite sides of the gap between the ships. Doyle, who had just come from below deck, was ordered to grab the wheel.

"Listen here," the captain began, but Tom didn't let him finish the sentence.

"Why wouldn't you come and kill the rotten, evil, no-good, villainous man who killed your wife, the man who killed your son's mother?"

"Thatch never killed your mother, Tom," Elliott burst out, "He didn't do it!"

At the last word of his sentence, Glove drew a sword, and it struck Elliott's cheek. "Liar!" he called, his face as red as blood, as red as war.

Queen Anne's Revenge

"I never killed your mother, son," Thatch said to Adam.

"It's not about my mother! I'm on about Tom's mother, Mary!" Adam shouted mostly from confusion.

"Has he truly denied you the right to know?" Thatch said, knowing the answer but pretending he didn't.

"The right to know what?"

"Mary was your mother, son!"

"But that would make me Tom's brother," Adam muttered, not believing him, "and we look nothing alike."

"In what way?"

"For one thing, my hair's black," Adam began, but pieced together the entire conversation, leaving this as all that needed to be said. His face, his tone and his volume all dropped.

"You said you did a lot of things to Mary," he asked, awkward from his phrasing, "was I one of them?"

"That's right, my boy! Welcome home!" Thatch was pleased with his intuition.

The Lady Mary

The harbinger of truth was the crystal, which Glove had reclaimed without Tom's recollection. It fell from the locket, and Glove fell with it. It was as if the ship had come to life in that instant, but a life lived many years ago. Those on it became ghosts, observing a past on the same ship they called home.

A blonde-haired woman, young and frail from bearing a child, stood away from a much younger Andrew Glove. The two were arguing.

"It all seems suspicious, Mary, that you spend so long a prisoner of Edward Thatch, then return to me, to bear a black-haired child!"

"You just said it yourself! I was a prisoner to Blackbeard!" she could clearly hold her own in an argument with a man of his temper.

"And you said yes to him?"

"No, of course I bloody didn't but you try saying no to Edward Thatch! He doesn't know the meaning of the word!" Mary sniffled as she walked away from Glove and leant herself against the railing to gaze out into the black horizon, "he only takes, and takes and takes some more. Till nothing is left. And still he isn't satisfied."

"How could you?"

"How could I? How couldn't I? I had no choice; he gave me no choice. Yet now I stand before the man I love, and that man blames me! I don't know what to say, I honestly don't. I really can't believe you, Andy. Have you forgotten who you're talking to, who I am? Have you forgotten who you are too?"

Suddenly a shot was fired, and Mary toppled over the railing and landed into the sea, face down. Andrew rushed over to see, and mortified, tossed a smoking pistol after her. The weapon sank, but Mary's body floated beside the ship, near where her name was painted, as the surrounding water turned red.

Andrew Glove fell to his knees and sobbed as a young boy, only seven or eight years old, ran below deck in panic. This boy, believe it or not, was the first-mate, Elliott Ethan.

The vision showed within Glove's cabin now — him with two children, one three years old and the other hardly a month. The older child was playing with dolls, the younger was in a crib. Glove sat still in his chair and thought before the child encouraged an interaction.

"And what's this one called?" he asked the boy, whose hair was blonde and already long, and who would make up a name for the toy. The two did this for several dolls, which appeared to be handmade, until Glove lifted his son onto his lap and pointed to the baby.

"And what's he called?" he asked, "Is he called Adam?"

The toddler mumbled sounds, not words, but to sound them out, it was something like "Luh-lodge."

"Come on, son, say 'Adam.' Say it," Glove repeated, to which the child said again, "Luh-lodge."

"Yeah, that's right," the young Andrew Glove smiled, closing his eyes and crying once more.

When Mary's body washed upon a barren shore, which was within the brackish waters of the Humber estuary, a man on a sickly pale horse found it. This man knew not who the dead woman was but thought it appropriate to bury her. So, he did, digging the grave by himself with a rusty old spade and having not the resources for a coffin. Mary Glove was buried in a grave marked only by five stones of varied lengths forming a cross, not known to her husband and young children.

The vision ended, Glove on his knees, crying, in the same spot his younger self had cried on the deck. He saw the stone and grabbed it, locking it back in the locket. Despite his pain, Elliott said, "Cut the rope."

The Flaming Cutlass

Tom got up, feeling what he could only think was terror. Elliott cut one rope for him, Noah handing Tom a sword and repeating, "Cut it. Cut the rope."

"Cut the rope before he can tighten it," Tom remembered these words, reciting them slowly, shaking. He did not take Noah's sword, but his own flaming one. He drew it and ignited the blade.

"Listen here," Glove said through cries of guilt, trying to fasten more rope to *The Flaming Cutlass*. But the burning steel of Tom's sword cut through the rope effortlessly, rocking the ships as the rope snapped. He ran immediately for the helm, took the wheel from Maddy, and turned it away from *The Lady Mary*. He pulled down hard on a lever, forcing more sails to open to their fullest. The ship picked up speed immediately, leaving a furious yet distraught Andrew Glove behind them.

Ahead of them now was the stone table, which *Queen Anne's Revenge* used first, then *The Flaming Cutlass* in pursuit of it. Glove saw no need to rush after them, nor did he have the energy. But he reached it, ending this act here.

Act 4: Ride On

Chapter I

Ganrudarbith: *The Lady Mary*

Elliott had mostly ignored his wound. Of course, he had wiped the dripping blood from his face; holding a cloth there until it clotted, but didn't talk about it. He didn't want to talk about it. Because he didn't know what he'd say.

He had taken the wheel from Doyle, who loitered but did not start a conversation just yet. The next planet was, as Elliott had gathered from the map, and as he had hoped, quite barren. It was, in fact, impossible for this planet not to be barren, because there was no land. To Elliott's relief, his compass was acting normal once again, so he figured out his heading despite the lack of landmarks.

Barren, however, does not mean easy to traverse. The Himalayas are barren; they are not easy to climb. The endless sea of this next planet, which was called Ganrudarbith, was as equally dangerous. Calm for an hour or so, the wind picked up. It was strong, stronger than anything *The Lady* had ever dealt with, seeming to fill the sails and overflow them. Rain joined in too, darkening the sky and worsening the mood of all the pirates.

Elliott did not have the skill as a helmsman to navigate the storm, nor did Doyle. The former handed the wheel to the latter and went himself to find the captain.

Captain's cabin

Elliott hesitated at the door to Glove's cabin and sighed. As he had many times before, he knocked on the door and entered carefully.

"Captain, we need you at the helm," he said, avoiding eye contact, and holding the cut side of his face away from him. Glove's eyes were red, his face as well. Elliott knew he had been crying, to an extent which only he, out of all the crew, had ever seen. He was also on the brink of sleeping, but rose slowly out of his chair. A wave, which crashed against the boat, threw him up and out of the door.

Main-deck

Glove dismissed the pair of pirates when he took the wheel himself, but asked them to stay on deck. So they did, a while away from the captain. It was Doyle who broke the silence between the two of them.

"You okay?"

"Yes, Doyle, thank you," Elliott replied briefly.

"I don't like it," Doyle persisted.

"Don't like what?" Elliott asked, balancing his volume to talk over the wind and waves, but not be heard by Glove.

"That he'd do that to you," Doyle whispered.

"He was in shock, he was scared."

"That doesn't make it alright" Doyle suggested, noticing that it had dripped blood again. He handed his friend the bandana from his forehead, "Here, wipe it with this."

The bandana was red, so it showed little blood on it. Elliott groaned as the pressure stung the cut, "Thank you, Doyle, I know I'm too harsh on you sometimes – we all are."

"No, I get it, Elliott, I should've told you about what I'd done. If I'd told you, Tudor wouldn't be dead, maybe Adam wouldn't have been taken from us."

"No, if you'd have told me, I'd have just wasted those ones too. We'd be in the same situation, so don't blame yourself."

"Oh, I will, believe me."

Glove stood at the helm, batting the wind and rain, which he was sailing into. He ached, he strained, and he was tired. His hand slipped, the wheel turning against him as *The Lady* forced herself to rotate away from the storm. The captain fell to the side, leaping back to grab hold of the wheel again, shouting in pain as he forced the ship to correct its course.

Doyle ran to help him, but knew he was too inexperienced to offer to take his place at the helm. Elliott too aided, the three men holding the wheel in place, and turning it together when they needed to. Doyle ran back and forth to alter the sails in response to the altered course, with the help of Lewis, who had not made it to *The Flaming Cutlass* before her departure.

"You boys have stuck with me; you two can appreciate the good I've done for you. Elliott, you know I've made you who you are, please don't forget that. We're almost there, just help me through, please," Glove said sleepily but with conviction. His weak body slumped against the shoulder of his first-mate.

"Go to sleep, captain," Elliott suggested, "We can try to take it from here."

"You can't, son," Glove said bluntly but truthfully.

"She can," Elliott said, thinking of their prisoner, "She's a better helmsman than Thatch."

"Are you suggesting releasing our hostage?" Glove said unhappily, "What good would that do?"

"She can take the wheel, give you a rest. We may be close, but we aren't there yet, you need to rest."

"Go and get her then, I'd like to see if Miss Sings lives up to her reputation."

The brig

"Miss Sings," Elliott called for her attention, but corrected himself, "Commander Sings."

"Just call me Amber," she replied, sitting on the cold, wooden floor of the cell.

"But Commander Amber is a bit of a mouthful," he laughed.

"Like you said, I'm not the commander of anything anymore."

"You can be now; we need someone at the helm."

"Why me? You must think me wicked."

"I'm no good, and the captain's growing tired. And I'm sure you're not wicked, you were only following orders."

"Does it matter if I was following orders?" Amber asked, "My crew must think me wicked – if they're alive. I've worked them to their death, came to kill you, and at the end of all this I'm supposed to kill everything. What bothered me most is that I don't actually remember it happening. I don't recall becoming wicked."

"But there's hardly a difference between falling from grace and never reaching it — you're still in the same place."

"So you're telling me I was born wicked?"

"I didn't mean that. But it's easier to get up when you haven't just fallen."

"Save me the poetry."

"Look, we've got some good men, my best friends, out there, trying to stop it. But they're outmatched. I want to help them, but we have to get through this storm to reach them, so do me a favour," Elliott said as he unlocked the door and opened it, "get up and take the wheel."

Queen Anne's Revenge

"Come on, son," Thatch said to Adam, "come and have some dinner with us."

Adam agreed, mostly because he didn't want to disagree with Thatch, nor did he know what else he'd do. So the two of them walked from the captain's cabin and below deck. On the main-deck, Adam saw a dozen men stand to attention as their captain walked past. The deck was tidy. It wasn't spotless or shiny, but as well kept as practically necessary to optimise functionality. Adam had never been on a ship with this large a crew, and, having the spatial awareness of a blind rhinoceros, barged into and through groups of men coming up the stairs and onto deck.

When they reached the dining area, a small table sat in the middle, with one seat at the head for the captain, and only six other chairs for other crew members. Thatch pointed Adam to an empty chair beside himself, which was for the quartermaster.

"Sit down there," Thatch instructed, "You killed my quartermaster, I suppose you better fill the position."

This comment angered the first-mate, and other senior crew members, as they believed they should be promoted rather than an outsider take the role. They of course didn't express this view, or else there would be more job vacancies.

Adam was quite disappointed by the spread of food provided by a pirate of Blackbeard's standing, but then again, he had also spent the past five years in Hell with them. Pickled eggs, ship's biscuits and cured meat were on the menu. Despite his ungratefulness, he ate all of it, and a lot of it. There wasn't much talking, which Adam was happy about, because it gave him time to plan. What he was planning was his escape. But it wasn't just his escape he had considered. He was aware, from a conversation he could just about remember, that the very ship he sat in was holding a herd of satanic cattle, bound to destroy Earth. Something else that he was aware of, and was hoping Thatch was not, was the fact that he had plucked the stone from Blackbeard's desk when he picked up the coats he had thrown on it.

He knew Thatch could not deliver the herd without the key, so wanted to depart the *Revenge* promptly as to certify this impossibility. He also, though he might not admit it, missed his crew's company. So, he observed, mentally mapping the ship and its layout, keeping track of who was posted where, and when this changed. To his misfortune, though in line with his expectation, he had gathered that there was no part of the ship left unguarded for sufficient time to warrant an undetected getaway. And he didn't have his gun either. He needed more information, so yawned exaggeratedly and asked to see the sleeping quarters. Thatch showed him to the communal sleeping area, then went to the helm, for the storm was worsening.

Adam sat down on the edge of the bed and laid his coat under it. He took off his boots and placed them beside the coat, but then jumped up in shock when he saw what he thought was the stone from the locket on the floor at the other end of the room. He checked no one was around and walked over to the item and picked it up. It was not what he had thought, but a non-Satanic piece of agate of similar dimensions, which had fallen from a chest of jewellery. He kept it anyway, then lay down to sleep.

The Flaming Cutlass

No one on *The Cutlass* had spoken for a while, other than orders and instructions and the exchange of information. Maddy had made herself comfortable in the crow's-nest, or at least as comfortable as she could be given the state of the weather. She had kept *Queen Anne's Revenge* and *The Bristol Dragon* in her sights, ensuring Tom that he was going in the right direction. But, as the other parties had experienced, the storm grew stronger, and the waves more violent.

Thomas Glove was not as strong a helmsman as his father, as Blackbeard, or as Amber. It was safe to say, in fact, that there was no way in which he could have successfully sailed through the storm while keeping his rival in his sights – if it weren't for the fact that he had two mermaids in his crew. Both Neve and Charlie had, though they hadn't thought to mention it until now, the ability of hydrokinesis. They warned it was only slight: they couldn't stop it from raining, but could shield them from the incoming waves.

Tom offered to have them lowered in a rowboat at the front of the ship, but the mermaids were happy to be in the water. So, that's what happened; the two of them dived into the restless ocean and swam at the front of the ship like dolphins, keeping up with it. Their power was limited to the repulsion of water, which seemed counter-intuitive for an aquatic creature, but was perfect for breaking waves before they collided into the timbers of the ship. As they swam towards a wave, it slowed, then switched its direction. The effect of this was not far-reaching, but between the two of them, a road of calmer water was paved in front of *The Cutlass*. This may not sound like much, but it was instrumental in speeding up the ship's journey, allowing them to pursue the *Revenge* regardless of the less concise steering.

"What's the plan?" Noah asked Tom, realising that they were both far enough ahead of *The Lady* and far enough behind the *Revenge* to begin a discussion.

"We bring him home," Tom replied, obviously talking about Adam.

"How? We surely can't just sail up to the *Revenge* and hope Blackbeard hands him over."

"No, I guess I still need to plan it," Tom suggested.

"I know," Noah said with a smile, "that's why I brought it up."

Tom put one hand on Noah's shoulder and asked, "Do you have anything in mind?"

"I didn't say I'd do the planning for you – I just knew it would have to be done."

"Then at least help me plan, so we don't both get blown to pieces."

Queen Anne's Revenge

Adam lay in the bed that he had been shown to and observed the surrounding room. He saw a pistol, which he would need, as well as a sword and some bullets. There was also a telescope, which could come in handy. Thinking back, he remembered that there was a rowboat suspended to be deployed at the back of the ship, for which he had a plan: a plan to escape.

But the bed he was in had become warm, and he found himself quite comfortable. So, instead of executing his plan, he fell asleep.

The Lady Mary

At first, Glove was reluctant to hand the wheel to Amber, but once the exchange had occurred, he promptly retreated to his quarters. Because of the powerful waves below them, Amber instructed that one man would still have to help her at the wheel, the other altering the sails. Doyle took the latter role, as he had before. She also demanded that the sails be altered more frequently than the crew was used to, giving Doyle no rest. The division of labour caused by the limited crew delayed any discussion between Elliott and Doyle. So, Elliott spoke to Amber instead, even when she asked him to be quiet while she was steering.

"What will you do now?" he asked.

"Now what?"

"Now you have your freedom."

"How am I free? I am still aboard another man's ship," she replied, making Elliott reevaluate his wording.

"We'll have you off it soon enough," he responded, "You might even get to go back to Earth."

"But will then I be free? Or will I still be bound to the whims of a captain?"

Not much more than an hour after Amber had taken the wheel did the storm wither entirely, leaving nothing above them but the black blanket speckled with white that was the sky itself. Glove, being as physically and mentally tired as he was, did not wake, so Amber stayed at the helm, no longer needing Elliott's aid. The time stood quietly at the helm gave Elliott time to think out a plan. He had decided that he wanted to help his friends return to Earth and live the lives that they'd had taken away from them. But he didn't want to leave his captain either.

He relayed his plans to Doyle, explaining, "I believe it would be good — I mean morally, that is — to give Thomas the locket and let them get to Earth."

"But the captain has it, and he'll never give it up."

"I know, but if we time it right, we could take it from him in his sleep, and hand it over."

"How? They're miles away now."

"We need to send them a message."

"Yes, but how?"

"Doyle!" Elliott smiled.

"What?"

"Not you," Elliott muttered, as he went to find Doyle the dragon.

Below deck

When he entered the office, Elliott saw the two cages. The first contained the small dragon, the other, the hideous insect bound to destroy the world. He looked at the latter and frowned. The nature of their voyage so far had felt like a more eventful and purposeful version of usual pirate life, distracting him from the truly satanic matter at hand. The ungodly sight of the animal made him disappointed with the nature of his captain's mission and angry. Drawing and loading a pistol where he stood, he shot the Locust twice. It flustered and screeched, but keeled over onto its back.

"Well, that's enough of that," he thought to himself, instantly worrying that he had just forfeited his soul to the Devil.

But nothing happened, so he lifted the dragon's cage and took it upstairs.

Main-deck

When he rejoined him, Elliott swiftly began explaining to Doyle, "There's no land on this planet, so if we let this little fella out, he should fly and land at the next ship, on *The Flaming Cutlass*. So, if we tie the message to his leg like a pigeon, he should carry it to them."

"Are you sure?"

"Well, hopefully. It's worth a shot anyway. Look, you can even see them now that the storm has lifted."

So, Elliott got a pencil and a small sheet of paper, and thought about what to write. Doyle found in his box a piece of string and handed it to his friend to tie the note to the animal's leg, a gesture Elliott met with gratitude.

"What if they don't come?" Doyle asked, "They need to keep up with Blackbeard to get Adam Back."

"They won't get Adam back, not without reinforcements," Elliott responded, "They are outgunned by Thatch and *Queen Anne's*

Revenge alone, not to mention the second ship. We'll give them the guns, some ammunition, and whatnot, you know, from the bazaar. Give them some barrels of gunpowder – and rum – just in case they need it. If Adam can get off the *Revenge*, then all they have to do is break it open, let the herd out."

He couldn't write and talk at the same time, so fell silent as he jotted down a message. He then rolled the paper up tightly and tied it up with a bow of string. Carefully, he grabbed Doyle (the dragon) by the body and lifted him out of the cage. He flapped with power, assuring Elliott he could make the journey. The man ignored the dragon biting at his hand as he used the other to tie the message to its foot, making sure it was secure. Doyle settled down and perched on Elliott's arm like a falcon mixed with a cat. He talked to him, though knew he wasn't listening, then pointed him towards *The Flaming Cutlass* and let go of its feet entirely.

Doyle sprang off his hand and flapped in bursts alternating with gliding, like a duck might. His crested tail trailed stiffly behind him like the rear of a plane as he circled around *The Lady* in search of food. Elliott tossed a scrap of meat in the intended direction, and the animal darted after it, snatching it from the water, then continuing in this direction until it was hardly a darker speck in the ready dark sky. "Let's hope he can see in the dark," Elliott muttered, as he watched the dragon fly away with hope.

Queen Anne's Revenge

Adam slept less stilly than he was used to. Maybe it was the change of bed, for he had slept in the same one for over twenty years, or the scratchier sheets. Or maybe it was the sounds he heard in his head.

Tossing and turning, sweat dripped from his head as his dreams took him back to the night on Oblitos, when he heard the growls of Queen Anne, and the gunfire. He recalled the sound of Tudor's scream, of a crunch of bone, and how he did nothing. These sounds seemed so unimportant to him when he heard them. But not now. Now, they woke him up, now it was too late to do anything.

Adam jumped out of his bed and panted. He grabbed his boots and put them on, grabbed his coats, tossing his old to the side and putting on the new one, layering over it the belts which carried weapons and ammunition. He then picked up his old coat and took from it any piece of ammunition he could find. One thing he realised was missing was the locket. He had put it in the pocket of his coat, bit couldn't feel it anywhere. Instead, he retrieved a piece of paper, which read, 'It must run in your blood.' It wasn't signed, but Adam knew it was from Thatch at once, and sighed.

He didn't dwell on this, and grabbed two pistols and all the bullets he could find, and the telescope. He loaded the guns, as well as two from his belt. With two double-barrelled and two standard pistols, he had six shots. And he knew that there'd be six men on deck, so he'd have to land each shot. Assuming Thatch had gone to bed, it was likely the helmsman wouldn't be prepared for him.

Holding his hands in his pockets and the loaded pistols in his hands, he walked down the corridor and up the stairs to the main-deck, and crouched, waiting to make his move. He had the five crew members he had expected to be there in his sights, knowing the helmsman was behind him on the higher quarterdeck. He could hear his heart thudding quickly against his chest — at least when his heavy breathing wasn't drowning it out.

Adam got the shock of his life when someone grabbed his left arm. At once, he pulled his right hand from his pocket and fired the pistol. The barrel of this gun, however, was crooked, so the shot missed the target and hit the wall.

"Calm down, son," Thatch said, "It's only your old man."

Adam searched his brain for something to say to sound innocent, so just said, "I couldn't sleep."

The Flaming Cutlass

"If we can get Adam off the ship, we just have to break into the sides enough to let the cattle out," Noah said, "But I don't know how we get to him without putting our own ship in danger."

Though the storm had cleared from the night sky, the mermaids still swam in the water to break the waves. "Maybe they could do it," Tom suggested, "They can get to and from the *Revenge* without being in a big ship, without attracting attention."

As he said this, Tom heard a faint flapping, like a bird flying overhead. Because it was dark, he couldn't yet see the animal, but knew something was circling the ship. The flapping stopped for a while, and only now did he see what it was. Doyle the dragon was gliding towards the deck. The creature flapped as I was about to land to reduce the impact, then skidded on all fours until reaching a stop.

"Doyle?" Tom called in delight and confusion, walking over to the dragon, though he had no food to win its favour.

Doyle approached him, though with a brief hesitation, stopping to scratch the string around his leg, drawing Tom's attention to it.

"What's this?" he said, though he knew the dragon would not answer him. He subtly tapped the floor and beckoned Doyle to him, which worked just well enough to allow him to grab the note, pulling the animal's foot with it. Doyle bit Tom's hand, and the note tore from the string, as the creature flew up onto a flagpole.

When Tom opened the piece of paper, he knew it was Elliott's writing. It read: 'Glove is asleep; come quickly and take what you need. I'll give you the stone. You are outgunned without this.' Tom passed the paper to Noah when he asked to see what it said, then checked in front and behind them. *The Flaming Cutlass* was still closer to *The Lady Mary* than it was to *Queen Anne's Revenge,* but Tom recognised that joining the former again would slow down the pursuit of the latter. But he then recognised that it's better to be prepared to face a problem than expect mermaids to solve it.

"We've shown we can catch up to the *Revenge*," Noah said, "and I do think he's right; we don't really stand a chance if it came down to it. I'm not a pirate, and I can see that."

"But we might lose him," Tom argued.

"He's already lost. You're lost, I'm lost, we're all lost. This is the sort of place you only get to when you're lost. If we continue as we are, we might get him back, but we still might not save Earth. And even if we do, your father will still have the stone to destroy Heaven. If we take that stone from him, that can't happen, and then we will be stronger to ensure Blackbeard does not destroy Earth."

"There's a lot of ifs there."

"When is there not? Look, I know he's your friend, but we're talking about everything here."

The bright stars shone bright in the sky between *The Cutlass* and *The Lady*, proving that the storm had dwindled from existence. The ship was sailing towards them, and with them sailing toward it, the journey would take half the time. "Alright, we're going," Tom said cautiously, as he turned the wheel and adjusted the sails from the comfort of the helm.

A feature that had made sailing easier, though he hadn't thought to give it credit, was powered-steering, making the wheel more responsive to him and less responsive to the waves.

"They've turned around," Elliott said happily, "It worked."

"What do we need to get ready?" Doyle asked him.

"You pile up all the spare weapons, those new ones from the bazaar. Give them a third of the cannonballs. Some food, maybe. Just do it quietly. I'll get the locket."

"Do you want me to get the stone," Doyle asked, "I may be more, you know, sneaky."

"That would be true anywhere else, but I know that room better than you, I know the captain better than you. Trust me, I'll get the stone."

So, the two set off to do just that, Lewis offering to help Doyle, who reminded him to be quiet as Elliott had told him before. They had quite a pile of things ready before the first-mate had even plucked up the courage to enter Glove's quarters.

Captain's cabin

Elliott stood at the door and prepared to knock in the fashion he always had, but stopped himself, remembering the gravity of stealth. So instead, he so very carefully twisted the handle of the door, and pushed it open just wide enough to peer through with one eye. To his relief, Glove had his hat over his head, and was fast asleep. He opened the door to allow himself through, then closed it without making a sound.

The locket was fastened around Glove's neck, his hair covering the chain at the back of his neck – covering the clamp which fastened it. Elliott paid attention to his own breathing, forcing it to be slower and quieter than his lungs were insisting. He tiptoed to the darker side of the room, avoiding two floorboards which he knew creaked. When he reached Glove, he ceased breathing entirely, and crouched behind his chair. Knowing he could not unclasp the piece of jewellery, he attempted to open the locket and take the stone out of it. Without moving the chain, he got as good a hold of it as he could, working around the edges to find the closing mechanism.

Before he could prize it open, Glove turned towards him. He let go of the jewel in fright and moved back behind the chair, out of sight. He let out a sigh as Glove snored. The locket was now suspended in the air, dangling from the captain's shoulder. Elliott reached for it, trying not to pull and disturb him. He located the latch that sealed the item shut, and twisted it. The stone's radiance grew brighter as Elliott removed the glass from in front of it, and the source of this glow slipped from its container, dropping onto the wooden floor.

With this thud, Elliott again dashed back to hide, clenching his eyes shut. He waited five seconds, still and overcome with dread, but with the lack of further sound, other than snoring, he slowly reached for the stone and picked it from the floor, placing it quickly into his pocket. First, after waiting a minute to collect himself, Elliott rose and walked out as cautiously as he had walked in. When he shut the door once again, he let out the deepest breath of his life, huffing in the process.

Main-deck

"I've got it," Elliott said, still panting, to Doyle as he returned to him. *The Flaming Cutlass* was not far away now. Elliott and Doyle stood awkwardly and impatiently for the exchange to occur. It felt that the sea had become still and silent just to make it even more tense. Elliott broke the quiet by saying, "You should go. When they get here, go with them."

"You should too," Doyle said happily.

"I can't leave Glove, he's made me who I am. And anyway, it's partly my fault his plan is going to fail, so I should at least stick with him."

"Even after all he's done to you?"

"It's a scratch, Doyle."

"Yes, but that's just the start; he's shown he's willing and able to turn on you."

"And in a more subtle way, I've also turned on him. I can't leave him, Doyle, I can't."

"Then I'm not leaving you," Doyle replied with a smile, "I can't leave you here, it wouldn't feel right."

"Doyle, you should really go, be free while you have the chance."

"I'm staying with you," Doyle said finally, "just to be sure."

Elliott wasn't convinced, but granted Doyle the right to decide for himself. He then thought of Amber and went to have a similar conversation with her.

"Amber," he said to get her attention, before becoming quieter again, "in a few minutes, *The Flaming Cutlass* will arrive, and I am going to give them the key to get out of here. I suggest you go aboard, then you can be free."

"Free to do what?"

"They're going to Earth, I believe. If you go, you'll get the chance to start afresh, to be free to not be wicked."

"And what will happen of you?"

"That's yet to be discovered, though I don't see this ship getting very far without you. But this is about you."

"It wouldn't be a great start, would it?" Amber replied, "To acquire the freedom to not be wicked, just to let the person who granted you that freedom face such an uncertain future."

"Don't worry about me, for God's sake," Elliott said, "just go and be free."

"We'll all have to serve somebody in this life. I'd rather serve alongside someone who wants me to be free. I'll stick with you, as thanks for saving me, and just maybe it all ends alright."

Again, Elliott would not force anyone to abandon him if it would affect their conscience. He offered the same proposal to Lewis, who at first simply said, "Ah, I'm fine here, mate," and left it at that, until Elliott successfully encouraged him to change his mind.

Queen Anne's Revenge

"You couldn't sleep?" Blackbeard called loudly, "Is that why you're on edge, or is there something else on your mind?"

466

Adam's heart was racing, and all he could find to say was, "I'm alright, I just needed some fresh air."

"Come on, son, walk with me," Thatch said calmly and without threat. He had the locket around his neck now, and Adam couldn't help but stare in frustration. The pair walked onto the deck and up to the helm. Thatch did not take the wheel, but instead gazed out across the navy-blue waters.

"My eyes are up here, son," Thatch said with a hearty laugh, "I see you looking at this old thing."

He was of course talking about the locket. Even so, Adam had few words to say.

"I don't blame you for stealing it," he continued, "I would have done just the same thing. That's how I caught you. But not to worry, son, you can have a share of the spoils. Endless riches — that's what's ahead of us. Absolutely everything you could want, I've been told. I know that sounds tempting, but just stick with me, you'll see it soon enough, no need to go your own way. And no need for your old crew, for that matter. No need for that liar, Glove — no need for any of them."

Adam was acutely aware that he could shoot Blackbeard as the two stood. He also realised that likely meant that Blackbeard was also aware of this, so would be prepared to shoot first. It was unlikely he could beat him in combat. Adam's greatest skill, however, according to himself, was 'bullshitting.' He could probably beat Blackbeard by bullshitting.

He walked further across the quarterdeck to the farthest back part of the ship, saying, "I'm sorry, I don't know what encouraged my behaviour. I suppose I thought that doing it myself would prove that I'm better than you."

All while he spoke, Adam observed the rigging and the small rowboat and oars suspended from it. He saw where to cut or untie to free the boat, and how he could reach it quickly.

The Flaming Cutlass

Tom was tense. He worried about several things. For one, this may or may not be the last time he sees some of his friends again, if his plan works out. Second, he dreaded the eventuality of his father waking and being furious. To allow for a swift departure if necessary, he sailed past *The Lady* and turned around, so the ships were facing the same direction when side by side. Elliott, when he could see the crew of *The Cutlass*, he put his finger to his lips to ensure that they remained quiet.

A plank was, as before, placed between the decks of the ships, on which Tom and Noah crossed to retrieve the collection of guns and cannonballs and ammunition, Lewis carrying some on his was to board *The Cutlass*. No one talked, though there was plenty of grave eye-contact since every person was as uneasy as the others. The majority of the operation was over quickly, though not yet had the stone been exchanged. Doyle kept his own elbow-knives and put them on.

"Tom," Elliott called as loud as was appropriate, "one last thing."

"What is it?" Tom asked, a tad impatient. Elliott looked around, worried, assessing for danger. When he observed that there was no danger, he took the shining stone from his pocket and placed it in Tom's hand.

"Go on, Tom Glove, do your best to save Earth from Edward Thatch, then go yourself. Grant our crew the freedom that was taken from them, and protect those who need your protection. That's an order."

"Come with us," Tom said.

"No, I'm not getting into this," Elliott replied, "Just go."

He then contradicted this by ordering, "Wait!"

Tom turned around and saw Elliott holding Adam's musket. He threw the weapon to him, saying, "You can't leave without this!"

The Lady Mary: **captain's cabin**

The sleeping Andrew Glove tossed his body to one side in his chair, his hat falling from his face. Torchlight immediately fell upon his eyes, which fluttered subtly, opening to a squint. He snored for a while still, despite the disturbance to his sleep, though this ended abruptly. He was not well-rested nor replenished to a great degree, but revitalised just enough to prevent him from drifting back to sleep. What truly woke him, however, was when his eyes looked down to see an empty, open locket.

He sprung from his seat, startled, and began searching on the cold, wooden floor. But there was no glow from the satanic rock, for it was not there.

Main-deck

After Tom had hugged Elliott and Doyle, he said goodbye, just in case it was the last time he would. He then took to the helm and sailed away, sighing that he had executed the exchange without confrontation.

The Cutlass was about three hundred yards away when Doyle stood beside Elliott and asked, "So what now?"

"Now?" Elliott thought for a second, "Now, I wait to endure the resulting fury of my captain, knowing I am ultimately moral in causing the chaos I have."

"But why should you endure any fury for being moral? He may be our captain, but he has no right, nor need, to punish the good."

"It was good enough for Nero," Elliott said, though this was sophistry, for he was masking his unwillingness to answer with poetry.

You know already what is about to happen, for you have seen what Elliott and Doyle have yet not. Glove returned to the helm in indignation, and upon seeing *The Flaming Cutlass* sailing away, his eyes grew unblinking and rabid.

"What have you done?" he said, first quietly, though he then repeated this in a cry of rage and despair.

Glove then drew his sword on impulse, and paced towards his first-mate, whose silence suggested guilt. But it wasn't Elliott who met the blade – it was Doyle. He had taken a sword of his own. It wasn't his usual choice of weapon, but he needed the range to combat the captain's cutlass. He did not fight to wound, though Glove was doing exactly that.

Doyle blocked most of the attacks, it not taking him long to disarm Glove by knocking away his sword. He seemed to overpower the older captain, likely because the defence of a friend is even more persuasive than fury. When Glove was disarmed, Doyle, through his instinct as a fighter, went in with an elbow, running the new blade from. Glove's right shoulder to the left side of his abdomen. This cut his linen shirt but was obstructed from reaching the flesh. Glove pushed Doyle away, where he fell into the railing at the side of the deck. With no care for the consequences, Doyle called, "It was me; I gave it away."

He then fell backwards into the sea. Not because he was clumsy, but because he had been shot. Glove, who held the smoking pistol, reloaded the weapon and placed it back into his belt. He looked over into the water, as Elliott joined him, and saw that Doyle Clementini was dead.

Chapter II

Queen Anne's Revenge

With his side facing away from Blackbeard, Adam slowly took a knife from his belt. He leant further over the rail, his head looking over his shoulder to the sea past Thatch. He frowned intentionally as if he had seen something, so his captor directed his gaze in the same direction. It was at that moment that he flung himself from the deck and landed on his rear I the rowboat, cutting the rope securing it as he fell. Only as he landed in it did the boat itself fall towards the ocean, hitting the water with a splash. He didn't have the locket; he hadn't released the herd early, but he had escaped. He had escaped, but he was still within firing range. To remove himself from the danger, he grabbed the oars in terror and rowed. He hadn't done much rowing in his life, but anyone can row a boat when you have a maniac with a gun twenty yards away.

The Flaming Cutlass

The shot of Glove's pistol could be heard from *The Cutlass*, naturally causing the crew to turn their heads. Maddy, being in the crow's-nest, had the job of identifying what had happened. Through her telescope. "I think it's Doyle," she said, "He's shot Doyle!"

Lewis and Noah ran to the back of the ship to observe and made the same conclusion.

They all fell silent. Unlike with Tudor's death, they couldn't avoid the stabbing pain of guilt in their guts when this news sunk in. The now quite still waters allowed the mermaids to return to deck, though the slower winds which caused this hindered the hopes of catching up to *Queen Anne's Revenge*. But with full sails, they returned on their journey, fleeing the scene behind them and aiming to put a good distance between them and Glove.

"I bet he did something stupid," Maddy said, talking about Doyle.

"Something stupid, to help us," Tom specified, "I bet he's died, hoping it means we don't."

Noah found glasses and a bottle of rum amongst the pile of goods just delivered to them. He placed a glass in front of everyone and poured a shot of rum in.

"To Doyle," Tom said, raising his glass.

Everyone else echoed this toast — except Maddy, who instead said, "Thanks, Doyle."

They could no longer see their rival ahead of them, though knew which direction to travel, *The Flaming Cutlass* has proved itself faster than *The Lady Mary*, making it faster still than *Queen Anne's Revenge*. It was inevitable that they would reach Blackbeard – provided that there was enough distance between him and the Gate of Ubyvis.

The Lady Mary

"What did he jump for?" Glove asked Elliott after a minute's silence. The first-mate just stared at his captain, dumbfounded. He realised now that he had chosen the wrong ship, regardless of loyalties. He still had in his possession Doyle's bandana. It was stained with Elliott's blood, but he clenched it in his hands and held it to his chest. When his captain looked away, a fear escaped from his eye.

"I'll take the wheel, Miss," he said to Amber, "We need all hands on deck now that the traitors have left us."

"What's going to happen, Captain?" Elliott muttered, still facing away from him.

"We're going to get that stone back. It's my only way to her, so we have to get it. Mark my words. I'll get it one way or another."

Elliott and Amber had to labour hard at adjusting the sails, loading cannons, and preparing the vessel for pursuit. They did not speak, communicating with glances alone. Amber looked at a pistol and then at Glove, silently suggesting a plan, which Elliott rejected with a shake of his head. This may sound like he was simply remaining loyal, but it would be easier to reach *The Flaming Cutlass* with three people than with two, and there'd be no point freeing themselves of Glove to sit idly on a barren planet.

While *The Lady* was slower than *The Cutlass*, this was insignificant enough to allow Glove to keep a constant distance between the two, as the wind-speed was the limiting factor. There was half a mile between the two boats now; enough to keep it tense but make any attack impossible. The horizon was so dark, the sky and sea bled together, and it felt like they were sailing into oblivion. Elliott made the observation that the stars were fewer and did not arrange themselves into the usual constellations. Nor was there a moon to scatter light across the softly rolling waves.

The Bristol Dragon

Adam rowed frantically, unable to process the lack of gunfire he was receiving. He continued the stroke of his oars but found that the boat grew slower, then noticed that his feet were wet. He looked down at his sodden boots and saw that there was a leak in the bottom of the boat. To his credit, the hole was under the seat, so was obstructed from his view from the deck. But it was causing to sink, whether he had noticed it.

"Mother-fucker," he said, realising now why Thatch had not just shot him. He looked behind him, and Blackbeard's silhouette had disappeared from the torch-lit deck.

There was no way he'd make it back to the *Revenge*, nor any reason he would want to risk the consequences. *The Bristol Dragon*, however unimportant it had been thus far, was within reach. He constructed a plant in a heartbeat, thinking that he'd give bullshitting another try.

So he rowed to the best of his ability to *The Dragon*, the rowboat sinking as he reached the ladder up to it. "Don't shoot!" he called as he was about to reach the top, "I have a message from Blackbeard!"

There were four sailors on deck, with Commander Teddy Feather at the helm, who all looked as confused at each other.

"Who are you?" Teddy said in a way that was presumably supposed to sound intimidating, "Where did you come from?"

"The sky," Adam replied sarcastically, "Where'd you think?"

"Ah, you're the boy."

"I'm hardly younger than you, mate,"

"But you're Blackbeard's boy," Teddy said to him.

"Yes, but it doesn't matter who I am!" Adam shouted, "I have a message, that's why I'm here." Adam's plan was detailed for its speedy creation, and he drew the piece of paper Thatch had replaced the locket with and pretended to read a different message from it.

"He needs," he paused, trying to gauge how many sailors were on *The Bristol Dragon*, "a dozen men – at least a dozen men – need to row over and sort something out."

"What are you on about?" the commander responded, "Don't they have enough men?"

"There's been an issue with the herd. Repairs are necessary quickly and with as much help as you can spare."

"What kind of repairs?"

"There's no time to discuss the repairs, we need the men."

Teddy looked Adam up and down and up again, locking eyes with him and waiting for his bluff to fail. But there was not a tremble of doubt on Adam's expression, so he simply said, "Let me see that note," though Adam had 'dropped' it before he had finished this sentence and it drifted into the water. Teddy looked sternly at him but was ultimately convinced to instruct fourteen men to row to *Queen Anne's Revenge*. He sailed his ship to overtake the flagship to allow it easy passage.

This left Adam on deck with Teddy Feather and ten men below deck, who had not yet come above deck to claim the positions of their crewmates. Still having a pistol loaded in his pocket, so shot the commander while there were no witnesses, pushing his body into the sea after collecting his guns. He then ran to the helm and steered the ship out of firing range of the *Revenge*, reloading his own guns as he did. That left ten men to convince to sail for him or kill, and four loaded guns to achieve this.

No expert as a helmsman, he left the ship on the new course, sailing with the wind away from the *Revenge*, and went below deck.

Below deck

"Alright, men!" Adam called to whoever could hear him, "Do not be alarmed, but the commander has deserted us! I'm in charge now, as an appointment of my father, Blackbeard himself!"

One man met him and stared blankly, to which Adam replied, "Take the wheel, lad! We've altered course."

The man was confused but was convinced to follow this instruction simply by the volume at which out was shouted. Adam found more men sitting with no jobs, so ordered them, "Come on! Grab the sails! On deck, all of you! Get her going straight and good!"

Queen Anne's Revenge

Thatch was sitting in his chair at his desk when there was a knock on the door to his cabin. It was an officer asking for what reason fourteen men had been sent to the *Revenge*.

"I called for no men at all," he remarked dully, then, seeing the huddle of pirates standing aimlessly behind the door. They stepped out of the way when they heard Blackbeard's boots thud against the floor as he marched to take the wheel. "That bastard boy!" he called before he had reached it.

"What's going on, sir?" one man asked Thatch timidly.

"Grab the sails, you no-good deck-apes!" he ordered with fury, "Man the guns, tie the ropes, do something useful or God help you!"

Thatch spun the wheel mightily and turned the boat around and in pursuit of *The Bristol Dragon*.

The Flaming Cutlass

"Does it bother you?" Tom said to Noah, who was the only one stood beside him, "Does it bother you that if Blackbeard gets there before we can get to him, he will get vast riches and immortality, when we get to watch our friends drop off, one by one?"

"Yes, it bothers me, but that's why we're here, is it not? To stop that from happening?"

"But like Elliott said, we are no longer the crew of *The Lady Mary*. We are not bound to go to Heaven by destroying it, nor are we bound to go to Earth."

"What's your point?"

"What would be so wrong with going to Heaven, now we don't have to destroy it? I've seen the visions from the stone, of Pestilence and

War and Famine and Death, so why put ourselves through it when others are getting rewarded?"

"The people in Heaven don't need help. The people on Earth, who have to go through all that Pestilence and War and Famine and Death, who could benefit from your strength as a pirate captain."

"So you want me to be a hero? Seems like an awful lot to ask."

"You don't have to be a hero to everyone. But if you can be a hero to someone, to anyone – anyone deserving at all – that's surely the best use of this chance."

The Bristol Dragon

Adam did not do anything to directly impact the ship's operations besides shout old enough at its crew to ensure it kept its course.

"Why's the *Revenge* following us, sir?" a man asked Adam.

"Because," he laughed, wanting to know the answer himself, "because we're going the same direction! He expressly said that we are to stay ahead of them, so hurry up, fellas, don't want to hold up ol' Blackbeard!"

Adam had no idea whether *The Bristol Dragon* could outpace *Queen Anne's Revenge*. Evidence to the contrary was the decreasing distance between the two. He knew not how much longer he could keep us his façade, nor how much longer he had until the two ships were again side by side – the ideal arrangement for a fight.

He knew he was out of time when a shot hit the stern of the ship. "Bugger!" he exclaimed, realising that the *Revenge* had front cannons, and was close enough to use them. "Just keep going!" he shouted at them as he ran below deck. He heard the lowing of the Devil's herd below his feet. His plan was now simple: let the herd out, so that they cannot be delivered, and hope he can get away in a rowboat without being killed. The barrels of gunpowder and rum had already been un-stowed to make room for the cattle. All he had to do was roll them into one place and light them up.

Adam had gathered from the lack of subsequent shots that Blackbeard had either given up or simply didn't want to damage his own ship, especially if that meant freeing the herd. He ran back onto the main-deck to see, proving the tater to be true. He made sure he knew where the rowboat was, being thankful that there even was one, and ran back below deck before Thatch gained the chance to board.

"Here goes fuck-all," he whispered, lighting a fuse into the gunpowder and sprinting as fast as he could away from it. Seeing a harpoon on the way out, he bent down to grab it, then leapt onto the boat and forced it into the water.

He rowed, and rowed, and rowed to get away from the chaos he had created, waiting to hear the imminent explosion. This sound did occur, but the herd was not released. So, in panic and disappointment, he just kept rowing. Eventually, his nose caught the smell of burning wood, as various pirates leapt from the ship t avoid the secondary explosions. The sound of horns against weaker timber signalled the success of the plan; bull after cow after bull after cow dashed out of the ship. Some flew above the waves and carried on, others were not so smart, so ended up swimming frantically away, being pushed by those behind them.

Adam wasn't far enough away to simply observe this; he still needed to get out of harm's way. But he couldn't out-row a flying bull, so the beasts soon were at his heels. A flying brute even overtook him – but this was why he picked up the harpoon. He tied the line to his seat and threw the weapon while he was close enough to get a well-aimed shot. It bellowed as the barbs hooked into its flesh, and the weight of the boat with Adam in it added resistance to its movement. This had left him travelling in his intended direction, which was back to his crew, though occasionally he used a spare rope as a whip to correct it.

Queen Anne's Revenge

At the sight of the cattle pouring from his second ship, Thatch spun the wheel in the other direction. If he were merciful, he would have briefly stopped to allow *The Bristol Dragon*'s crew to board. Ill let you guess whether or not that happened. He saw Adam in his rowboat, but with the satanic herd between them, he saw no logic in going after him.

"That boy!" he called, mostly furious though slightly proud, "Not to worry, *Queen Anne's Revenge* is still shipshape, we'll still make it, boys!"

Chapter III

The Lady Mary

The wind again had changed in magnitude and direction. This time, it was in favour of the pirates, blowing right the way they were going. It had proven just short of impossible to sail a ship of *The Lady*'s size with only three people, so they were lucky they had no reason to man the guns or do any real navigation. After Elliott and Amber had adjusted the sails for the new wind direction, Amber took the wheel from Glove. The captain went to his quarters but left the door open onto the deck. He still needed to rest, but he did not sleep.

In theory, Glove would be able to hear through the boards, so Elliott, who stood near Amber in the helm, whispered, as he had become accustomed to doing.

"If we reach *The Flaming Cutlass*," he said, "just get on it. The crew of this ship is cursed to forfeit their souls to Satan – you don't need to be included in that."

"Nor do you," Amber replied.

"Maybe I'll get what I deserve. I made a deal with the Devil to destroy Earth; you didn't."

"Did you or did your captain?"

"The captain I supported."

"Then stop supporting him."

"That doesn't make up for it, though, does it?"

"Freeing me — that makes up for it. Accepting you're wrong and changing – and encouraging others to change – that makes up for it."

"Does it really, though?"

"Yes, it does, as long as you prove it. What you oughtn't do is write yourself off. What good is that? You'd want the same for everyone else, I know that."

Elliott replied to this with hesitation, "Doyle's dead, when it should've been me."

"But it isn't you. And it's no good being both of you."

"Well," he thought, "we're not there yet."

The Flaming Cutlass

"I don't understand," Tom said, "why you wouldn't be happy saving the Earth, then going somewhere better."

"Because that's only better for us," Noah said.

"But we'd be heroes, wouldn't we?"

"That is a status that you must maintain. There're more men than Blackbeard who would see the world burn."

"And plenty more men than me to stop it."

"But many less able to."

"Why are you pressuring me?"

Noah did not answer but instead grabbed the stone from Tom's hand and held it over the sea. Tom looked at him sternly, his cheek twitching. Noah threatened, "I'll do it! I'll throw this away if you're just going to waste it."

"Don't you dare!" Tom burst out as he tackled Noah to the deck, trying the grab the stone back from him. Noah threw the stone, but it landed five yards away and down onto the main-deck. The two got up and ran down the stairs, pushing each other out of the way. Noah dived to reach it first but could not grab it, for Tom had got hold of his leg and swung him back. He leapt forward to get it, but Noah had placed his hand over it. Both men laid on their bellies on the wooden floor with their arms stretched. Tom made a fast and slammed down onto Noah's knuckles until he was forced to let go – but he did this by sliding it away further, then both crawled after it.

When Tom had again been beaten to the stone, he got up and picked the smaller man up from the ground, shaking him.

"Give me the stone," he grumbled, before marching to the side of the deck, carrying Noah with him, "If you're going to throw it, I'll throw you after it!"

Noah squealed as he tried to get out of Tom's arms, and then again when he became free, but fell off the boat and into the water.

Neve and Charlie, who had watched on, quite amused by the squabble, walked as quick as their anatomy allowed to see what had happened. Noah splashed around in the sea as waves rushed over him. "You ass!" he called once he had put his head out of the water.

"Sack the juggler!" Neve said, not entirely sure if this idiom applied here or not.

"I think you've got to jump in now, Tom!" Charlie said.

"Yes, encore!" Neve added.

"Have you still got it?" Tom asked, shouting down to Noah in the water.

"Erm, no," Noah said.

"I'm not getting you out then."

"What do you mean 'you're not getting me then'?"

"I mean, I'm not getting you."

"You are getting me."

"Have you got it?"

"No."

"Then I'm not getting you."

"You are getting me."

"No, I'm not."

"Yes, you are."

"No."

"Yes."

"Get the rope, then," Tom gave up and threw a line to Noah, circling the ship around the man to allow him to climb up the ladder, before adding unnecessarily, "dickhead."

When Noah reached the deck again, he removed his jacket and shook himself dry. He and Tom looked at each other in despair, but couldn't help laughing. "I guess we'll just have to get Blackbeard's," Tom said, masking his disapproval.

"I'm sure that will be straightforward," Noah said back.

"For fuck's sake," Tom said, eyeballing Noah, "you bell-end."

Adam's boat

Adam had been travelling for a quarter of an hour — though it felt like less — when the line holding the harpoon to the boat snapped, and the bull flew off, free from its symbiotic passenger. The small rowboat skidded across the water before slowing, only to be moved by the waves. He finally found the nerve to look behind him and saw that he was no longer being followed by the *Revenge*. He then thought about what it was he had actually just pulled off. This notion caused him to let out a loud cheer, which turned to a prideful laugh.

Through the darkness of night, he couldn't see his friends, but found relief in escaping Blackbeard. Taking the oars out slowly, he began rowing towards *The Lady Mary*. He put little effort into rowing, knowing that the ship was itself sailing towards him. He granted himself a rest, for he had just released half of the Devil's herd before they could do any damage.

He then reached into his sock, which was wet with seawater, and retrieved a small object. It was flat, red, and radiant: it was the stone, which he had removed from the locket and hidden. He looked at in and chuckled. However he had got it, this is an important revelation; he had taken the key to the Gate of Ubyvis, so prevented the other half of the herd from reaching their destination.

He felt inclined to sleep. But this time, he resisted. He remembered that with no other hope of a way out, Thatch would come for the stone when he realised its absence, so put a bit more effort into rowing.

The Flaming Cutlass

Tom looked to the horizon, which had on it a faint scratch of red to define it from the sea. The water scattered blue light through its depths once again, and Doyle the dragon began to chirp high in the sails. More importantly, the brightening landscape provided just enough contrast to the distant shape of a ship and its sails.

"I can only see one ship," Tom said, confused as to the whereabouts of the second ship in Blackbeard's fleet.

"Maybe the other is just ahead of it, and that's why we can't see it," Noah suggested, not really getting a clear look without a telescope.

"We'll see soon enough," Tom remarked, before calling to the crew, "There she is: *Queen Anne's Revenge*, we're almost to them."

Charlie and Neve made their way up the stairs to the helm as best as their anatomy could manage, Noah going over to help them up.

"What will happen when we get to them?" Neve asked curiously.

"We'll have to fight them," Tom answered, "to get Adam back, and to get the stone."

"What do we need the stone for?"

"It's the key out of here."

"Where are we going?"

"Earth," Noah answered, "where we're from."

"Well, I'm afraid we aren't much good at fighting on land," Charlie stated.

"You said something about being able to get legs?" Noah asked.

"Erm," the mermaid chuckled, "we could cast a spell, if we had a pair of human legs."

"That can be your job," Tom said to Noah quickly, "when you get the chance, saw off a pair of legs."

"A pair of pairs of legs," Neve reminded.

"Whose legs?" Noah said, high-pitched.

"The first pair of free legs you find," Tom replied, "someone's bound to die when we fight Blackbeard."

"Why is it my job?"

"You know you want to," Tom replied.

"No, I don't."

Queen Anne's Revenge

Blackbeard had sailed his now lonely flagship until the herd of cattle was no more than a fiery light in the distance. The sky had made its best efforts to return to a paler blue, though streaks of amber and scarlet lingered behind the clouds. Flickering through the wind, the feather of the captain's hat blew around, indicating that the strength of the wind had once again picked up. The direction of this, however, was more compliant with the plans of the pirates.

Thatch put the fourteen men who had fallen for Adam's trick to work, making sure every rope, knot and sail were exactly how they ought to be. He knew that there was not much more distance between them and the final stone table before the Gate of Ubyvis. He felt the locket, which hung just below the plaits of his beard, but did not look at it. In the piece of jewellery was not the stone to get them out, but simply a similar-looking piece of agate. But for now, as Blackbeard had not realised this, he sailed forwards, and he did so keenly.

The Lady Mary

The dawn, which had revealed the *Revenge* to *The Cutlass*, also revealed *The Cutlass* to *The Lady*. It wasn't clear if they were gaining on them, but showed that they were close enough to anticipate action.

After tying a rope and adjusting a sail, Elliott trotted down from the quarterdeck and entered the captain's quarters.

"Any further plans on how we acquire the stone, captain?" he asked cautiously.

Glove huffed and paused, giving it away that he hadn't been giving the subject its due thought, "Erm, well," he said, "he won't shoot at you, son. *The Lady* is safe with you aboard it. I can board and take it."

"Just take it?" Elliott asked. "Just like that?"

"Well, I fear is may be more difficult than that. That was my worry which his careless invitation of other people: the crew is not all loyal to me anymore, so we'll have to be careful."

"Well, we're not too far away now," Elliott reminded his captain, before again returning to the quarterdeck.

Adam's boat

Though he had tried his best to avoid it, the restlessness of the past night forced sleep over Adam. The gentle white noise of the waves and breeze only deepened this spell, and so Adam became oblivious to the urgent world around him. He had no torch to light up his little boat, so he just floated in the fleeting darkness of dawn.

He had returned the stone to his sock, for he thought this was the safest location for it. What he had failed to notice before drifting asleep was the approaching ship, *The Flaming Cutlass*. Or perhaps he had noticed but was so exhausted that he could not muster the strength to act upon it, or instead the mental strength to process the matter. No matter the reality, the ship, which Adam had not yet been aboard, sailed steadfastly towards him, though it hadn't noticed him either.

The Flaming Cutlass

"Maybe you don't need to fight on land with us," Noah suggested to the mermaids, "I mean, your water-powers, what do you call it?"

"Hydrokinesis," Charlie answered.

"Yes, hydrokinesis — that's pretty cool."

"Yes, but it won't be much help against an entire pirate ship and crew. I want to fight like a real pirate – that would be cool."

"You can man the cannons," Tom suggested, "That's a real pirate job, and we'll need people to do that when we fight Blackbeard."

"Could I really?" Charlie's teak-coloured eyes lit up.

"Yeah, and that way you wouldn't need legs – they're overrated, anyway."

"They look less stupid, though," Charlie commented with comically exaggerated frustration.

"Look!" Maddy called down from the crow's-nest, pointing to the port-side of the ship. All but Tom at the wheel rushed to view the sight to which they had been directed. It was a small boat, drifting smugly on the waves, with a man laid face-down in it.

"Adam!" Noah called, "It's Adam!"

Hearing this, Tom left the helm unattended and took a look for himself. "Adam! Adam!" he called, with no immediate response, then ordered the crew to throw a rope down. When his friend did not react to the calls, nor the rope which brushed his arm, Tom, without thinking, jumped into the water, a second line in his hand. He splashed to make his way to the boat and shook it when he reached it.

Adam, snoring, flinched, his eyes squinting in the new sun's light. He took his jolly time to wake fully, but when he did, swapped snoring for panting, as if his nervous system had failed to assess the now less perilous situation. Tom pushed water into his face to speed up the recovery, shouting, "Adam! Adam! Get up! We're here!"

"Bugger off!" Adam replied, still quite thoughtless.

"Get up, you arse!" Tom grabbed him by the shoulder and shook him. So, he got up, and the two climbed back to *The Flaming Cutlass*.

"What the Hell happened to you?" Tom began, not getting an answer.

"What the Hell happened to *The Lady*?"

"Long story, I need a first-mate though."

"That black-bearded bastard kidnapped me. Where's the captain?"

"I'm the captain," Tom answered softly.

"What about Elliott?" Adam answered the earlier question.

"Elliott's still on *The Lady*," Tom explained, watching Adam's face furrow and wrinkle as he contemplated all the information.

"Are you asking me?"

"Asking you what?" Tom decided that the conversation had to be restarted, because his friend was confusing him too much, "Right, I bought this ship and came to save your arse. Dad didn't want to come, so the crew split up. Elliott and Doyle stayed, the rest of us are here. So, do me a favour, be my first-mate, and come and blow up that 'black-bearded bastard'."

"Well," Adam chuckled, "that – that settles it."

Queen Anne's Revenge

Thatch took his telescope down from his face, allowing his blue eyes to shine and a grin to form across his mouth.

"There she is, boys," he began with resolve, "the final stone-henge: leading us to the final treacherous planet on our journey out of here. Soon — soon — soon, we will have it all. Soon, I'll have it all. All the riches of all the universe. And when you have all the money, you have all the power. I will become untouchable, unconquerable, indomitable," this list subsided as Thatch's vocabulary of adjectives dwindled.

The crew were indeed inspired by this speech, and their work ethic conveyed this. They managed to influence *Queen Anne's Revenge* into accelerating fast towards their target. But then, the smile of delight dropped from Thatch's face, a tremble of fear taking its place. His aged, pink skin drained of its colour. He had not experienced fear like this when confronted with the Devil. That was because he knew not what the Devil could do. What he saw before him: he knew all too well what it was capable of.

The sea around the stones, which stood out as obelisks from it, bubbled with a swirling boil. Even the tallest waves broke and joined a spiral of water glowing blue-green. And from the water, circling also, were great fins and uneven spines that sat on a submerged and endless, serpentine body. The enveloping ocean of this planet had been, until this point, void of life. Now, Blackbeard could see why.

"What's that?" the navigator asked.

"What's that?" Thatch repeated sarcastically, "You know what that is! That is the ungodly bastard that doomed us to here! That is he, Leviathan!"

Chapter IV

The crew was now about ready for breakfast. Because of the responsibilities of captaining and steering the ship, as well as the impending danger both in front of and behind them, Tom provided only a simple meal. Crackers, ship's biscuits, a few pieces of gingerbread, and some sort of rehydrated broth were available. Tom returned to the helm to allow the crew to eat in relative leisure. So, everyone sat around the table and ate their fair share of food, ignoring their disappointment that they hadn't had the freshest or most satisfactory of meals. *The Flaming Cutlass* had too few plates for everyone to have their own, so people took from central plates of food, placing items they wished to reserve in front of them. Adam sat next to Lewis, who sat next to Noah, who sat next to Maddy. And Maddy sat beside Neve, who sat next to Charlie, who sat next to Adam, who was unfamiliar to her.

The entire group chatted busily to distract themselves from the fear of incoming dangers – and because the ship was now crewed by very many different types of people, who were still getting to know each other. Some topic or another had resulted in a split in the conversation. On one side of the table, the men discussed one thing. And on the other side, the women (mermaid or otherwise) discussed another thing. Neither party engaged with the other's conversation, not because the nature of it excluded them, but just because that was how the flow of talking had ended.

The talking distracted some from eating. Not Adam. Lewis noticed as he talked to him that his eyes went back and forth between the man talking and a piece of gingerbread placed in his vicinity.

"Is this anyone's?" Adam asked, with no hint of shame.

"Not mine," Lewis said.

Noah smiled at the corners of his mouth. After Adam received no more answers, he told him, "Ah, it's mine."

"What's it doing next to me?" Adam asked, slightly offended that someone claimed it.

"I didn't want it," Noah answered, "you can have it."

"Go on, then," Adam said, trying to sound reluctant as he snatched up the biscuit and ate it in two bites. Noah hid a laugh as he did this, but it was unclear why.

Queen Anne's Revenge

"Drop it!" Blackbeard called hoarsely, "Drop the anchor! Now!"

The great steel anchor shot straight out of rest, and soon its chain was pulled after it. The crew braced themselves for a thud as the anchor hit the seabed and dug itself in. They waited longer than usual –

because the thud never arrived. The *Revenge* slowed gradually, but the anchor never struck dirt. The sea was too deep for the anchor to find the floor, so instead it just dragged behind the ship, suspended.

Thatch was nervous to fold up the sails so that an escape would be rapid if required, so he let the *Revenge* dawdle slowly towards the ungodly serpent. Since Adam had escaped on one, the crew hauled out a second rowboat from storage. Three men, who had all been getting on Thatch's nerves for various reasons, were instructed to board this boat. Blackbeard took the stone that was in his locket and placed it in his pocket, not looking at it much in a hurry. He then handed the now-empty locket to the men, hoping it would serve as a distraction.

"Now get off my ship and row!" Thatch yelled in unprovoked fury, "over there!"

So, the men did. Sat huddled in a sad little rowboat, unsure of their aim nor fate, they rowed off to the west of the table, becoming closer to the Leviathan than the *Revenge* was.

"If that bastard goes for the bait," Thatch commanded the crew, "raise the anchor, and raise it fast."

The anchor slowed the ship just enough so that the rowboat could outpace it. As they approached the stone table, a fog of steam drifted across the swirling currents, which grew thicker the closer they got.

The coiling body of the hellish creature slowed its spiralling and submerged. When the rowboat found itself about three hundred yards from the Leviathan, they stopped rowing, unsure of what to do. The pirate in the middle raised up the locket, not sure of the consequences. They became even more confused when they noticed the beast guarding the stone-henge had disappeared. One man stared, to the best of his ability, into the water, looking for a sign of danger. This sign took the form of a glue-green light. The light was dim and quite distant; but growing. "Row," he muttered, and they all did – and did so quickly.

The rowing sped up when, about one hundred yards away from the rowboat, a colossal head raised its nostrils and eyes above the water. It looked like the head of a crocodile, but huffed in and out like a whale before submerging again.

Seeing the Leviathan distracted, Blackbeard shouted enthusiastically, "Raise the anchor! Raise it! Raise it now!"

The men did as asked, and the *Revenge* accelerated cautiously. This was not satisfactory to Thatch, who insisted, "All men to the capstan! Put your sorry backs into it or to Davy Jones with the lot of us!"

The leaden anchor was eventually wrestled out of the waves, it dripping with hot water as it nestled back to sleep, and the wind which filled the sails could once more drive the ship to its fullest, bound straight towards the now unprotected stone table. When the Leviathan raised its foul head again, it opened its mouth, exposing fangs like stalactites, and clamped it shut over the entire length of the rowboat. But, from the perspective of *Queen Anne's Revenge*, it was a success, and Blackbeard did indeed reach the last planet.

The Flaming Cutlass

Why Noah had found Adam eating a piece of gingerbread humorous became apparent when Charlie, who was sitting next to Adam but had not paid him much notice, placed her hand on the table. Her fingers, which were more webbed than a human's but less so than a duck's feet, felt around on the table for a piece of food. But there was no food – because Adam had taken it.

Charlie was about to ask what had happened, but that question was answered when she noticed Adam contentedly scoffing a piece of gingerbread.

"I know humans are supposed to be uncivilised," she began with a comment that offended all the crew, though none brought it up, "but I'd still expect you to ask before taking my food!"

Adam acknowledged these words but stared straight at Noah.

"You said it was yours, you bastard!" Adam shouted, but Charlie paid no attention to this.

"There's no more left, either," she added, "I was looking forward to that!"

Noah, still laughing in delight at his own trick, said, "Adam, you terrible person," just to wind him up further.

"You know what you've done," Adam said scornfully, but since everyone else decided to get in on the shouting, he never got the chance to explain himself. The overblown reaction received, to Adam, justified his actions, so he simply shut up, and let everyone get themselves annoyed.

The bickering ceased when a shout could be heard from the helm.

"Guys," Tom called, "you better come and see this!"

On deck

'This' is not a very descriptive word and failed to prepare the crew for what it was they were coming to see. 'This' was, as you have guessed, the same vast reptile which Thatch had just outsmarted: Leviathan. As it had before, it circled the stone-henge. Also, as it had before to the crew of *Queen Anne's Revenge*, it terrified the crew of this ship.

"Maybe it will move out of the way," Noah said optimistically.

"Fat chance," Tom laughed dully.

"Is that?" Neve asked in anticipation.

"The Leviathan," Lewis answered, "that beast isn't moving, not unless it wants to."

"Then we give it a reason," Tom argued.

"What kind of reason?" Noah said suspiciously.

"Those weapons," Tom replied, pointing to the stockpile they had taken from *The Lady Mary*, "maybe it's about time we used them."

"You'd better have bought some ruddy good weapons," Lewis said rather accurately.

It was clear that Thatch had already made his way to the next planet, which made any hesitation dangerous. *The Cutlass* did not have the time to spare for waiting simply for the hope that the Leviathan should move out of the way. She needed to reach the stone-henge, if they wanted any chance of stopping Armageddon, and they had to reach it promptly.

So, the crew wasted no time and went straight to rifling through the pile of weapons and trying to figure out which might be most suitable for slaying princes of Hell. One weapon, which Maddy had taken particular interest in, mostly since she had purchased it herself. She was forced to lose interest when Adam took the weapon from her grasp and started trying to figure it out for himself.

It was a piece of equipment Adam had recently familiarised himself with. In fact, this was the sort of weapon that had been instrumental in his escape during his exploits away from *Queen Anne's Revenge*. It was a harpoon gun: the biggest harpoon gun anyone had ever seen. And the harpoon within it – it was a huge and cruel harpoon. Even though it was twelve feet long and hideously barbed, the tip was as sharp and narrow as a new pin. The gun itself required slight assembly: for example, it needed fixing to the deck; and the flexible but powerful line tied to it from the harpoon. Also, the harpoon was currently in two pieces and needed to be screwed together in the middle. Rather conveniently, it was powered by gunpowder.

"Get us an 'ammer," Adam called, "and some nails."

People protested but realised that a harpoon was indeed the customary weapon for hunting giant marine vertebrates. So, a box of six-inch nails and an inappropriately small toffee hammer were brought to the deck, and the crew wrestled with the unfamiliar equipment and fastened it to the front of the deck.

Adam tossed a large handful of gunpowder into the harpoon cannon and took aim with a grin. They were still a little while away from the Leviathan and secretly hoped it would move itself before the eventuality of conflict. All but two of them. Adam and Maddy both stood, eager to figure the gun.

The Lady Mary

"When we get to *The Cutlass*, what are we actually doing?" Amber asked, still largely in the dark.

"We're supposed to be taking the stone off of them," Elliott answered dully.

"To do what with it?"

"To get out of here."

"And destroy Earth?"

"Well," Elliott said, abashed, "that was the deal."

"And how are you supposed to do that? You don't have a herd of demon cows."

"We have this –" Elliott paused, remembering how he had shot the Locust only a handful of hours ago. Without warning, he walked away and went below deck.

Below deck

Elliott crept below deck to his study, where he expected to find the inverted corpse of the hellish insect. To his horror, the very much alive and evil little face of the Locust looked right at him. His heart sunk. If it were still alive — he still had to release it. He imagined shooting it a second time would have little effect — in fact — he imagined it was rather indestructible. (He failed to think of drowning it, largely because he didn't wish to go anywhere near it.) The Locust was stiller than before, but spasmed violently from time to time. Disgusted, Elliott left the creature to bother itself.

The helm

"It's still there," he informed solemnly.

"What is?"

"That rotten thing."

"What thing?" Amber said, raising the pitch of her voice.

"Our doom? I suppose. A creature of God's wrath – though to be honest I don't see much Godly about it," Elliott got himself distracted by the matter, and trailed off, "though I suppose we may be acting out God's will. But then again, how can God's will be orchestrated by the Devil?"

"The world was meant to end somehow, that's God's will."

"But that end is supposed to be brought about by angels and their kin, not by man – and not ending with Satan's victory."

"Then why are you doing it?"

"I'm not," Elliott pushed away the notion, "but I fear my captain might."

"Well, you're not stopping him," Amber said disapprovingly.

"It's his decision, he has free will and all."

"You could free him to make the right decision."

"I've tried killing the thing, it didn't die!"

"Have you actually tried to reason with him?" Amber said.

"Well, not directly," Elliott answered, "I have, in little ways, but what else can I do? He's the captain, and he's always done his best thus far."

"You know what he wants to do is wrong, and you're complicit. For what? Because he was good in the past? Because you feel you owe it to him?"

"Yes, is that really unfair?"

"A fallen man is owed nothing but guidance back to the light! Helping this evil: that's not helping him; that's not doing anyone a favour."

"What do you actually want me to do?"

"Just talk to him, Elliott, and give him a chance to change his mind."

"And if he doesn't?"

"Then forget about all you think you owe him. He can't sail there by himself, we can go and fight on the right side."

It bothered Elliott slightly that Amber had both read him so well and rivalled him in wit. Though he wasn't devoid of stubbornness or pettiness, he had enough levels of morality to look past this. He took a deep breath, for now he was feeling rather sick, and ruminated about what he should say to Glove and just how to say it. It pained him a tad, but he said to Amber, "You're right, I'll speak to him in a minute."

The Flaming Cutlass

The Leviathan sprayed mist from its nose as it raised its immense head from the water both to breathe and to open its jaws. Its body wriggled from side to side like an anaconda swimming, but it did so with less awkwardness than a snake may. The creature's breath as it left its vocal cords could be heard, accompanied by the blue glow of its flame.

"Shoot it then!" Maddy shouted at Adam, "Get it before it can get us!" Adam was aghast when Maddy forcefully shoved him to the side and fired the weapon herself. He watched carefully, monitoring her aim, planning to correct it. But he didn't have to (to his discontent). The grim steel harpoon left its cannon with a racket, whistling and rotating along its length until it struck its target. Said target — the Leviathan — bellowed when the spike struck the end of its snout and lodged into its armoured hide. Leviathan breached the water like a whale, submerging on the return until the chain of the harpoon was taut.

The flaw in the decision to use the harpoon was the fact that now the Leviathan was bound to *The Cutlass*, and she to him. Due to the demon's (for the serpent is still a demon) superior speed and manoeuvrability in the waters, which were now steaming, the pirate ship was plucked from its course and after the fleeing beast.

"Get rid of it!" Tom called, trying to steer his ship towards the stone-hedge. The harpoon gun itself was fastened too tightly to the deck, so Adam and Maddy struggled to break the chain connecting it to the harpoon.

The pair were relieved of their efforts when the might of the serpent tore the harpoon from its skin, leaving it bleeding black blood. Adam wound in the chain to retrieve the harpoon while the rest of the crew flustered about to observe their aggressor. The mermaids, with the guidance of Lewis, were stationed at the cannons as promised, and waited should Leviathan turn back around.

Gun-deck

Of course, he did, swimming at an equal pace alongside *The Flaming Cutlass*, hesitant to attack. Again, Leviathan leapt from the water, his head observing the boat before flopping below the waves, his body following, and tail never leaving.

"Next time," Lewis said to Charlie, who seemed more interested in the defensive operations than Neve, "next time, we'll get him."

This was incorrect, however, as when the beast breached again, it received no cannon fire. When its crooked, clawed fins exited the water, Leviathan brushed them against the side of *The Cutlass*, rocking the ship.

Main-deck

"Adam!" Thomas called as Noah briefly took the wheel, "Here!"

He tossed Adam his musket, which Elliott had ensured to give him. Glad to be reunited with his weapon of choice, Adam neglected the harpoon gun and loaded his gun. He too waited for Leviathan to emerge from the sea before firing.

The Lady Mary: **captain's cabin**

"Captain?" Elliott addressed as he entered, his eyes fixed to the floor.

"What, son?" Glove replied, himself not looking up from his desk.

"About the plan," Elliott murmured.

"Aye, 'bout the plan," Glove carried on himself, "I've been doing some thinking 'bout the plan."

"And what have you been thinking?" The first-mate asked, uplifted by hopefulness, soon to be shot down.

"I think you should board *The Cutlass*."

"What?"

"You should board; they won't fight you. I can trust you to get the stone somehow."

"What if," Elliott tried to interrupt with his own idea, "what if we didn't take the stone?"

"What are you talking about, lad?"

"What if we let them get to Earth? What if we let them go home, and didn't destroy Heaven or Earth with eldritch creatures!"

"Enough with that, you daft boy! You don't know what you're talking about."

"I know that what you're doing is wicked. And it's the Devil's work. And it needs to stop!"

"You know full well why I'm doing this! You know I'm not wicked!"

"It's not your motives that worry me – it's the outcome of this damned quest!"

"It will be worth it! You know I reward loyalty."

Elliott said this quietly but poignantly, "and kill for a lack thereof."

Glove stopped himself from reacting emotionally, and instead delivered a short and decisive response: "Precisely, my boy."

Elliott hesitated. He was not expecting this answer, but appreciated that he had, in a way, encouraged it. While he was scared, his temper had finally worn thin, so he responded respectfully but assertively, "You can't kill me. You need me."

"I know that," Glove said, chuckling, "but those traitors on *The Flaming Cutlass*, I don't need them. Those mer-folk, Lewis, Noah: I don't need them. Miss Casserole, Lumberlodge, well."

"What would she say?"

"Who?"

"You know who I mean," Elliott said, at last looking his captain in the eyes, "Mary."

"She'll never know. Because you'll never tell her. Now, get out."

The Flaming Cutlass: main-deck

Adam watched Leviathan intently, waiting for a flick of his flippers or tail as a sign he should burst from the waves. He had loaded his musket with more powder than usual, for he could see the beast's scales were hard, and his skin thick. Something else he had noticed, from the corner of his eye and much less in the forefront of his mind, was that they were steadily approaching the stone-henge. They wouldn't have to slay Leviathan – they simply had to stay alive long enough to reach their destination.

As the crew had expected, Leviathan breached the water again, where he was greeted with munitions. Higher than before, the great reptilian face peered at the deck for a moment before it again made a splash. Musket shot hit the muscles of his jaws as his mouth opened, preventing him from biting a mast.

Gun-deck

With the beast's head out of reach, the cannons had their best aim at the uncoiled body which trailed behind it. To her delight, Charlie successfully shot Leviathan with her cannon. The jubilation prevented observation of the actual effects of this, but it had to count for something. It was the Leviathan itself that confirmed this, as his hunting tactics were soon altered.

But to those on the gun-deck, who could not see much of the sea in its entirety, there was a brief moment of triumph – in the misplaced belief that Leviathan had retreated.

Main-deck

Leviathan disappeared from sight. No one saw him near the ship, but no one saw him swim away either. His whereabouts were identified when *The Flaming Cutlass* began to wobble. She then began to tremble. Then shook. Then stumbled. The Prince of Hell was beneath them. Tom, when he realised this, steered to move his ship out of harm's way. But Leviathan, with his snakelike body, looped in front of the bow of the ship and caused it to cease progress with a great thud. This proved effective, though a loud and low hiss suggested discomfort on the creature's behalf as well.

Now ahead of *The Cutlass*, Leviathan raised his head from the water, swimming like the Loch Ness Monster. His throat glowed with blue flame, and his forked tongue flickered jealously at his adversary.

Adam reloaded his gun — not with lead shot but with the new bullets he had discarded into his pocket. He was at this point certain that they would have no effect on gravity in any way, but thought that it might be worth a shot anyway. So, as Leviathan turned to face them, Adam shot the bullet into his mouth. Both his assumptions were correct: the bullet did not inflict any non-contact forces upon the reptile, but was worth it, as his head soon shot back into the blue.

Tom stared at the stone-henge, seeing it only one hundred yards away. He then stared at the water to see if and where Leviathan would pop back out and attack. He then stared at the stone-henge again, and so forth.

With the sweat of his forehead reaching his top lip, he drove *The Flaming Cutlass* to momentary safety, as she was flung through space once again, to join *Queen Anne's Revenge* on the final planet of Hell's solar system.

The Lady Mary: the helm

Elliott, sorrowful from the reminder of his captain's stubbornness, knew his cause was lost and went back to the helm. He said nothing at first, and neither did Amber, which made Elliott feel awkward, so he said, "He's not budging. And I'm not sure he ever will."

"Well, there's not much time left to find out," Amber said through gritted teeth, as she pointed to the stone-henge a mile ahead.

No Prince of Hell turned chaotic sea-serpent awaited *The Lady* for some reason or another, so she sailed straight and simply, and too made her way towards the other ships, and the Gate of Ubyvis.

Captain's quarters

Glove looked up at the painting of Mary on the wall and sighed. "I'll be with you soon," he said.

Act 5: Bat Out of Hell

Chapter I

Krykrakon: *Queen Anne's Revenge*

As soon as *Queen Anne's Revenge* reached the last planet, Krykrakon, Thatch wasted no time and set out towards the Gate of Ubyvis. The Gate stood proudly on the horizon, sat itself within a protruding island and was showered by a great waterfall. The Gate behind the waterfall shone with a glow that called to Thatch like a flame might to an insect. Silent but strong, it beckoned him, and he knew it was his destination. The drenched arches shimmered in gold and silver, standing maybe two-hundred feet high, though this was hard to tell from the distance.

The seas were large but littered with small islands and sea-stacks, so *Queen Anne's Revenge* had to weave her way around them occasionally, though this was by no means a challenge. With Blackbeard at the wheel, they were sailing for maybe twenty minutes before a truer obstacle presented itself. A wall of rock: low, but still impossible to sail across. It appeared fast and with little warning, masked by waves which scattered over it, causing a very sudden change in direction from the pirate ship.

"We have a map," Thatch remembered, no longer going simply off his instincts, "look at the map."

So, the navigator looked at the map and saw across the centre of the planet, a straight and continuous wall. However, marked obviously, was a small passage through it, about a mile west of them. They soon reached it and found the gap featured an old but large metal gate. It was just about wide enough for the *Revenge* to squeeze through, and was open, appearing to have been left open for many years.

Beside the gate were two short pedestals. One was empty but featured circling stone serpents carved into its base. The pedestal on the right was not empty. An unclear figure occupied it. The figure was cloaked in darkness, or at least a very black cloak, but it was indistinguishable from darkness itself. His face was set back within the hood and devoured by this darkness, so was invisible. In his hand was the handle of a scythe, but it was without a blade.

The figure held out the wooden handle as to instruct the boat to stop. Thatch was hesitant to, but the figure seemed important. He observed that neither *The Flaming Cutlass* nor *The Lady Mary* were behind, so ordered for the anchor to be lowered. When the boat stopped, halfway between either side of the gate, firm footsteps could be heard. The footsteps were walking up the side of the ship.

Blackbeard looked at the haunting spectre and dared to ask, "Are you Death?"

"I am he," Death answered both quietly and loudly.

"Who are you here for?" Thatch just about mumbled before his lip became stiff and silent.

"I have been waiting for passage from this realm to seek the soul-razing blade of my scythe. But I see you are of no service to me, for you don't have a key out of here."

Blackbeard did not speak but lifted the stone from his pocket for Death to see.

"It's not real," Death spoke, "If you ever had it, it's been replaced."

The blood once drained from Thatch's face returned in an instant when he realised. He looked at the stone, which he had taken for granted, and realised it was a simple piece of agate. With a face of brutal red, he launched the stone in the direction of Death, but he wasn't there. "That wicked boy!" he called, unable to be proud of Adam's trick for sheer fury.

The anchor was lifted, the boat awkwardly manoeuvred around and back through the old gate, and they made way for the first ship they could find.

The Flaming Cutlass

"I suppose it's time you explained to us just how you got here," Noah asked Adam, who was standing beside him at the helm, with Tom steering. So, Adam did so with joy and an already deep nostalgia for his antics. He did, of course, exaggerate liberally, having no witnesses to correct his retelling. Perhaps the most detailed event in his story was the blowing up of *The Bristol Dragon*, Adam making sure he received praise for limiting Thatch's potential for destruction. While they knew a lot of the story would be fictitious, both Tom and Noah were truly delighted to listen to it – and did indeed give him due credit.

"And that reminds me," Adam said, the grin on his face growing by the second. He crouched down to do what appeared to be the scratching of his foot but returned to eye-level with something in his hand: the stone. He was preparing for a smug explanation of how he had acquired it but was cut off by his contented friends.

"Adam, you brilliant bastard," Tom said, giving him a friendly push on the shoulder.

"This is fantastic," Noah laughed, "Now, we don't even have to fight him. Now, he's got no way out — no way to the Earth. No way to destroy it!"

"He will come for it, you know," Adam dampened the moon with this reality.

"But now we only have to survive it, and keep it safe. We don't have to fight him beyond necessity; we just need to get home quickly."

"You know what," Adam began thoughtfully, "I am starting to look forward to getting home, I have some ideas on what we can do when we get there."

"We are going home, right?" Noah stared into Tom's eyes, frightened of the answer.

"Yes," Tom looked at both his friends and chuckled, "we're going home. And we're going to get there, trust me."

The Lady Mary

Glove marched onto the deck hastily, but insisted Amber not give up the wheel. Instead, he joined Elliott in religiously altering the sails, ordering Amber to sail as concisely and effectively as possible. While *The Flaming Cutlass* had proven itself faster, it was being steered clumsily, giving them the perfect opportunity to reach her. This was an opportunity Glove was eager to capitalise on. He knew, given the circumstances and size of the crew, this arrangement would be more effective than if he himself were at the wheel, not that he announced that.

It was indeed a successful arrangement; Amber gave the best performance as a helmsman as she could, neatly swerving around obstacles without losing speed or covering unnecessary distance. Glove pulled on ropes and tied them up swiftly and accurately, ensuring the sails served their fullest purpose. Even Elliott, while less skilled at the task, kept the ship and its rig ticking by assisting his captain, and spotting the best times to make an alteration.

If they were to maintain the velocity they were going, they were soon to catch up with *The Cutlass*. And maintain it they did. With skill and toil, they hunted down the others like a missile, and so they prepared.

"It's about time, son," Glove said to Elliott, "Miss Sings will sail us ahead of *The Cutlass*, so you can row to them. We'll then slow down so that you can be dropped off when *The Cutlass* catches up."

"I'd like to go with him," Amber made a hopeful attempt to rescue them both, "to give him some back-up."

"No thank you, Miss Sings, we need you at the wheel."

"We could anchor," she argued.

"We don't have the manpower to lift it again," Glove said truthfully, "You're staying aboard, and that's final."

Amber and Elliott looked at each other with disappointment. Elliott had just come around to Amber's idea of joining Tom's crew, but he had no plans to leave her behind.

The Flaming Cutlass

"She's on our six!" Maddy called, referring to the location of *The Lady Mary*, "And she's closing in on us!"

"Adam, my first-mate!" Tom called, "Alert the gun-deck, prepare for cannon-fire!"

Adam began yelling orders, starting with, "Now, you fish-tailed freaks!"

"Nicely!" Noah added, an instruction Adam ignored.

"Where's she gone?" Tom asked, losing sight of the other boat.

"They've gone behind that island!" Maddy described, being able to see the sails of *The Lady* from the crow's-nest, "She's level to us!"

When Adam returned, Tom asked him to take his musket to the crow's-nest and wait for instructions to fire. So, he did, taking with him some biscuits to 'share' with Maddy.

"They're ahead of us now!" he called on his way up, a little confused as to why.

"How far ahead?"

"Even more now!" Maddy said.

"What the Hell's that?" Adam asked, stealing Maddy's telescope.

Maddy, stealing it back, explained, "I think it's a rowboat."

Adam stole the telescope again, "It's Elliott!"

Elliott's rowboat

Elliott Ethan looked grimly back at *The Lady*, his new friend stuck aboard it. He then looked longingly but sadly at *The Cutlass*. He said to himself, "Oh, Elliott, what have you gotten yourself into? What are you even doing? What are you going to do? They're not going to just give it to you."

He rowed his boat sadly and will-lessly into the course of *The Flaming Cutlass*, knowing they would notice him and allow him aboard. He heard calls from the ship but did not engage thus far. *The Cutlass* was hurrying, but when Elliott's little boat nudged against it, he tied a rope to a step of the ladder so that they were secured.

The Flaming Cutlass: **Crow's-nest**

"Can you see Glove?" Maddy asked Adam as the two looked out for *The Cutlass*.

"No, why?" Adam said, paying more attention to Elliott in his rowboat.

"Because we could shoot him if we could. If you could, I mean. Kill him before he can kill any more of us."

"What do you mean 'kill more of us'?" Adam said, frowning, "Who's he killed?"

"He shot Doyle."

"Oh, for fuck's sake."

"Are you alright?"

"Well, it's going to make fighting him a little easier."

Maindeck

With hesitation, he then climbed the ladder and emerged onto the deck ungainly.

"Elliott!" Tom said simply, smiling.

"Don't be so excited," Elliott answered, melancholic.

"What is it?" Noah asked, with a subtle and unintended hint of threat.

"I've come to get it," Elliott said, not advancing to take the stone.

"What?"

"The stone."

"You think we're just going to give it to you?" Noah said with a sarcastic laugh, "so you can destroy the Heavens and Earth?"

"Listen to me," Elliott said strongly, "I don't want to destroy it. All this time, I've been trying to stop it. But if I don't get the stone, Glove may kill some of you, and he'll keep Amber captive. All I need is the

stone so we can avoid that, then I'll have to think of a way to get it —
and us — back to you."

Adam climbed down from the crow's-nest, since it was he who had
the stone in his sock (not that he planned to give it over). "Look!"
Maddy interrupted this exchange, resulting in Elliott's words falling
redundant, "They're coming!"

"So it was a trap?" Noah asked accusatorially.

"No, look," Elliott replied, "that isn't *The Lady*."

Tom specified, "It's *Queen Anne's Revenge*!"

Indeed, Blackbeard's ship sailed surely towards them, approaching
fast and threateningly. Tom became clearly flustered, sweating and
shaking his hand, which was not on the wheel.

"What are we going to do?" Noah asked him.

"Maybe we give it over," Tom said, not thinking straight.

"You what?" Adam said, "No!"

"Why not?" Tom whined, "It's a coincidence I even have it. It's a coincidence we found you before they did. It's a coincidence we were even here in the first place!"

"Not everything's a coincidence," Noah argued, shaking Tom by the shoulder.

"It's a coincidence we were even born," Tom added needlessly.

"We may all be born by coincidence," Adam said thoughtfully, "but after that, what we do — that's no coincidence, that's on us."

With this comment, Elliott looked praiseful-ly at Adam, despite the hindrance to his own cause. Adam, however, lost his calmness and called out, "He knows! That's why he's coming! He knows I took the stone!"

"You took the stone?" Elliott said in shock, "What about the other one?"

"Someone lost the other one," Tom said, glancing at Noah.

"Actually," the cowboy said slowly, lifting something from his pockets. It was the stone. "I never lost it."

"What?" Tom shouted, high-pitched.

"Then give me that one," Elliott said while observing Thatch with his telescope.

"No," Noah replied quickly, "because we still can't let it end up in the wrong hands."

"He's right," Tom said, "I can't do it."

"That there," Elliott said, pointing to the *Revenge*, "that's the wrong hands. You can't risk fighting him. I have a plan, trust me. Just give me the spare, and I promise I'll throw it in the sea before he can use it."

Everyone exchanged looks and frowns and glances, trying to evaluate the situation. This ended shortly, as they all noticed the fact that Thatch was even closer. "Give it to him," Tom said momentously, "Let's hope his plan works."

With reluctance, Noah handed him the stone, and Elliott embraced the group. "It will work, I think. But don't wait for me if not," he said, before he departed *The Cutlass* and returned to his rowboat.

Elliott's rowboat

As planned, *The Lady* had fallen behind *The Cutlass* to allow Elliott to sail to it easily. There was, however, still a furlong between the two, with the approaching silhouette of *Queen Anne's Revenge* between them. Still holding the stone in his hand, he lifted it up to the view of Glove, who smiled back.

When he reached *The Lady*, he tied the rowboat behind it and boarded.

Queen Anne's Revenge

Thatch was no longer at the wheel, as, when in a combat situation, the role of captain demanded much attention to the crew, which would distract from precise steering. He was standing at the helm, peering wilfully through his telescope to observe the two ships.

"That's new," he observed, "They have two ships."

He didn't say much more about this, as he could not foresee the relationship between the crews of either vessel. He focussed on an object floating between the pair of ships.

"It's the first-mate boy," he narrated, "and he's taken the stone. He's got the stone!"

"Orders, captain?" the helmsman asked him.

"Full speed towards *The Lady Mary*! The second ship is likely backup only."

The Lady Mary

When Elliott reached the deck of *The Lady*, his captain, who said, "Well done, my boy," instantly hugged him. However, at the same time, he reached his hand into Elliott's and snatched the stone straight from it. Elliott bit his lip to avoid an exclamation, for the very first part of his plan had failed.

"Take us around!" the captain ordered Amber, "Put some distance between us and the other ships — before we overtake them!"

"What are we doing about that?" Elliott asked, pointing to the *Revenge*.

"Man the guns," the captain said in conclusion, as he loaded a pistol.

Chapter II

The Flaming Cutlass

The Flaming Cutlass paced forward towards the *Revenge*, not slowing. The fact of the matter was that Thatch was approaching nonetheless, so there was no point in slowing down. It was noticed that *The Lady* was going wide, spacing itself from *The Cutlass*.

"Who's he going to go for?" Adam said in anticipation.

They all stood at the edge of their metaphorical seats, waiting to see which ship the *Revenge* would veer off towards.

"She's gone for *The Lady Mary*!" Maddy called down, noticing a slight change in course from the view of the crow's-nest.

"Full speed ahead it is!" Adam called, trying to make the most of his high rank.

"What about Elliott?" Tom said, flustered.

"You heard him; he told us not to wait for him," Noah supported Adam's idea.

"Exactly," Adam said, "so full speed ahead!"

"I'm going full speed!" Tom yelled, "We've been going. Full speed this entire time."

"Then steer better!"

Queen Anne's Revenge

A fog drifted across the water, which did not aid Thatch's view of his target. He had a mental map of where each ship was, but not in his mind was the geomorphology of the area.

"What's the plan, captain," the first-mate asked him.

"We go to the right of her, fire a shot if we can. Then, we circle around, putting ourselves on the inside. When they reach the gate with Death there, we can catch up and board."

"Okay, sir," came a reply, though in this time, Blackbeard thought to himself about his plan and realised the inefficiency of it.

"Belay that," he said, "Turn around now, head straight for the gate."

The first-mate passed this order on to the helmsman, and to the second-mate, who passed it on to the lower-ranking crew-members on the deck. The ship, being as large and grand as it was, did not have the best turning circle, so had to loop around many landforms. During this manoeuvre, they lost sight of *The Lady* through the fog. *The Cutlass* too was undetectable. Working hard and under strict supervision, the crew of the *Revenge* did their best to turn the ship around swiftly. The glow of the Gate of Ubyvis was no longer visible, so the compass alone told the navigator the correct direction.

When they reached the old gate, they did not stop for Death, nor did Death address them. The *Revenge* continued course, decelerating. After a while, the waters on either side of the boat turned perilous. They were, in fact, impossible to traverse in a large vessel, for they were lined with shards of rock so tightly packed that not even a rowboat would have been safe. These peripheral seas were also steaming warm and had a subtle glow of red. The only waters that were safe formed a linear path, straight toward the Gate of Ubyvis, or at least where it was expected to be, should the fog lift.

Captain's cabin

Thatch ordered the ship to be slowed to wait for the others. He strolled to his cabin and placed his hat upside down on his desk. The second-mate then delivered to him a small box, and opened it before presenting it to his captain. In it were a small pair of scissors and a spindle of cannon-fuse. Blackbeard cut strands of fuse one by one until he had a dozen or so, then he plaited them within the strands of his beard. He then took the remaining pieces and held them to the flame of a lamp so they lit, and used them to light the others. These fuses were then tossed into his hat, which was returned to his head.

The Flaming Cutlass

Tom successfully sailed *The Cutlass* to the stone wall, which ran across the planet, colliding with it because of the ship's speed and lack of visibility. In a sudden moment, his innards churned, and he felt very sick, as he assumed he had sunk the ship. Instinctively, he spun the wheel to the side to turn the boat away from the obstacle, taking a bit more time to sort out the sails accordingly. His heart thudded as he waited for the front of the ship to dip down – but it never did.

Sighing a sigh of relief, he made his way to the gate too, instructed by Adam, who recalled the map from some time ago. When he reached it, he hardly noticed its ghostly guard, and sailed straight through it. His eyes were instead fixed on the *Revenge*, for he could now see its dark shape again.

"Maybe give her some space?" Noah advised. Tom tried that and found there was no more width of water to move into.

"She's slow," Tom said, "Maybe we can get past unharmed."

"Maybe hide Adam," Noah suggested, "so he doesn't think we have his stone."

Before he could answer, Adam went to the gun-deck, where the mermaids were sitting patiently, not talking much to Lewis. They were, despite the silence, they were taking turns to poke the pirate when he wasn't looking, making him turn around to figure out which one of them had done it.

"I've got my eye on Blackbeard," Maddy assured from her vantage point, "He's looking at something else."

The Lady Mary

Glove looked through his telescope. What he saw was his rival, Blackbeard, looking back at him. Just as his son had, he ignored Death and sailed through the ancient gate, which shut behind them noisily. Glove looked at the unappealing sight of both ships ahead of him, "It's my only way to her: right between them."

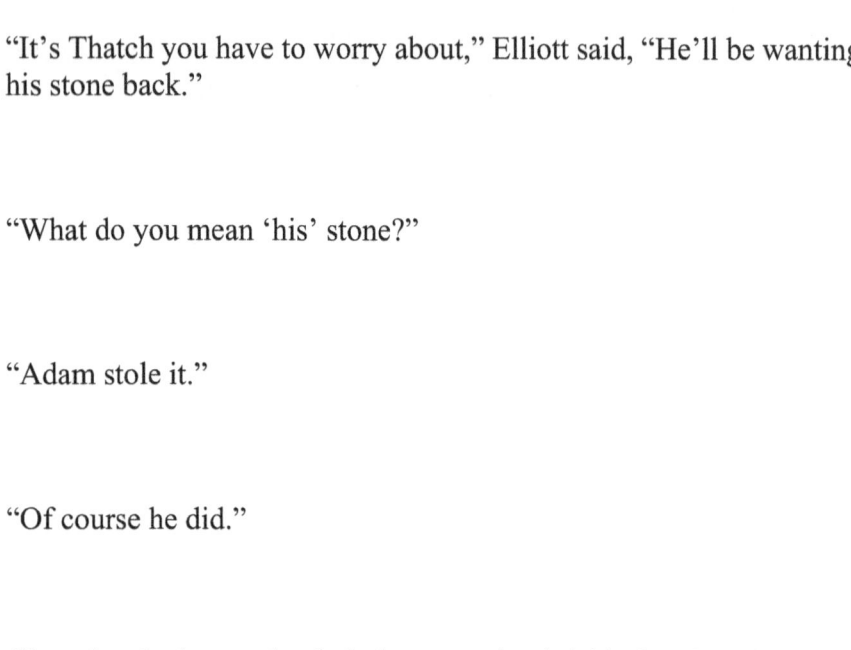

"It's Thatch you have to worry about," Elliott said, "He'll be wanting his stone back."

"What do you mean 'his' stone?"

"Adam stole it."

"Of course he did."

Glove laughed a nasal exhale in a way that left his face in a frown.

"Just get us through, please," he said, not sure himself as to whom this was aimed at. Even if he had wanted to, there was not enough crew to lift the sails nor operate the anchor, so slowing down was not a viable option. He slotted his ship in between the two others, closer to *The Cutlass*, and progressed until they were level. Putting his hands together and to his face, he said under his breath, "I'll be with you soon enough, my love."

Queen Anne's Revenge

"Close in on *The Lady*," Thatch calmly ordered his helmsman, who did just as instructed. The ships were not simply level, but their sails interlocked with one another, preventing anyone from overtaking or falling behind. *The Cutlass* did its best to avoid this – but it could not

542

afford to sail any closer to the rocks at its side, so remained conjoined with *The Lady*.

"Old Glove!" Thatch said with a grin, smoke drifting from his beard to form a cloud of grimness around him. He observed Glove momentarily close his eyes and breathe through a closed mouth. "On my instruction," Blackbeard called to his crew, "board, and fight to the death for that key out of here!"

One dozen men took up one or two of the twenty cannons facing *The Lady*, with a dozen more lining up to board it. A dozen men carried the task of maintaining course, and the few others were on standby.

"Now!" Thatch shouted, red in the face yet eager for the fight.

The Flaming Cutlass

"We need to stop him somehow," Noah reminded Tom, "Here's the chance."

"How though?" Tom asked, "Our guns can't reach, and we're outnumbered terribly."

"There's only your father, Elliott, and Commander Sings on *The Lady*. We outnumber them, so we can use their guns."

Tom looked at him, his eyes lighting up as he saw the plan formulate.

"You keep the wheel," Noah built on his idea, "I'll get sort out everyone else. We'll board *The Lady* and fight."

Gun-deck

"Everyone out!" Noah called to those on the gun-deck, "We need you!"

"For what?" Adam asked.

"We're boarding *The Lady Mary*, and using her guns to attack the *Revenge!*"

"Everybody out!" Adam iterated as he, Noah and Lewis aided the mermaids to the deck.

Main-deck

"Your musket's up 'ere!" Maddy shouted at Adam, "Swap with me, we need your aim up 'ere!"

"I want to fight!" Adam said heartily, "Throw the gun down!"

"I think she's right," Tom said, "You'll fight your best fight up there."

"A'ight," Adam said, climbing up to the crow's-nest as Maddy climbed down. Maddy, Noah, Lewis, Neve and Charlie stood, shoulder to shoulder, looking towards *The Lady*, which they could board with a mere jump. Each drew weapons: swords, guns, grenades, knives and whatever else they had fancied from the bazaar's loot.

When they heard Blackbeard command his crew to attack, they too sprung to action, joining them in combat on the deck of the central ship, *The Lady Mary*.

Chapter III

The Lady Mary

"Get to the gun-deck!" Noah called to the mermaids, who waddled their way there as best as they could, striking men with cutlasses as they did. The pirates themselves stuck to fighting off Blackbeard's crew. The gun that Maddy had picked up was most notable, for it was automatic – a feature she had never seen, being from Georgian England. This weapon had powerful recoil, soon teaching her to hold the weapon with both hands as she, quite aimlessly, sprayed bullets towards *Queen Anne's Revenge*.

A brave man, who jumped down from the higher deck of the *Revenge*, ran at her with a sword and primitive pistol. This soon obstructed her military dominance. He knocked the gun from her hands and cleanly cut a few locks of hair from her head. Noah found a gun that comfortably resembled the type of revolver he was familiar with and shot the man before he could harm his ally further. He did not kill the pirate, however, as Adam beat him to it with a single shot of his old-fashioned musket.

Gun-deck

Neve and Charlie located the cannonballs and gunpowder, though the cannons were loaded already, and found a lit torch. From the torch, a second was lit, and they sat themselves beside the cannons.

"Do we wait for orders?" Charlie asked.

"No, I say we blow them up now!" Neve said enthusiastically, doing just that. Charlie followed suit, neither knowing what to expect in return from *Queen Anne's Revenge*.

Queen Anne's Revenge

"Orders to fire, captain?" An officer asked.

"Not yet," Thatch answered, "Wait until either a third round of fire, or until we get the stone back."

The Lady Mary: main-deck

Though he was the captain, Glove had mysteriously disappeared from the scene of action. Amber bit her lip, trying to focus on steering and hoping to avoid combat, but shooting from a pistol she had handy when she thought it necessary or helpful. Elliott, fighting pirates himself, made his way over to Noah and whispered to him, "He's got it. Glove's got the stone," before the flow of the battle carried the two away from each other.

The first wave of Thatch's crew had experienced great casualties, so the reserves, and some of those previously on other jobs, replaced them in an attempt to overwhelm the combined crew of *The Lady Mary* and *The Flaming Cutlass*. Elliott reached the helm and provided protection to Amber so she could keep the ship straight.

"It's right there," he said, nodding towards *The Cutlass*, "get on it."

"Not yet," Amber answered, "we're not done yet. Take the wheel. And pass me a gun."

Elliott did not expect quite as much in response, but took the wheel, leaving it occasionally to fight, since the other two ships were mostly keeping his own on track.

"Elliott!" a voice called from *The Lady*. It was Tom, holding up his sword, and then throwing it over to him. Elliott picked up the sword, set it alight, and nodded in thanks to Tom.

Queen Anne's Revenge

Amber had left the helm for a reason that was apparent when she hauled herself up to her old flagship. In a heartbeat, she shot the first-mate, stabbed an officer, reloaded her gun, and shot the helmsman. She could have shot Thatch, the captain, but wanted him to watch his crew fall apart.

"Miss Sings!" Blackbeard called, ten yards away at most, "I sentence you for treason!"

The bullet from Thatch's gun scraped the leather of Amber's coat, as a look of regret fell upon her face. Her former captain drew his cutlass and walked over to deliver his sentence. Though he was an inch off a foot taller than she, Amber did not retreat from the fight. In fact, she initiated it, slashing her sword high towards Blackbeard's face and striking off a plait of his beard, burning fuse and all.

Thatch's sword soon after tore down her front and split the belt hanging over her. The blade then knocked off her hat. Amber thrust again, grazing his side, but was then flung to the ground when the flat edge of the sword struck her face. Unrelenting, Blackbeard's boot stomped towards her, though she didn't look up to see him. She turned over only when the whistling of Thatch's sword sounded through the air.

His blade did not meet hers, but a flaming one. Elliott had left *The Lady* under the control of Noah, and successfully disarmed Thatch of his sword. He helped Amber up, gave her a loaded gun, and defended himself from Thatch's fists. The burning blade cut his leather gloves as Blackbeard grabbed the flaming sword with both hands and tried to prize it away. Frustrated, he kicked Elliott away from him, drawing a pistol in either hand before Amber could get a clear shot at him.

The Flaming Cutlass

Eager to assist the fight, Tom prodded various buttons on a console beside the wheel to see what they did. After some lucky combination, a voice played, saying, "Autopilot on."

He then observed the wheel turn itself the correct way, laughing in delight. "Pure magic," he said, picking up his secondary cutlass and a brace of pistols.

Tom prepared to board *The Lady* when Adam stumbled down from the rigging, musket over his shoulder. He said, "I have an idea," without elaboration, picking up as many grenades as he could stuff in his pockets, and boarding instantly.

The Lady Mary: gun-deck

"I guess we go again," Charlie suggested after seeing not much consequence of the first shots. So, they moved over to another pair of loaded cannons, and fired them again. The *Revenge* rocked, and *The Lady* rocked with it. The support the ships provided each other, since they were so close, prevented any response from the *Revenge* regarding her injuries.

Through the ships' walls, the mermaids could hear the crew talking to each other, but they never fired back at them.

"Again?" Neve asked.

"Wait one minute," Charlie decided, for uncertain reasons. The truth was that both mermaids had been thrown in at the deep end in terms of pirating. Never had they touched a cannon until the fight with Leviathan, so they were not accustomed to how they should be operated during ship-to-ship combat. But they tried their best — and (Neve in particular) had a thirst for violence.

The helm

Noah was distracted from steering when a man, larger than he and holding a sword, began to fight him. He threw a plank of wood at the cowboy, which both blocked the shots from his revolver and knocked the gun from him. Taking up a sword, Noah attempted to fight the man close up. This was a mistake, as Blackbeard's man far outmatched him.

His saviour came when Maddy regained hold of her automatic rifle and fired it indiscriminately. Noah had to fall onto the ground rapidly to avoid being shot himself but did this successfully — while his larger opponent did not.

When he looked up, Tom was there to help him to his feet.

"I don't know where he is," Noah told Tom, "but your father has the stone."

"Leave it to me," Tom frowned, then went in search of Glove.

Queen Anne's Revenge

Adam ignored any enemy on the deck of *The Lady* and progressed straight to the *Revenge*. On Blackbeard's ship, the captain stood, pointing a pistol at both Elliott and Amber. Between the three, fell a small, round object, which began releasing a cloud of white smoke when it landed. Not one of them could see, nor did they wish to fire a gun.

Thatch stood still and tense. He fired his pistol only when he noticed something strange. The burning fuses from under his hat fell to his boots, for the top of his head was now exposed. He knew exactly who had taken the hat, and the same man fired a gun at him. It was a musket shot. Neither shot landed through the smoke cloud, and the glow of the flaming cutlass in Elliott's hand had disappeared.

When the smoke cleared, Thatch expected to see Adam on the deck. He had a gun prepared to shoot him, though never got to use it, as he was not there. Instead, he was back on *The Lady Mary*, with both Elliott and Amber, Blackbeard's hat atop his head. Adam left something behind for Thatch: fistfuls of grenades. One by one, the bombs exploded across the deck. Blackbeard was thrown across his ship, running below deck to safety.

He was not safe there, however, as a pile of explosives here outnumbered those on deck. All he could do was crouch down and brace for impact. When the dust settled, he saw his ship alight.

"Fire!" he called to those on the gun-deck, "Fire all!"

The Lady Mary

Amber took the wheel again, and Elliott joined Noah, Adam, Maddy and Lewis in the fight. Even Oliver, the miniature donkey, had found himself aboard *The Lady* and offered his help in the form of head-butts and kicks.

"*The Lady* is your best defence from Thatch's cannons!" Elliott called to the crew of *The Cutlass*, "Help us keep her on track!"

Lewis retied some ropes and helped Elliott correct the sails, but of course, the chief priority was fighting the still-invading crew of the *Revenge*. They had battled all on deck, so formed a defensive line to face *Queen Anne's Revenge* and together shot down fresh waves of attackers.

Between Adam's accuracy, the unending stream of bullets from Maddy's gun, the flame of the cutlass, and the help of everyone else, no pirate successfully broke through their defences.

But then, the cannons sounded, throwing everyone onto their backs.

Gun-deck

Neve and Charlie were entirely unprepared for the twelve simultaneous cannonballs that blew through the wall of *The Lady* and completely stunned them. Men left their stations at the cannons and climbed through the side of the ship, ignoring the unconscious mermaids in search of the stone.

Chapter IV

The Lady Mary: **captain's cabin**

Tom found his father just where he expected to: in his seat, sword in one hand and gun in his other. He had it the stone back into his locket and fastened it with a small chain around it. Glove did not speak, he just stared blankly at his son, then at the map in front of him.

"We can't let you do this," Tom said with no hint of fear or uncertainty. With these words, Glove looked not at his son but at the painting of his wife upon the wall.

"I have to do it," he replied, "for her."

"It's not for her — you killed her. She wouldn't want you!"

Main-deck

Blackbeard's crew emerged from both sides around the protagonists, armed and loaded. "I have a plan," Elliott muttered to Noah, "get everyone onto *The Cutlass*, and wait at the helm for my next instruction."

Noah looked back at Elliott with desperation in his eyes, and shook his head.

"This better work," he said, turning to Adam to tell him to, "Hold them off."

Below deck

Noah ran to the gun-deck, Elliott two going to a lower level.

"Come on!" the cowboy called to the mermaids, though he needed to help them back to consciousness. The pirate first went all the way to the bottom deck of the ship and opened the gate to the chicken pen. As he ran away from the brig, several birds chased after him, quite hungry.

The main reason he had come below deck was something else, however. He entered his study and grabbed the cage containing the Locust with both hands, disgusted but protective.

Main-deck

The crew had reduced Blackbeard's army down to one dozen, though at this point, Maddy's rifle ran out of ammunition. To make it worse, Thatch himself jumped down onto *The Lady*, bringing with him the smell of burning. The fuses in his black beard had become short, and left soot within the lines of his mad, red face. He approached Adam while he was midway through reloading, brushed his musket away and said, "That's enough, where's the stone?"

"Right in that locket of yours," Adam answered with an inappropriate display of un-seriousness which caused Blackbeard to punch him to the ground.

"At least we know where you get it from," he said to Adam, who kicked from the ground. As he did, his sock slipped down his ankle and exposed the actual stone.

Thatch struck a sword down through his sock and pinned it to the wooden floor, cutting through skin at the same time. Adam was in pain and hopeless, so Thatch slowly, for all help was distracted, took the stone from his sock. He left the sword in Adam's leg where he lay, drawing a gun to shoot him.

In panic, Noah assisted everyone he could across to *The Cutlass*, ignoring Adam and the danger he was in. A large barrel of flaming rum flew towards those escaping to *The Cutlass*. However, the mermaids got to use their skills in the fight after all. Rum is largely water, and even its alcoholic content has similar properties on a chemical level. At least close enough so that the whole fiery wave was repelled when Charlie jumped in front of Noah. Hydrokinesis had saved him, and caused and antagonist to burn instead. To return the favour, the cowboy assisted the mermaid onto the deck of *The Flaming Cutlass*.

Thankfully, Elliott did not fail to notice Blackbeard, and threw the cage containing the Locust, the door of which was open, at Thatch, striking him clean in the temple with the metal container. The small beast inside fluttered out in rage and clung to Thatch's face, gnawing at it. Blindly, the pirate shot his gun, which hit Lewis in the chest. Blackbeard screamed uncharacteristically and ran, stone in his locket, towards his own ship, so that he could try to break free of *The Lady* and reach the Gate of Ubyvis first. The Gate was close now, and clearly visible in all its grandeur. The water spilling over it dwindled and stopped, revealing behind it the seas of Earth.

"Retreat, all!" He called to the survivors of his crew, "I have it!"

Oliver the donkey jumped over to his owner and buried his face in his clothes, which reddened fast. Lewis just about mumbled something to his companion before passing away, "I'm alright, little fella." But the animal stood guard of its owner regardless, despite everyone else fleeing.

Eventually, the Locus let go of Blackbeard and landed on the deck of *The Lady*. Elliott shot it – to no avail. He then tried to cut it in half, or to squish it with his boot, but the wicked animal was too nimble and bit his ankles. Then, something darted down to get it. Doyle the dragon, who had been resting a while, saw the beast as food. He took it to the flagpole and wrestled with it, bashing it against the timbers as he clasped it in his beak. Though it was larger than his head, Doyle rocked back and forth and tried to swallow the Locust. His best efforts left no more than the creature's gangly legs and powerful wings hanging from his wedge-shaped bill, as yellow pus spewed from the Locust's body.

Elliott assisted Adam, whose leg was bleeding, by quickly removing the sword and helping him up. On *The Cutlass*, Noah grabbed hold of his arms to aid him over. Before he went, Adam called to his friend, Lewis, but received no answer, for he was dead. Though he was in agony, Adam delayed his return to *The Cutlass* to kneel by his deceased friend. He checked his pulse and kept hold of his hand even after he knew the result. Putting his other hand on the donkey's head and patting it, he said, "Until I see you again, old boy. I'll buy you a drink next time." Knowing the time was short, Adam took Oliver the donkey in both arms, and carried him with him to *The Flaming Cutlass*, wobbling like a concussed giraffe.

Elliott stayed on *The Lady* and developed his plan to Noah, saying, "When I get to the wheel, turn *The Cutlass* port-side – as sharply as possible."

"Not yet," Noah said, "Tom is still fighting for the stone."

"Tom? Where is he?"

Noah nodded toward Glove's cabin before Adam added, yelling in horror as he had remembered, "We need their stone, 'cause Blackbeard has mine!"

Captain's cabin

Of the three men left on *The Lady Mary*, two of them, Glove and his son, were in the captain's cabin. At the sound of his son's previous words, "she wouldn't want you," Glove flipped over his desk. He sprung from his seat and shot in anger, missing, but shattering the glass window on the door. He then took his cutlass to his son's neck and held him against the wall.

"Take that back," he said gravely.

"That can't be done. You can't change the past, it's done, already written," Tom said, trying not to escalate, "It's a fate you chose — you can't undo it. I'm just trying to fix it."

The door swung open, and through it came Elliott Ethan, flaming sword in hand. He used the weapon and swiftly sliced the locket from Glove's neck, and then pushed him away. Tom dived to retrieve the jewel, though his father soon met him with a sword.

"Tom," Elliott called, tossing his friend his flaming cutlass. Tom used it defensively, throwing Elliott the locket in exchange.

"Go!" he called to Elliott, though he didn't leave right away. Instead, Elliott pleaded with his captain.

"Andrew Glove, end this wickedness! This mission has torn your family apart, not protected it! Tudor, Doyle, now Lewis: they're dead because of this madness! Can't you see? The ship's going down. Thatch has a stone, and the Gate is right there. You don't have much time, but you can still do the right thing."

"Just go, Elliott!" Tom called, "Go now!"

This time, Elliott wasted no more time and sprinted from the room. A shot caught his side as he did, and he fell down to the floor. Glove pursued, but his son booted the door shut. So, the two fought with cutlasses, both unyielding. The fight lasted many minutes, both anticipating the other's moves and retaliating with resolve. But the older man tired faster, occasionally letting a strike past. The burning sword struck his face, blinding his eye.

In sheer instinctual defensiveness, Glove grabbed the sword with his bare hands, receiving excruciating burns and cuts, though caring none, and tore the sword from his son's grasp with a great groan. He flung it behind him, instantly hearing a rip, which gave way to the fluttering sound of a fire. It was the painting of Mary, his wife. The flaming sword had cut straight down its centre and started a blaze.

"No!" Glove called when he turned around to observe it.

Tom did not want to risk losing the chance to escape, so unbolted and forced open the door, and made his way to Elliott, who bled on the deck.

"It's alright," he said to his friend, helping him up to his feet.

"Son!" Glove called from the blazing room behind him. He perhaps shouldn't have, but he stopped to turn around and look at his father. Something about the tone seemed less threatening than before, more painful.

The waters had widened, and the three ships' sails were no longer folded together. *Queen Anne's Revenge*, the slower and heavier ship, was behind *The Lady*, though *The Cutlass* had managed to fall further behind. Blackbeard ordered a round of cannon fire, which struck both ships.

"Son," Glove repeated, catching up to his son and first-mate. Though his hands were in agony, he passed Thomas his flaming cutlass.

"My boys, if you go through with this, you may no longer be immortal," he said, both to Tom and Elliott.

"We know," Elliott said.

"But it's not us we're doing it for," Tom added.

"Forgive me," Glove said as he brushed the back of his hand on Elliott's face, where he had cut it earlier. He then took his hat off his head and placed it on his son's head. Then he took his own sword, now in its scabbard, and gave it to Elliott.

"Captain Thomas Glove, Elliott Ethan, go and save them. Forget about me, I'll buy you some time."

"Come with us," Elliott said, before becoming delirious and speechless from bleeding.

"No, son," Glove said tearfully, "go now."

Adam jumped to *The Lady* despite his wounded leg. Before he could help Elliott across, Glove beckoned him and whispered in his ear, "I know he's your father, but I should have acted like one. I'm sorry for that." He then spoke to the three of them, "I know I have failed you all, but please remember all I have taught you. And all you've taught each other."

Once Tom, Elliott and Adam — and the big old rooster, which had flown over — had reached *The Flaming Cutlass*, Andrew Glove waved to his former crew. He then looked at Edward Thatch, who was steering *Queen Anne's Revenge*, smiling slightly. He stumbled to the helm of his own ship, which was sinking on one side now, though it was still slightly ahead of the *Revenge*. Doyle the dragon, who had a full and bloated belly, took off the best he could and landed on Elliott's shoulder.

"Oh, Edward!" he called audibly to Blackbeard, who frowned at him, "This is for Mary!"

Thatch widened his eyes and mouthed, 'no,' as he watched Glove grab the wheel with both blistered hands and swing the wheel with full force anticlockwise. *The Lady Mary* swung with might to her left, just in time to collide with the bow of *Queen Anne's Revenge*. Not only did this cause the front of both ships to splinter, but forced the *Revenge* into the deadly waters to its side. The razors of stone shredded the hull of Thatch's ship, slowing it as it crumbled into the water.

This freed the Devil's herd at once, furthering damage to the ships, which toppled over each other in a heap of burning timber. The men on board were flattened beneath the carcasses of their vessels or landed in the swirling, steaming water.

The Flaming Cutlass

As for the crew of our heroes, there was little more to say. No longer on autopilot, *The Flaming Cutlass* sailed quickly towards the Gate of Ubyvis. Gobsmacked, no one spoke, both looked up in awe at the shining structure. The sea around them began to run and spill through the Gate, accelerating the ship even more. Tom took the stone from the locket and held it up. Even if they had changed their minds, there was no way to turn back now; the waters took through the Gate of Ubyvis, and the waterfall ran again over it to obstruct the view of its magic. Thomas Glove and his friends, new and old, had escaped Hell.

Chapter V

And as for Andrew Glove: the man came tumbling out of the wreckage and fell into the violent waters. The current pulled at him, as if there were sirens below, trying to drown the unfortunate soul within the depths. He flapped his arms about to grasp at the floating debris. Eventually, he lifted his tired body onto the timbers that were once the side of his ship. His face rested on the faint mark, which he himself had painted. *The Lady Mary*. He placed his hand on the name.

A shadow now loomed above him. It was Blackbeard. His sword was drawn, Glove's was not. However, a fiery bull who had broken off from the herd charged past and flung the pirate through the air, landing on the timbers Glove floated on. Glove used this time to draw his cutlass. Both burst towards each other on their knees. Thatch's sword scraped Glove's arm, though the man using it let go of the weapon and fell past him. Glove then turned, holding his sword inverted, and attempted to stab him, but he blocked with a plank of wood, knocking the sword from his hand. He then leapt onto him, and they wrestled and fought like dogs. Exhausted, they both stopped to catch a breath, as the wood they lay on slept and the two floated away from each other. Seeing a sword out of the corner of his eye, Glove rose to his knees and sunk it into Blackbeard's shoulder, and then into the wood.

Thatch gasped in pain, fear, and relief. Glove did the same. The mist and waves had smothered the flame of the fuses on Thatch's beard and smudged the soot across his face, turning it grey.

"Andrew," Blackbeard cried tearfully, "kill me, Andrew. You deserve to. Don't make me face him."

Glove located a pistol and shot at Thatch's head. But the bullet did not land in his skull, but on the wood it was laid on. Glove shook his head and said, "No."

He fell onto his back as Blackbeard floated away from him, whimpering.

His own raft drifted onto a small patch of mud, which barely reached out of the water. He looked up. Frankly, he had been so sure that he was ultimately going to die because of his sacrificial play; he wasn't fully conscious of what was going on. But above him stood the Gate of Ubyvis. Its waterfall falling in front of him as the mist sprayed his face. But as he gathered his senses and stood up to admire the very thing which he had been seeking for all this time, the water again stopped falling. And now its waters revealed something that cannot truly be described with words alone. A soft, light blue sky was illuminated, though neither sun nor star sat within it. It seemed as if the light came from within the very fabric of its being. The walls were carved in such a way you would assume they were marble — if it weren't for the fact that they were so purely white it would be difficult to believe they could experience any form of ageing. Two grand pillars divided this, so grand in fact they appeared to be holding up the sky itself. From each pillar hung a great, golden gate.

Behind the gate, he saw a throne sitting high on top of steps, with four cherubim around it. On the throne was a slaughtered lamb, emitting a light so strong that it blinded the observer from noticing any other details.

Glove looked around him and then saw a glow from his pocket. He reached into it. Quickly, he snatched the item out from within. It was another stone, another key. He grasped it tightly to his chest and advanced, fighting through the mud as he struggled towards the gate. He paused to catch his breath, though failed. A tear fell down his face.

"Mary," he choked.

So, he stood in front of the gates of Heaven, and fell to his knees, raising the stone up as if it were a gift, and a pledge. He tried to slide his knees towards the gate but couldn't help but momentarily freeze.

But he was not alone. The Devil's herd stampeded furiously. In all directions. Including his.

So, under the pounding of steely hooves, Andrew Glove was proven vincible, and his body was devoured by the mud.

Epilogue: Still Breathing

Earth: The English Channel

The Flaming Cutlass

Disoriented, feeling rather sick, and suddenly realising the mental and bodily exhaustion they all faced, the crew of *The Flaming Cutlass* fell into each other and sighed, contented. Wounds were dealt with to the best of their ability, and they all sat on the floor of the helm in a happy daze. They were entranced for what could have been seconds, minutes, or hours, until they were rudely interrupted.

A sort of flying machine, comprising a round capsule, tail and propeller above, flew noisily towards them. Three small but rapid red boats triangulated around *The Cutlass* and approached. Both the boats and flying machine had 'HM Coastguard' written on their sides. Out the window of the flying machine leant an elderly man with a full grey beard and dark suit, holding a cone to his mouth. From the cone, his voice projected over the sound of the propeller.

"I am Detective Walter Arkwright, please state your intent!"

Hell: Pandæmonium

The Fates presented themselves to Satan and informed him, "The souls of Thatch's crew are yours; he failed at the last stretch."

"What about the others?"

"Some sort of technicality," the first Fate said, grinning.

"What technicality?"

"They escaped under a different flag. Their souls were not bound to contract if they were not serving under Andrew Glove," the second Fate answered, before the three of them disappeared.

"Does that mean Armageddon cannot begin?" Beelzebub asked his master.

"Did you actually think this was about Armageddon?" Satan said, Beelzebub looking blankly back at him, "Armageddon cannot begin with me in mortal form! The trumpets can wait — my ledger of souls cannot."

"So, this was about souls?"

"I need one thousand of them to break free from this prison; this was just the start. The Revelation is a waiting game; it can only begin when all the pieces fall into place."

The Flaming Cutlass will return

www.ingramcontent.com/pod-product-compliance
Lightning Source LLC
Chambersburg PA
CBHW060210030726
47499CB00004B/981